THE

DIALOGUES OF DEVILS,

ON THE

MANY VICES WHICH ABOUND IN THE CIVIL AND RELIGIOUS WORLD.

BY THE

REV. JOHN MACGOWAN, V.D.M.

LATE MINISTER OF THE GOSPEL, DEVONSHIRE SQUARE, LONDON.

PHILADELPHIA:
LEARY, GETZ & CO.
224 NORTH SECOND STREET.
1860.

INTRODUCTION.

Nothing can be more various and opposite than the opinions of mankind, respecting the influence and agency of infernal spirits. Some continually throw the blame of their vices upon the poor devil. Take their word for it, and they are upon all occasions the innocent dupes to his subtilty and malice. They represent him as the prime agent in all their complicated schemes of wickedness; and would fain persuade us that, so far from being the objects of our just aversion, they deserve all our commiseration and pity. From such representations one would be tempted to think, that if malicious and busy devils did but stay in their own country, mankind would be as harmless as lambs, and every species of wickedness be soon banished from our then agreeable world.

Others there be, who fall into the opposite extreme, and with all their power endeavor to clear the devil of the slanders thrown upon him. Whether he hath retained them as his advocates I pretend not to say: but they tell you that he has no hand in all the wickedness committed under the sun; that it is impossible he should have any influence on the minds and manners of men. Nay, some go farther still, even doubt of his very existence, and are confident that all their wickedness ariseth from another quarter.

My mind, I must confess, was long agitated between these widely different opinions: now I verged towards the one, now towards the other extreme; and for a long time continued in such painful suspense, that I would have given a world to have been satisfied in a matter of such vast importance in human life. But at length I obtained a full and most convincing discovery of this very intricate affair, and let who will deny it, I am perfectly satisfied that, however justly the guilt of men may be charged on their own corruptions, infernal spirits do exist; and are fully employed in forwarding their wicked designs and purposes. Yea, I have learned so much of the art and address of diabolical spirits in this matter, that as I shall, I trust, avail *myself* much of the very singular discovery, so, from a principle of benevolence to mankind, I think myself fully justified, without further apology, in communicating it to the public.

Know then, that not far from my humble cot, there is a widely extended, most tremendous, and gloomy Vale, first formed, as is supposed, by some dreadful earthquake, or some other remarkable convulsion in nature. The confines of this valley, on the outside, are everywhere nearly level with the surface of the ground; but the precipice within is to the last degree horrible, insomuch that few have had fortitude enough to approach it. The ancient bards very justly called it HORRIDA VALLIS, and we, from them, the Vale of Horrors. This horrid vale has long been supposed, by the credulous vulgar, to be the haunt of infernal spirits; and some people imagine that it is the only place on earth where they freely converse about the dark designs of their mal-administration.

My curiosity continually prompting me, at last conquered my native timidity, and I resolved, if possible, to find an entrance into this unfrequented, unknown, and dreadful place.

But many months, I may say some years, were spent in this fruitless search, and I despaired of success. At length, however, having entered a very large and unfrequented wood, one side of which led to the very edge of the precipice, as I walked a few furlongs down a gradual descent, gloomy beyond whatever I had seen before, I came to a huge rock, all overgrown with ivy and moss. It had the appearance of an ancient ruin, somewhat in the form of a pyramid; the bottom occupied a considerable space, and the spiral top was hardly concealed by the highest branches of the tall and aged oaks, which surrounded it. Near the ground, by chance, I discovered an opening, almost choked up with baleful hemlock and nightshade. At first I thought that this could be no other than the cave of some ancient Druid; but approaching it, and having, with much toil, cleared away the noxious weeds, I found what I had long sought for, an entrance into the dreadful cavity.

Here my resolution almost failed me, and I was at the point of relinquishing the long projected enterprise. At length I recollected myself a little, and resolved to descend into the place, though, as I thought, not much less horrible than hell. The passage, a little within the entrance, led downwards almost in a perpendicular direction: but its straitness, and the natural unevenness of the rocks that formed it, rendered my descent more practicable and safe than I at first expected. Down, however, I went, fathoms I know not how many, ere I found myself at the bottom, and from an easy opening entered the *Gloomy Vale.*

Looking up, I saw rocks upon rocks projecting over my timorous head; and I perceived myself to be within the most hideous inclosure that sure ever mortal eyes beheld.

The vale being solitary and gloomy as death itself, I said in my heart, Surely if damned spirits are permitted to visit the earth, this must be their rendezvous, and two to one I shall see some of them. I therefore observed carefully my retreat, and by several marks on the rocks which formed it, I hoped that, on any emergency, I might be directed to the entrance of the cave, by which alone I could return to the society of mortals.

I soon found that my precautions were far from being unnecessary; for I saw, by the feeble light, which glimmered in the place, a form most frightful, making directly towards me. My heart bounded in my breast with terror: and swift as a hare, pressed by sanguine hounds, I ran to my little sanctuary. No sooner had I entered it, but the fiend stalked up to the very door of it. The hair of my head stood upright, the blood ran down my back as cold as Greenland ice, and I looked on myself as a dead man; having often heard of miserable wretches being torn in pieces by the talons of merciless infernals. But, as the hideous form attempted not to penetrate into the cave, nor seemed at all conscious of my being there, I recovered myself a little, and reviewed it with less apprehension of danger. At length he espied another of his clan, to whom he called, and with whom he held the following dialogue, which made such an impression on my mind, that I afterwards recollected the most part of it; and here present it to the worthy reader. The name of this devil, as I afterwards understood, was Avaro, and that of the other Fas[illegible]

DIALOGUES OF DEVILS.

DIALOGUE I.

FASTOSUS AND AVARO.

AVARO. So ho! Fastosus, whither so fast at this time of the morning? Be not in such a hurry: but let a kindred devil exchange a few words with you. Pray, how do you do, uncle?

FASTOSUS. Hah! my nephew Avaro! I little thought of finding you in the vale at present. But I am glad to see you. Pray, how do you do?

AVARO. I thank you, sir, I am pretty well, only tired with much exercise. But pray where were you going in such a hurry? When I called to you, you seemed to outfly the wind!

FASTOSUS. Indeed, Avaro, I should not be willing to discover my concerns to every inquirer; but I condescend to make free with you, on account of our near kindred; and knowing you to be a true son of Beelzebub, I can trust you with any secret. As for my present hurry, the occasion of it is this, The right honorable *Madame de la Coquette* having an inclination to a suit, of some fashion never before invented, was thrown into a violent fever, through the dullness of the mantua-makers, who could devise no *cut* suitable to her ladyship's desire. Finding her life to be in danger, unless she was gratified, I was last night dispatched to hell, to procure a new pattern from the best artists there; and having got it, I was going post to France, to assist my lady's mantua-maker in cutting and finishing it: which done, I suppose I shall have a trip to London, to accommodate the countess of *Prudeland* with a suit against the next court-day.

AVARO. What! the courtly Fastosus become mantua-maker! I should never have thought of such an employment, for my part. You have *now* descended low, indeed, uncle!

FASTOSUS. Indeed, Avaro, your ignorance almost provokes me to be angry with you. But you need not be so much surprised at my concerns with the mantua-makers; for I assure you I am so much admired for my skill in dress, by both sexes of the human race, that there is scarcely a suit of clothes made, either for man or woman, without my direction. Nor shall you find a peruke-maker hardy enough to venture a wig on the block, ere he has had my opinion of it. In short, cousin, there is very little done, and in dress there is nothing done, in high life or low, but I have a hand in it.

Avaro. If I have offended my honored uncle, I humbly beg your pardon. I assure you, I said nothing out of disrespect to you. We all know that your spirit is princely, your monarchy great, and your dominion very extensive. But indeed I never thought of your being conversant with tailors, barbers, and mantua-makers.

Fastosus. Nay, nephew, I am not angry. Nevertheless, you ought to revere me as your elder and better, and not take upon you to call in question the truth of what I say. As for the barbers, they are a set of transformists established wholly by my dexterity; and but for my sovereignty over man, these transformations had never been introduced. Now the transforming trade goes on so successfully, that there is reason to hope very many will be at last transformed into the likeness and nature of our sable fraternity.

Avaro. Pray, uncle, be not angry with me, if I do not speak altogether as you would have me; for you know I never had any inclination to learning or politeness; and I cannot help expressing my wonder at some things you say. Besides, I am amazed to see you look so thin; why you look like a skeleton! What have you been doing, or where have you been? By your looks, you might have travelled barefooted to the holy land, or crept on your hands and feet to Medina, and wept forty days by the tomb of our dear friend Mahomet. You have not been on pilgrimage, sure!

Fastosus. I thought, from what I had said, you might have known that I have not been on pilgrimage very lately; though I assure you, I have often travelled to Jerusalem and to Mecca as a guide to those holy pilgrims. There is not one of all the bare-legged travellers, who will stir their foot from home, until their good friend Fastosus is equipped in palmerian habiliments, to press forward in the van as their protector. Nor are these pilgrims my only vassals; for the superstitious, of all denominations, have with one consent devoted themselves to me.

AVARO. Well, but, uncle, I am sure they worship me with sincere regard, as well as they do you; and I either attend them in person, or pour my influences upon every one of them, in all their religious journeys to Jerusalem, Mecca, or elsewhere.

FASTOSUS. It may be so, Avaro; but their prostitution to covetousness hinders not their devotion to pride; for I have conducted many of this fraternity to the supposed sepulchre of Jesus of Nazareth, who, in their own opinion, were made so holy thereby, that when they returned to their native country, they thought the earth itself unworthy to bear the pressure of a foot, which had trod the threshold of the adored sepulchre. These religious adventurers, (especially if they obtain some precious relics, of which there are great store in Palestine) generally lift them so far above their fellow creatures that thenceforward they can hold no intercourse with the common people, lest their supposed spotless garments should be polluted with worldly filthiness. Nor is it uncommon for these fantastical devotees to imagine, that by their journeys to Judea they have gained considerably above the price of heaven. So that when they come to die, they have holiness sufficient for themselves, and a handsome legacy to bequeath, as an help-out to some poor brother, who loves home better than the holy land.

AVARO. Ay, Fastosus; but then you may thank my brother Falax and me for your Jerusalem journeys: none of them would have been instituted but through falsehood, deceit, and covetousness. And I really think that we did excellent service to the great Beelzebub and the sublime porte of hell, in imposing that cheat upon mankind. Though, by the way, one would wonder that the reasonable mind should be so easily deceived, seeing there is nothing in any of these pilgrimages, that has so much as the appearance of religion.

Often have I laughed in my sleeve to see the poor pilgrims, with holy awe and profound reverence, approach a log of rotten wood, fully believing it to be part of the cross on which Immanuel was crucified. Oh! how have I seen them congratulate themselves on their supposed happiness, if by any means they had procured a diminutive chip of an old gate-post, from the hand of a venerable priest, with his holy word upon it, that it was part of the cross! And, to speak the truth, which you know I am not very fond of, these reverend gentlemen have words and wood equally plenty; for when one log is sold off, they immediately replace it with another; so that this market will not stop for want of merchandise, whilst there is a tree left in the forest of Lebanon. I would not, on any account, that the world should know that the traffic in relics is all a cheat, by the help whereof my dear children, the Jerusalem priests, get more money for chips of rotten wood, than the greatest merchant in Norway gets for his masts, and yards, &c.

Fastosus. By what you say, and I own it to be right, cousin, you and I must share the persons and divide the spoil betwixt us, on the day of reckoning. You and cousin Falax have laid the snare very craftily, and I, by my haughty influences, drive the fools to it. Good Avaro, your game would not go well without my assistance; and while you and I continue to play into each other's hand, we can readily bring the two fools to meet, each deceiving and being deceived. I mean, we can bring the covetous fool and the credulous fool together. The credulous deceives the covetous fool with his money, and the covetous deceives the credulous fool with his rotten wood. Dear Avaro, our work goes forward apace, and we shall have them both at last.

Avaro. No doubt of it, Fastosus; for both the covetous and over-credulous are ours, by common consent. Our game could not well go better than it doth at present; for all ranks and degrees of people are subjected to our potent sway. No doubt but you have heard of that noble piece of architecture called the Triple-Crown, which I and my brother Falax made for our worthy friend and stedfast ally the *pope* of Rome.

Fastosus. Heard of it! Surely I have. Was not I the principal person concerned in the work? But, Avaro, you have an ugly way of denying people the due honors of their labor. But for me, his Holiness would never have thought of such an invention. And as I had the principal hand in it, I aver, that the best mathematician in hell could not have invented a more excellent piece. I have thought, ever since, that the artful Falax acted his part with as much dexterity m the formation of that capital ornament as, when he and we assisted our venerable friend, Mahomet, in composing the Alcoran. But the chief beauty of it was, to see our hoary friend, the pope, with greater confidence than if he had been one of ourselves, exalt the papal chair above all that is called God. So that now, in the sense of the Romish impostor, saving and damning depend no longer on the justice and mercy of the Eternal, but upon the will and pleasure of him who fills the infallible chair.

Were we any thing but Devils whose hatred to Truth i implacable, it would have grieved us to see how she sighed and sobbed, as if her heart would break, when the impostors assumed the character of infallibility. She knocked with violence at the gates of the bishop's palace: but there was no admission for her there. She begged and prayed that the inferior ranks of the reverend clergy would receive her; but no one of them would suffer her to come under their roof; so that the poor heaven-born lady swooned in the streets, and there was none to assist her. Her eyes became as fountains of briny tears, trickling down her radiant cheeks; her locks were dishevelled, and her apparel hung dangling around her. In this mournful plight she went through all the streets of the mystic Babylon, uttering her lamentations in every public place, and in every concourse of the people. But, as in former times she had piped to them, and none of the worshippers of the Beast would dance; so now she mourned to them, but none of them would lament. She stretched forth her hands all the day long, but none of them would attend to her; the venerable pope, father of the world, having published a decree that none of them should suffer her under their roof, nor administer the least comfort to her in her calamity, under pain of the Rack, the Gibbet, the Wheel, or Fire and Fagot. Yea, more; when his Holiness saw the importunity of Divine Truth, and perceived that she would be a perpetual thorn in his side, if not timely and wisely prevented, by forcing her out of the world, he clad himself in Vulcanian armor, sought for her in every corner of Babylon; when he met with her, lanched his fatal spear with papal force against her, that wounding her so deeply, she fainted and fell to the ground, and no doubt had died had she not been immortal. When the most holy bishop had thus deprest her, he cried out in devilish triumph, "*I am the successor of Peter, the vicar of Christ, the pillar of truth, the porter of heaven, and the supreme head of the church.*" At which words, Truth entirely disappeared, and to this day has not been suffered to set one foot within the limits of the papacy.

AVARO. It was a noble enterprise; nothing could exceed it. I am persuaded, that the man who was in-dwelt by our brother Legion, and resided among the tombs, was never capable of coming so near to us devils in cruelty, deceit, and falsehood, as that same venerable man, his infallible holiness, hath upon every occasion.

FASTOSUS. Indeed, Avaro, Legion, though a many-viced devil, is but a fool when compared to his holiness; but it is highly necessary that he should be well qualified in devilism, seeing he is appointed Beelzebub's great vicegerent in the Christian world.

AVARO. Great are the abilities requisite to such a station; and his holiness possesseth them liberally. Did you ever hear, Fastosus, the manner in which our Italian success was received by Beelzebub the great, and his infernal nobility?

FASTOSUS. I suppose I have; but I have so many things to think of, that at present it has escaped my memory; therefore, if you remember it, I shall be obliged to you for the recital.

AVARO. With all my heart. I assure you it is well worth your hearing, for thereby it appeared that his infernal majesty had the deepest sense of our services, and conceived the strongest hope of the increase of his kingdom from the alliance formed betwixt the sublime porte of hell, and the apostolic chair at Rome.

As soon as swift-winged Fame arrived at the gate, known by the name of earth-gate, she knocked violently, as you know is customary with her upon any emergent occasion. Our friend Cerberus, the porter, no sooner saw that it was Fame, but he immediately sent a messenger to court, to inform his majesty and peers, that the ambassadress Fame was arrived. In shorter time than a lawyer could frame a lie, hell was all in an uproar, every inhabitant being big with expectation of some important news from our friends on earth. Fifty of the nobility were dispatched from court, to congratulate Fame on her arrival, and to conduct her in state to the court-end of the city. The mighty Beelzebub ascended the flaming throne, to receive the ambassadress with imperial grandeur; and as soon as she arrived, she was introduced to his sublime presence, by Lucifer, prime minister of state, and in full court related all that had passed concerning the change at Rome in the system of religion: which desirable news was received with all the demonstrations of joy damned spirits are capable of. Fame having finished her relation, the mighty prince, who sat on the stupendous throne, arrayed in all the majesty becoming his elevated station, lifted his warlike arm, waved the imperial sceptre for audience, and thus addressed his courtiers, his eyes blazing as burning furnaces, while he spake.

"My lords, my brethren in sovereignty, and sharers of my glory; from the just sense I have of your steady attachment to my interest and government, as hath always appeared from your unwearied study, as far as possible, to destroy the creatures of our arch-enemy, whom, constrained, we call the Almighty; and promoting to the utmost our common interest among mankind. From such considerations, I cannot forbear congratulating your highnesses on the happy turn our affairs on the earth have taken, by the indefatigable pains and vigilant endeavors of our worthy friends and genuine descendants, Fastosus, Avaro, Falax, &c. &c.: as appears by the report you have just now heard from the mouth of our swift-winged ambassadress, Fame. By the industry of those worthy spirits, worms of the earth are wrought up to such a degree of pride and self-conceit, as to undertake enterprises that we, who are of angelic race, could not accomplish; yea, even to assume prerogatives, which never once came into our minds. My noble lords, there is reason to believe that this revolution will prove a leading step towards a very plentiful harvest. I signify therefore as my will and pleasure, that your highnesses take special care that the lodgings at the court-end of the city are kept in due repair, as henceforth we may expect at every term, numerous shoals of popish priests of all ranks, to take up their residence with us; and you may be sure they will take it very ill, if they are not accommodated according to their quality.

"I think, my lords, it is worthy of observation, that all the missionaries we ever dispatched among the heathens, could not prevail with poor pagan priests to aspire to that degree of impiety, which the pope hath now assumed. I hope, my lords, that truth and holiness are in a fair way of being banished from the face of the earth; for I am persuaded, that this universal father, his cardinals, legates, and bishops, will exert all their influence to promote our interest in the suppression of our enemies." Having said this, a flaming billow rolled over the imperial seat, and so stunned the good old prince, that he could speak no more for a season.

FASTOSUS. All those things I well remember, now you have mentioned them. But I want to know what you have got in that leather bag. You have not become nailer, sure!

AVARO. This bag, sir, contains a thousand pounds, which a certain attorney, a dear child of mine, wants to have deposited in some place of security, as he has not at present an opportunity of putting it out to generate, an increasing faculty with which all his other cash is endued. This same gentleman is a person of great worth, ready to assist the rich and great, provided always that his good deeds are handsomely rewarded. But so cautious and prudent is he, that he utterly abhors parting with even so small a pittance as a guinea, to relieve a poor distressed tradesman; and indeed for this very sufficient reason, that he cannot, in such a case, obtain land security for his money; so that if the poor man is ever so honest and industrious, he must even reconcile his thoughts to a dungeon, or seek relief from another quarter; for our worthy lawyer would part with no money to deliver him from it. His present fear is, lest any of his poor neighbors, knowing that he has plenty of money by him, should, by their pressing solicitations, over-persuade him to part with a little to help them in their distresses; for he, like many other honest men, is determined to keep what he has got, if one half of the parish should die for want of bread.

FASTOSUS. By your description of the worthy lawyer, I may expect his children as my pupils after his decease. I warrrant me, Avaro, before their father is half consumed by the worms, I shall have them bowing and cringing to me as their god. I have remarked, for some thousands of years, that when the parents have worshipped the god Avaro, by giving themselves up to covetousness, for the most part, after their decease, the children have made choice of me and our cousin Profanity for their patrons. Surely, if covetous parents knew what courses children would follow when their heads are laid low in the grave, and their souls still lower in hell, they would quarrel with their god Avaro, or die with grief on the prospect.

AVARO. Ay, uncle; but there is not one of all my numerous disciples, who knows me by my proper name; and I am by far too subtle for them to find out the cheat. My English vassals, for instance, commonly worship me under the false names of industry or frugality, prudence or laudable care; but there is not one of them who can be prevailed with to believe himself a worshipper of the devil Avaro, which is, you know, my true and proper name.

FASTOSUS. Nothing equals our success; for you damn the parents by covetousness, and we damn the children by pride and profanity. Good Avaro, we have them hip and thigh; it is but a few of all the mundane race that we lose; and those also we should have, if they were not forcibly taken from us: but this is one comfort, that if we must have the mortification of seeing any of the human race get safe to heaven, we have also the pleasure of disturbing and distracting their minds on the journey; and many of them we bring to the stake or gibbet, under the direction of our good friend Crudelis, who presides over those hells upon earth, known by the name of the holy inquisitions.

AVARO. Hells, did you say? Right, hells indeed! One holy inquisitor goes beyond an hundred of our fraternity in the art of cruelty, which you know is the first of the learned sciences at Rome. Such wonderful inventions of torturing, one would have thought, could never have been contrived. What ingenuity does the rack display! How excellently formed for exquisite torture! What an apt resemblance of the infernal furnace is the dry-pan! A contrivance worthy the most skilful among the Beelzebubian artists. But their watery torment, the gag and pitcher, is what raises them most in my esteem. Almost every blockhead hath some notion of a hell of fire; but it is peculiar to the skill of an holy inquisitor to contrive a hell of water. In this, Fastosus, we must all knock under to them, for indeed they are our betters. And, to enhance their merit, their torments are inflicted upon the unhappy wretches who fall into their hands, under a show of the greatest sanctity towards God, and pity to the unhappy victim of their cruelty. And so very strictly do they and their assisting familiars observe the rules of inviolable secrecy, that the world can never know the hundredth part of their villany.

Fastosus. Secrecy is indispensably necessary to a people so much devoted to our interest as the worthy inquisitors and the rest of the Romish clergy are. Were it known to the world what methods they take to aggrandize themselves and support the papal hierarchy, the cheat would be discovered, the fabric would fall to the ground, the craft by which they have their wealth would soon be at an end, and their reverences be brought into contempt.

Certainly the great Beelzebub will deal gratefully with the holy father at Rome, and his cardinals, inquisitors and bishops, when they arrive in hell. For my own part, I stedfastly believe that if our good friends the popes and inquisitors are not served below their quality, they will be put in possession of the seats on the right hand of his majesty's throne, as our friend Mahomet and his mufties were in those on the left. And when their extraordinary merit is considered, our infernal nobility will have no reason to grumble at their advancement; for nothing less can be deemed adequate to their uncommon merit and usefulness in confirming our dominion over mankind. And so fervently have they our interest at heart, that it would be very extraordinary indeed, if any of them should be lost, and fall short of our dreary abode.

Avaro. The basest ingratitude to use them otherwise, Fastosus. For my own part, I shall always give place to a pope or inquisitor, and I think it is the duty of all our sable fraternity so to do; for when their inferior species is considered, it will appear that they not only vie with, but even exceed the most dexterous among us in many things.

Fastosus. I am thinking, Avaro, of the easy station you have got, in comparison of mine. You are concerned but with a few, I am concerned with every one. You chiefly serve the higher ranks of people, but I am hackneyed night and day by all sorts of men, from his holiness the pope to the hermit in his cell, from the queen on the throne to Bridget the farmer's maid. But was it not that I find my account in it, and by that means am adored as a divinity my princely mind would never submit to such constant drudgery.

AVARO. Good Fastosus, I speak it with reverence, but you are exceedingly mistaken in my business. I assure you, it increaseth every day upon my hands, and requires very constant application; insomuch, that for these twelve years I have not had time to close my eyes for one refreshing nap. Ah, uncle! I am concerned with, and for many; and with none more than with the sons of the mystic whore. This old bawd, with the scarlet gown, hath many children, who swarm as locusts along the face of many European countries, and eat up the good of the land before them. And there is not one amongst them, who knows how to spend a day without my company. When I would gladly lay me down for a little rest, one or other of them conjures me up to inquire after pay for this funeral mass, that dispensation, or the other pardon. For, you may know, that with them there is nothing to be done without ready cash; for they never give credit.

FASTOSUS. That old proverb, "Money answereth all things," seems well adapted to the tenets of your disciples, Avaro.

AVARO. Wonderfully adapted, sir! very wonderfully adapted; for money forwards their devotion vastly, and helps them strangely on, in their way to heaven. Dear children of mine I own them to be! for, notwithstanding their pretended love to devotion and the souls of their fellow creatures; if a poor man travelling from earth to heaven, should happen to be arrested by any of the officers of purgatory, (who make it their business to waylay travellers) and be turned over to the tormentors; if such a man has not left a sufficient sum for purgatorial masses, and no well-disposed lay person is found to supply the deficient assets of the prisoner, he may lie, if it be possible, until he is burned to tinder, ere any parson of the convent will put one hand to help him out of those dreary flames. But, on the other hand, if a sufficient sum is left for masses to be said to the lady of Loretto, St. Dominick, St. Dennis, or any other eloquent saint, all the parsons will apply as cheerfully as young dromedaries, and put their shoulders to the work, like so many bulls in a yoke, until they have cleared him of his prison. You may always be sure that with them, according to the well-known proverb, "It is money that makes the mare to go."

FASTOSUS. I pray you, Avaro, where does this same purgatory stand? I have often heard of it, but never could meet with it, either in this or the other world, notwithstanding I have sought it with care.

AVARO. You have sought for it in the wrong place, uncle; you should have ransacked the brains of the pope and his clergy; for there, and nowhere else, the chimera is to be found. It is only a scheme to get money, that I contrived for them; and hitherto it has answered our highest expectations; for by this craft the parsons have great emolument.

FASTOSUS. This I do know, that nothing is more attractive of the attention of their reverences, than brilliant gold; for the sake of which, systems the most absurd are imposed upon mankind, with the sanction of priestly authority. Indeed, it is presumed that these holy men will authorize nothing but what is lucrative. O the wonderful trade of priestcraft! Indeed, Avaro, I begin to think you a devil of good abilities, and an honor to the race of Beelzebub.

AVARO. I am highly obliged to you for your good opinion, sir; and assure you, that were you acquainted with the system of our government, I should go near to rivet myself in your esteem; an honor which I much desire, and in order to which, I shall relate a certain affair which wonderfully displays the genius of priestcraft, and gives the most just idea of the doctrine of purgatory.

FASTOSUS. I shall be glad to hear it another time, cousin; but for the present I must be gone, to forward my lady's robes; for the mantua-maker dare not touch them before my arrival at Paris. Exactly four hours hence I shall give you the meeting.

AVARO. I shall think of the appointment, uncle. Success to your enterprise.

DIALOGUE II.

FASTOSUS AND AVARO.

Being acquainted with the appointment, I chose to wait for their coming; but was so alarmed at what I had heard and seen, that I lurked close in my retreat, not daring to attempt any discoveries. At the time appointed, I perceived them walking up the valley; and as they drew near,

Fastosus said, Yes, Avaro, I assure you there was great joy in the court of Versailles on account of my arrival, and that both amongst the French and English ladies: the latter of whom are the humble servile imitators of the former; which tends so to chagrin some, and give pleasure to others of them, that by this means contentions run very high among the French ladies. One part complains of the English, as no more than the apes of the French; these are they who would monopolize all the finery to themselves; therefore their censure of the English ladies is not to be regarded. The others boast of their superiority, and are not a little proud of their dominion over the fair Anglicans; who, they suppose, dare not attempt to introduce so much as the pattern of an head-dress, until it hath the approbation of the French. But to drop this for the present, Avaro, I shall be glad to hear the story you mentioned before we parted.

Avaro. It was this, sir. There was a gentleman in Provence, a steady member of the holy Roman Catholic church, who died lately, and as soon as dead, his pious relations made his death known to their reverences the priests, in order to procure their good offices, in behalf of their departed friend, whose soul, it was upon no ill ground feared, was hardly white enough for heaven, and would therefore be obliged to call at purgatory, for an effectual cleansing, ere he could proceed further upon his journey. The venerable priests no sooner heard of the gentleman's death, than they prudently began to consult the good of the church, and what means appeared to them the most likely to feather their own nest; as this must needs be done, either by the life or death of the laity. This being their sole intent, it was unanimously agreed to refer themselves to my direc tion, and an interview in the apartment of the principal was requested. Being at that time in the neighborhood, I immediately granted their petition, and presented myself among them in the principal's chamber; a place very familiar to me. The reverend old father was no sooner aware of my arrival, than he arose from his seat, fell prostrate before me, to do me humble greeting, withal expressing the most grateful sense of my care and condescension, in coming so soon to their assistance.

Humble salutation past, the principal addressed me in the following learned manner. "Worshipful Prudence," for that is the name I am known by among them, "we have an affair of great importance to lay before you; and with the profoundest humility will we thank you for your advice."

FASTOSUS. Nay, Avaro, if you talk any thing about that same humility, I will not stay a moment longer, for I hate the nature of it.

AVARO. You need not be offended, sir; for the gentlemen in question have as little of that as your heart could wish for. It is not the nature, but the mere name of humility which serves the purposes of priestcraft; and which he and his brethren so much admired. And you know, sir, that the name without the nature of humility, is nothing but pride in disguise.

FASTOSUS. Well, I am glad they have no more of it; for that Humility is a fellow whom I abhor; but I thank my stars it is very seldom that I meet with him; however, when he and I do meet, we as naturally quarrel as the elephant and the rhinoceros.

AVARO. I assured them of my assistance, and the old parson went on with his story. "O! thou priest-governing spirit, (said he,) thou must know, that about eleven of the clock, last night, a neighboring gentleman went out of this into the other world, leaving behind him an estate, upwards of ten thousand pounds per annum, devolving to an only son, and to this convent has left no more than fourscore crowns, for the salutary work of delivering his poor soul from the dreadful flames of purgatory. I do not know, indeed, but our great lady, whom we serve, might be satisfied with half the sum; but we thy servants are not so easily pleased. It is our pious desire to procure as much of the young man's estate, as by any means we can, for our own private use; as none of us can tell what we may want before we die. Besides, we do not know but so large an estate, devolving unencumbered upon him, may be the means of ruining the soul and body of the inexperienced youth. Now, we, as the holy guardians of his salvation, think it necessary, for the good of his soul, to cut off as much as we can of the fuel of his lusts; well knowing how dangerous riches are to the laity. Thus, great patron, I have revealed the pious intent of our venerable brotherhood; and, lovely spirit, if thou canst by thy advice serve us in this matter, we entreat thee to do it; for our eyes are to thee, and our hearts are open to receive thy instructions."

FASTOSUS. Who could have thought, Avaro, of any of your disciples being exposed to such exalted piety? However, it was piety of the true Romish stamp, greatly admired by the venerable clergy.

AVARO. Well, said I, most reverend father, let not your pious mind be afflicted about the young gentleman's soul. Let you and your worthy brethren observe my instructions; and I shall undertake to put you in possession of the greatest part of his estate; which, as you justly observe, will greatly redound to the safety of his soul.

Be sure that you bury the old gentleman, with as much seeming sorrow and devotion as might be expected from a well-paid parson; yea, with as much feigned courtesy to the heir, as if the deceased had left you five hundred pounds. Then be sure to say mass for him to your lady, St. Dominick, St. Francis, or to the saint of your convent, as soon as possible. That being done, let a skilful messenger from your reverences wait on the son and heir, to tell him that, alas! his poor father has got much deeper into purgatory than was expected, on account of some sins which he had concealed from his confessor; which sins, because they are hidden, will take a great deal of burning, unless expiated in time by frequent masses. Tell him that you are not certain, but you hope, about two hundred crowns, laid out in masses to some favorite, loquacious saint, may go near to procure his deliverance. This news will probably so surprise the youth, that the messenger will receive the money, and his hearty prayers into the bargain: for if he is a good churchman, it will not be easy to persuade him that your reverences only aim at picking his pockets.

Having received the money, you must take care not to go any more to the young gentleman, until the time that all the masses might have been said: then go to him again, and tell him that by fervent application you have at last got his father's soul within a few yards of the surface of the flames, that you cannot possibly restore him an inch farther, until more masses are said for him; and that you think an hundred crowns' worth more may, in all probability, clear him. This being received, take care not to visit him again too soon, but wait until another quantity of masses might have been said. At a proper time go to him again: expatiate much upon the piety of your brethren: Tell him, that by their endeavors, his father was quite discharged from the court of purgatory, and was just going to be turned out at the head-end of the town, when it happened, most unluckily, that there came up the soul of a woman, whom he had debauched in his life-time; that this malicious woman had brought an action against him, the bill was found, and the poor old gentleman condemned to fiercer burnings than before, which may last for many years, unless a speedy supply of money is granted, to procure friends in heaven to intercede for his release. This scheme will procure you double the former sums. You know, father, hidden sins take a great deal of burning.

Six or eight months afterwards, go to the young gentleman again, and tell him that you laid out his last money to the best advantage, that with it you procured half a dozen of the best orators in heaven to plead his father's cause; who, by their fervent supplications, had at last prevailed; that the old gentleman was delivered from his torments, and was led in triumph to the gates, to be dispatched immediately for glory. But, as his unlucky stars would have it, just as the porter opened the gate, there came up the soul of a mendicant friar, whom the old gentleman had in his life-time unhappily beat, and now openly accused him of this almost unpardonable crime: on which account he was remanded back to more exquisite torments than ever. Tell the young gentleman that this unhappy accident caused such grief to the brethren, that there is hardly any one of them able to say Ave-Maria; and that some of them intend, as soon as their strength will admit, to go to Jerusalem, to try if by any means they can procure his deliverance at the holy cross or sepulchre.

You know very well, reverend father, in what tender and pious strain to tell your story; and to make it penetrate the deeper, you can shed a few crocodile tears over it. If you manage wisely, you may, in this case, sell your tears at more than a crown each. Be sure thus always to find out some impediment or other to the old man's release. You may bring him often to the gates, but if once you let him go through, all your hopes are over from this quarter. Care should also be taken to inform the young heir of the tremendous curses the pope has denounced against those impious children, who enjoy their wealth and ease, whilst they suffer their poor unhappy parents to lie roasting in purgatory, rather than pay the priests for delivering them.

Fastosus. Ay, Avaro! But what if the young gentleman should have sense enough to see through the villany of the parsons, and courage enough to refuse the money! How then, cousin?

Avaro. That was what I was going to tell you, sir. For, continued I, if, sir, young 'squire Great-purse should have sagacity enough to see through your scheme, and deny you the money, let one of your most devout brethren assume the ghost, from night to night haunt his dwelling, and, in an articulate manner, utter, in the name of the father deceased, the most dreadful curses against his undutiful son, who possesseth a large estate in peace and pleasure, whilst his poor father lies broiling in the flames of purgatory. By these means you may procure either all or most of the estate to yourselves.

Fastosus. An excellent scheme! and, from what I have known of those reverend worthies, exactly suited to their taste and principles.

Avaro. It was so, as you shall hear: For I had no sooner finished, but the aged father, who was not likely to live to say many more masses, arose, and, with tears in his eyes, thanked me a thousand times for my cordial advice; protesting that nothing could be better adapted to the end proposed, or more agreeable to the principles both of him and his brethren; assuring me that they would follow my directions, as invariably as Saturn does his orbit.

FASTOSUS. By this account of the Romish priests, it appears that they are at no loss for merchandise. Purgatorial fire, holy water, masses, dispensations, pardons, &c. are commodities which do not require a very large capital, and yet are attended with considerable profits. The great parsons, over and above the tythe of the lands, have very advantageous craft by this means. But between you and me, cousin, it is all the merchandise of the scarlet strumpet.

AVARO. It would be dangerous to our interest, if the world should know the truth. Then our great vicegerent would be worshipped as a god no more. The wondrous beast which ascended out of the sea of ignorance and error, would be torn limb from limb, and his carcass given to the hawks and ravens.

FASTOSUS. So then I find you are a papist as well as me. I myself have large concerns among the clergy, and with none more than his holiness the pope, the great parson at Rome; the parson of the parsons. This universal parson, though he pretends to be descended from Peter, my enemy, hath conceived such a good opinion of my abilities, that he will not make a decree, nor publish a bull, until I have put the finishing hand to it. You know, cousin, that I am none of those who are backward in showing their opinion, but readily dictate to all who refer themselves to my direction. As to his holiness, notwithstanding he is the father of the whole church, he is my humble servant; and, as I said before, consults me upon all occasions. The advice that I give, in general, is, that by all means he take care to keep up his authority over the consciences and liberties of mankind: and the same advice I give to the clergy in general. Hence every parson attempts to reign within his own district, despotic and supreme over the consciences of the people, who are obliged, under pain of damnation, to honor him as the plenipotentiary of heaven, and the arbitrary distributer of blessings and curses. I advise his holiness at all events, to support his infallibility beyond the scriptures of truth, and his supremacy above the laws of God or man. This same advice I whisper in the ear of my clergy in general, who, to a man, agree that the scripture shall not pass with toleration, unless it is dressed in the garb of their interpretations. As such, and only as such, it is imposed on their parishioners. The good old vicar never contradicts any thing I say, notwithstanding he knows, at the same time, his pretensions to be a cheat; but to the utmost of his power, follows the directions of his adored Fastosus; and never did mortal man show more implicit obedience to the monarch of darkness.

AVARO. So then the papists worship his holiness the pope, and he worships the devil Fastosus. Is not this the system of the popish divinity in a few words, uncle?

FASTOSUS. It is so; and a system adhered to by many who are called Protestants. For, with such love to wealth and honor have you and I inspired them, that although, as reasonable beings, they must know that the Almighty Ruler will bring their ways into impartial scrutiny, and judge them for their fallacious guile; yet, for the sake of worldly riches and honor, at all events, they resolutely follow our directions.

AVARO. Ay, sir, that is the heaven of the priests. They both seek and have their reward. The fat of the land is in their possession, and they are honored as the directors of conscience. And yet they are the successors of the apostles, who had neither silver nor gold; and yet they are the ministers of Jesus, who would not receive honors from men. And yet they are the most humble creatures that ever lived; and yet it is death to contradict them.

FASTOSUS. Having made sure of the mighty father of the world, his holiness of Rome, to join issue with us in promoting our interest among men; I have an excellent device to insure all the other ranks of his dependent clergy to our interest likewise. The patriarchs and cardinals are sure to prove loyal to the pope, and, of consequence, to us, from a hope, which I have inspired each of them with, of one day ascending the papal throne himself. The loyalty of the archbishops is insured by the hope of a cardinal's hat, and their right reverences the bishops are sure to remain inoffensive animals, in hope of attaining in some future period the archiepiscopal dignity. The same device runs through all the other ranks of the clergy, and thereby they are all rendered my humble servants. By these things it appears that we are likely to have a very plentiful harvest.

AVARO. Doubt it not, Fastosus. Beelzebub's regions will be well provided with gentlemen in holy orders, who are so dexterous in managing the cheat, that it is carried on, un perceived by their adorers. Look ye, Fastosus! who comes? It is Crudelis! Where do you think that deformed spirit can be going now?

FASTOSUS. He is on the scent of blood, I warrant him. By his nature he might have been got by a panther, and nursed by a mountain bear.

AVARO. Let us call him, sir; perhaps we may learn some news of him. So, ho! Crudelis; what, not a word with you?

CRUDELIS. Hah, gentlemen! are you here? I did not think of meeting with you, my dear friends and fellow de stroyers. How do you do, Fastosus? And how do you do Avaro?

BOTH. We are pretty well, cousin; only jaded a little with constant application to business. But pray, Crudelis, how have you been employed of late?

CRUDELIS. Employed, do you say? Never fear me. I have not been idle, I assure you. Do you suppose that I can pick up no game in Britain, in this golden age? If you do, you are greatly mistaken. It is true, that some of the late kings of England have been my avowed enemies, and as far as in them lay, have expelled me the kingdom. But be they as vigilant as they will, I find opportunity of breaking through the fences which they have reared against me, when you may be sure, if I cannot get great, I pick up small game, of which I can only give you a very small specimen at present. In one place I persuaded an ambitious child to poison, or otherwise kill, an old cumbersome parent, who will not die without violent measures. I prevailed with a rogue, in another place, to dispatch his woman, and her brat, to preserve his own reputation and estate. In a third, I stir up an ambitious servant to kill and plunder his master. And frequently I can prevail with one gentleman to kill another in a duel, on some punctilio of false honor. And sometimes I persuade the despairing wretch to lay violent hands on himself, destroy his own miserable life, and by doing so, enter upon another infinitely more miserable. Then I take to my heels, and am followed with a hue and cry all over the nation. But thank you, I am too swift for them all. I never give them time to say, "Crudelis is here." But they often say, "These are the tricks of that horrid devil Crudelis."

Yesterday I was attending a duel, which I myself stirred up, (as I suppose you know that all duels are of my instigation.) so it was here; I persuaded the gentlemen combatants to fight with sword and pistol, hoping that both would have fallen in the action. But though my design was good, as ill-luck would have it, it miscarried, and only one of them bit the ground. However, I am not without hope that the other will be hanged for the murder, and, if so, then I have my design. I assure you, gentlemen, I use my utmost endeavors to throng the nether regions. O, my brother destroyers! I could tell you such stories as would make you bless yourselves, and adore the prince Crudelis. These are but trifling things, thrown in to whet your appetite against the next opportunity. Then you shall hear. But for this time I must be going. Adieu, gentry, for I smell blood at a distance.

Fastosus. It is amazing what power this deformed fiend hath obtained over mankind. What ills, so very different from the principles of humanity, he hath by his barbarous insinuations introduced. What is very surprising, he hath made mankind more cruel to one another, than we infernal spirits are among ourselves. He stirs them up to destroy and devour one another: but we are never known to quarrel among ourselves, nor to make war upon our own race. Be that the part of foolish man: We devils are masters of better policy. This very Crudelis himself, sanguine as he is to devour blinded mortals, lays aside all his voracity, when he joins our black assembly, and is as tame a devil as any of us. Well may you and I destroy with success, when such a deformed lump of hell as Crudelis, is made welcome among them.

Avaro. But with your leave, sir, as Crudelis is gone, let us resume our discourse. I remember, before he interrupted us, you briefly hinted that you were somewhat addicted to religion, and that you are a papist too. I was never wont to consider you as a religious devil; much less did I think that you assumed to yourself any of those distinctions, which divide the professedly Christian world. I thought, formerly, that the great Fastosus had dwelt only in kings' courts, with people of soft raiment, and occasionally waited on the nobility and gentry, at their country-seats. What! the devil Fastosus a papist too!

FASTOSUS. In reality, Avaro, (to make use of a human phrase) your ignorance is enough to provoke the very devil. Do you not know yet, if I were not jack of all trades and religions, I could never maintain my sway over men as I do. I have very great concern in religious matters, I assure you, and that among more denominations than some people like to hear of. Sometimes I am among the Pagans worshipped as an arch-flamin, and president of all their religious orders. Very frequently I have the honor of filling the papal chair. Then I am adored under the venerable names of Pius, Innocent, Benedict, &c. accounted the universal pastor, head of the church, and father of the whole world. Occasionally I sit as judge in the holy inquisitive tribunal, where Concupiscentia and I are adored as divinities. Now I am an holy mussulman, and styled his reverence mufti, Muly Alab. Then, before you are aware, I am shut up in a cloister with the nuns and friars, whom I make more proud of their pretended chastity than a thousand saints are of their real graces. On such occasions, I am known by the name of the venerable matron Humility. It happens, also, that I am obliged to metamorphose myself into a capuchin, or a Palmerian friar, and in that show of self-denial I beg my bread from door to door. By these means I teach the fantastical devotees to be more proud of their awkward form, and voluntary humility, than a wise earl would be of all his landgraviate. Anon, I change my station, and find myself an abbot of a convent, where my depending priests and brethren worship me under the name of the holy father. Then, very soon after, you will find me attending the worthy confessor in his visitation; when, to be sure, I persuade his self-conceited reverence that he is well-nigh as pure as the most holy mother pope Joan, a fortunate lady, who, a few centuries ago, became head of the church, and mother of the whole world. The hermit, in his cell, on the mountains of Ararat, frequently offers his adoration to me, and, for my part, in return for his obsequiousness, I am in no wise sparing of my exalting influence. I persuade the world-abdicating wretch that his solitary residence in that holy asylum, far more than merits a mansion in heaven, and at his peril, that he stir not one foot from thence, to go down into an ungodly world: the mountain-top, or a cell in the desert, being the best place imaginable, in which to merit everlasting glory. The worthy hermit admits my doctrine to be true, his favorite passion is gratified, and he obeys implicitly my directions.

AVARO. Then his eremitical reverence never questions the goodness of his heart, I perceive. He knows not that he carries a spring of iniquity within himself, even to the desert, or the mountain's top.

FASTOSUS. No, no, he fears no evil from within. If he gets to a distance remote enough from the rest of mankind, he can repose the greatest confidence in his own heart; and thereby proclaims his folly to all the world. I assure him, that if he will remain during life in his cell, when he comes to die, he will have holiness sufficient for himself; and a large redundancy, by which he may help some poor friend out of purgatory.

AVARO. Hey day! how different was Paul's doctrine from yours and the hermit's, Fastosus! He asserted that by the works of the law no flesh living should be justified; but you and he believe that by the works of the law a man may be more than justified. Yea, that by observing of things nowhere commanded in the law, such as forsaking society, counting beads, and mumbling prayers, he may not only justify himself, but help another to justification.

FASTOSUS. Ay, Avaro, the hermit believes so; but for my part I believe no such thing. I know better, though I thus delude him. But to pass on with my story, I can tell you, I have a good deal of employment among your disciples, cousin, and with them I work wonders of compelled generosity. I meet with many, who never had the heart to perform one virtuous, benevolent action, whilst health continued; who, when they perceive that they must come to a reckoning in the other world, are very assiduous to have their accounts balanced aforehand. I persuade them to leave a massy sum to this hospital, to the other parish, or to certain meeting-houses. When I thus direct the will of devotees, one leaves gold enough to build a chapel for our lady, a second doth the like for St. Peter, and a third for St. Dominick. But in general they are most fond of saints of their own rearing, the greatest part of whom are now made constellations in the nether sky, and courtiers to the prince

Beelzebub. Ask you me, Avaro, what end the testator has in those pious legacies? I tell you, by this time he sees that the manner in which he got and kept his money, has not the least tendency to save him from destruction; and he knows but one way to avert the impending judgment; that is, to leave his so and so gotten money for the good of the church; and that, he is told, never fails to sanctify every measure to procure it. Some of those deluded testators are not without hope, that, in some future period, their names will be enrolled in the pope's bible; and their shrines adored in the Christian pantheon, at Rome, where all the gods of the papal hierarchy are enshrined.

Avaro. Good Fastosus, I really think, that, if the papists would act in character, they should dedicate their temples to St. Judas, St. Demas, St. Demetrius, St. Alexander the coppersmith, &c. for they are the genuine offspring of those celebrated heroes.

Fastosus. Their very descendants, cousin. You and I, who know what we see, can discern no essential difference between the holy Roman Catholic religion, and that of the ancient pagans. It was the most excellent device imaginable to introduce paganism under the specious show of orthodox and infallible Christianity. And I can tell you, there is no essential difference between the popish religion, and that of some sects of very staunch Protestants; but these things we must keep to ourselves; for I would not, for ever so much, our people should know that the popish religion is diabolic.

Avaro. I should be glad to hear it made out, uncle, how the religion of some Protestants is much the same with that of the papists: this being well cleared up will yield me great pleasure.

Fastosus. I can clear it up, Avaro. And shall, at a time convenient; but not now. I must go and put the finishing hand to my lady's robes. To-morrow I shall meet you here. Adieu.

Avaro. Well, seeing my uncle is gone, I'll go and hide the lawyer's money in a place of safety, and return to some business which I promised to transact for my worthy children.

DIALOGUE III.

INFIDELIS AND IMPIATOR.

THE way being clear by the departure of Fastosus and Avaro, I came out of my lurking place, in order to make what discoveries I could in the valley, which I now knew to be a rendezvous for those evil spirits, who so dreadfully have enslaved mankind. I had not gone far, before my alarmed imagination transformed every thing I saw into a devil; the croaking of the raven was as dreadful as the voice of an hobgoblin; and the shrieking of the owl as terrible as the roaring of Apollyon. Every distant bush seemed to bear the aspect of some devouring fiend, so powerful was the influence of my imagination. Curiosity, however, had still the ascendency over my fears; and I wandered from place to place, seeking for something new. At length I saw, at some distance, a tall gigantic form, slowly moving towards me. A form nearly as huge as the steeple of St. Cuthbert's church, at Dulmensis. Every time he contracted his extensive chest, he darkened the air with the breath which issued from his expanded nostrils, as pillars of smoke from the chimney of a fire-engine: smaller streams of the same darkening vapor came curling forth from his armpits, and every pore of his skin, so that wherever he came he blackened the air around him.

Now, thought I, my life is not worth two-pence, if yonder demon lay hold on me. Therefore I ran with full speed to the cliff of the rock, where I had lurked so secure before: and having taken sanctuary in the subterraneous cell, I gathered so much courage as to peep out, that I might learn what was become of the terrible monster. I saw that he was got almost to the door of my cave. Frightened I was, you may be sure; nevertheless, I comforted myself with the thought, that such a tremendous bulk could not enter my narrow retreat. He said to himself (his voice as he spoke resembling hollow thunder) "I thought I had seen the honorable Fastosus, and the careful Avaro, walking here just now; but I might be mistaken; or if they have been here, they are gone on our great father's business, no doubt. Well, seeing it is so, I will take a turn or two in the vale, and then return to my business again."

Notwithstanding all the tremor of my mind, I was eager to know what he was, and how he came hither; but durst not discover myself, lest he should prove a devil of the cannibal kind, which if he should, I thought that he would scarce make one mouthful of my diminutive carcass. But when he mentioned going to business again, I queried whether he might not be one of Vulcan's smiths, come out of the forge to take a refreshing walk; then I recollected, and asked myself, "If he is one of the cyclops, how came he to be acquainted with the devils Fastosus and Avaro?" I continued in this dreadful suspense for some time, until at last seeing one of his companions, he entered into discourse with him. I found that his name was INFIDELIS, and that of the other IMPIATOR.

INFIDELIS. Impiator, my child, how do you do? I am glad to meet my son in the vale of horrors, in so lucky an hour.

IMPIATOR. Hah, my worshipful father, Infidelis! Am I so happy as to meet with you here? My venerable sire, how do you do?

INFIDELIS. I thank you, son, very well. Notwithstanding my great age, and hurry of business, I do not find the least decay in my constitution, but rather seem to grow stronger; and indeed there is a prediction on record, that I shall be strongest at the last.

What pleasure does it give me, my dear Impiator, to hear that you are so successful, in ensnaring the minds and corrupting the morals of mankind, throughout every nation of the world. If what I hear of you be true, you approve yourself a right chip of the old block. I rejoice that some of all ranks and degrees of people are so subjected to our sway. I am told that many, even of the professors of religion, fondly caress you, my son.

IMPIATOR. Indeed, sir, it must not be denied that my kingdom is in a growing condition, all over the world. I think I was hardly ever so much, and never more caressed than I am now. Even in pagan nations, heretofore remarkable for uprightness and temperance, I have introduced the fashionable vices of the Christian world: so that an Indian will drink and swear even with an Englishman; and lie and cheat as fast as a Gaul or an Hollander. Greatly am I beholden to a certain company for instructing the eastern world in the learned arts of violence, rapine, and murder. Not to dwell, however, on the conversion of the pagans to the vices of nominal Christians, much improvement has been made even in Christendom itself, of which, take the following instances out of many that might be given.

It is not a vast number of years since your son Impiator was held in perfect disdain in Scotland; but now I have chosen many legions of the Caledonians for myself. I think I ought rather to say, that being quite tired of the service of Sobriety, a prince of another family, they made choice of me for their ruler. But you know, father, that I am no scholar, therefore improprieties in my speech are not at all to be wondered at. However, I have reduced the Scotch to such a veneration for my once hated person, that they have cordially embraced the ornamental vices of the English nation; such as sabbath-breaking, whoring, drunkenness, swearing, gambling, &c.; but whether they will be as successful in obtaining pensions from the government, after they have gambled away their estates, is not so easy to determine. The conquest of the Scotch, sir, is the more agreeable to me, because, as I said, there was a time, when those vices were hardly so much as known in that country; now, who but Profanity in all their towns? Nor am I without my worshippers in the country, even among their Presbyterian parsons themselves.

INFIDELIS. Glad am I that my lovely child has subdued the stubborn Scotch. For I well know that the Presbyterians there resisted your influence long after I had erected my standard in the land; yea, after multitudes flocked to it, and swore allegiance to the great Infidelis. But how, my son, hast thou so happily accomplished this change?

IMPIATOR. Really, sir, I obtained help from a quarter whence there was not the least reason to expect it. I mean from the parsons, the spiritual guides of the people. It hap pened thus: The parsons of the kirk quarrelled among themselves, and divided into two parties; one of which forsook their mother kirk, and very solemnly delivered up the other party to the devil; on the other hand, the reverend gentlemen, who abode in the kirk, in the like spirit of devotion, delivered up the schismatics, parson and people, tc

Beelzebub. Beelzebub, who you know is never backward in receiving a gift of this kind, finding that all the presbyterians in Scotland were thus in full tale made over to him, laid his hands upon as many of them as he could conveniently reach, and made such use of them as greatly assisted my operations. Little was now to be heard in the pulpit, except railing, scolding, calling ill names, and tossing anathemas, from one party to the other. Thus while they went on bandying curses, we went on persuading the people that religion is a farce, and that true happiness consists in present gratification; and this doctrine, readily affecting the heart and senses, was eagerly received, and my government established.

INFIDELIS. It was a favorable juncture indeed; and I have often remarked, that if there was any turn of religious affairs much in our favor, for the most part, we have parsons to thank for their assistance in it. Many instances of this might be given. But I pray thee, my son, didst thou ever hear of my original, and the nature of my government?

IMPIATOR. No, not I, indeed. You know, sir, I was born with evident signs of stupidity, and therefore could never read; and, to tell you the truth, all my cares are in the present tense, without inquiring into either originals or terminations.

INFIDELIS. All this I know, my child. But, as we are secure from mortal auditors, being in Horrida Vallis, if you can spare a little time, I will give you some account of my rise and progress. Perhaps it may have a happy tendency to promote your destructive designs, and so strengthen the pillars of the elevated throne of great Profanity. What I relate you may depend upon for truth: for, although we seldom speak any thing but lies to mankind, one devil may well enough depend upon the word of another.

IMPIATOR. Yes, that we may, sir; and I presume if mankind were to hear what passeth at our private conferences, they would not continue long so fond of our service as they are at present. As to your story, sir, I am ready to hear it. Perhaps, as you say, I may profit by it.

INFIDELIS. Well then, my son, you will observe that I am of a very great age, well-nigh as old as the world, which you see is worn quite threadbare, and will in a little time be folded up as an old garment of no use. As to my original

I can tell you that I am well descended; of royal lineage, I assure you. Great Beelzebub himself begat me, and my sister Ignorantia, on Eve, the mother of all living on earth. When I came to years of maturity, he gave me Ignorantia, my fellow-twin, to wife; and by her I had you, with your worthy brethren, Avaro, Falax, Crudelis, and your sisters, Perfidia, Concupiscentia, &c. At the same time my elder brother Fastosus, who had Inscientia, a lady of remarkable beauty, given him to wife, begat on her Ambitiosus, Contumax, Discordans, and their sisters Malevolentia, Iracundia, and a large train of excellent worthies, famous in the annals of the nether regions.

As soon as I was born, I stood up like a stupendous wall betwixt the Creator and the creature, so that blessings, of a spiritual kind, could not descend from God to man, nor could obedience ascend from man to God. One of the first things I did was to maim their moral powers, and accomplish an union betwixt them and my great father Beelzebub. Such an union I did establish, as nothing natural shall ever be able to dissolve.

IMPIATOR. Ha! my sire, you began very early indeed. You spent little idle time in your infancy; and proved very successful in your first enterprise too!

INFIDELIS. I have no reason to complain for want of success, I assure you. But you shall hear. The very moment I was brought forth, the great Beelzebub gazed upon me with all the admiration of a father infernal, and said, that I was the loveliest babe his eyes ever beheld. Multitudes of his sable menials, flocking together, were likewise astonished at my beauties. Such majestic grace displayed itself in my countenance, though then but an infant, that all agreed "I was father's own child." Moreover, such were their hopes of my usefulness, that great Beelzebub, and his peers, did what they could, sparing neither pains nor expense, to have me transported to hell, to be nursed up at the infernal court; believing that my presence would greatly alleviate their distress, and prevent their trembling on the thoughts of futurity. But my constitution being altogether earthy, it was found by experience that the infernal air was too hot for me, and that I could not live within the confines of the damned. Earth, my child, only earth is my habitation. Here I was born, and here I suppose I must die.

Impiator. With your leave, father, I think I have somewhere heard, that all who are now the inhabitants of the deep are unbelievers. How comes this to pass, if the great Infidelis cannot live in those torrid regions.

Infidelis. I perceive, child, that you are no great proficient in theology. As for me, I have dealt against divine matters all my days. It is your province to counteract moral principles, not interfering much with things divine; and my province to oppose truth, rather than promote immorality; therefore I shall inform you how it comes to pass. Know then, that what a man is when he dies, such he is in the eye of the moral law to all eternity; for death casts the die, and in the same posture in which the tree falls it must lie for ever: but with infidelity they never more agree. For instance, many of them, whilst on earth, could not be prevailed on to believe that there is a God; but in hell they are feelingly convinced of the truth of this doctrine. Now they believe that there is a terrible God, and that they are fallen into his dreadful hands. Search hell through all its corners, ransack every furnace in the fiery world, and you will find never an atheist therein. Others, whilst on earth, were not quite so stupid as to imagine that this beautiful world, and all things therein, came into existence of themselves, and that the economy of nature is wholly effected by chance: therefore, they assented to the being of God; but deemed it enthusiasm to suppose that this God should subject his creatures unto a written law. They sneered at the authority of the scriptures; ridiculed every part of instituted worship; and gloried in their infidelity. But now, they are sentenced to hell, and have had a specimen of eternal torment, they most sincerely believe the veracity of the scriptures; finding themselves to have been judged acccording to what is written in them. Others, whilst health and strength continued with them, supposed God was only jesting, when he threatened the sinner with the vengeance of eternal fire; but now they are in hell, enduring that vengeance, they verily believe that he was in earnest. In short, son, many of them disbelieved that there is either God or devil, heaven or hell; but now, all these things are certain, even to demonstration, with them; they having been driven to associate with the peers of darkness.

The very best of historical faith is to be found in hell.

There are millions now inhabiting there, who, when on earth, could boast that they had good hearts, and believed well all their days, but who never began in reality to believe the report of the bible, until they tasted the sulphur of the lake. Then they believed very sincerely, though very much against their inclination. Now do you understand me, when I tell you that unbelief cannot live in hell?

IMPIATOR. Yes; but you amaze me, sir! I never heard so much before. What a learned devil you are! The famous pope Hellbrand himself could not have discussed the subject with greater accuracy. One may see from you what it is to be conversant with popes, councils, convocations, and the clergy. But in our country all the conversation runs upon horse-coursing, card-playing, cock-fighting, fox-hunting, whore-making, swearing, lying, cheating and drinking. Not a word about religion, unless it is to damn the parson for a sanctified hypocrite. And more, sir, I never knew that I had so many brethren and sisters before. Right well I knew that I was begotten by you; but I looked on myself as your only son by Ignorantia, my mother. Those honorable spirits, whom you mention as my brethren, I always took to have been sons of Beelzebub, your brethren and my uncles. I should never have thought of a fraternal relation subsisting between them and myself, in any other way than co-operation.

INFIDELIS. You have been greatly mistaken, Impiator; for Beelzebub never begat a son besides myself, and my brother Fastosus, who is something older than I. I am aware that there are some who allege that Contumax, Crudelis, Discordans, &c. are the natural children of the great Beelzebub; but it is a mistake; for they are only his grandchildren, sons to my brother Fastosus. The very moment that Contumax was brought forth, our great father Beelzebub, with all his adherents, were cast down from the ineffable heights of primeval glory, to the depths of bottomless perdition; and, according to a certain historian, were nine natural days in falling. Now, my dear Impiator, by this account, Contumax is your cousin, and my nephew. So that you are not only a brother in government with those illustrious princes; but sprung from the same famous ancestors with them.

IMPIATOR. Indeed, sir, I am astonished at your story;

but you know that I am no scholar, and that ought to excuse for my ignorance of matters so profound. Besides, such things very seldom make a great impression on my mind, being quite out of my latitude. However, I should be glad to know how your extensive government was established.

INFIDELIS. How it elates my mind, to hear my dear Impiator express desire after instruction! I will inform you as far as I myself have known. My kingdom, which is indeed extensive, was established as follows. As soon as I was born, I began to call in question the truth, goodness, and authority of the Almighty; and in every respect set myself to oppose the Eternal, by contradicting every word which he spake to man.

For instance, when God said to man, "Thou shalt not eat of the fruit of such and such a tree;" although then in my infancy, I stepped up to man, and thus interrogated him: Hath God indeed said so? are you sure of it? are you not mistaken, think you? You must needs have misunderstood him; for it cannot be consistent with the goodness of such a being as God is, to forbid your eating the fruit of such a divine tree. And as God had said, "In the day you eat thereof you shall surely die," I addressed myself to man after this manner. Die too! nay, ye shall not die. That is only an empty threatening, to keep your conscience in awe; for God doth very well know, that if you eat of that precious fruit ye shall be Gods, like himself, having knowledge of good and evil. For this it is that he hath prohibited the use of this divine tree. My brother, Fastosus, also performed wonders on this occasion. By these means I brought over man to my obedience. Thus I established my interest upon earth, and hitherto I have maintained it. With safety may I say that my good friends, both parsons and people, to this day, love me as their lives, and at any time sooner take the bare word of the adored Infidelis, than the word and oath of the God of Heaven.

IMPIATOR. Why sir, you began from a child to work the delightful works of darkness.

INFIDELIS. Yes, I am the eldest of all the Beelzebubian offspring, Fastosus alone excepted; and I yield in point of government to none of the princes. Fastosus and I, indeed, have a dispute between us, concerning the extent of our earthly territories. I can freely allow him the pre-eminence with respect to his angelic dominions; but I can never be brought to own that his sway over mankind is more extensive than mine, nor yet more sovereign. I yield to none in this debate; for all men are included under my government: and what makes greatly for my interest is, that the far greater part of them cannot be persuaded that I have any real existence. Thus it is, my dear Impiator, I reign almost universally over mankind, and they perceive it not. Many thousands of those good people, who believe nothing of my existence, and who, in their own imagination, had believed well all their days, have I conducted very safely down to the dark abodes of ever-gnawing anguish; within which they were no sooner entered and began to taste of the entertainment, than they were fully convinced they had never believed aright. It is the unparalleled dexterity of our administration, that all our works are performed in obscurity. And, let me tell thee, child, it will require a better light, than any natural ray of the human understanding, to trace and detect our deep intrigues. Thus far, with respect to myself and government. I shall take it kind if you will, in your turn, oblige me with some account of yours, my son.

IMPIATOR. Yes, sir, your command shall be instantly obeyed; yet upon this condition only, that you excuse my inaccuracies; because I know myself to be the most illiterate devil of the fraternity, and cannot speak like the courtly Fastosus, the reverend Infidelis, or the intelligent Falax.

INFIDELIS. No apologies, Impiator. We all know that neither you, nor your disciples, have any taste for learning. Therefore, we expect not to hear you speak as an orator, but as a plain, illiterate devil.

IMPIATOR. Then I proceed. My kingdom doth not consist of all the land known by the name of Impiety-Real, as some geographers allege, several provinces being made over, by treaty, to my uncle Fastosus; such as the provinces of Civility, Legality, Presumption and Formality. I reign openly only over the land called Impiety Enormous; and in our country the laws are as black as the bottomless pit; for there iniquity is established by authority. As to the rest of my kingdom, it was, like all the branches of Beelzebub's government, accomplished by subtilty and guile. For man, considered simply as a creature, could never have been subjected to my sway; for this reason I was put to my shifts, to find out some proper method for introducing my rega power.

So violent was the opposition to it, that my brain was put to the utmost torture; and after all I should have been obliged to return to my native country, with my finger in my mouth, had it not been for the timely assistance I received from my worthy friends and relations. My good old mother, who, you know, hath an excellent hand at a dead lift, by means peculiar to herself, kicked up such a dust as almost put out the eyes of one of the most vigilant and formidable of my numerous adversaries: a captain, from whose hand I had much to fear. His name was Intellectus. From that time to this, he hath been incapable of discerning my deformities, and the danger to which men are exposed by my dominion. And what makes very much for me, the old gentleman can hardly be persuaded but his eyesight is now as good as ever it was. I need not tell you the advantages that resulted to me from this his deception. At the same time my worthy uncle Fastosus came up to the second, a sturdy chief, whose name was Volens, as tradition says, and he gave his back a most dreadful wrench, insomuch that he has never recovered his former posture. I myself took a poisonous, or rather an intoxicating apple, and having gilded it over with leaf-gold, presented it to the third, whose name, if I remember right, was Rationalis. It answered my expectation. He swallowed the bait, and ever since has called bitter sweet, and sweet he hath called bitter.

This triumvirate being thus disabled, I found my conquest extremely easy; and, without any struggle, on the part of the rest, I confined them to incessant labor and drudgery, in the different parts of my extended territories, where they are as content as possible with their condition, many of them believing they are still in the garden of paradise.

INFIDELIS. Indeed, learned or unlearned, you display uncommon merit. Great is my honor and happiness in having such a son. The potent Impiator will do honor to the venerable name of Infidelis to the end of the world. Well, my son, will you please to proceed?

IMPIATOR. Perhaps you have heard that my kingdom is divided into several cantons, according to the dispositions of my subjects, each canton having its proper employments.

1. There is a canton of drunkards, out of which I select

all my courtiers, and officers in general. This canton has several communications with all the other parts of my dominions; and this we call the royal canton.

2. There is a swearer's canton, a set of people the most unaccountably foolish of all my subjects; but a people very profitable to our government.

3. There is a canton of thieves, to which all pilferers, robbers, gamesters, and deceitful dealers belong. A very populous and splendid canton this is.

4. There is the liars' canton. These are a people possessed of two tongues; a people who have very much of the features of great Beelzebub; and a very populous and polite canton it is also.

5. There is the canton of Sabbath-breakers. Here there is hardly room enough for the inhabitants, they are so exceedingly numerous.

6. There is the adulterers' canton. This is a very dark place; seldom visited by the rays of the sun. The fornicators cohabit with them.

7. There is the murderers' canton, the darkest and the most miserable place in all my dominions; yet for all that, it is very well peopled. For here are ranked not only those who cut one another's throats, like the Alexanders, Tamerlanes, Philips, Louises, &c. but also oppressors of every sort, cruel husbands and wives, disobedient children, who break their parents' hearts, false friends, backbiters, and calumniators. Indeed all who wanton in the unhappiness of their fellow creatures, like corn factors and carcass butchers: so that you see here are many inhabitants, and that too of considerable figure. It is worthy of observation, that all the cantons have easy passages from one another; so that although the employment in each is different from that of the rest, they all hold communication with one another, as subjects of the same prince, and heirs of the same inheritance.

Yea, so numerous are the roads that lead from one to the other, that if a man gets into any one of my cantons, it requires no less power than omnipotent power, and wisdom equal to omniscient, to extricate him from a labyrinth so dangerous. And it is well for me that it is so; for some of my subjects are frequently terrified, especially those that work in the deep mines, lest they dig themselves through the earth, and tumble into hell. But a little time discovers that their efforts to deliver themselves are all ineffectual; for the road by which they escape from one canton, leads them into another equally dangerous. Many ways there are to throw a man down into my mines; but, believe me, if ever any one comes up again, it must cost the Almighty an errand from heaven to rescue him. I assure you, sir, that by the help of these subtle passages and intricate turnings, I keep my subjects enslaved, with as little trouble to myself as any master devil that ever ascended out of the bottomless pit. But, by the way, I am constantly employed in planning out fresh measures for the slaves to pursue. Oh! sir, the end will show that I give ample demonstration of my fidelity to my royal grandfather, Beelzebub, of whom I hold my lands by fief.

INFIDELIS. My dear son, how it rejoiceth my aged heart to hear of your wise administration! However infatuated your foolish subjects may be, the great Impiator lacketh not craftiness. By you, my son, shall my name be perpetuated when I am dead and gone. For I must die, my child. As soon as the mighty angel shall sound the dead-awakening trumpet, the great, the far-famed Infidelis must resign his breath. Yet, be not you discouraged, Impiator; for you shall live for ever. You know how I fostered you in my bosom, and endued you with qualifications to sit on the throne of Profanity, where so successfully you reign.—Permit me now to tell you, that knowing that I must die, I have, like all other wise people, made my will, and, for your encouragement, I have appointed you, my son, with your uncle Fastosus, your highly honored brother Desperando, and your cousins Contumax and Discordans, the joint executors thereof, and sole heirs unto all my dominions and subjects, who, at my decease, are to be transported to the land of torment; there you shall reign in eternal triumph over them. Then it will be, and not before, that great Impiator shall arrive at the zenith of his glory.

IMPIATOR. I suppose so, sir; for I am told that, about that time, the provinces of Civility, Formality, Presumption, Legality and Hypocrisy, so famous in the empire of Fastosus, are all to be annexed to my dominions, which will then be very extensive, and the government of Profanity very respectable.

Infidelis. I would ask you now, my son, for a description of those famous cantons you mentioned; but as affairs of importance call me hence, could not you favor me with an interview for this purpose, to-morrow, precisely at twelve o'clock?

Impiator. I will, sir. Fare you well.

DIALOGUE IV.

FASTOSUS AND AVARO.

Being privy to the appointment betwixt Fastosus and Avaro, I took care to arrive in the valley time enough to hear all that passed. For now my business was left to shift for itself, and every thing gave place to the force of curiosity, which bore down, like an inundation, every thing before it. If my wife consulted me in any thing, I would answer, "Fastosus." If my children told me of their progress at school, I would abruptly reply, "horrida Vallis!" When my journeymen, or apprentices, talked to me about the shop business, my answer was, "the great Avaro." And if they said any thing about my good friend, the parson, I would say, "Oh! the wonderful Infidelis!" In fact, I could think about nothing but the devils in the valley. Therefore, I took care to provide myself with every thing necessary, and away I went to the vale of horrors, and had not long been there ere I saw Fastosus and Avaro come travelling towards me. And thus they began their discourse.

Avaro. I am glad, very glad, sir, that you are here so soon. I was afraid that you would find much business at Paris, besides finishing my lady's robes.

Fastosus. I did find more than I expected, cousin; for I had no sooner finished with the mantua-maker, than I was waited upon by a hatter, who begged to be informed, whether it was most genteel to fix the loops of a hat an inch and a half, or only one bare inch in depth; and whether a gentleman is most of a cavalier with his hat cocked in right angles, or with one obtuse and two acute angles. Before I had well satisfied the hatter, in came a gentleman peruke-maker, who humbly asked me whether a nobleman looks most like a hero when he has one, or when he has two curls bobbing over his ears. Provoked that the gentlemen mechanics should suppose I had nothing to do but to cock hats, and adjust wigs, I wrinkled my forehead into a most majestic frown, and made the following answer: "Get hence, thou shrinking cur. I have known a lord before now that had his ears so covered with tiers of curls, that he could not hear the commands of his superiors. The brave princes Ferdinand and Frederick of Brunswick, and the noble marquis of Granby, will soon break through all the redoubts of a barber's fortifications."* The words were no sooner out of my mouth, than I was sent for by his grace the d—e of C——ll, to inform him whether it was most graceful for a courtier to wear his hat with the front declining on the right or the left side of the brow. To whom I said, "Good my lord, you may soon resolve this difficulty, without seeking to the devil for advice. If your grace will only mark well to which side of the block the hats of the vulgar incline; then be sure to let the hats of the courtiers turn always contrary to the vulgar method." No sooner had I satisfied his grace, than L—s desired to know which was his best way to keep up his character, and support his dignity in Europe, on the loss of his dominions in America. For answer, I referred him to good Mr. Maubert, of Brussels, who hath as good a hand at a dead lift, as if he had been bred a priest. And so, cousin, with no small difficulty, I broke loose, and am come hither according to appointment.

Avaro. By what you say, honored sir, I perceive that, wheresoever idleness prevails, it is not among us; for we have no rest day or night, but go about plotting the destruction of mankind.

For my own part, I assure you, I have had but little rest since I saw you last; and so very fond are mankind of my counsels, that I expect but very little rest for the time to come. You know I was going to secrete a bag of money in the valley, when you and I met. This was no sooner done than I was waited on by a parson, who had his eyes upon a good living, with a view to receive directions about obtaining it. And he was followed by a tradesman, who had a desire to make a profitable break of it; but begged

* This was written before the conclusion of the late war.

directions how he might do it honorably. I referred him to the goddesses Perfidia and Fallacia for instructions, as they more immediately preside in that department. This honorable gentleman dispatched, I was attended by a certain curate, who having never had inclination nor opportunity to examine the canons of a certain church, came to consult me whether it was lawful to christen a child, if the parents had not money enough to pay the fees. I told him, by no means; for if you once begin to officiate gratis, you will have enough of it, and the parson's trade will be worse than an attorney's clerkship. The gentleman took my advice, being determined to seek the good of the church; and truly, because the mother had not two shillings and sixpence to pay the parson, she could not have her son made a child of God, and an heir of the kingdom of heaven.

Fastosus. Well, but cousin, is that matter of fact?

Avaro. Indeed, sir, it is what actually happened not five hundred miles from London bridge; and there is a certain gentleman alive who could avouch the truth of it, if he thought proper.

Having dispatched the journeyman parson, I was sent for, in all haste, by my good friend the attorney. He, worthy gentleman, has undertaken a cause which, he very well knows, can never be defended upon principles of honor and honesty; but his client is a rich man, can well bear fleecing, and therefore he could not in conscience put him aside. He knows exceeding well how to turn the rich man's cause to his own emolument, if he could but manage it so as not to injure his own credit. That was the perplexity which he begged me to clear up. Said he, within himself, "Can I but get this cause to depend in chancery for a few years, (which by the way is the highest point in law for a desperate cause) I shall gain some hundreds of pounds by it." As soon as he had done his duty to me, he very humbly laid the matter without reserve before me. Then said I, My good sir, let not the suit disturb you. I will manage it both for your honor and profit; never fear me. Who is he that is employed against you? To which he replied, "Oh! a very skilful man. No less a person than the great Mr. Falsehood,—a very eminent attorney indeed!" Come, said I, let him be sent for. This was done, and the lawyer Falsehood attended accordingly.

Being both seated in my client's great parlor, the good man addressed Mr. Falsehood, thus, "My best friend Mr. Falsehood, you and I are engaged as opponents in this suit; both of the gentlemen are resolute, and will bear a good deal of fleecing; you know what I mean, sir. Now all is as yet uncertain, and the issue will greatly depend upon the measures to be taken by you and me. I would therefore, good sir, that we make it certain. If right take place, it will be speedily over, and we shall make but a poor job of it; but if it is well managed, it may produce some hundreds a-piece. My advice is, sir, that it shall hang in chancery, like a poor man's soul in purgatory. What do you say, Mr. Falsehood?"

Mr. Falsehood replied, "It will never do, good sir, it will never do, to bring it to a speedy issue; that is certain. But I'll tell you what we will do. You know that you have the worst side of the cause, and if I act the part of an honest man, you will soon be obliged to give up; but I shall act the part of a skilful lawyer, which will suit both of our purposes much better. I shall give you all the advantages that I can, in order to keep the cause depending, until the patience of our clients is quite exhausted, and they agree to put the matter to arbitration. As they are both men of resolution, by that time it will be a job worth gathering."

So having set the two worthy lawyers to drink a bottle to the good luck of it, I left them, took wing and came hither. But I can tell you, if I had not soared aloft I had not been here so soon; for I saw a great number of parsons, lawyers, and farmers watching for me. I gave them the slip, however, and artfully dropt my influences upon them. Surely they may allow their master sometimes to converse with his friends.

Fastosus. Ah! Avaro, when we subjected man to our powers, we planned out a great deal of employment for ourselves: for so fond are they of us, that they will do nothing, unless one or other of our fraternity preside over every action.

Avaro. Sir, if it would not be offensive to you, I should be glad to hear some account of your origin, and of the nature of your government.

Fastosus. Avaro, a spirit earth-born, as you are, must be too grovelling in his genius to understand much of my history, dominion, and operations; otherwise, I would with all my heart favor you with the relation you desire.

AVARO. Well, sir, but I am willing to learn of you, if you will condescend to instruct me. However untractable I am among mankind, you shall find me teachable enough with you.

FASTOSUS. You promise fair, cousin. I love your submission, and therefore shall begin. Observe then, I am of high parentage, as well as of heroic deeds. I was born in heaven, cousin. It was there that Satan the great archangel begat me, upon himself; and as soon as I was begotten, I in return begat him; and the very moment I was begotten I was brought forth, and instantly killed my father.

AVARO. Indeed, uncle, you start high. You told me that I could not understand you, and now I perceive the truth of it; for really I understand not one word of all you have said. I hope, sir, you will condescend to explain your parables.

FASTOSUS. Well, if you understand me not, I shall descend lower, though indeed, I hate to speak of my own affairs in a vulgar style, so as to be understood by every petty spirit. But as you, Avaro, are of excellent use to my operations, I shall stand upon no distance, but avoid all ceremonies with you. Understand me then. When God Almighty had created all the hosts of heaven, every angel was perfectly pleased with his station; the most solid and joyous contentment reigned among them, and united the etherial inhabitants, who were, in those days, very numerous. No one so much as wished his station altered. No one thought himself capable of higher felicity and preferment than he enjoyed. The adventurous Satan himself, though he has not been blest with one moment's rest ever since I was born, before that time possessed all the sublime and refined pleasures his exalted capacity was capable of. And well might he be pleased with his station, seeing he was a mighty prince among the angels, next in greatness to the Son of God, who was appointed lord-lieutenant of the creation. And a mighty prince in heaven he would have continued, had he not afterwards become a candidate for omnipotence. As for me I was not born then, but I have heard old Satan, my father, with flames of malice and indignation darting from his eyes, tell how the most perfect harmony existed among the hosts of paradise; until it happened that a declaration was made from the lofty throne, that the Son of God was predestinated, at a time appointed, to assume a nature inferior to that of angels; and the Most High commanded that, in that nature, all the angels of God should worship the Son, even as they worship the Father, and that all should submit to the government of the man whom God delighted to honor.

At this instant I was begotten in Satan's alarmed breast, and cried out, 'Tis enough that such exalted spirits as we submit to him in his present unincarnate state. But worship and submit to him in an inferior nature, let who will, I will not. What does he mean? will the Almighty debase his first and best, and make us subject to an inferior nature? No, it shall never be said, that Satan the archangel stooped so low! The great archangel's voice was heard, his resolution was approved of, the standard of rebellion set up in heaven, and many millions of angels, whose natures I had changed, joined in that day, and fell into the depths of bottomless perdition. Now do you understand me?

AVARO. I understand you pretty well when you say that Satan begat you; but you say, that you begat him, and millions of devils besides. It ran always in my head that God had made every devil in the bottomless pit; but if I understand you aright, you say you made them all.

FASTOSUS. True, I do say so, and I will not quit an hair's breadth of my just prerogative. God never did, nor ever could, make any sinner, either angelic or human. Mind well what I say; for I perceive you are dull of apprehension, and but of a shallow judgment. It was not I, but God, who made them creatures. God created them in a holy, pure, and glorious state, and endued them with powers to preserve their primitive station, in the upper skies: but it was I, not God, who, from angels of light transformed them into devils of darkness. The very moment I was conceived, I changed them from light to darkness; from holiness to sin; from glory to dishonor; and thus, though not as creatures, yet as devils they are wholly of my formation. Do you understand me now?

AVARO. Yes, sir, I understand you as to that; but you said just now, that the moment you were brought forth you killed your father. Great sir, these are dark sayings.

FASTOSUS. Ay, Avaro, to such as you they are dark; but I'll explain them. I did not mean that I annihilated his angelic nature; no, he is an angel still, although a black one. But I meant that I slew all his primitive disposition to goodness, killed the life of holiness that once was in him; deprived him of the favor of God, which some people prefer even unto life. I made him that crooked, perverse monster, which you see he now is. I opened the overflowing sluices of divine indignation, which continually pour down upon him, whatever he is doing or wherever he flies, and not upon him only, but upon all his adherents. Was not this killing him to purpose, think you?

AVARO. Indeed it was. You had not hurt him half so much, uncle, if you had deprived him of being. I wonder that he can endure the sight of you, after all that has befallen him on your account! You have deprived him of every good, and brought every evil upon him; and yet he loves you as he does his own soul. 'Tis strange! wondrous strange, Fastosus!

FASTOSUS. You'll think it stranger still, when I tell you that he is so far from hating me, that he will do nothing, either in earth or hell, amongst men or devils, but as he is directed and prompted to it by me. And so far is he from repenting of what he hath done, that he hath told me a thousand times, if it were to do again he would do it. Nothing grieves the heart of old Satan so much as this,—the very man whose exaltation he opposed, whose sway he resisted, and whose person he hath still in the most perfect abhorrence, is dignified, not only by a personal union with Jehovah; but by all judgment being committed into his hand, and the public administration of all the affairs of heaven, earth, and hell devolving upon him. Great is his torment, from the consideration that he, with all his adherents, must receive their final sentence from the same person, who, of all beings, he hates with the most consummate hatred, and on whose account he hates and seeks the destruction of all the creatures of God.

'Tis a perpetual hell to him, that the object of his greatest aversion sitteth on the circle of heaven, and holdeth him continually as with bit and bridle; limiteth his operations at pleasure, and sovereignly appoints his license by an unalterable determination. When, through confirmed malice and desperate resolution, Satan struggles for larger scope, Immanuel gives him a check, saying, "Hitherto thou mayest go, but no farther." And sometimes so severe is the check, that the prince of darkness is quite overturned; and whilst sprawling on his back, for very vexation that he can go no further, he rageth, and roareth louder than a thousand lions, so that all the arches of gloomy Tartarus resound. Then in the anguish of horrid despair, he bites his adamantine chains, foams at his mouth, and utters such dreadful blasphemies as none but himself can utter. What is the most remarkable of all is, that the more rapidly the torrent of the Almighty's wrath pours in upon him, the fonder he is of me, the cause of all his misery.

AVARO. Sir, you say that Beelzebub will do nothing without your direction. If I understand this right, it is not he, but you who are governor of hell. Pray, sir, where are all his princely prerogatives then?

FASTOSUS. It is not fitting, Avaro, that you should criticise upon my doctrine. You ought to embrace it implicitly as I deliver it to you.

AVARO. Pardon me, great sir; you put me in mind of some of the modern parsons; for that is the very way that they want their doctrine to be embraced, implicitly, without questioning its currency. 'Tis merry enough to hear them exhort their hearers, to search the scriptures, to try the spirits, to take heed what they hear, &c. and yet after all, if any of their hearers attempt to bring the parson's own sermon to trial by the scriptures, he is deemed a troublesome, self-conceited fellow, and if he happens to disprove his doctrine by the scripture, he is presently dealt with, and excommunicated as troubler of Israel. For the parson would have other people's doctrine tried, and, if false, refuted; but it is impious to do so by his own. Brave days, Fastosus, are these! It is quite laughable to hear the modern clergymen tell their hearers, that they have a right to private judgment, and to know the mind of God for themselves; and at the same time obliging them implicitly to abide by the confession of faith already authenticated. That is, uncle, the clergy will allow you to controvert the scriptures if you choose it; but their own articles must have your implicit submission.

FASTOSUS. Well, cousin, you have fairly laughed me out

of my resentment, by the droll conduct of your parsons. However, what I said, Avaro, I will maintain. It shall never be said that the devil, Fastosus, did at any time eat his words; but I will condescend to explain myself. Without me, Beelzebub would be none other than an angel; but mixing myself with his angelic faculties, I render him a perfect devil. The same I do with all the rest of my infernal subjects. Beelzebub himself is but a titular prince. 'Tis I who instigate him, that am the great devil of all. To tell you more, it is I who formed hell itself, as a place of punishment. Such is the rectitude and equity of his nature, that God never would, nor could, inflict any punishment without my intervention. He was ever guided in all his works by his own perfections, and therefore could never have punished sinless beings. All beings would have remained sinless, but for me. So in making sin, I made the punishment of it. For if once sin is introduced, punishment follows of course; it being as natural for sin to bring forth punishment, as it is for the sun to send forth light and heat.

No being possibly can be a devil, but the being who is possessed and governed by me. Every being thus possessed and governed, whether angel or man, is a devil. But for distinction's sake, we ascribe only the plain name of fiends, to the angels whom I govern, and to men and women under my dominion, we give the names of devils incarnate, because they inhabit bodies of flesh. The difference in the stature of devils is not, that one is less devilish than the other, but their being possessed of more noble endowments, and more extensive qualities than others. So you see the devils of quality among us, are more intelligent, more subtle and crafty than devils of a vulgar race. The reason why Beelzebub is head over all the infernal tribes also, is not because he is more depraved than his adherents; but because he was originally created in a more glorious station, possessed of endowments more exalted, and blest with more extensive natural powers. As such, being once depraved, he is capable of excelling his fellows as far, in diabolical achievements, as at first he excelled them in their heavenly station. The same rule holds good, through the various ranks of my subjects. Were you to ask me, why it is that devils without a body, are capable of exceeding in sweet rebellion, those spirits who are embodied? I would answer without hesitation, "Not because the one is less vicious, or one whit less depraved, than the other; but for the following two very good and substantial reasons.

1. Although I reign and rule in the heart of every one of them, yet whilst they are in the body, they are laid under particular restrictions by the Almighty; so that they cannot do all the evil which in their hearts I prompt them to do; and therefore they cannot be so much like Beelzebub, in their actions, as they would be. Fear and shame very often prevent people from gratifying their impious and unclean inclinations, when a love of virtue, and the fear of God, are absolutely out of the question.

2. Because the natural powers of man are very far inferior to the powers of infernal spirits. The more extensive a man's natural capacity, the nearer he may arrive to the stature of Satan, if unrestrained by the grace of God. Hence a crafty and learned pope, is by far more like the devil than an ignorant, swag-bellied friar. Yea, Avaro, the more enlarged the capacity of either man or devil may be, as it makes him capable of the higher degrees of wickedness, even so in proportion to the natural abilities of both shall the punishment inflicted be. No wicked being is so capable of being wicked as the crafty and understanding person; who, if he is not truly virtuous and holy, must be truly wicked and devilish. Hence one Hume, one Voltaire, is an hundred times more capable of being useful to us, than fifty H—w—ds, or even five times the number of popish priests. You may take this as a general maxim, that the most enlarged soul must be the most tormented, if not saved.

Avaro. One may see by your learning, sir, what it is to be born among spirits. Why, you converse as freely and fluently about the nature of angels and men, as I can do about gold and silver coin. Great, great, sir, is your merit.

Fastosus. How should it be otherwise, Avaro, when you consider the subtility of my nature? I am the very soul of Beelzebub, and all his vassals. Petty spirits may boast of their conquests one to another, but they must all be silent when courtly Fastosus opens his mouth. You, Avaro, Impiator, Discordans, &c. have all of you made as great inroads upon mankind as can possibly be expected from such unseemly spirits as you be; but as for me, you see I am a spirit of a comely deportment, and caressed by all. Indeed many people are now a days of opinion, that a spice of my nature is absolutely necessary, in order to make them respectable in the world, and prevent the injuries which otherwise might be offered to them. Nor is there any who can discern the fatal consequences of being under my direction, except, those who are enlightened from above, by him who was given for a light to the Gentiles. I lodge securely in the secret caverns of the heart, and from thence I convey my influence so imperceptibly through all the words of the mouth, and actions of the life, that you rarely meet with a man or woman, who will own that they have the least acquaintance with me; though with many of them, the judicious beholder will easily perceive, that I am deeply concerned in all they do or say.

Avaro. Indeed I have often heard people declare, that they never saw the devil Fastosus, nor had the least acquaintance with pride. Yet, they said, a little spirit ought to be shown, that every one might know his proper place. But I perceive now, that pride itself is that same spirit which they deem so necessary, notwithstanding their supposed freedom from it, and aversion to it.

Fastosus. The very same spirit, Avaro, though they do not know it; for I deceive them at every turn, being capable of transforming myself into so many different shapes, and bearing a name so suitable to each, that even when I lord it over them with the greatest power, they remain utterly ignorant of their subjection to me. Sometimes I assume the appearance and bear the name of my avowed enemy, Humility. Then you will see people of fashion, or those who think themselves such, descending lower than their station, for no other reason than to get a good name. At another time you may see me transformed into the likeness of Charity, and I prompt my slaves to bestow their alms, in order to be esteemed benevolent and generous. I have seen a man of wealth and industry, perform such actions with this and no other view. And he has made his poor belly to suffer for it many days to come, when at the same time he had his thousands out at use. Then I take upon me the name of Decency, and am greatly employed in regulating domestic affairs, descending even so low, as to take cognizance of meat and drink, dress and company

Then you may see madam extremely diligent in persuading Miss Prim and Miss Stiff not to be seen in the company of those of an inferior station. Ere you are aware, I have got the pride of good breeding; and oh! what wonders of fashionable civilities I work, and forward the great designs of hell. At this time you'll see my lady, who having forgotten the fashions prevailing about twenty years ago, when she was under forty, is as careful as possible not to deviate in the least from the customs of them who were born since she was a wife and mother. Sometimes I bear the name of a spirit of honor. Under this name I prevailed in ancient Rome, and now reign over many of our European cavaliers. In this character I do great execution among the British gods at the west end of London, where the greatest enormities are deemed excusable, but the putting up with an affront an unpardonable evil.

AVARO. There would be nothing done, in comparison of what there is, among mankind, if we appeared in our own likeness, and went by our proper names: for there are thousands that love us extremely while in disguise, who would be ashamed of us, if we went by our proper names of Covetousness and Pride. As for my part, I am fain to perform all my works in disguise; bearing the feigned names of Industry, Frugality, &c. But, sir, will it please you to give me some account how you first made your entrance good amongst mankind.

FASTOSUS. I have already told you, that as soon as I was born, I obtained full dominion over the adherents of Beelzebub; this taught the angels of the deep that the only way to seduce innocent beings, was to inject my nature into them; and that the seeds of pride being once sown, they could not fail of most abundant fruitfulness. Man was originally created in a holy and happy estate, a perfect stranger to those evils which now prevail over, and reign predominant in the natural and moral world. You could not have seen so much as one symptom of pride or covetousness, or other vice, either in Adam or Eve, in their primitive state. They loved without unchastity, and enjoyed without uncleanliness; nor were they in the least acquainted with the racking torments of jealousy. No anxious thoughts, perplexing fears, nor distracting cares, disturbed their peaceful hearts. Envy, anger, shame, and resentment, were strangers to the new-created pair, and never set foot in paradise before my arrival there Their sole delight was to contemplate the beneficence of their God.

Our eagle-eyed angels, when they saw the noble deport ment of man, soon perceived that he was of the same nature which the son of God was predestined to assume, (for as some think, he might, out of love to the human nature, appear occasionally to the heavenly hosts in the form of man*) for the resisting of which decree, they were damned to the depths of ever-burning hell. The first discovery Beelzebub made of the blessed situation in which man was created, filled his noble mind with such violent agitations of rage, envy, malice, and pride, that his fury burst beyond all bounds. He stamped and raged in a most tempestuous manner; insomuch that he shook the sable firmament of hell, and brought his confederates to inquire the cause of his anguish. A council thus convened, after the prince had a little recovered from the first shock of transporting rage, he related to them what he had discovered, concerning the inhabitants of Eden, and asked advice of his senators, who, to a devil, vowed speedy destruction to man. Some demur there was respecting the plan of their operations: for the impolitic part of the assembly, finding the smallness of their number, were for having man assaulted by storm: but the more sage politicians voted for craft, as the likeliest method to seduce them. At last the august assembly came to this unanimous resolution, "That the great Beelzebub should, by certain means, by him to be devised, inspire them with my nature, nothing doubting, but if that could be done, they would soon declare in favor of the devil's government.

After he had well weighed every circumstance, the arch-apostate undertook the enterprise; but did not judge it proper to exercise force against them, knowning well that if their resistance proved equal to their power, all his destructive measures must unavoidably be broken, and the enterprise miscarry. Therefore, like a wise hero and consummate

---

* Some may think that this parenthesis is an impeachment of the knowledge of Fastosus, supposing that himself was ignorant, whether the Son of God did or did not assume the form of man in his intercourse with the heavenly legions. But it ought to be observed, that this judicious devil is relating transactions which were antecedent to the time when he professes to have been born.

politician, he resolved to accomplish, by craft and subtilty, what was not to be done by open assault; nor did he think it advisable to address them in his own form, lest he should frighten them at his first appearance, and by that means render their seduction for ever after impracticable: but judiciously concluded that the most promising method was, to assume the body of one of their familiar domestic animals, which were daily under their observation. Accordingly, after long consultation with himself, and strictly examining the brutal tribes, he possessed a beauteous serpent, perceiving that it was head of the reptile world, and best fitted for converse with man, with whom also it was more familiar than all the beasts beside. Thus equipped for executing the deep projected scheme, he still acted with caution becoming the most consummate experience. He cared not to attack them both at once, lest by any means they should see through his disguise, and he should occasion his own repulse; therefore he craftily lurked near them, and overheard their discourse, that he might better learn which of them was the weaker vessel.

Being a spirit of great penetration, he soon found that the woman was not only the weakest but the youngest; and what greatly encouraged his hope was, that the man loved the woman with the most tender affection, a circumstance very painful for him to behold. Peace being now a stranger to his own bosom, it was grievous for him to see the felicity of the human pair. In consequence of these discoveries, he made no attempts upon the man; but bent all his endeavors to seduce the woman, not doubting, but if that could be effected, the man would come of course, so strongly was he attached to his yoke-fellow.

I would tell you the whole now, cousin, but I must go and assist my lady Gaiety to dress; for she is to dine with my lord Frolic to-day. About four o'clock I'll meet you here.

DIALOGUE V.

INFIDELIS AND IMPIATOR.

FASTOSUS and Avaro had not been long gone, before I saw Infidelis and Impiator, stalking up to the rendezvous, and as they walked, thus conversing:

IMPIATOR. But is it possible, sir, that the papists should ascribe an equal, if not a greater glory to the blessed virgin, than to the Son of God.

INFIDELIS. It is not only possible, but certain; and, as a proof of it, I shall repeat to you one of their prayers to her; a prayer which can by no means be offensive to any of our people. "O Mary! the star of the sea; the heaven of health; the learned advocate of the guilty; the only hope of the desperate; the saviour of sinners. Thou callest thyself the handmaid of Jesus Christ, but art his lady; for right and reason willeth that the mother be above the son. Pray him, and command him from above, that he lead us to his kingdom, at the world's end." Here, you see, child, that although he was believed by his apostles to be God over all; the papists have found out a way to put him under the command of his virgin mother. Not only so, but they have put him under the command of St. Ann, reputed by them to have been his grandmother, as may be seen in that famous prayer, approved and authorized by the doctors of the Sorbonne, in Paris. I'll repeat the passage, being the fourth paragraph in the prayer. "In homage of the right and power (of mother) which you had over your daughter, (Mary) and of grandmother over her son, and of their (Mary's and Jesus's) submission, which they render you." Here you see he is supposed to submit to his grandmother Ann, as well as to be under the government of his mother Mary. I could tell you strange things, son, about the popish religion, and I intend it ere long; but, for the present, I would beg of you to give me some further account of the different cantons of your devotees. I think they were seven in number.

IMPIATOR. I shall describe them to you, sir. And it would be proper to begin with the canton of drunkards, because that is the royal canton, where I keep my court, but with your good leave, I shall defer the description of it to the last.

INFIDELIS. Son, your will is your law in this particular take whatever method your thoughts suggest as best.

IMPIATOR. Then I begin with the canton of swearers the most foolish and unaccountable set of people, upon the face of the earth. This canton is divided into two provinces, both which are full of people. In the first province dwell the false swearers, and the profane swearers in the second.

The province of false swearers is divided into three districts, the first of which is inhabited by knights of the post, a set of gentry who get their living by giving evidence in causes to which they are perfect strangers. These knights commonly make their court to the c—k of arr–igns, whom, they know, is best capable of finding them employment. It is not a great many years since, a gentleman, walking in the sessions-house, in the Old Bailey, was accosted by one of these knights with, "Pray, sir, do you want a witness? Sir, I'll serve you as cheap and as well as any man." Gardiner, bishop of Winchester, formerly was a mighty protector of this order of knights: and, at this day, our good friend, the father of the world, his worthy inquisitors, and not a few right reverend prelates, are head men in the district of false swearers. Many a good Christian has been brought to the stake, or gallows, by their assiduity, both among papists and pagans; and more especially the former who are far from being so honest as the latter; and not by half so consistent.

The second district is inhabited by the mercenary swearers. This is a race supposed to be descended from the knights of the post, and to be sure there is great likeness betwixt the two. The mercenary swearers will buy a piece of goods for five shillings, and as soon as a buyer presents himself, tells him that, upon his life and soul, it cost him six shillings. When he meets with another seller of the same commodity, in order to obtain a good pennyworth, he shows him the goods for which he paid five shillings, and tells the stranger, that, "As he hopes to be saved, he gave no more than four and sixpence for it." The dealers in horses, drovers, and butchers, are singularly dexterous in this kind of swearing In this district, it is a prevalent opinion, that a man is not fit to live in the world, unless he can swear to a lie.

The third division is inhabited by the foolish swearers, a people the most remarkably stupid of any under the government of hell. Some of them are so accustomed to it from their infancy, that they do not so much as know when they swear, and are as destitute of design in the practice as the parrot when it scolds the chambermaid, or as many good people when they say their prayers at church. Othe. seem to have such a low opinion of their own probity, that they imagine no one will believe what they say, unless every sentence is ushered in with an oath in the van, and confirmed by another in the rear. Gentlemen of family, fortune, and fashion, are stationed in this class, and are extremely dexterous here. Nor are the officers of the fleet and army less learned, or devoid of those embellishments. The greatest part of the English officers, indeed, marine and military, esteem a man not fit to carry a musket, unless he can swear a hundred oaths in a quarter of an hour, without any qualms of conscience.

The British army so far excels in this fine art, that they can fairly curse the French off the field of battle, without ever striking a blow: so terrified are the French at the oaths of the English. Ay, father, I assure you, that this heroic practice is now so prevalent among the basest of the multitude, that I could pick you out a low-lifed boatswain, who will vie with an admiral; and a dwarfish drummer, who will swear with a lieutenant-general, for any money. Yea, I could pick you out a fellow, who cannot procure whole shoes to his feet, that yet will match any nobleman or esquire in the land at swearing. And, sir, if honor consists in being adapts here, the vilest pedlar may vie with the best of the gentry, and the very footpad may challenge a peer of the realm. The canton of swearers is a very populous and very honorable place. Here are dukes, knights of all orders, marquises, and earls. And a very worshipful canton it is too; for numbers of very respectable corporations, and many justices of the peace reside in it.

I have often laughed to see a delinquent brought before a magistrate, and by him be obliged to pay two shillings for every attested oath, when the magistrate himself had no.

manhood enough to maintain conversation for ten minutes, without being guilty of profane swearing.

INFIDELIS. Pray thee, my son, what are the qualifications requisite to a justice of the peace in thy country?

IMPIATOR. Two qualifications, sir, only are requisite. The first is, that the gentleman be pretty well to live in the world, and the second, that he shall be an obsequious tool to administration. As to knowledge of the law, love to the people, regard to moral principles, and all such stuff, they are altogether out of the question.

I was going to say, it is a very religious canton, too, because here you may find a considerable number of reverend parsons, both Papists and Protestants. As for their oaths in use, they are various, as the fancy of the swearers inclines them. Some swear by heaven, others by the God of heaven; some swear by Christ, others by his blood and wounds; some by St. Peter, others by St. Paul; some by St. Mary, others by her virginity; some swear by the pope, others by his holiness, and by his infallibility; some by the life of their sovereign; some by the life of the devil, and some by their own lives. Some there are who swear by the church; others by the liturgy and mass; and some, for want of a better epithet, swear by their own eyes and limbs.

INFIDELIS. Indeed, son, these are a set of as foolish people as one would wish to meet with. The devil himself would not wish them to be more foolish. One would wonder to see men of distinction, who disdain to conform to the vulgar, in other particulars, rank themselves with gypsies and sturdy beggars, in the most abject and unmanly practice. Sensible people, and some there are still among men do not esteem a man the more for his acres or pension, but for his virtue and good sense; and hence a swearing gypsy and a swearing gentleman are held as equally dishonorable. But no more of this; I intend not to become a moralist at this time.

IMPIATOR. I assure you, profitable as they are to me, I am ready to crack my sides with laughing, to see how foolishly they fight and broil, curse and damn each other, and how ready they are to forward the devil's interest, notwithstanding it is to their own everlasting ruin.

The second canton is that of thieves; and a very flourishing canton it is, notwithstanding we every session send a freight over the Stygian lake,* who no more return to their native country. This canton being very extensive, is likewise divided into several lesser cantons. The first of which contains the gentlemen thieves. A very courtly, polite, and fashionable set of people. Gentlemen thieves are such who enjoy places of honor and trust, and are not careful of their duty to their king and country. It is observable of them, that when they are out of place, they are the greatest enemies to corruption, and the staunchest friends to liberty in the world. They are capable of no influence, but that of patriotism, so long as unprovided for; but the moment their happy stars make them placemen, they forget their patriotism, drop their enmity to venality, and seek nothing so much as their own emolument, leaving the public to shift for itself. It is thought that not a few gentlemen thieves live within a hundred miles of famous Tyburn; and some people farther think, it is great pity that solemn tree is not more frequently graced with them: but in modern times it is quite unfashionable to hang any but the little thieves.† Those gentlemen having no principles, above ambition and avarice, to influence them, being once in place, are capable of being more injurious to the commonwealth, each of them, than an hundred highwaymen; and yet Tyburn is not hon-

* The author has often lamented the unhappy untimely end of the malefactors hung up every session; sometimes for things perhaps comparatively trifling, and which in themselves cannot merit so severe a punishment. It does not appear from Scripture or reason, that common theft should be punished with the gallows; and especially when the matter stolen is of little value. Nor does it appear to be good policy to deprive society of a member, who might afterwards be useful, on account of some rash and unguarded invasion of his neighbor's property. Hang them once, and their services are for ever lost to the community. If other methods were taken, villany would be more successfully suppressed, and the members of society spared for usefulness. The British senators must needs see, that the hanging trade does not lessen the number of rogues, nor the untimely end of one leave suitable impressions upon the minds of others. To be bound to hard labor for the space of one year, would be more terrible than to be transported for seven: and besides, use might introduce a laborious habit, which would render stealing unnecessary. I am persuaded, that to a dissolute young man, who hates labor, to be chained to a dung-cart, or placed in some other servile station, would be more dreadful than Tyburn itself.

† If an ingenious mechanic should die for filing a single guinea; an extravagant youth be hanged, without mercy, for putting one in bodily fear, on the highway; or a vain girl, in the prime of life, be executed for stealing a few yards of lace, and others plunder the nation of thousands with impunity, it shows that there must be a defect somewhere.

ored with a gentleman thief, above once in a century, much to the grief of real patriots.

Another class of gentlemen thieves, are our officers by sea and land, who impose upon their king and country by false musters: and in a very peculiar manner those who make their own fortunes, (no matter whether in the East or West Indies) by the fatigue of their men, who are left to remain in their original penury. These, together with the commissaries for the army, agents for regiments, &c. are all stationed here.

The second subdivision is peopled by what we call the fashionable thieves. A prodigious populous place is this. Here dwell legions of attorneys; vermin, who, for five shillings' worth of labor, will charge their clients near the same number of pounds; and very conscientiously take pay, for wilfully perverting and defeating a just cause. Here you may find gentlemen, who can procure witnesses to swear just as you would have them, and pack a jury that can give a clear verdict, over the belly of the most consistent evidence. Such a jury hath, ere now, saved a noble neck from the deserved cord, through the all-subduing power of money. To this famous division belongs the tradesman, who will take more from an unskilful buyer, than he knows in his conscience his goods are worth: a thing very common among dealers. Also, the wealthy gentleman, who, in buying, will take advantage of the indigence of the seller, and pay, if he can, less than the real worth of what he buys. This practice is now so very near to universal, that tradesmen deal with one another, for the most part, as if they were all known to be rogues and cheats; and he is the best tradesman, that can best guard against the villany of his neighbors.

Here dwells the careful tradesman, who, if a man once owes him five pounds, would write down five pounds ten shillings. This method is so much in vogue, that many people dare not trust their names on the tradesmen's books. As for my friend, Sir Roger Latepay, he has had such experience of it, that his wood is in danger. In this fashionable division dwells the tradesman, who, conscious that his own capital is expended, supports his luxury and grandeur at the expense of his dealers; and many such there be in town and country. The avaricious farmers, manufacturers and householders, who make their servants and mechanics work under their usual wages, from the pretence of deadness of trade, &c. The buyer, who is conscious of his present inability, and spends without any probable view of being hereafter able to pay, dwells in the very heart of this division; and hard by him dwells the father, who, to gratify a depraved taste, squanders away his estate, to the defrauding of his wife and children. All of these, sir, are very fashionable people.

The third division is that of holy thieves. That is, men whose theft is in holy things. By holy thieves, I mean unholy men, sustaining holy offices. Such is he, who enters into orders, merely for the sake of a good living. All who climb over the wall, and come not in by the door, are thieves and robbers. Thieves, because they steal the portion of the priests; for, having no right to the sacerdotal function, their participation of the altar is sacrilegious theft. Robbers, because they make havoc of the church, and deprive God's children of the food allowed them by their heavenly father. Here dwell shoals of popish priests, and very considerable numbers of protestant clergy, of various denominations, as well as the total sum of pagan and mahometan mufties. His holiness, the pope of Rome, is indeed president in this division, for he steals the prerogatives of God and applies them to his own private use.

The fourth division in the canton of thieves, are those whom we call the sporting thieves. Such are card-players, cock-fighters, horse-coursers, and gamblers of all sorts. I know of none of my sporting subjects, but what will win if they can, either by upright, or inequitable means. Therefore, with us it is an established maxim, that the true gambler is the certain thief. Here too you may find princes, nobles, spiritual and temporal, and judges of every rank. Ha! ha! ha! how have I been ready to split my sides with laughing, to see an archbishop lay aside his mitre, and take up a pack of cards; and the sacred judge, after having passed sentence on a criminal, lay aside all his solemnity, and put on the sprightly sportsman! Then cried I, O! the bench! O! the pulpit! O! the gambler!

The fifth division in the canton of thieves, is inhabited by what we call fantastic thieves. A very contemptible canton this is with sensible people. Yet foolish as they are with their nostrums, they make it appear, that there are people more foolish than themselves; for they pick the pockets of the neighboring cantons very cleverly. Here dwell your Duffies, Godfries, Stoughtons, Fluggers, Lowthers, Jameses, Turlingtons, &c. Here the famous Mr. Mountebank is president, and Mr. Andrew Archee is his deputy. In this division nothing is heard of but pills, lozenges, troches, balsams, elixirs, drops, cordials, and the ready coin; for the fantastical thieves can give no credit.

The sixth division consists of plain honest highwaymen. Honest, when compared with many of the others; for when the thieves are about to rob a man, they very honestly tell him their design, and stake but a few high words, and the mouth of the pistol, against the purse and all that is in it, which, notwithstanding the odds be greatly on the traveller's side, the highwayman carries lightly off, with the watch into the bargain. Whereas many of the gentlemen thieves carry on their work so slily, that you know not their intention of robbing you, until long after the robbery is committed. O! Tyburn, Tyburn, thou hast long groaned for such men as these!

Here too are many venerable priests, who, by pretended pardons, dispensations, &c. play the pick-pocket to great advantage. Much could I say about this class of veterans in the thieving trade, were I not afraid of exciting their resentment, which would be very detrimental to my designs, as they lead the consciences of the laity just which way they please.

Infidelis. Indeed, my son, by your account of them, the highwayman and pick-pockets are less prejudicial to society, than many who are held to be men of great renown.

Impiator. Ay, sir, a thousand times, and I can tell you that some of the greatest names are enrolled in the annals of this canton of thieves. There are the Grecian and Roman heroes, almost in general, particularly great Alexander, and Julius Cæsar. There is Tamerlane, there is Kouli Khan, there is Philip of Spain, and there is L——s of France, who has as good an inclination to thieving as any body. Poor gentleman! it is not half a century since he put forth his hand to pick the pocket of George king of Britain; but he got his fingers most wofully bitten, before he could pull them in again. But what is bred in the bones will never be out of the flesh; therefore, as the English did not take care effectually to secure themselves when they had it in their power, they must expect further experience of French theft.

INFIDELIS. One would have thought that the English have had so many instances of royal theft, from that quarter, that they would have effectually prevented future danger from thence. Nor are our good friends the Spaniards less inclined to the thievish practice than their neighbors. Witness Peru and Mexico, those once opulent and populous kingdoms, which now belong to them, in the same manner as the purse of gold belongs to the highwayman, who took it from the gentleman whom he murdered.

IMPIATOR. Ay, sir, great thieves are abundantly more hurtful to mankind, than thieves of a dwarfish size; though famous Tyburn, and the places akin to it, seldom have the honor of ushering them into the other world.

The third canton is the liars' canton, a people with double tongues, and of the nature of an otter, amphibious. The great Beelzebub is grand president here, but is represented by two famous deputies, namely, the artful Mahomet, and the good old gentleman at Rome. Of the two, the latter is most in favor at court, because Beelzebub says, he is so very much of his own image; although, it must be owned, Mahomet bears a very great resemblance. All the holy fathers, my lords the inquisitors, with their assistant familiars. All the venerable patriarchs, and princely cardinals, reside in the metropolis, near the exchange, in the principal street, which is a straight thoroughfare to hell. The bishops, of both ranks, are stationed next to them, and greatly facilitate the journey of passengers. The very populous suburbs are inhabited by the sons of St. Ignatius; than whom, none are more excellent at the arts of lying and evasion. And here too are abundance of friars, of every order, who, though less crafty than the Jesuits, are very diligent in the great work of deceit. In this country, politeness and learning have arrived at the greatest perfection. Here are abundance of courtiers, and statesmen, besides atheists and deists, highly esteemed by our people, for their learning and sense.

The famous court liars are like a dead fish. They always swim with the stream of power. They are for or against stamp-acts, and general warrants, just as the sentiments of their superiors direct. They are Protestants, or intolerant papists, or neither, just as their prince is inclined, or as their own interests require. Their consciences are tender as a willow, and will turn any way with the application of a purse of gold, a place, a pension, or a peerage. When it serves their low and base purposes, you will find them patriots; but if the good of the nation clashes with their sinister views, you may find them traitors either to church or state, or to both. Of this class were Bonner and Gardiner, zealous Protestants in the days of Edward the Sixth, and bloody papists in the reign of his sister of scarlet memory. To this class also belonged Sharp, the archbishop of St. Andrew's; for it was not conviction, but gold, that changed his sentiments from presbytery to prelacy. All the arguments which my lords, the bishops of England, had advanced, made no more impression upon him, than an arrow would have made upon a rock of flint; but when his majesty came, in a rhetorical manner, to press him home with a heavy purse of gold, a coach and six, and a bishopric, he was quite confounded, and had not a word to say for mother kirk of Scotland. Such court arguments as this, sir, stop the mouths of many a patriot; Lord C——m is a recent proof of this. Such was the force of his elocution that it could gain battles, subdue states, reverse laws, and make placemen tremble, until he was unhappily confounded by a place, a pension, and a peerage; and now, poor gentleman, he has nothing left to gratify his ambition, but the melancholy reflection of what he once was.

There is another herd of court liars, (excuse the phrase, sir, because it is the common opinion, that of all vermin, court liars are the most detestable) who fawn like a spaniel upon every prince that ascends the throne, in order to ingratiate themselves into his favor, thereby to make sure of their own emolument. If the manners of the prince are ever so dissolute, they caress him as their most wise and amiable monarch. Though he were as much of a dastard as Sardanapalus, they will persuade him that he will vie with Hector for magnanimity. If he is a drunkard, or glutton, they will flatter him with his temperance; or represent his luxury as a princely virtue, very becoming a royal personage; even if one half of his subjects be famishing for want of bread. Some of those court liars will tell their prince, that it is no crime at all for him to enter his neighbor's territories, and murder twenty or thirty thousand of his subjects, though there is really no cause given on their part, for the hostile invasion. Some such villians precipitated Lewis of France into a war with Britain, which would infallibly have proved his ruin, had he not been well befriended by some people near St. James's.

A truly patriotic courtier is a strong pillar to the throne; but court liars are the destruction of that prince whose ear they govern.

It is my opinion, that a prince has need either to be a very wise man himself, or to have very honest men about him. Happy is that nation, who has a wise and prudent king, and at the same time honest and faithful ministers. Earthly thrones are so infested with fawning flatterers! that if the prince is not very well acquainted with his Bible, it is difficult for him to know, whether he is virtuous or vicious.

INFIDELIS. That is a book in little esteem. Great men are for the most part too polite to trouble themselves with its contents, because they are so unfavorable to their practices.

IMPIATOR. True, and by those means princes are the more readily deceived. For a mitred courtier may, perhaps, tell his prince, that it is lawful for a royal personage, to debauch the wife or daughter of one of an inferior rank, but unlawful for a plebeian; notwithstanding his spiritual lordship knows very well, that when God said, "Whoremongers and adulterers I will judge," he exempted not the prince any more than the peasant; for with him there is no respect of persons on account of their worldly dignity.

Another right reverend courtier tells his prince, that it is allowable enough in him, on the Sabbath, after the irksome service is over at church, to divert himself with a quiet, civil game at chess, quadrille, or whatever his pious inclination leads him to; and that it may be lawful for some favorite nobility to assist at the sport; but, says he, it is utterly unlawful for the husbandman and low mechanic; though the downy doctor knows well enough, that when the Almighty sanctified the Sabbath, it was not a part only, but the whole Sabbath he intended.

INFIDELIS. Well, Impiator, whatever license the right reverends allow at court, their sable brethren in the country are not less indulgent; for in most parishes in England, the people may swear or pray, get drunk or communicate, go to church or stay at home, get to heaven or hell, just as their inclination leads them, for any concern his reverence the parson gives himself, provided always he is not cheated of his dues.

Impiator. I know I am well befriended by many clergymen. But to return to the prince, I assure you I have often thought that, of all men, it is the greatest difficulty for him to be a good man, and get safe to heaven: he has so many about him, who are base enough to commend even his vices, and but very few who love him well enough to correct his errors. But if I become a moralist now, you'll suppose I act out of character. However, though many have exhausted all their wit and good nature upon the court liars, they are still the same, they lie as fast as ever for the sake of money, estates, high places, &c.: therefore some people call them mercenary liars.

But many of the inhabitants of this canton are less ambitious, and will very freely tell lies for a penny gain; amongst those are the travelling tradesmen, who carry their shops upon their backs. Them we call the petty dealers, and the humble liars. But we have others more generous still, who will give you a lie fresh from the mint, with no other view but to raise a laugh. These we call the merry liars, because they go laughing to hell. Others we have, who stand in the capacity of god-fathers and god-mothers, who very roundly promise and vow to do, for the child, what they never intend to perform. Some people call them the foolhardy liars. Next to them reside a very venerable tribe, called by the name of reverend liars. Reverend, because in holy orders; and liars, because they tell my lord bishop that they are moved by the Holy Ghost, to take upon them the office of a deacon, whereas they are moved by the hope of a good living, not knowing that there is such a being as the Holy Ghost; and deeming it enthusiasm to profess to be moved by him. When once put into orders, and a benefice, those worthy gentlemen rave against all who profess to be influenced in their devotion, by the Holy Spirit, as fanatics, enthusiasts, and madmen. Now, either my good friend the parson lies to my lord bishop, or his congregation; but the truth is, he lies to both.

The fourth canton is, that of sabbath-breakers, which is a

very populous, polite and opulent canton indeed. The far greater part of the nobility, and other gentlemen of rank and fortune, reside here. They are too well-bred to worship God on Sunday, in public or private. They scorn to suppose themselves indebted to the Almighty for life, and breath, and all things; or to be accountable to him for the use they make of their time, estates, and talents. They leave it to the low-lifed mechanics, to go to church or meeting, or when there, to be devout, and take notice of what they are about. Let the parson talk about heaven, or hell, or what they will, they are unconcerned, never once supposing themselves endued with immortal souls.

There is my good friend, my lord Timelagg, a nobleman of the first distinction; he is so taken up through the week, with contriving how to provide for himself and his creatures, that he is in no condition to go to church on Sunday, but chooses some convenient part of it for an airing, either in the coach with my lady, or on horseback with his cousin, 'squire Idle. Mrs. Housekeeper also is very closely employed in preparing tea and chocolate against their return. Mr. Steward is very busy in preparing his rent-rolls, studiously contriving how to extract an estate for himself, out of his master's, so that he cannot go to church at any rate. The footman, and my lady's woman must needs attend their master and mistress; the coachman and postilion must guide the machine; the butler and groom must be within call, one to take care of the horses, and the other to furnish with claret or champaign; so that the minister is very little obliged to his lordship for finding him an auditory to preach to.

The London tradesmen come up as near to his lordship's example as their circumstances will admit of. Their spirits are quite exhausted with the fatigues of weekly business; therefore, instead of leading their families duly to church, you may meet squadrons of them every Saturday night and Sunday morning, going to regale themselves with a Sunday's pleasure, which consists in eating, carousing and riding.

Then there is your sabbath-day visitors; very genteel people. The tea-table gossips are much concerned here: you may find hundreds of tables, the conversation of which is supported at the expense of the reputation of some absent

For it must be observed that our gossips are so absolutely destitute of innate ideas, and are such perfect strangers to the affairs of civil life, that they cannot support conversation five minutes at a sitting, but by the help of slander. Hence some people have said, that slander is the very soul of conversation. And sure enough, if you pick out all the slanderous expressions from the conversation of our gossips, you will have but a very scanty fragment remaining.

There are others so given up to indolence, that they keep great part of the Sabbath in bed, on a couch, or in the easy chair. These people are so exceedingly opprest with the weight of their own bodies that they can attend at neither church nor chapel, although active enough the other parts of the week: and yet they are good Christians, and hope to go to heaven when they die. And yet they seldom think of any thing but living for ever; in order to which they eat, drink, and sleep away the sabbath. These go by the name of lazy sabbath-breakers; and all who are employed the whole morning, in preparing superfluities for dinner, live along with them.

Another class of sabbath-breakers consists of the petty dealers, who buy or sell commodities, for back or belly, on the sabbath day. We call them the mistrustful sabbath-breakers, because they cannot trust God with their customers; and slothful sabbath-breakers, because they do not provide for their families, on the six days appointed for labor. England, with all its bravery, is horribly disgraced by a set of profane people, such as grocers, chandlers, butchers, barbers and bakers, who will not miss the taking a penny on the sabbath, any more than another day. Besides them, there are tailors, mantua and shoemakers, who, with their late finishes, make great encroachments on the sabbath, and that in the most open manner.

Infidelis. I thought in England, the law had made provision against such enormous breaches of the sabbath.

Impiator. Yes, the laws do indeed make provision for the suppression of such vices: but I have the pleasure of seeing the enforcing of those laws, very often left with people who are entirely devoted to my interest; so the laws are frequently asleep, when I am awake and upon my rounds.

But there is another tribe against whom there is no hu

man law. I mean the thinking sabbath-breakers; a careful industrious set of people, esteemed by all and known but to few. They are constantly employed through the week, and are glad of the sabbath's approach, that they may repair their bodily fatigue, and give a free scope to their plodding minds. When they awake on the Sabbath morning, they are deeply contemplating some transactions of the past week, or concerting measures proper to be followed in the ensuing. Nor does the man alter his subject when he goes to church. No, he is quite uniform. Try him, and you will find him all of a piece. Let the parson choose what subject he will, the other sticks to his text; so that it often happens when the minister thinks his auditory is collected, and the bulk of his parish appear at church, he is mistaken; for the greatest part of those whom he thinks to be present, are only there in appearance; their minds, their better part, being absent on other occasions.

For instance, the parson sometimes thinks that he sees 'squire Folly and madam his lady, in the front pew of the right-hand gallery: but he is mistaken; for only their bodies are there; their minds are absent. As for the 'squire, he is busy chasing the hare or fox, over all the hedges and ditches in his manor; and his lady is mentally at this ball, or the other assembly; or at this play or the other opera; or perhaps she is cheapening silks, at Mr. Cant's, silk-mercer, on Ludgate-hill.

Sometimes the merchant seems to be at church: however, he is only there in body, his soul having sailed in the good ship Bonadventure, to buy slaves on the coast of Guinea, or barter goods at Bengal or Malabar. The mercer, draper, and grocer, seem sometimes to be there; but frequently it is an imposition: for although their bodies may indeed be present, their souls are gone on a journey, to visit their customers, or left at home, in the counting-house, balancing their books, or examining their tradesmen's bills, that they may know with whom they can deal to the greatest advantage; perhaps issuing forth a capias against 'squire Latepay, a gentleman well known to those dealers; or it may be, the soul is busy, entering protests against certain extravagant manufacturers.

As for the industrious farmer, you may well think he

has something else to employ his mind, than either sermon or prayers; for it must needs require much thought and forecast to determine right, where to sow his wheat, where his clover, and what land to set apart for hemp, how to dispose of his young colt, and the gray horse, who is in danger of losing his eyes. And he, good man, hath found from long experience, that he can contrive better at church than anywhere else; and being willing to thrive in the world, he will let slip no opportunity proper for advantageous consideration.

But I can tell you, sir, if the people so frequently put the cheat upon their parson, he in his turn retaliates upon them; and many times when the congregation flatter themselves that they see the parson in, and hear his voice from the pulpit, they are mistaken; for it is only his body, his soul being attending the levee of this nobleman, or the other bishop, making his court for a fatter benefice. These, sir, are some of the thinking sabbath-breakers.

Then there are the mad sabbath-breakers, a set of the very dregs of humanity; and yet by some means or other their impious practices are connived at, notwithstanding interdicted by all laws divine and human. Such are our pellet throwers in Yorkshire and Durham; our foot-ball tossers, who are found all over the nation; our leapers, runners, tavern-haunters, and all of every denomination, who exercise themselves in any sport on the sabbath, are stationed along with the mad sabbath-breakers.

Last of all these are our religious sabbath-breakers, a district that is formed of party zealots and self-seekers, both preachers and hearers. As for the former, their doctrine is various. One man preaches the pope, another preaches the councils. One preaches St. Dominick, another St. Francis. One preaches episcopacy like the great Sacheverel, another preaches presbytery, as the only way of salvation. One preaches up mankind in general, and another preaches his own personal endowments in particulars; but as for preaching Jesus Christ, that is quite foreign to their purpose, and is therefore left to be performed by others. Thus, sire, you have had a view of the canton of sabbath-breakers.

INFIDELIS. And a noble canton it is, my son, both rich and populous, of great service to us, and vast enlargemen to the territories of Beelzebub. How illustrious is the throne of great Impiator! I long to have a description of the rest of your kingdom, but for the present I must be gone, my son. Will you please to give me the meeting here to-morrow morning?

IMPIATOR. I will, sir. Adieu.

DIALOGUE VI.

FASTOSUS AND AVARO.

PRIVY to the appointment betwixt Fastosus and Avaro, I resolved to stay their coming, and had not been long before I saw them at a distance, walking up the valley towards me. Arrived at the usual place of conference, Fastosus struck twice with his rod on the earth, and instantly there arose two thrones of the blackest ebony, one of which he occupied himself, and the other was filled by his cousin, Avaro. Thus enthroned, Fastosus opened the conversation, whilst I seized my pen, and sat eager to catch the fleeting sound.

FASTOSUS. You know, Avaro, when we parted in the morning, I was going to assist my lady Gaiety, to dress for her visit to my good lord Frolic. I went accordingly, and hard work I assure you we had of it. As soon as I appeared before the toilet, I received orders to render myself invisible, and not to depart the room, that I might be in readiness to adjust the head-dress, and bosom ornaments. Yes, madam, said I, I will give your ladyship due attendance. With that I rendered myself invisible to her, but continued visible to all other beholders. So to dressing we went. First we ornamented the feet, which was attended with very considerable difficulty. It cost us several tyings and untyings before her ladyship was pleased with her own foot. At last, having finished the feet, and my lady viewed them several times in every position, we proceeded to other parts of the important work. First we did and then we undid every part of the finery. But our hardest work about the head and bosom was, how to put one as much as possible out of its native form, and to expose the other so as to make sure of attracting the eyes of beholders. Monsieur Frisseur, who was our assistant, gave it as his opinion, that to come up to the very zenith of the mode, it was necessary she should bear an head as much as possible in resemblance to a ram without horns; and Mrs. Prude, my lady's woman, told us plainly, that Mrs. Pander, whose province it is to establish female customs, had expressly declared, every lady worth above one hundred a year, ought, in a full dress, to wear her bosom quite naked. My lady is adorned with excellent hair; but it will not serve her except it bear a look the most unnatural possible. Her skin, fair as alabaster, we were obliged to daub with patches, the color of Beelzebub's coat, as a token of her loyalty to the black prince of the nether regions. But how to place these patches was a question of no ordinary concern, and hardly resolved at last. First we tried one large patch on her chin; but my lady soon perceived, that it hid the beauteous dimple, which nature had there impressed, and therefore it was presently removed. Then we tried how the cheek would answer; but alas! it obscured the lively rose, which is a native there, and which my lady takes great delight to view in her glass; on this account we exempted the cheek from the burden. At last, after much anxiety, and very serious consideration, it was resolved that we should fix it on the middle of her forehead, resembling the eye of a cyclops, and put a little one, on the left side of her chin, bearing the likeness of a mole. However, it cost several trials with them in both places, ere the patches would lie agreeably to her ladyship's fancy.

AVARO. Ah! Fastosus, if the ladies only knew how ridiculous they make themselves look in the eyes of the judicious, they would be very loth thus to deform their native beauty. What delicate beauty! what perfect comeliness do we see rendered disagreeable and ridiculous, by these transformations! And how can they be but disagreeable and ridiculous, when all the decorations of nature lie concealed, and nothing appears but the manufactory of art, that great supplanter of nature? Such ladies are certainly greatly deceived by you, Fastosus; for the end proposed by all those metamorphoses is to render themselves agreeable to the gentlemen, whereas they produce the contrary effect. Art can never beget love. This is nature's work alone. Art may indeed excite lust; but nature alone begets that love which a virtuous lady would strive to obtain. It is strange, Fastosus, that nature has so little, and affectation such great concern among people of fashion as at this day. Well, I hope you pleased her at last?

Fastosus. Yes, yes, I hope I did; but my work did not end with madam: for Mrs. Prude, her woman, who was assisting us in the equipment of her lady, and often put her tongue into her cheek, and bit her lip, to prevent her laughing out, and when she saw her mistress's vanity, as soon as I had done with her lady, beseeched me that I would put a few pins into her clothes, because she was to attend her mistress to lord Frolic's; and, notwithstanding my patience was almost spent before, I was obliged to stay ever so long, pinning and unpinning her; for Mrs. Prude affected the fine gentlewoman, almost as much as her mistress.

But what vexed me worse than all the rest was, just as I got to the bottom of the stairs, to make my escape, the cook maid caught me in her greasy arms, and begged me to assist her to dress herself in her half-holiday clothes, as her sweetheart was to take the advantage of her lady's absence to come and visit her. I could not deny the girl, because I thought she really had need of considerable amendment, before she presented herself to her lover. So after we had pinned and unpinned a considerable time, I burst through the casement, to avoid the importunity of the laundry and chamber maids, whom I saw coming. Thus I gave them the slip; for those ladies and their female attendants, would drudge any devil in hell off his feet, might they have their own way. But I am right glad that I am come hither from among them.

Avaro. Then, sir, I perceive with all your greatness, you have no objections to assisting a waiting woman or a cook-maid occasionally.

Fastosus. No objection at all, cousin. The soul of a waiting woman will fill a vacancy in hell, as well as that of her lady. The difference is this; the lady of honor is capable of drawing more to hell along with her, than her waiting woman can; therefore I choose to make sure of the mistress, and for the most part the maid comes along by her example. But as soon as we get them safely inclosed within our flaming prison, we let them see we are no respecters of persons; for the mistress and her maids, my lord and his valet, the 'squire and his groom, have all the same apartment allotted to them, feed all at the same table, drink of the same cup, and are served by the same devil, whom they never find to be sparing of his liquor; but to serve them plenteously, though much contrary to their inclinations.

AVARO. That doctrine you unpreach when you attend upon them, Fastosus. You wisely keep your thumb upon that. And indeed it is well so to do; for comely as your appearance is, they would discard you else. Serious thoughts of futurity would spoil all our sport, uncle.

FASTOSUS. Indeed, Avaro, I am not such an half-wit as to tell my lord, that his riches and grandeur, if not duly improved, will sink him lower in the bottomless abyss than the rustic plebeian; nor am I such an inconsiderate devil, as to tell him that his hunting, hawking, horse-coursing, cock-fighting, card-playing, drinking, swearing, whoring, &c. are the broad way to never-ending torment. Neither do I foolishly tell my lady, that balls, assemblies, plays, &c. are the rosy paths which lead most infallibly to ruin. No, no, let me alone for that; I warrant me I can keep my counsel well enough; and as for them they will find all out at last, without any instruction.

AVARO. If I remember right, Fastosus, when we parted last, you were relating the manner in which you made your entrance good amongst men. I should be glad, sir, if you will be so obliging as to finish that account.

FASTOSUS. I purpose it, Avaro. You may remember I told you that great Beelzebub, having discovered the woman to be the weaker vessel, he made no attempts upon the virtue of the man, but resolved, by all means, to seduce the woman; not doubting but she would bring over her husband to our interest along with her. It happened one night that Adam had a dream, ominous of our conquest, which made him very fearful, lest any part of his, or his wife's conduct, should promote the dire event; therefore he reasoned with her, concerning their duty to their Creator, gave her the strictest charge to keep out of the way of temptation, and withal informed her, that he was not without his fears, even upon her account. But she, for her part, just as the devil would have it, resolved to separate herself from her husband that day, which she had never done before. Whether she thought to endear herself more to him, by letting him see how well she would resist temptation, if any should offer, or took it rather ill to be under his tutorage, I pretend not to say; but, maugre all his entreaties, she would go forth, by herself, into a distant walk, to gather some delicious berries, for an innocent repast for her and her lord, at noon.

This was an opportunity just to Beelzebub's wish, and he took care to improve it to advantage. I told you before, that previous to this, he had possessed the body of a beautiful snake, in those days man's familiar domestic; and now finding Eve at a distance from her husband, the serpent discovered himself to her, and with more than animal gestures attracted her eye. Captivated with its unusual motion, she stood ravished with its beauties, and admiring its agility. As it drew near to her, she put forth her gentle hand, stroked its skin, and the subtle animal, after its manner, returned the compliment, by laying its shining head on her lap. Their station was near to the tree of knowledge of good and evil, upon which the forbidden fruit luxuriantly hung. To this tree the serpent frequently looked, with all the languishment of ardent desire, until once he made sure that the woman observed it. "Lie still, thou pretty creature, said she, (stroking it,) what makes thee look so earnestly at that prohibited fruit?" "Ah! thou fair goddess, returned the serpent, I have good reason to admire the sovereign virtue of that delicious tree: for I was created only in a brutal station, without consciousness of mind, or the use of my tongue; until, being on my thoughtless ramble yesterday, I chanced to espy this amazing tree, whose fruit hangs in such luxuriance. After a short pause, such as a brute may be capable of, I climbed up the tree, and began to feast on the most delicious fruit that ever was eaten. Joyful at my happy fate, I soon became sensible of a self-conscious mind, capable of discerning between good and evil. Soon my tongue, which before cleaved to the roof of my mouth, was untied, and I could express sentiments of joy in the most rational manner. And now, when I met with you, I was going to renew my repast on the fruit of that sovereign tree."

AVARO. Oh, Fastosus! The most subtle scheme that ever

was heard of! Well, this may be spoken to the honor of Beelzebub, when I am dead and gone.

FASTOSUS. Well, but Satan did not then know of the happy consequences that have since arisen from this affair, to some part of the human race. However, having laid his snare with all the subtilty he was master of, he thought it well to assault the pure mind of Eve with unbelief.* He asked her, if the reason why she was so divinely beautiful, was not her feeding often upon the fruit of that so sovereign a tree? The woman answered, "No, we have never so much as once tasted of it, but invariably observed the command of our Creator, who hath put us into this garden, and said unto us, Of every tree of the garden ye may freely eat, but the fruit of the tree of knowledge of good and evil, ye may not eat; for in the day ye eat thereof ye shall surely die." To whom the serpent. "Indeed! Did he really say so? Are you not mistaken, think you? Die too! Why am not I dead then, I who have eaten of it so plenteously? No, no, you shall not die. That is only an empty threatening, to keep you in subjection to him; for he very well knows, that the moment you eat thereof, you shall be like himself, knowing good and evil; no longer be man and woman, but become gods."

The woman replied, "Ay, but my pretty creature, how shall I know that I shall be a goddess, if I should venture to eat of that desirable fruit?" "Know! said the serpent; you may easily know it, if you consider that, if I, who was created only a brute beast, am by eating the fruit of this tree, exalted to humanity, you, who are more than half a God already, shall certainly, by so doing, be exalted to real divinity." With these words he injected into her bosom some seeds of my nature, which fermented to that degree, that nothing would now serve her turn but to be deified. Sagacious Beelzebub, perceiving the uproar I had made in her mind, introduced all the train of real vices, which now infect the human species; subjected her wholly to his sway; and she, as his instrument, could have no rest until she got her husband's neck also fast in Beelzebub's yoke.

Thus was pride first introduced into the terrene creation; and thus was man subjected to my powerful sway. Being

---

* See p. 38.

b ght forth in the heart of man, I arrived instantly at full g wth; involved them in sorrow; enveloped them in blindness and ignorance; and instead of that happiness and dignity which Beelzebub had promised them, of becoming gods, I brought forth in them trusty Shame, the elder born of my earthly family, and he, as a spirit of great power, made Adam and Eve fly to a thicket, to hide themselves from the presence of an offended God. Instead of becoming gods, I transformed them into the image and likeness of father Beelzebub, in which image they begat and brought forth their children. It was now that I begat the lovely Discordans; to us the more lovely because he is anti-natural. No sooner was he born, but he sounded a trumpet, and cried, "To arms! to arms!" Then you might have seen the rhinoceros and elephant, the eagle and dragon, the lion, panther, and wolf, appear in all the fury of martial spirit, and proclaim an eternal war against one another: nor were Adam and Eve exempted from domestic uneasiness themselves.

Avaro. All this worked just as the devil would have it; and greatly enlarged the territories of hell, by annexing earth to the infernal crown. Well, uncle, I perceive, by your account, that you are the father of sin, in the mind of both angels and men.

Fastosus. True, Avaro, I am; and so well is my power established, that I am the very last that shall be subdued, and rooted out of the hearts, even of those that hate me, and who at last shall be delivered from my yoke. This is true, cousin, whether you believe it or not; and I assure you, that I have the pleasure of giving many a painful heart-pang, even to those who curse my name and nature. But to my story, cousin. I manifested my powerful sway over man, in the case of my faithful servant Cain; not only in his bloody revenge against his brother Abel, who had revolted from our government, but in making him despair under his punishment.

I triumphed gloriously over the inhabitants of the antediluvian world, who, for my sake, scorned to submit to the commandments of God, resolving to be guided by the thoughts of their own hearts, all of which were inspired by me; therefore every thought and imagination of the heart was only evil continually. I wrought them up to such a degree of rebellion, that the Almighty resolved to bear with them no longer, but to sweep them away with the be som of destruction; yet he would not do it without giving them proper warning, and calling them to repentance and reformation. One Noah, a famous preacher of righteousness, was the instrument raised up, on this occasion; and to be sure the man preached faithfully and fervently: but I had the pleasure of hardening the people's hearts to that degree, that he met with nothing but abuse for his pains. Every body accounted him to be a frantic enthusiast, fanatic, or Methodist; until the divine patience was quite worn out, and their destruction came upon them by a deluge, which swept them all from the face of the earth, except this same Noah and his family; and for my part I do not remember a time, on which hell had so many visitants at once as then.

AVARO. But how could Noah and his family be saved, when the deluge came upon all the earth?

FASTOSUS. Why, Avaro, it was by the help of a ship, which he was taught to build. For this same Noah was the first ship-carpenter in the world; and although a prince, he was not above laboring with his hands. But it galls me to think how the Almighty mixes mercy with judgment; for in this destruction, which he brought upon the old world, he taught the new world the most necessary and useful art of navigation, by means of which he will spread the knowledge of himself over all the earth.

After this I set up my lofty standard on the plains of Shinar. Multitudes flocked to it, and became my humble servants. It was now I projected a scheme of erecting a tower, equal in altitude to Jacob's ladder. Two special advantages, I alleged to them, would accrue from it when finished. The first, to perpetuate their name to the latest posterity. The second and greatest advantage would be, that thereby they might bid defiance to the Almighty. Such provision being made for their safety, that, on the first appearances of judgment begun, they might retire to the tower, where the waters could not follow them. But here, you may observe, I played the devil with the children of men; for although I flattered them with such advantages, I believed in my heart that such a presumptuous, daring undertaking, would have provoked the Almighty utterly to have destroyed them root and branch. And, indeed, at one time I thought I had gained my point; for he did come down and confound their language, in such a manner that the great design miscarried. It was diverting to hear the brick-layer call for mortar, and, Lo! a box of brick was brought him. Another calls for bricks, and the server runs for a board of mortar. One calls out for a level, and he receives a plumb-line. Another asks for a square, and a level is brought him. The bricklayers, provoked to see themselves mocked by their servants, not as yet knowing their language to be confounded, began to lay their resentment upon the bones of their laborers; and the laborers, considering themselves as very ill used, returned the abuse upon the builders; and thus they quarrelled and bickered, until they were fain to leave off the work, and betake themselves to other employments.

But, alas! cousin, in this affair the devil was outwitted; for we all thought that this haughty attempt would have provoked God utterly to destroy them. But he made use of our project only to send them abroad to people the earth, the more widely to make his glories known. And to the deep mortification of all our black fraternity, especially father Beelzebub, upon the ruins of the tower was written, in everlasting characters, the following motto: "Here the devil overshot himself." But this was a trifling disappointment in comparison of many others, some of which I may perhaps give you an account of.

Wherever the sons of Noah went, I went along with them; and not a great number of years had the earth been dry, before I persuaded them to forge, found, and carve to themselves objects of religious adoration, more agreeable to their fancy, than the God who made them. And by this means it was, that pagan idolatry was introduced, which, strictly speaking, is the religion of pride alone; even as the present Roman Catholic religion is that of pride and covetousness.

I will tell you strange things, of my government, Avaro, at a time convenient; but as we were coming along, you mentioned somewhat about the clergy of France. Pray, what of them, cousin?

Avaro. I have often, sir, made honorable mention of the dutiful disposition of my dear children, the French parsons. But I had, some years ago, occasion to try an experiment, which greatly quickened their devotion, and clothed the face of all the country with poignant sorrow. By their unwearied pursuit of the interest of the church, that is to say, by their coaxing, wheedling, and threatening of people, out of their goods and chattels, for the benefit of the clergy, they were grown so fat and purse-proud, they were not able to say half of the masses they were paid for, nor to attend upon the duties of their pretended devotion; which, persisting in, they themselves would have contributed to the opening of people's eyes to discover the cheat.

I imagined that nothing could be more suitable, than physic, to purge off some of their grossness. I went straight to Versailles, demanded an interview with the most Christian Louis, and accordingly was introduced by one of the lords of his bed-chamber. As soon as he had done me greeting after the royal manner, proportionable to his very great esteem for me, I opened the conversation in the following manner: "My royal friend, said I, perceiving that you have been ransacking the world lately, in quest of gold, to supply your pressing and growing wants, I am come to inform you where you may meet with store of moidores, yea, treasures in abundance, without travelling out of your own dominions." "Is it possible? said he. I pray thee, lovely spirit, where are the golden heaps to be found?" I replied, "The clergy, the clergy, sir, are so overgrown in riches, that they are hardly able to say an hospitable mass for the dead, or even to go about to cheat and defraud people out of their money and souls as heretofore." "Ungrateful villains, said he, to hoard up their money to lie by them useless, when I, their king, am just at the point of becoming bankrupt. I will ease them of their burden, I warrant you. I will let them for once know, that they have another master besides the pope, and leave it to them to replace their stores the nearest way they can." I was not afraid but my scheme would work to my mind; for I took him at the very nick of time, when the king of England had emptied his coffers, by destroying his naval force and trade; and, poor gentleman, he knew not well how to fill them again.

Glad of such an opportunity, he assembled the heads of the clergy, and demanded of them an exorbitant sum, in the way of a free gift. A very genteel way of robbing the church indeed! The holy gownsmen, like dear children of their good Avaro, showed themselves as tenacious of their gold as the paw of a lion is of its prey. They used every argument which priestly subtilty could invent; they lugged in both heaven and earth as protectors of their property. Yea, they even told him that to command them to part with their money, was no less than robbing the Almighty; just as if the Almighty and them were partners in the trade of priestcraft. But clergymen have the advantage of all princes, in that their cause is always the cause of God; although God has, in reality, nothing to do with them or it. They held both with teeth and hands, rather than generously to assist their sovereign, though now become almost insolvent. But you know the proverb, "The weaker goes to the wall." And so it was with them. He, being stronger than they, prevailed; and, although their money came from their coffers like blood from their hearts, they were obliged to comply. But I can assure you, the parting with it cost them more real distress of soul, than ever the selling of their consciences to obtain it had done. The sorrow of the priests is, for the most part, a farce; but their sorrow on this occasion, was deep and unfeigned.

It was not a great while after, that moidores failed a second time, and other resources being drained, he again had recourse to the sons of the clergy; and did by them as they commonly do by the laity. I mean, their money being gone, he was content with stripping them of their plate; so that were you now to see the cabinet of a French priest, you would find it as empty of plate as Glaud the shepherd's pantry. And I am of opinion that Louis, having once found the way to their nest, he will take care they be no more overgrown in riches. But to repair their late losses, they can now look out for a prey, with as much penetration as an eagle, and are as rapid as a panther in seizing on it.

Fastosus. It is my opinion, cousin, that, if princes were to take care that the church should not become too rich, there would not be so many religions as there are. But who would not be a priest or a nun, when they may roll amidst the blessings of both worlds, and under the pretence of religious retirement, enjoy every thing grateful to the flesh, in the greatest luxuriance, without any labor or toil of their own? I assure you, cousin, if I were not a devil, I would choose to be a priest myself.

Avaro. Being a priest is not such a great privilege now

as it has been; though it is still preferable to any trade or the lay kind. The expulsion of the Jesuits has been very injurious to priestcraft. The church is sure to thrive in the reign of a prince, who is under the direction of a jesuitical confessor; and the priesthood will always find in him a powerful protector. But I fear much that the princes of Europe, from their late advances, will at last throw off the yoke of ecclesiastical tyranny.

FASTOSUS. In fact, cousin, it is not a little strange, that they have not done it ere now. Nothing can be more preposterous, than for a prince who hath sovereign sway over extensive dominions, to be under the control of an arrogant priest, as if it were by him that kings reign and princes decree judgment; or as if he were the prince of the kings of the earth.

However, cousin, you forget that it is time for us to go on our nocturnal circuits. Mine is very extensive; I must, therefore, bid you adieu. To-morrow morning let us meet here.

DIALOGUE VII.

INFIDELIS AND IMPIATOR.

FROM what I had heard and seen, you may think I took care not to be too late, in attending the sable gentry in Horrida Vallis, where I was hid before any of them arrived, and prepared for taking down their discourse; the first of which, that I heard, was by Infidelis to Impiator.

INFIDELIS. How illustrious is thy throne! How extensive are thy dominions! Oh, great Impiator, my son! Before you, the greatest grandees of the earth do bow. Will you please, my son, to finish your account of the remaining part of your territories?

IMPIATOR. I will, sir. And you may observe that the fifth canton is that of the adulterers and fornicators. These are divided into literal and mystical. The class of literal adulterers and fornicators are so fashionable and notorious a people, that a description of them seems unnecessary; and so very disagreeable, that it would be offensive to you. I shall therefore do no more than describe their dwelling, and assure you, sire, that every individual of them is a very humble servant to your son Impiator. Their dwelling is on the banks of a river, the source of which is in the court, which runs through every part of the king's dominions, carrying the inhabitants along with it; and at last disembogues itself into hell, where all adulterers and fornicators shall infallibly be tormented, as a proper counterbalance for their fleshly pleasures; where, instead of women, they shall have devils; instead of wine, the sulphurous liquid; and instead of beds of down, the boisterous billows of Phlegethon.

Next to them are the mystical adulterers and fornicators. By whom I mean all that have any commerce with the whore of Rome, that old bawd with the scarlet gown: or, in other words, all who have the mark of the beast, either on their foreheads, or their right hands, and such who have this mark upon both.

By those who have the mark of the beast upon their foreheads, I mean the worthy preachers and hearers of the Armenian doctrine of the church of Rome; as also the strait-hooped gentlemen, who believe with the charitable Italians, that there can be no true faith but that which they profess, nor salvation but in their community. The far greater part of the clergy belong to the former, and the good Sandemanians belong to the latter class of doctrinal priests, or mystical adulterers.

By those who have the mark of the beast upon their right hand, I mean the practical papists, the whole bulk of the holy Catholic church; and besides them, all that do the works of the beast, after the example of that orthodox church. By the works of the beast some understand every part of religion, which is not founded upon scripture institution. Such, say they, are consecrating of churches, and baptizing of bells; dedication of meeting-houses to certain saints or angels, as the patrons of parishes; the worshipping of saints and angels, by celebrating an annual festival in honor of their name; such are your observers of high festivals, abstinences from meat at certain seasons of the year; worshipping towards the east, as if God were not everywhere present; bowing at the name of Jesus, as if it was more august than that of Jehovah, &c. Such, sir, with many more whom I might name, are the mystical adulterers and fornicators.

INFIDELIS. Ay, but my son, you have not told me which are the fornicators, and which the adulterers. I want to hear that; for the one is usually distinguished from the other.

IMPIATOR. Yes, sir, they are distinguishable enough; for the practical professed papists, who profess not the least degree of relation to Jesus Christ, as the head of the Christian church; but own themselves to be the adorers of the whore, who sits on many waters, are held to be the fornicators; whereas nominal Protestants profess themselves married to Jesus Christ, as the great head of the Christian church, and notwithstanding this pretended marriage with him, maintain a doctrinal commerce with the whore of Rome; on which account they are to be held as the adulterers.

The sixth canton is the murderers' habitation, which is divided into two grand divisions. In the first are murderers of others. These are subdivided into petty cantons. In the first of which live the mental murderers, just upon the frontiers of the country. They are a people who, without just cause, are angry with their neighbors. This lambent flame they inwardly cherish, until revenge is begotten along with hatred, envy, and malice. With them, therefore, nothing is wanting but opportunity to destroy the reputation and life of the object of their hatred, with safety to themselves; but very often it happens that their hatred and revenge destroy their subjects ere they have an opportunity of avenging themselves. The verbal murderers live next to them, in a very spacious country, because they are very numerous. By the verbal murderers I mean those who withhold from the character of others the good which they do deserve, and speak of them the evil which they do not deserve, or even the evil which they do deserve, in a way in which they would not wish others to speak of themselves, in like circumstance. I attend, for my part, in many companies, where the conversation cannot possibly be supported for a quarter of an hour but at the expense of some absent acquaintance. And so fashionable is this in polite life, that it is become a proverb, "That scandal is the very life and soul of conversation." To this petty canton belong all talebearers, backbiters, railers, evil surmisers, and particularly the very obliging gentry, who tack *but* to the end of all their encomiums on others· as, "He is a good sort of a gentleman, but—" or, "She is an agreeable lady enough, but—" where you may observe that little unintelligible word but, stabs the gentleman and lady's reputation through and through.

Having passed through this, you come into the country of those who murder with their looks. In this country you may see an eye to curse a man to hell and damnation, and an eyebrow call a man a scoundrel, and knock him down The Rev. Mr. Adam Gib, primate of the associate synod in Scotland, has lately had his heart wounded so deeply, by the looks of some of his elders, that it is thought he cannot recover the stroke as long as he lives: but, for the good of the public, he hath prosecuted them before the presbytery, who, without inquiring into facts, sentenced the reputation of the irreverend elders to be hanged, drawn, and quartered, to the great consolation of the pious sufferer. As soon as you get out of this country, you come,

Fourthly, into a very extensive plain, inhabited by what may be called domestic murderers; a set of beings who murder without impunity, no suitable laws being provided against them.

Here dwells the parent, who spends wastefully what should regularly support his family, so that his children are brought up in the most dissolute and irreligious manner, as a preparative to the most vicious practices: hence, whether the children prove virtuous or vicious, strict equity accounts the profuse and careless parent the murderer. Near to those murderous parents lives the lascivious husband, who estrangeth himself from his lawful consort, and frequenteth the company of lewd women. Many you may find here, who, as the very worst of felons, rob their wives and children of their legal property, to support the most infamous strumpets, who, like the horseleech, are continually saying, Give, give. Such men are sure to find the truth of that saying, "A whore is a deep ditch." Here it is a very common thing to see the most virtuous women, so ill used by their murderous husbands, that they languish and grieve under their affliction, until at last they die of a broken heart. No assassin ever better deserved the gallows, than such husbands; for no assassin ever put the person whom he murdered to equal torture. The very same may be said of the lascivious strumpet, of high or low degree, who is false to her husband.

Among domestic murderers live the parents, who, for the sake of an agreeable settlement, oblige their children to marry with persons, whom they cannot possibly love. This lays a sure foundation for certain murder, and brings the party to the grave in the most distressing manner.

But if covetous parents would only consider, that a compelled marriage is worse than a poisoned dagger plunged into the bosom of their offspring, they would certainly have more compassion than to persist in the iniquitous measure. Here likewise live those, who restrain their children from marrying the objects of their choice, merely because there is a deficiency of a few hundreds, or thousands, in the fortune. Parents who can relish nothing but money, and have a wrong notion of honor, make no scruple of conscience, to render their children miserable all their days, rather than suffer them to marry a degree and a half below themselves. It is very strange, that the laws of nations should make no provision against this murder; and stranger still, that those of Britain countenance and encourage it.

However, marriages are seldom happy, where the affections are not joined, prior to the matrimonial ceremony. Money may unite the persons, but it cannot unite the affections, as appears in numberless instances: of which disconsolate, dull, and heavy husbands, broken-hearted wives, frequent divorces, elopements, domestic quarrels, and divided families, the natural effect of forced marriages, are evidences.

There is yet another species of domestic murderers, connived at by the law. They are such who not only train up their children in idleness, but in luxury and wantonness. By these means their spendthrift sons, if of high birth, are fitted to become robbers of the nation, when their own fortunes are spent; and if of middle life, they are fitted for the highway, and consequently for the halter. Nor is this method of training up less fatal in its influence on the female sex; for it prepares them for the stews, or the suburbs of the stews, where gentlemen's courtesans dwell, perhaps for theft and then for the gallows. Idleness and luxury are as rank poison to the mind, as arsenic is to the body. Many people, indeed, lament the young gentleman's unhappy fate, when he is going to Tyburn; but very few censure his parents, as the first cause of his untimely end, by the manner in which they brought him up. This is some comfort to us, however, that though such domestic murderers act with impunity from man, the law of God will take such notice of them as to bring them to hell, if their crimes are not repented of. To be sure it would be more agreeable to us, to see them enter hell by way of Tyburn: but the devil cannot always have his will.

Another sort are very careful to preserve the bodies of their children, by providing diligently for them the necessaries and conveniences of life; as they grow up, are very careful to preserve them from the highway and the stews, by putting into their hands a business by which to obtain a comfortable livelihood; and, after all, prove the murderers of their children. For, on the one hand, they restrain them not from bad company, which leads to destruction; company that corrupts the principles, vitiates the conduct, and leads into bad practices, such as sabbath-breaking, gaming, lying, swearing, &c. Nor on the other hand, do they take any pains to cultivate their infant minds, further than to know how, when, and to whom, they should make a genteel bow, and courtesy, and how to express the modish compliments in a graceful manner. They never once deem it necessary to instil into their minds an early sense of religion and virtue.

Many parents, if their children learn a little polite behavior, do not much care whether they read the Bible at all.

In this country too dwell duellers, boxers, boasters, and provokers; all the bands of assassins, and intriguers against men's lives. His hoary holiness is captain general of this band, and his cardinals and inquisitors are next to him in honor. Here dwell persecutors, of every name, popish, episcopal or presbyterian; all who impose religion on men's consciences by the power of the sword.

The second division is that of self-murderers; and I assure you, sir, this is a very populous place, more crowded than the former. Here dwell gluttons, drunkards, and intemperate persons in general; for there are more who eat and drink themselves to death, than the fever, the consumption, and the sword destroy. Idle, lazy, and slothful persons, live here, under the character of second-hand murderers; their idle habits introducing diseases of the most fatal nature. The immoderately careful, also, kill themselves with mere anxiety. In the next town the envious are stationed, those who are as mortally wounded, by the prosperity of their neighbor, as any man can be by a dagger. In the suburbs live those whom we call the impatient; for trouble is not so very deathly as impatience under it. Over the bridge live the ambitious, a people of lofty views, who crack their heart-strings by climbing. In the neighborhood of the latter live the lascivious, who kill themselves by little and little, and parboil their flesh ere they present it to the worms. I might add to this list a prodigious number besides, known among us by the name of soul-murderers. But as I was never remarkable for knowledge in casuistical divinity, I shall leave this to others, and proceed to,

The seventh and royal canton of drunkards; which is divided into two very grand divisions, the first of which is inhabited by the sot, and the second by merry companions. The soaking sots are a well-seasoned race, who seem as if some of their ancestors had been of the bristly kind. They are a swinish set of people, always grunting, but when their lips are in the cup; unless it may be that the calf mounts them in the morning, and rides them until half past two, then dismounts just in the middle of dinner, and the eager swain vaults into the saddle, and rides them until they are lame. The ensign of the sots' division is a long tobacco-pipe, and greasy fore-breasts of a coat; and if any man have business with them, he would do well to wait on them in the morning, before the calf dismounts; for after that they can do nothing but grunt, until sleep dismounts the pig again. Thus they are ridden alternately by the calf and the pig. The sots drink merely for the sake of liquor; and in process of time their blood becomes so inflamed, that they carry the arms of their company upon their faces, which are dyed into a kind of bastard scarlet color, and grow as rough as the skin of a shark, with preternatural pimples.

The second division is that of merry companions, or, according to men of learning, good-fellows. They abhor the name, yet love the practice of drunkards. You could not affront them worse, than by telling them they are in love with the landlady, for the sake of her liquor. Were you to ask them their reasons for frequenting the tavern, they would soon tell you, that it is not for any love they have to the liquor, but they go there merely for the sake of good company. By the way, sire, they go to the wrong place to seek for it; for no good company haunts taverns and ale-houses. Good company is most likely to be found in good places; but taverns and ale-houses are quite of another cast, being public portals, through which many pass to the nether regions. Yea, such a good opinion has Beelzebub conceived of them, that many of the landladies, and their daughters, are appointed his factors and agents upon earth.

It is the practice of merry companions to meet at the tavern, or some other place of public resort, as many evenings in the week as business will admit of, to read and expound the newspapers, give their opinion of the proceedings of the ministry, of commercial transactions, or to comment on the operations of war. Sometimes they meet to play what they call a civil game of cards, backgammon, &c. or it may be to reproach some neighboring Presbyterian parson for his affected sanctity: for you must know, that they not only hate sanctity itself, but its very appearance. Often you may hear them deride the fanatic, for what they call his narrow and bigoted spirit, and, at the same time, applaud the reverend Mr. Liveloose, for an affable, free, and generous soul. Many of those merry companions, who will by no means bear the name of drunkard, I can pick you out, who will drink a bottle or two at a sitting, and go home betwixt one and two in the morning, with eyes as fierce as those of an hyena.

In short, sir, if you were to go through my canton of drunkards, when our men are all at work, you would hear a great noise as if Vulcan with his cyclops were there, hammering thunderbolts for Jupiter. And would certainly imagine, that hell had burst its belly, and poured out its entrails amongst us, on account of the hideous cursing, swearing, damning, singing, scolding and bawling, tearing and fighting, boasting, lying, cheating, and unclean words, looks, and gestures, which there abound. This, sir, is the royal canton, out of which I choose all my principal men; which you must own to be sound policy; for if ever I can get a man to become a drunkard, I can cause him to commit what wickedness I please; and I must tell you, that this canton is inhabited by men of all ranks, occupations, and persuasions.

Thus, reverend father, I have given you a brief account of my dominions; but if you were to pass through the several cantons, and see them all yourself, you would say, that the hundredth part has not been told you.

Infidelis. Oh, my child! my dear Impiator, how my aged heart is filled with joy, on hearing your pleasing story! Illustrious indeed is the kingdom of Profanity! You honor me, my son! Your success does great honor to the name of Infidelis. But, I pray, do you know any thing of a set of people whom they call Nazarenes? They are the only people in the world who have cast off my yoke. Oh! how it would rejoice me to hear that your craftiness had engaged them in your service!

Impiator. I know them very well. A small body of despised, precise creatures, hated by all the world. I assure you, sir, I have done all that lies in my power to bring them under our dominion. But mortified I am to tell you, that I have never been able to conquer one of them. Immanuel hath published very strict laws in his kingdom, absolutely prohibiting his subjects from touching, tasting, or handling any thing that belongs to us, or so much as visiting our cantons; and they are so firmly attached to his government, that it is with the greatest difficulty, now and then, we get one of them down into our mines. But when such a thing does happen, my subjects have a good day of feasting and mirth; send gifts to one another, of such things as they have; and the shouts of joy, "So we would have it," may he heard in all the cantons of our dominions.

For instance, it happened once that Noah, who was, in the main, an utter enemy to our government, was induced to make a visit to the drunkard's country, which caused much gladness through all the land. The triumphal flag was displayed upon the tents of Ham, wherever the news was spread; and every man reported to his neighbor, saying, "Behold, he is become like one of us." At the same time, the confederates of Shem covered themselves with sackcloth, put ashes on their heads, exchanged their pleasant songs for lamentations, mourning, and woe; until the patriarch was safely returned to his own country again.

It happened also, on a certain time, that I was happy enough to inveigle David the great, within the borders of the adulterers' canton; who, to cover the infamy of such an expedition, rushed, with violent precipitation, into the very heart of the canton of murderers. The monarch's arrival was soon proclaimed among all the murderers and adulterers, who made a grand entertainment on the occasion, and invited the blasphemers to partake with them. Oh! Infidelis, if you were there, certainly you would have tired your sides with laughing, to see how they footed the treble dance, whilst the music played, "The best of them are as bad as ourselves." And all joined together in this chorus—

"What we do in public, they do in private,
The difference is only in show."

Then they clapped their hands, and shouted, "So, ho! brave boys. Now we are all on one side. The man after God's own heart hath joined our communion. The psalmist of Israel is now one of ourselves. Hypocrites, altogether, who pretend to more religion than others." Thus, sire, from the fall of one, our people concluded that all were bad.

The like fell out in the case of Peter, the apostle, who, on a very dark night, missing his way, was first trapped in the liar's snare, and then in the swearer's gin, so that he denied the Lord who bought him, and cursed and swore that he did not so much as know Jesus of Nazareth. I can tell you, when such a thing does happen, that we entrap one of the Nazarenes, it greatly increaseth the industry of my subjects, and bends them more than ever under my yoke. Indeed, as there is no other way to Zion, but what lies directly through the very heart of my dominions, there is now and then one of them tumbles into our mines, especially in the dark and long nights of winter.

Infidelis. Now and then, child! I thought you had often companies of them at once in your dominions.

Impiator. No, sir, I cannot say so. I will tell you how the mistake happens. We frequently have companies of those who are called Nazarenes, it is true; but then the name and the nature are two different things all the world over. In order to bring true Christianity into disgrace, the great and wise Beelzebub stirs up some of our country people to put on the outward habit of the Nazarenes, join their company, and travel with them, almost to the borders of the kingdom of Profanity; but not one of them can be persuaded to set a foot out of their own country. As those people pass along the road, in their own country, it is not much to be wondered at, if they do occasionally try their hands at their old employments. But as for the real Nazarenes, I assure you, I very seldom meet with one, who has curiosity so much as to view our land as he passes through it. Even when our subtle emissaries do entrap one, let me and my chivalry do what we can, we never detain him beyond a certain time; when some powerful messenger is dispatched from the skies, to deliver him out of our tenacious hands. But we have the satisfaction of often procuring them an hearty drubbing, so that many of them go halting to their grave. I, myself, have seen Immanuel meet them, in the very midst of our kingdom, seize, bind, and chastise them, until with blurred faces, they humbly submitted to kiss the rod, and heartily blessed God that ever the birch tree was planted.

INFIDELIS. Ay, child, they are made to kiss the rod, that is the plague of it; for then they bid farewell to the pleasures of profanity. Oh! were it but possible by any means to harden them against the rod, what advantages might we reap from it! Or, indeed, could we, as I have often strove to do, make them faint under it, it would answer the same end. But, beyond all our power to hinder, Immanuel does somehow, along with the stroke, convey sustaining strength. Yea, sometimes even makes the rod itself, in some respects, pleasant, and at all times profitable to them. Ah! my son, we shall never be able to rob him of one of his own, for when he chastiseth them with a visible hand, he sustaineth and comforteth them with a hand invisible.

But let us not be discouraged, nor yield the contest. Let us destroy whom we can, and let us disturb and distract the minds of those whom we cannot destroy. Let us think of the great Beelzebub, what achievements he is daily performing, notwithstanding he groans in the yoke of eternal despair. And for your encouragement, my dear Impiator, let me tell you, such is your care to maintain a despotic sway over your subjects, and such is their attachment to your person and government, that both you and they may be assured of warm lodgings in the palace of great Beelzebub, as soon as this world ceaseth to be the stage of action.

IMPIATOR. Yes, sir, such is the flourishing state of my kingdom at present; but I have my shocks at one time and another. It is but a few years since I was terribly afraid, lest I should have lost my British subjects.

INFIDELIS. Lost your British subjects, my son! Who, or what is he, who dared to attempt any thing against the great Profanity?

IMPIATOR. Ah! sire, a powerful enemy; no less a person than George III. He was an enemy to my powerful sway when he was only prince of Wales; and as soon as he ascended the throne, he more openly showed his dislike me; published an edict for banishing me from his dominions; enjoined his officers to apprehend me wherever I was to be found; and, under the penalty of his displeasure, prohibited his subjects from entertaining me at any time, especially upon the sabbath-day; a day on which I am used to get above double business done for Beelzebub. Had I not been well befriended by the British nobility, as well as by the commons of the land, bad days had come upon me; for what will not precept, enforced by example, be able to accomplish?

Had he, like many princes before him, only enacted laws against me, and still continued to correspond with me himself, I should have had little to fear; but would you think it, sir, he actually attempted to clear the court of me; will suffer no swearing in his presence, nor gaming on the Sabbath evenings in his palace, and even discourageth drunkenness and debauchery. Indeed, sir, if inferior magistrates had all been of the same disposition with their king, poor Impiator had been obliged to quit the realm, and live in exile, like the devil Crudelis.

INFIDELIS. That the king of England is a sober and virtuous prince, will admit of no dispute; but the case of Impiator can never be desperate, whilst you and I are in such high esteem with so many magistrates and placemen. We shall be regarded much sooner than he. So long as inferior magistrates can be kept in subjection to us, there is no fear of our interest, let the prince be ever so virtuous. I, as an old stander in the world, have seen much of mankind, and out of my consummate experience shall offer some things for your encouragement.

A good king may enact good laws; but it is impossible he should execute them, without the assistance of his subjects; therefore your kingdom, my son, can never suffer, until a law be made, which shall render all common drunkards, swearers, sabbath-breakers, whoremongers, extortioners, &c. incapable of the office of a magistrate. Whilst magistrates can suffer buying and selling on the sabbath-day; whoredom, drunkenness, and swearing to abound in the streets, with impunity, what hath Impiator to fear? Doth it not demonstratively prove, that such magistrates are firmly attached to the devil Impiator? No danger, my son, no danger at all! Let the king and queen both abhor you ever so much, unless they can get men of virtuous dispositions established in places of trust, the devil Impiator shall reign, in spite of all they can do to prevent it.

Do you think that a magistrate, who is himself a drunkard, will ever strive to suppress the beastly sin of drunkenness in others? Or that he, who is a profane swearer, and tolerates the practice of swearing in his own household, will ever exert his power to suppress it in others? Can it be thought, that a man who keeps his woman, instead of his wife, will be very assiduous to suppress the reigning sin of whoredom? Or, that he who can, without conscience, grind the faces of the poor, will ever be a promoter of piety? Never fear it, Impiator. All you have to do is to debauch the minds of as many magistrates as you can; then you will have the vulgar of course, when they see vice reign with impunity.*

IMPIATOR. After all, sir, I think there is reason for some fear, when we consider the power of example. You remember how, according to tradition, it turned the heads of all the Macedonian army, to the one shoulder, in the days of Alexander, and how it raised a hump upon most of the genteel backs in England, in the days of king Richard the third, of bloody memory. Now, sir, if example were to have the like effect at present, Impiator could not live in England.

INFIDELIS. I am sensible, son, that a virtuous example is

* This second-sighted devil seems to have judged rightly of the case; for profaneness of every kind has made most awful advances in the present reign, notwithstanding the virtue of the sovereign. Divorces, consequent upon conjugal infidelity, were never so rife, since England became a nation. Masquerades and routs, which received but little countenance in some former reigns, in this, meet with all that the vainest heart can wish for. That this is the case, let Connelly's, the pantheon and the female coterie, bear witness.

not without its proper influence; but this I have always seen, people are more easily drawn by example, into vice, or even into things indifferent, than into virtue. Assure yourself it will require a stronger power than the example of the best and wisest of men, to draw a vicious person to the love of virtue.

Should the virtuous example of a prince have any influence upon others, you must take care to nick-name them, get them pointed and hissed at, and despised, and all will go on very quietly.

Let us now go in quest of our kindred, my son. I expected to have seen some of them here this morning.

DIALOGUE VIII.

INFIDELIS, AVARO, FASTOSUS, IMPIATOR, AND DISCORDANS.

Infidelis and Impiator had but just done talking togeth er, and were about departing, when Fastosus, Avaro, and Discordans came up the valley, and saluted each his kindred; in which salutation Infidelis thus began:

Infidelis. Honor and renown, to the great Fastosus! Furious contentions, to restless Discordans! and heaps of glittering wealth, to the careful Avaro! To which infernal salutation,

Fastosus replied, Darkness and confusion surround my brother Infidelis! Lewdness and debauchery attend my cousin Impiator! I am glad to see so many of our family in the valley at once.

Infidelis. I pray you, cousin Discordans, how do you do! These many weeks have passed since I saw you.

Discordans. Even jaded out of breath, uncle. How do you do, most Rev. sir? and how do you, my worthy cousin?

Infidelis. Having, with great care, caused our influences to rest upon our subjects, we came hither to the valley to regale ourselves with a dish of sweet conversation, which we hope will now be more agreeable, on the arrival of so many celebrated worthies. But I would know, cousin, where you have been so long?

Discordans. Been! I have been busy, wandering to and

fro, on the face of the earth, as usual, promoting the interests of great Beelzebub. So diligent have I been, that I have had no time, since I saw you last, so much as to take a nap. But, as you observed just now, having left my influences upon mankind, I hope to enjoy the pleasure of my uncle's company for a season.

INFIDELIS. How, cousin? Are you so close at it? I thought your affairs had been urgent only upon certain occasions.

DISCORDANS. Indeed, sir, mankind are fond of me, almost to distraction. I believe I have as much business, now-a-days, as any devil of the club; and I manage my affairs with as much dexterity too.

INFIDELIS. What is that staff, you have in your hand, cousin? And what is that looking-glass, that hangs by your side? By your looks you are too vigorous to need a staff to lean upon; and to judge by the appearance of your person and dress, I should have thought you had as little need of a looking-glass.

DISCORDANS. You are pleased to banter a little, sir: but that which is well received, is never ill delivered. This you call a staff, sir, is my telescope. And this glass is my inverting mirror. The two chosen instruments by which I carry on all my operations.

IMPIATOR. I thought, cousin, we devils have no need of glasses, either perspective or visual. What! is your sight bad, Discordans?

DISCORDANS. No, no, my sight is as piercing as the eye of an eagle; but piercing as it is, I cannot do without my glasses.

IMPIATOR. Then, I suppose, the glasses are for the use of your subjects. Indeed, cousin, I never took you to be a friendly devil before.

DISCORDANS. Not so friendly as you imagine, coz, nor are the glasses for their use but for their abuse. For there is not one who makes use of either glass, but he is abused, as sure as ever he uses it. This is no very great friendship, sir, is it?

INFIDELIS. No, cousin, if so you approve yourself the offspring of great Beelzebub. I should be glad to hear something of their uses, and the manner of your operation by them.

DISCORDANS. I am ready to oblige you, sir, if the great Fastosus is pleased to permit me.

FASTOSUS. You do me honor, my son. I permit you, with all my heart.

DISCORDANS. Then, sir, if you please, you shall try my telescope first. Take it in your hand, sir, and put it to your eye. Now, sir, what do you see?

INFIDELIS. See! I see the greatest mountain that ever I beheld! The top of it reacheth even to the stars. Strange! I did not think there had been such a thing in the world! Why, the highest mountain in Armenia is but a hillock, when compared to this?

DISCORDANS. Now, sir, be pleased to take down the glass; look the same way with your naked eye, and try what you can discover.

INFIDELIS. Nay, now I can see nothing at all, but a molehill, about a score of yards from us. But what is gone with the mountain, think you?

DISCORDANS. That very molehill, sir, is the mountain which you saw. To convince you of it, Impiator shall make the trial likewise. Now, Impiator, what do you see?

IMPIATOR. See! why I see the wondrous mountain; and I see a prodigious number of monsters, ten times as big as an elephant, travelling up the sides of it!

DISCORDANS. Now, sir, the molehill is the mountain, and the ants are the monsters that inhabit it.

INFIDELIS. Amazing! that any instrument can change the appearance of things, so much from the reality. Indeed, Discordans, I can hardly believe my own eyes.

DISCORDANS. Sir, you shall have full conviction. Put the glass to your eye, and mind well, when I roll this ball on the green, and tell me what it appears to you to be.—Now, sir, you have seen it, what do you say?

INFIDELIS. I am more astonished than ever. It appeared to be well-nigh as huge as the body of Saturn, and seemed to roll through immeasurable space. Now I am convinced, incredulous as I am.

DISCORDANS. All is well so far. Now you shall try the other end of the telescope, and learn the wonders of miniature. Let us look towards the other side of the valley. You see a very large oak, whose arms are extended at least two hundred feet in breadth. Do you not see it, sir?

INFIDELIS. See it! How you talk! I might see that tree without spectacles, if I were three-fourths blind.

DISCORDANS. Be not too positive, sir. Take a good view of it now, lest you should not readily apprehend it with the glass.

INFIDELIS. Why, cousin, I cannot fail seeing this tree at the first trial, it is such a large one, and just at hand too!

DISCORDANS. Well then, please to put the glass to your eye, the contrary way to what you did before.—Now, sir what do you see?

INFIDELIS. I can see nothing at all. What is become of the tree think you?

DISCORDANS. Look better, sir. The tree stands just where it did, I assure you.

IMPIATOR. I suppose my father has not the glass right at his eye; has he, cousin?

DISCORDANS. Yes, yes, it is very right. Do you discover any thing of the tree yet?

INFIDELIS. No, nothing at all. Is not the glass fallen out, think you?

DISCORDANS. No, sir, the glass is all right. But tell me, do you see nothing of any kind?

INFIDELIS. Yes, I see, at a prodigious distance, some kind of a shrub, about the size of a common thistle. To me it appears to be about fifteen inches high.

DISCORDANS. Look stedfastly at it, sir, and see if you can find out what species it is of?

INFIDELIS. I take it to be a small oak plant; but at such a distance, it is not easy to distinguish the species of such a diminutive shrub.

DISCORDANS. Now, sir, I perceive you discern it right· if you please, you may take down the glass. You see, sir, the oak tree stands just where it did; and now you discover nothing of the shrub. Believe me, sir, the plant which you saw, is none other than that stately oak, magically diminished in its appearance, by the power of the glass. The oak itself has undergone no change, neither did the ball, nor the molehill. All the change is only in appearance.

INFIDELIS. I am amazed at the astonishing powers of this instrument. When it is used one way, it magnifies a molehill to a stupendous mountain, and a tennis-ball to a world; and when used the contrary way, it reduceth an oak of the most gigantic stature, into one of the most dwarfish shrubs. I pray you, cousin, what is the name of this instrument, and where was it invented?

DISCORDANS. Sir, the name of this amazing instrument, is Prejudice; it was invented by Lucifer, the most famous mathematician in hell; and is of excellent use, in forwarding the delightful works of darkness, and securing the dominion of Beelzebub, over mankind, upon earth.

INFIDELIS. Dear cousin, I am quite impatient to have a description of its uses. It cannot fail of being of excellent service, if skilfully managed, as I doubt not it is, in the hand of Discordans.

DISCORDANS. Sir, having already seen something of its amazing effects, you may well believe it is very useful to me. By this partial glass it is I sow contention, strife and discord, wherever I come. It is my custom when I begin my operations, and intend to set people together by the ears, to visit each of them separately; apply my glass to his eye, in the magnifying way; and, as you see it is so constructed that it will turn any way, I turn it towards himself, by which he obtains a partial view of his own virtue and merit. Then I apply the glass the contrary way, and direct my dupe to consider his vices in the diminishing medium, by which he almost, if not wholly, loseth sight of them. Having had such a partial view of his own virtues and vices, the fool takes the former to be a thousand times greater, and the latter a thousand times less, than they really are. By these means he is prejudiced in his own favor so far, that he is ready to quarrel with all, who think not as well of him as he does of himself. Thus, I prejudice almost every man in his own favor, so far, that each looks upon himself as most worthy of general regard. From this it is, that you may meet with a drummer, who looks upon himself as more able to command well, than his colonel: or a catchpole, who deems himself fit for an alderman; and a scurvy attorney, who flatters himself, that he knows more than the lord chancellor of the realm.

But for this prejudice in their own favor, you should never hear of revolutions of state, destructive wars, cruel assassinations, and domestic broils, among mankind, so grateful to us infernal spirits. It is by this device, you will find one fool wiser in his own conceit than ten men who can render a reason. Yea, gentlemen, it is from the good opinion almost every man hath of himself, originally derived from the use of my partial telescope, that all divisions and animosities of every kind, and amongst every people, in church and state, do flow. Though, indeed, the gentlemen concerned in religious contentions would persuade the world that it is the glory of God, and the furtherance of the gospel, they have in view, in all their curses and anathemas, which they toss and retoss against one another. The vulgar take it for granted to be so, and therefore readily join with their reverend leaders.

In the mean while, man being sufficiently prejudiced in his own favor, I betake me to the following operations, from whence all jealousies, backbitings, murmurings, evil surmisings, &c. spring. I put the diminishing end of my telescope to the eye of my dupe, and direct him thus, to behold the virtues of his neighbor. The instance of the oak, reduced to the most diminutive shrub, will convince you that a man's virtues will appear little enough, if at all discernible, when viewed with my partial glass. So when the man with it examines the virtue of his neighbors, he is put to his wit's end to find any virtue at all, just as you were to find out the oak: but he sees, as he thinks, too much cause to conclude, that his neighbor is a very bad man. And if such a thing should be, that a man's virtue is so strong that it forceth evidence, even over the belly of prejudice, by its own native lustre, its appearance is changed from its reality, as the oak to the shrub, in the foregoing experiment.

Then I direct my disciple to apply the magnifying end of the telescope, and to take an ample view of his neighbor's vices and deformity; and this he doth to the greatest advantage. The two instances of a molehill transformed to a mountain, and a rolling ball to a revolving world, will convince you how glaring a man's vices will be, when viewed with the magnifying end of my valuable telescope, prejudice.

On obtaining this discovery, says my dupe, Ah! how glaring his vices appear! When I sought for virtue, I could not discern so much as the smallest of her traces in him; but now I seek for his vices, truly there is nothing else to be seen. Can he be a Christian? No, surely! If this be Christianity, I will for ever renounce it." Thus, my reverend uncle, I frequently persuade people who are really worthless, to despise, revile, and contemn those who are, in every respect, much preferable to themselves; to deny the character of virtuous men, even to the most virtuous of their day.

INFIDELIS. Now, nephew, you delight my ear indeed; and I freely own you of my illustrious kindred; nor are you less dexterous in pursuit of your calling, than the greatest of all our fraternity; the great Fastosus and I only excepted.

IMPIATOR. Gentlemen, I have been silent a long time, which I believe I am as little given to as any; but now, wonder unbraces my tongue, and I cannot but admire the art and industry of my cousin Discordans.

DISCORDANS. Although I am no way remarkable for gratitude, I thank you, cousin Impiator, for your compliment. There is this glass, which likewise demands your attention. Will you please to examine it, gentlemen?

INFIDELIS. Come, cousin, I will. Please to let me look at it.

DISCORDANS. Now for a fresh surprise. Do you please to place the mirror, and look into it.

INFIDELIS. I will, cousin. But what is the matter, think you? I see nothing but gross darkness. How comes this to pass, Discordans?

DISCORDANS. It is the nature of the instrument. Be pleased to turn yourself so as to look upon either, or all of us, in it. Now, sir, what do you see?

INFIDELIS. Strange! you all appear as angels of light. Did I not perfectly know the contrary, I could have sworn upon the alcoran, or the mass book, that Impiator had been Uriel; Avaro had been the genius of benevolence; that Fastosus had been humility; and you, Discordans, the angel of peace.

This glass is really more wonderful than the former. What an amazing power of inversion it hath, cousin! Why it transformeth light into darkness, and darkness into light; changeth the appearance of devils into that of angels of light. Well, Discordans, if this will not answer your end, I do not know what will. I pray you, cousin, what do you call it?

DISCORDANS. This, sir, I call my inverting mirror: but the proper name of it is *false reasoning*. An instrument of the true Luciferian construction, and most admirably adapted to my dividing purposes. It is the oracle at which, for the most part, mankind inquire after the truth of any matter. But, from what you have seen, you will readily believe that there is no truth in it; therefore, its discoveries, if the truth were known, would be deemed absolute falsehood. But I am very careful to keep up its honor with the people, as I could do but little business without it.

FASTOSUS. Right, my son, and it proves to be in high esteem: for the ancients were not more fond of our brother Apollo, who kept his court at Delphos, than the moderns are of the inverting mirror of false reasoning.

INFIDELIS. Good cousin, a word or two concerning its uses; yea, make an oration of it, if you please; for it will be very agreeable, even to Impiator himself, I dare say.

IMPIATOR. No danger of me, I assure you! I begin now to have some taste for information, all that I have heard being so very agreeable. Cousin Discordans, you may freely proceed without any fear of being too hard upon my patience.

DISCORDANS. But for this inverting mirror, gentlemen, I could do but little against the children of men; for excellent as my telescope of prejudice is, it would be altogether useless, but for the mirror: but, by the help of this, the telescope performeth mighty deeds in favor of our government.

By this mirror it is, I cause offence to be taken when none is offered nor designed; yea, even when the good of the party is sought after; and thus I foment differences, amidst the most fervent solicitations for unity. A certain great man, some thousand years since, had such a proof of this, that he complained bitterly against our people, saying, "When I am for peace, they are for war."

By this mirror it is, that public or private reproof is not only rendered useless, but even hurtful to the party reproved, and frequently prejudicial to society. So very much are people given to examine all matters in our famous mirror, that it is almost impossible to point out one man in a whole county, who hath wisdom enough to bear reproof with becoming patience. So that if it is an argument of folly, to turn away the ear from reproof, or to harden the heart against rebuke, these are brave days for folly.

By this wonderful mirror, I make even the preached word, not only useless to many, but offensive to some. For instance, it sometimes happens, that the preacher, as it is his duty, exclaims against drunkenness. At that instant I step up to the drunkard, and hold the mirror before his eyes; immediately he begins to view the parson's conduct in a very uncharitable light; and, as a guilty conscience needs no accuser, he concludes it is himself that is aimed at. "Well, says he, I see how it is; some spiteful person hath told him that I was drunk the other night, and he is wicked enough to expose me to all the congregation. Has he no faults of his own, that he can be so free in trumping up other people's failings? Cannot he preach the gospel without railing against individuals?

INFIDELIS. I have often seen it to be dangerous to our interests, for a person to go with a guilty conscience to where there is a faithful ministry.

DISCORDANS. By this time, I clap my telescope to his eye, and direct him to view the parson with it; which is no sooner done, than he exclaims, "Ay, ay, his vices are as great as mine, and greater too. If he is not a drunkard, he is something as bad; he is covetous; all know that: and he is uncharitable and spiteful." Then I turn the end of my telescope towards himself. "Well, saith he, the parson himself is more wicked by one half than I am. I meddle with no man's character. I am in charity with all men. I am just and honest in all my dealings. If I hurt anybody, it is myself, and what can the meddling fellow have to do with that?"

Thus doth this wonderful instrument invert the nature of things, so as to turn a well-meant admonition into a piece of envious raillery; what is really in itself a virtue, is changed in its appearance to a vice; and if the least degree of zeal appears in the delivery of reproof, it is traduced as passion and ill-nature. By the use of these two famous instruments, I set one great man to pull the ears of another, at the various courts of earthly princes; where, by my management, the truly worthy are frequently disgraced, and the worthless advanced to power. What ups and downs succeeded each other in the court of Versailles, in the days of madame Pompadour, when not the merit of the hero, but his attachment to that lady, was considered! If he was a true Pompadorian, he was sure to be advanced, however much of the calf his disposition had imbibed; but if an anti-pompadorian, down he came, though he were as wise as Ulysses, and valiant as the son of Thetis. And so it fared with them in their bad success in the late war.

FASTOSUS. I suppose the public would never object to their prince enjoying the common privilege of man, in having a favorite friend near his person, were it not that the party selected for that person is apt, insolently and inconsiderately, to crowd his own dependants, qualified or unqualified, into places under the government. But what France suffered for such misconduct in the last war, will be a warning to neighboring nations.

INFIDELIS. I should like to have the history of your glasses, cousin. And I imagine a few instances of your operations by them will be exceedingly agreeable to all the company, if you will be so obliging as to favor us with them.

DISCORDANS. With all my heart, sir. The first instance I remember, was in the case of Cain and Abel. As for Abel, you know he was a rebel against our government, enlisted under the banner of Immanuel, and bore arms against the monarch of darkness, to whom trusty Cain was firmly attached. Abel was well acquainted with the acceptable atonement, then to be made by Jesus of Nazareth, and had respect to it, in all the services which he offered to Deity. His sacrifices and services were therefore the fruits of faith, and consequently acceptable to God, whom he served. On the other hand, our friend Cain had no respect for the mediation of Immanuel, but considered his services as well deserving acceptance with Deity, in virtue of their own intrinsic excellence. Of course, both him and his services were rejected. For you know whatever is not of faith, is sin, and consequently detestable to the Almighty. Abel offered his sacrifice, and Cain presented his gift, the one in faith, and the other without faith; the result was, Abel was accepted and Cain rejected.

As soon as I was aware of this, and saw discontent visible upon his countenance, I went up to Cain, and began to ply him with my instrument. "Let my lord Cain," said I, "try his brother's conduct in this faithful mirror."

Accordingly he viewed it, and as he viewed, he said, "Ah! now I see how it is. He knew that a lamb or kid would be more acceptable to God than corn; but he would not inform me, I suppose, lest I should share in the blessing. Is this acting the part of a brother? I see now through all his pretended love, his whining advices and hypocritical cant."

This wrought just as I would have it. Then I desired him to view himself with my telescope, which he did, and thus exclaimed, "Why, I am a thousand times better than my brother Abel! I have as much righteousness in my one hand, as he hath in his whole person." Said I, "Now take a full view of your brother with this glass." He did, and as he looked, he said, "My brother is the most contemptible creature I ever beheld. I wonder not now to hear him complain of his unworthiness, as he does in his whining way." "Look again," I said. Then said Cain, "Why, Abel is so swelled with pride, that he cannot contain himself." "Look farther," said I: "Ay, replied he, I see what he aims at. He thinks I shall be his servant, and no longer his superior as elder brother."

You know it is usual for my worthy friends, Envy, Revenge, and Cruelty, to follow me in most of my enterprises. It so fell out, at this time, that those three diabolians were present; but none of them attempted to speak a word, until Cain had viewed his brother Abel with my instruments, in a light the most disadvantageous to him that could be. But Cain having obtained this view of Abel, up comes Envy, and thus addressed him: "Friend Cain, I am heartily sorry for your disgrace, and am grieved when I observe to you, that, it is my opinion you will never be able to endure your brother's greatness and prosperity, now he is accepted, and you are rejected. I am much mistaken, if his ambition ceaseth to operate, until he enslaves you entirely under his yoke. I much fear that it is what he aims at. Now, my friend, as you are the elder born, it is but reasonable that you should be ruler; but for the elder to be subject to the younger, is what I would advise you never to submit to." Then, said Revenge, if honest Cain will be ruled by me, he will make himself amends for all the grief he has sustained. To whom Cain: "I pray thee thou sweet spirit, which way shall I do it? Shall I burn his tents, or destroy his flocks? What shall I do to make myself amends?" Do, said Crudelis, what should you do? Knock him on the head at once.

"else, said Envy, he will be an eye-sore to you, all the days of your life."

Thus the matter was determined, and, accordingly, Cain took an opportunity one day in the field to murder him. In this instance, Abel's virtue and faith were considered as vicious craftiness; his sincere aiming at the glory of God, and his self-denial, were, by my inverting instruments, interpreted pride and ambition. Deluded Cain revenged himself, not according to reality, but according to his own jealous suspicions and groundless surmises.

Infidelis. Realities seldom appear, Discordans, where you reign, or your operations would not be so successful as they are in common.

Discordans. True, sir, there is no possibility of maintaining strife and contention, but by inspiring one man with mistaken notions of another, and each with a good opinion of himself. This is the spring of all contention.

I remember I made rude work between Jacob's wives; I think their names were Leah and Rachel, the daughters of your friend Laban, Avaro; and that too, for what neither one nor the other could possibly help. Rachel was plump, fair, and beautiful, but withal for many years barren. Leah was less beautiful, being afflicted with tender eyes. And from these two sources I let the world see the inconveniency of polygamy or bigamy. But to pass from the discord of the women, I come to their sons, amongst whom I made a pretty sort of an inroad, which for a season yielded me exquisite pleasure.

You must know it is always more pleasure to me to stir up discord among the good and virtuous, than any people whatever; although, by the way, it is much more irrational in them to quarrel with one another, than for those who are strangers to equal privileges. Yet, such is my dexterity, that, whilst they are in this world, I can make them very often behave to one another, more like enemies than friends and brethren. However, they escape my tyranny the moment they forsake their clay, and I am for ever banished from their peaceful mansions in the other world.

To return to my story. Young Joseph, son of deceased Rachel, was his father's favorite; and the fond patriarch, to evince his distinguishing regard to him, clothed him in garments of many colors. This badge of affection sat very uneasy on the minds of his brethren, who, to a man, resolved to teach future parents the folly of partiality towards their children; yet had conduct enough to bridle their resentment until a favorable opportunity should offer. It was not many years before an opportunity offered; for Joseph had a dream divinely inspired, of which I made very suitable improvement. He dreamed "that he and his brethren were all reaping together in the field, and lo! ere he was aware, his sheaf stood upright in the midst, and all his brethren's sheaves stood round and made obeisance to it."

Young Joseph, suspecting no harm, in his simplicity, told his dream to his brethren. Not long after, he dreamed that the sun, moon, and eleven stars, made obeisance to him; and, in the same simplicity of heart, told his brethren this dream also, never once suspecting that they would comment upon it to his injury.

At this time I happened to make a visit to them; and having the matter without reserve laid before me, I requested them to examine it with my instruments, as you know I am never backward when there is any hope of business. As they examined it, they were unanimously of opinion, that the haughty boy was but too sensible of his father's over-esteem for him. "Vain youth, said they, he can think of nothing but being lord over his brethren: it is evident, from his repeated dreams, his mind runs upon it through the day; for what people ruminate in the day, they are apt to dream of at night." Such was the sense my mirror gave of the affair. Then, said I, gentlemen, be pleased to survey the matter with this telescope, meaning prejudice. They did so, and said, "Did ever any body see such a haughty, presumptuous youth as this stripling of a brother of ours is? It may be, the young ambitious wretch feigned his dreams, the more easily to introduce his supremacy! He be our lord! Must he? His pride is boundless. It is not enough that he hopes to lord it over his brethren, but his old father must, it seems, make obeisance to his arrogance."

It was now I called on my brother Revenge to appear, to whom I willed them to make their case known. This they did; and he, without hesitation, (as you know he is a ready-witted spirit) gave them his advice. "Gentlemen, said he, the fact is evident; but why do you perplex yourselves? You have it in your power to prevent his aggrandizement

K

Yonder he comes, and here is a pit hard by: drown him in it, and see what will become of his dreams." "By all means, said Envy; for you see the old man is so dotingly fond of him, that he is ready to take his dreams to be divinely inspired; and the more foolishly the youth can dream, the fonder his father is of him; so that it is now, if Joseph is well, he cares little what becomes of the rest of his children."

The sons of Jacob, in part, followed our advice. They cast Joseph into the pit, which happened to be dry: but the angel of compassion wrought so far upon them, that they spared his life, and sold him to a band of Ishmaelites, who were to take care to dispose of him in a foreign market, far enough from home. So you see it was by the help of my incomparable instruments, Joseph was separated from his brethren.

INFIDELIS. If right reason had been director, they would have allowed it possible that God might speak in a dream, or in a vision of the night, to the lad; and that it was time enough to punish him, when he actually became guilty of usurpation. But in your way, right reason is quite out of the question, cousin.

If agreeable to the great Fastosus, I hold it good we disperse for the present, that our affairs on earth be not neglected; and let us meet here to-morrow morning for fresh conversation.

FASTOSUS. It is very agreeable to me, sir.

DIALOGUE IX.

FASTOSUS, INFIDELIS, IMPIATOR, DISCORDANS, AND AVARO.

IT was my business to mind the appointment, and give due attendance; which I resolved to do, whatever should be the consequence: accordingly I was there ere the arrival of the infernal gentry, whom I waited for with impatience. At last, they all came up the valley to the place of conference; where five sable thrones were ready to receive them. As soon as seated, the following converse began:

INFIDELIS. Indeed! is it possible that my lovely Impiator hath so far prevailed, as to make a reverend vicar drink until he is fuddled? Such a conquest as this makes greatly for our interest; for when the parishioners know that the parson himself was drunk in the week, they will pay very little regard to his sermon the ensuing sabbath. Let him preach repentance and reformation, with all the zeal he may assume, every hearer will say in his heart, "Physician, heal thyself." I always knew that you, Avaro, had large dealings with many of the clergy; but not until now, that my son Impiator had obtained such great power over them. What! and swear too! To see a parson get drunk, or to hear him profanely swear, would give joy to the devil himself, amidst all his disappointments. I assure you, in the days of the Puritans, I would have crept forty miles on my hands and knees to have heard the one, or seen the other. But thou, my son——

IMPIATOR. Indeed, sire, you may depend on what I say. Great and formidable are my enterprises. These eyes of mine have seen the foot-ball thrown down at the church-door, on Sunday after service, in the presence of the parson; who, like the father of his people, gathered up his gown, and stood patiently to see which of his flock could with greatest dexterity make it skim the sky. This, you will say, was a pretty sort of transit, made by the holy man, from worshipping the God of heaven to serve the famous devil Impiator. Ah, gentlemen, were I but an eloquent spirit, I could tell you such wonders about the profaneness of both priest and people, as would rejoice your hearts, and make you confess that few devils have more ascendency over mankind than myself. O! the young students who are training up for the ministry, are charming lads. It is but a few years since, a nymph, who had been under the tuition of some of those young clergymen, came to an overseer of the poor of the parish, near a certain university, and desired to speak with him. What is your will? said he. I am with child, said she. I see that, returned he; but who is its father? Three gentlemen of ——— Hall, said she. What do you talk of three for, said he; only one of them can be its father. Indeed, sir, they are all three the fathers of my child, and are all willing to give security to the parish: ana three very civil gentlemen they are, I assure you. I think, said the overseer, they have not behaved very civilly to you, seeing you are with child by them. O! sir, said she, they behaved very civilly to me. They got me to their room, and kept me there for above a fortnight, and all the while I ate with them, and slept with them at free cost.

AVARO. Well, but, brother, can you assert that as fact upon your own knowledge?

IMPIATOR. Yes, Avaro, I can; and more than that, the overseer is yet alive, and can at any time attest the truth of it.

INFIDELIS. Well, I think they are hopeful gentlemen of which to make ministers of the gospel; gentlemen who may be of great service to our government.

IMPIATOR. It is on that account I mention the affair. And I could tell you a hundred such pretty little stories.

FASTOSUS. Supposing my reverend brother Infidelis, for the information of these younger devils, were to relate part of his history, might it not be well?

INFIDELIS. I am ready to do any thing that tends to the prosperity of our common cause: with a view to this, I have already given Impiator some account of my birth, and first enterprises; and now, for common instruction, shall proceed. Having ascended the throne of Infidelity, the first thing I attempted was, to lull men into a persuasion, that I did not at all exist, and that there is no such devil as unbelief in being. When I could not so universally prevail in this as I wished, I endeavored to persuade each of them separately, that however Infidelis might reign over others, for their part, he had no dominion over them. For, said I, you have a good heart, and have believed well all your days. Although, as I said before, I have conducted many of those, who fancied they had believed so well in their life-time, very safely down to the chambers of horrible despair where they were soon convinced, they never believed at al aright.

Then I endeavored to persuade the people, that the threatenings of God's law, against sin, ought to be considered as a fancy; and, to strengthen this doctrine, I thus preached; (for you must know I have been a great preacher in my time,) " Look you, you timorous-minded mortals: vou may clearly see that God hath created you, with all the passions and appetites that attend you; and can you believe that he did this with a design to prohibit the gratification of them? No, surely! Could it be consistent with the character of that God, whose goodness is unto all, and whose tender mercies are over all his works, to endue you with these passions and appetites, and then damn you for gratifying them? No, no, those threatenings are exhibited only to keep your consciences in awe; but never designed to be rigorously executed. The law will make large allowances, for the inclinations, passions, and infirmities of the human nature; never fear it. The soul that sinneth need not to fear dying, as the scripture has threatened; and man shall not be cursed, though he continue not in all things written in the law to do them."

Here, gentlemen, you may see my fallacy, in dealing with mortals; for although all the faculties and passions of the soul were indeed essential to its created state, none of them were then irregular; none acted from improper influence; for every passion centred in its lawful and proper object. Besides, all sinful motions and desires of the heart are the effects of my dominion over man.

Then I proceeded to persuade them that God had forsaken the earth, and took now no notice of the deeds of men, so that every man might, with the greatest safety, gratify his peculiar inclination. By these means it was, the great Impiator was brought into existence, whose dominion has increased, every year, with great rapidity.

I persuaded men, that this world is the most certain good. A bird in the hand, said I, is worth two in the bush. Make sure of this world, and never fear for the other. Do you consider this as your abiding place, and build your nest in its highest branches, if possible. In this I succeeded so well, that every man by nature, and almost all by practice, look upon the present world as the chiefest good. Then it was that Avaro was born in our family, and Ambitiosus was born in the family of Fastosus.

All this, you must observe, I did in disguise, or rather in a state of invisibility. I dare not tell a man, when I wait upon him, that my name is Infidelis: for, although they are fond of my nature, even to distraction, there is not one of them but what hates to be told that he is concerned with me.

Indeed you cannot affront any of my subjects worse, than by naming him after me, and calling him Infidel.

IMPIATOR. That is the very case with my subjects: for, although they love my service with all their hearts, they hate to be told of it. If a man should at any time reprove one of them for his enormities, you would soon hear him damn the reprover, for a methodist, a puritan, or a sanctified hypocrite.

INFIDELIS. It is no manner of difficulty for me to lurk, unperceived by them, in the corners of their dwellings; but I cannot possibly hide myself from Moses, the vicegerent of the Highest. He is a person of a most piercing eye, and can trace all the motions of spirit; therefore it comes to pass, that he and I have frequent bickerings. Moses being the perfection of light, and I the most consummate darkness, there is an eternal war proclaimed betwixt us, and we never meet but we are at daggers' drawing.

Sometimes he comes, knocking with a tremendous hammer at the doors and windows of my lodging, as if he would lay the house in a heap of ruins; whilst the people within start and tremble at every thunder-clap of his hammer. Amidst their consternation, you may hear him, from without, call to them within, with a voice louder than many thunders, in the name of his august Master, to bring forth the devil Infidelis, and all his train, to public execution. But I am always well befriended by the people of the house, who, for the most part, tell him that neither Infidelis, nor any of his train, live with them, and that his excellency must needs have mistaken the door. They tell him he would do better to inquire at the house of Tom Drunkard, or Jack the swearer, where, very probably, say they, that evil spirit may dwell.

This is often the beginning of a rupture betwixt him and them; for he is not to be so easily deceived. He shooteth his burning arrows with deathly vengeance in at the windows, against the people of the house, whom I exhort, by all possible means, to resist to the last extremity. Never did you see the warlike Corsicans exert themselves with such ardor in defence of their liberties, as my subjects in defence of my government.

Sometimes they so besmear his heavenly face, with the filth they throw upon him, calling him severe tyrant, covetous extortioner, unjust villain, and the like, that he gives over the assault, and leaves them to my quiet possession. Then I take my seal, and seal them to destruction. For you must know, it is but in some places he exerts his unfrustrable influence.

It is likewise observable, that although my subjects will give Moses a good character, while he keeps at a distance from them, every one will fight to the knees in blood, when assaulted by him, ere they submit; so fond are they of my person and government. Sometimes it hath happened, that by irresistible force, he hath broken open the doors, seized the people of the house by the collar, dragged them to the brink of a pit called Despondency, into which he tumbled them headlong, and left them shut up in that dreary dungeon.

As soon as he is departed, I go to work, and turn some neighboring brook into the pit, with a design to drown them, or throw down earth, stones, &c. on purpose to smother them; and so I continue to pester and disturb them, until I am frightened away by the sound of Immanuel's trumpet, as he himself approaches for their deliverance: for you must know, I cannot stand my ground, but take to my heels, when he appears. Many a time do I hear myself cursed for an hellish brat, even by those who, but very lately, would have risked life and fortune, and, with the greatest bravery, fought in the cause of prince Infidelis. But as soon as they obtain a glimpse of Immanuel's glory, they have done with my yoke, and I lose their affection for ever.

However, as I cannot endure that rational scripture light should shine into the hearts of men, I have often been puzzled to find out proper methods to resist the power of Moses; for he is excessively turbulent sometimes, and frighteneth my subjects into a pretended service of his Lord. In order to appease him, the sons of men agreed to build a temple, and dedicate it to the Most High; rather choosing to worship him, than be destroyed by the artillery of Sinai. Accordingly, to work they went, and built a sumptuous dome for divine worship, in order to stop the mouth of that never-ceasing accuser. Now, thought I, things are likely to take an awkward turn with me; if this worship is not interrupted, I shall lose many of my present slaves. So I put my plodding brain to the torture, in order to find out proper methods of prevention; and I can tell you, gentlemen, I went wisely to work. You remember that, Avaro, for you were my helper.

The case was this. We prepared the image of a woman, fair and beautiful to the eye; she was inwardly made of clay, and outwardly adorned with the appearance of burnished gold. In her right hand was a regal sceptre, titles of state, and plumes of honor, &c. In her left she carried a heavy purse of money, and a casket of oriental jewels. Upon her head was an Imperial crown, studded with sparkling gems, which dazzled the eyes of beholders, whilst they read the following motto, which was written in all languages on her forehead, "I am the mistress of the whole world." We secretly conveyed this image into one corner of the temple, and placed it in such a manner as to be seen of all who entered.

I soon perceived, that the bait was suitably drest, and our idol had charms enough to attract the attention of the people. Ha, ha, ha, you would have laughed, until your sides were tired, had you been there, to see how the slaves looked asquint upon the idol, as they approached the altar of God. Ay, and, in the midst of their devotion, how they cast the tail of their eye towards the place where she stood. After their worship was over, O how they bowed and cringed before her ladyship! The very parson himself did her humble reverence, and many times embraced her in the most affectionate manner. Then said I, "A fig for Moses and all his threatening. I have the slaves as fast as ever."

Impiator. Indeed, sire, you played the devil with them then. But what said Moses? Did he calmly yield the debate?

Infidelis. No, no, he is none of your easy tempered people, I assure you. His eagle eye soon discovered the cheat, and as soon did he resolve on vengeance, as appeared by the event. Laden with burning fagots, he came to the temple, and, roaring like many thunders, he said, the flashes of lightning bursting as he spake, "This people draweth near to me with their lips, but their hearts are far from me Put away from among you that accursed evil, and worship the Lord with your souls, as well as your bodies, with your hearts as well as your voices, or look for destruction, even in the embraces of your idol."

This said, he hurled his brands amongst the people, and terribly disturbed many of them. Indeed it was something alarming to see them look so ghastly, and tremble at his fearful menaces. In their first alarm, they were for removing the goddess out of the temple, for fear of immediate destruction; but being a little recovered from their fright, the far greater part found such relentings towards her ladyship, that they could not bear the thoughts of parting with her; believing still, in despite of Moses, that her comely presence was highly necessary, to render religion tolerable; and rather than part with her, they resolved to part with the temple of God itself.

Some few of them, indeed, were resolute for her removal, deeming the urgent command of the heavenly accuser not at all unreasonable; but their company was very inconsiderable, and their strength inadequate to the enterprise. When they attempted to remove her, they could not so much as move her feet off from the pedestal; and notwithstanding the command was urgent, the far greater part of the people could not help, even in the midst of their devotion, looking towards the idol, with an approving countenance; and there she stands to this day, adored by most, and a snare even to the virtuous and good.

AVARO. Great and manifold are the services which that ornamented idol had done to our government, among both preachers and others; for many of the sacerdotal tribe have not the least view in their preaching, beyond a genteel living, and further preferment; to which end, adulation and flattery is more studied than the gospel. If they can but get the world to smile upon them, they desire no more. Give them riches and honor, they may preach the gospel who will, for them. Let the people only pay their dues punctually, they may choose, for the parson, whether they will serve God or the devil, whether they will go to heaven or hell. Brave days, gentlemen!

INFIDELIS. Yes, Avaro, the times are not to be complained of; nor indeed have they been bad for many hundreds of years, if circumstances are duly attended to. But to my story. In process of time, men became sensible, that unless the heart were fixed upon God, in acts of religious worship, their services could not be acceptable; but how to fix them they could not find. Being afraid the result of their inquiries might prove dangerous to my interest, if not interrupted, I advised them to make to themselves representations of God, in wood, stone, brass, or iron, but rather of silver or gold, alleging that, the more valuable the metal, the more acceptable the sacrifice would be.

The sons of men no sooner heard, than approved of my scheme, and resolved forthwith to put it in execution. Then, ere you were aware, every village was furnished with one or two god-makers; a set of artificers, from whom our present saint-makers in Italy, Spain, Portugal, &c. are descended; for modern times have not changed, but only given a different name to this craft, by which the popish parsons get their wealth.

But, alas! having never seen the shape of God, at any time, they were obliged to form their images in the mould of their own fancies, which being various, it came to pass that in one place the invisible Deity was likened to an old man with a venerable long beard, grasping a bunch of reeds which they called thunder. In another place he was represented as half man and half beast; yea, so various were the fancies of the artists, that in one place God Almighty was made like a fish, in another like an eagle or hawk, and in another like a log of wood, and indeed sometimes like a beast with four feet. So very briskly was this trade carried on, that all who were able to buy, had, in a few years, one or more god almighties, of man's making, in their own houses. The very same as our good friends the papists, have got almost every one a savior in his pocket or chamber. In the holy Roman church, you may find in every house, a Jesus Christ of one kind or another; for there be many sorts of Jesus Christs, as golden Jesus Christs, silver Jesus Christs, wooden, and even paper Jesus Christs, all made with as much craft as the ancient pagan gods.

Avaro. That trade of shrine-making among the papists, is a good sort of trade; but I can tell you, it falls far short of the craft of saint-worshipping, by which the priests get their wealth. Many a wooden saint there is in the holy church, which hath brought into the priests' treasury above six times its weight in gold. And indeed the pagan priests reaped equal benefit from their gods; from whence we learn that priestcraft hath been the same in all ages.

Infidelis. Some people there were, of more refined

knowledge than their neighbors, who advised against the trade of god-making, saying, "We must not bow down to graven nor molten images, nor in any wise worship them."—My priests, according to my directions, answered as follows: "It is not the image which you worship, nor do you at all bow your knee to it; but being emblematic of the divine presence, it greatly assists you in your devotion." This learned reasoning calmed the consciences of most of the dissenters, won them over to the religion by law established, and greatly wrought for the good of the church.

DISCORDANS. Why, sir, that is the very apology which the papists make for image worship, relic adoration, &c. but indeed it is no wonder, seeing their religion is one and the same with that of the pagans.

INFIDELIS. Some few there were, rigid nonconformists, who insisted that God must be worshipped in spirit and in truth; insisted that all idolatrous lumber should be cast out of the temple; by which the worthy clergymen, of that age, were so grievously galled, that they were forced, in a pious and tender manner, first to give up the heretics to the devil and then put the flesh to death for the salvation of the soul: in the very same manner (and for much the same cause) as the holy Romish fathers excommunicated and burned the Protestants. But the devil knows, by his experience, that the church has not half the power she pretends to; for out of the vast numbers, which she hath generously given to him, it is but a very few he hath been able to receive. Notwithstanding, both the pagan, papal, and other churches, have hereby shown the good will, which, all along, they have borne to him and his interest.

Having fairly introduced idolatry, I tried, if possible, to lead men further off from their Maker still; and for this end, I brought in gods and goddesses, a numerous train. For instance, if any man was more remarkable than others, for murdering his neighbors, or for giving large gifts to the church, that is, the clergy, I got him deified as soon as he died, and had worship offered to him, in the same degree with saint-worship in the church of Rome; for saint-worship and hero-worship, differ only in name.

Indeed, it is but doing justice to saints, in the Romish calendar, to observe, that the greatest part of them obtained their saintship for murdering of princes, massacring

Protestants, robbing their heirs for the good of the church, or for raving mad enthusiasm. Well, I went on and prospered, until I had brought all the world, a few individuals excepted, to worship the works of the mason, carpenter, blacksmith, or founder. Encourage but any trade, and it is sure to prosper: the god-making trade, being universally encouraged, prospered exceedingly; for in a little time there were national gods, much the same with the seven champions of Christendom; provincial gods; county gods parish gods; and even household gods, to the great emolument of the clergy. I think, gentlemen, you must all allow, that I have not spent my time in idleness among mankind.

Fastosus. No, no, brother, idleness don't suit you and me. We will leave it to foolish men and women so to spend their lives; but we will fulfil the old proverb used among them, viz. The devil is never idle. Let them enjoy their idleness in this world; we shall very likely find them enough to do in the next.

Infidelis. I think it is something more than seventeen hundred and sixty years ago that I had a trial of a very extraordinary nature to grapple with, such as I never had before then, nor ever shall encounter while I breathe the sulphurous smoke of the pit. Oh, it was a sore trial, gentlemen. Immanuel, a very dear lover of men, having sat on the circle of heaven for near four thousand years, with much relenting of mind, and longings for human happiness, from thence beheld the dreadful havoc I made in the world, rendering the whole posterity of Adam the children of wrath. Often did he call to the inhabitants of the earth to take me up, and burn me for a witch; but they were too much my friends to regard his advice: and, indeed, had they regarded it, it would have been an undertaking such as they could not execute without auxiliary strength. He sat long, and long he wondered that there was no friend, to help against so potent an adversary; when at last he saw there were none to help, he arose from his jasper seat, and in a transport of love, declared that his own arm should bring salvation. According to this high determination, he dismantled himself of the robes of manifest glory, laid aside his imperial diadem, which irradiates all the coasts of light, posted down to this world, on the wings of compassion, resolved to encounter me by dying

Alarmed at such an unprecedented enterprise, I dispatched our swift-winged courier, with all possible speed, to hell, to inform my great father, and the infernal divan, of the astonishing event. As soon as Fame reported her story, the monarch summoned his peers, to meet him in the flaming council chamber, there to deliberate on the matter; and having maturely weighed every circumstance of it, it was resolved to dispatch the devil Malevolus to Fastosus and me, with directions suitable to the occasion. That he, with Ambitiosus, Perfidia, Falax, and me, should take up our residence at Jerusalem, with the scribes, pharisees, and doctors of the law. We immediately obeyed our instructions, and succeeded admirably in our embassy. At the same time, Crudelis and Concupiscentia were appointed plenipotentiaries to the tetrarchical court of Galilee, where they received infallible testimonies of Herod's esteem.

Against the time that Immanuel was to be revealed, Herod admitted our cousin Suspiciosus to frequent audiences, of which the devil Crudelis, to his everlasting honor, greatly availed himself. He persuaded the tetrarch, that, for his own safety, it was highly necessary he should kill, destroy, and cause to perish, all the children in Bethlehem, from two years old, and under, in order that young Immanuel, who was formerly called the Ancient of Days, might be involved in the general massacre. This was the opening of our evangelic campaign; since which time, we have caused the shedding of as much Christian blood, as, if collected into one mass, would make a tide as deep as ever was seen at London-bridge.

At this time there appeared one John Baptist, a zealous Nazarene, and harbinger to Immanuel. He was likely to do great injury to our interest; therefore it was thought best to have him destroyed, which, by thy means, Discordans, we happily accomplished in part. Perhaps, Discordans, you can give a better account of that affair than I, as you were more deeply concerned in it.

Discordans. I do not know that, uncle; but I am ready to tell you what hand I had in it. You all know the man, and a trusty friend of ours he was, as any in his day. You know he most inordinately loved Herodias, his own brother Philip's wife; and by the direction of our friend Concupiscentia, he added incest to his adultery, by taking her to his bed. It was about this time, that this famous Baptist, the founder of the sect called by his name, began his public ministry; and, fearless of man, exclaimed against all manner of uncleanliness; for he was faithful to his commission. Well, this same austere Baptist took occasion one day, in the following manner, to reprove the tetrarch for his lewdness; "Herod, said he, the God who made thee, hath, for his own glory, exalted thee to the tetrarchical dignity; but, far from studying his honor, thou actest most unworthily, and turnest his goodness to thee into wantonness. Dost not thou know, that the same God who made thee ruler in Galilee, hath said, "Thou shalt not commit adultery." Put her therefore away from thee; if thou dost not, thou must expect, that the Most High will mingle for thee the cup of his indignation."

I was then at the court of Galilee, and did not fail to improve the Baptist's admonition to the most fatal purposes. I transformed myself into the likeness of a grave courtier, a form very familiar to me, went up to the king, and held my inverting mirror before his eyes, bidding him to take a full view of the matter thus. As my humble servant he did as I directed, and immediately said, "I perceive this field-preacher, this same Baptist, is an enemy to the Roman government, and, because I am a friend to Cæsar, he hath taken this advantage against me doubtless to prejudice the minds of the people, either to the divesting me of the tetrarchical power, or to the subversion of Cæsar's government."

When I had brought him thus to misconstrue the honest designs of the Baptist, I held my partial telescope to his eye, through which he looked with great attention, and as he looked said, "What a presumptuous wretch is this, to take upon him to reprove me! Me, who am his lord and master, and can soon destroy both him and his father's house. Must Herod be reproved by this despicable fellow with the rough garment? Is it now so low with Cæsar's deputy, the tetrarch of Galilee, that he must mildly bear the insolence of every snarling peasant? No, it is inconsistent with our dignity, to let such daring boldness pass with impunity. If a courtier, or nobleman clothed in soft raiment, had taken a little liberty with me, it might have been borne. But for this field-preacher! This Baptist, hah!"

By this time the great Revenge, that famous devil, whose history is so tragical, thought it time for him to appear at court, and as soon as he judged it convenient, thus accosted the offended king. "My lord the king, if your highness suffers such insolence as this to go unpunished, your nobles will contemn you; every paltry priest will say, Yonder goes the incestuous Herod; ay, the very publicans and Herodians will allege, that you are unworthy of the dignity you sustain, and all will censure your pusillanimity, in letting such daring insolence pass with impunity. Remember, my lord, that if wide-mouthed fame should, as is very likely, report the matter in Cæsar's ear, it is ten to one but he will cashier you, either for your reputed incest, or your want of magnanimity. Sir, for your honor's sake, cast John into prison." Herod was easily persuaded, and John was committed to jail.

On mature deliberation, however, he was afraid of putting him to death, for he knew that the people had a good opinion of the renowned Baptist; therefore he lived in prison, notwithstanding Revenge made daily solicitation for his blood. On every occasion when he met with Herod, he thus accosted him, "Well, sir, is the Baptist dead yet? What! not yet, sir? What do you mean by sparing him so long, sir? I assure you, sir, he ought to die for his insolence. Sir, his crime is no less than high treason against your person." Thus he plied him daily.

It happened, at a certain time, that Herod made a great festival in honor of his own name, which festival proved fatal to the innocent Baptist; for, ever since he had given offence, the devil Revenge had taken up his lodgings with Herodias the tetrarchess. She very well knew how foolishly precipitate Herod was wont to be in his wine, and how much his eye was to be allured with a well-performed dance, especially if performed by a handsome young lady. Not at all doubting but Herodina her daughter, would captivate the king, so far as to bring about the much desired death of John Baptist, she decked her in superb array, instructed her what to ask, if he should be pleased with her, then led her into the hall, where Herod and his nobles were carousing. There she footed the hornpipe with such exactness, that the mistaken eye of the tetrarch took her for a divinity, and swore that he would offer a great sacrifice to her, to the value of one-half of his kingdom, if her highness would only deign to inform him what sacrifices were most acceptable to her. She replied, "Human sacrifices are my delight. Give me then the Baptist's head in a charger."

Now there began a horrid scuffle in the tetrarch's breast. If he fulfilled not his oath, he thought he lost his reputation with his nobles, who sat at table with him; and if he did behead John Baptist, according to his oath, he exposed himself to the resentment of the people.

In the midst of this scuffle, in came Revenge, and addressed the king—"I assure you, sir, John deserves a thousand deaths, for his insolence to your highness." "Besides, said Fastosus, who was then at court, the great tetrarch hath no way left but this to preserve his own character unblamed." Then cried Herod, "Who will go for us to prison, and behead the Baptist." To which Crudelis replied, "Here am I, send me." Accordingly, having obtained Herod's consent, (for we can do nothing against mankind but by their own consent,) he went and beheaded Immanuel's harbinger.

Thus, gentlemen, you see, that by my famous instruments, false reasoning and prejudice, I cause offence to be taken where there is none intended. John only fulfilled his divine mission, and sought the good of the tetrarch, by calling him to repentance; but my mirror interpreted his honesty into treachery and insolence; which clearly shows that it changeth the appearance, quite contrary to the nature of things. But, reverend uncle, I prevent your proceeding with your story.

Infidelis. The cumbersome Baptist thus dispatched, we united all our forces against Immanuel himself, who was by the Jews called Jesus of Nazareth. Many were the conferences which we had with the Jewish rabbins, doctors, priests, scribes, and pharisees, in which all our debates turned upon that object of our common hatred. The high-priest, Fastosus, Malevolus, and me, were always placed at the head of the assembly, and every article was finally referred to us for decision. The venerable high-priest addressing himself to me, asked what I thought concerning the pretensions of this Galilean? To whom I replied, "If it please your reverence, I think he is an arrant impostor; for his father you know, and his mother you know, his brethren and sisters are they not all with you? But, continued I, when

Messiah shall come, no man can tell whence he cometh, nor whither he goeth." Gentlemen, you will always know my style by its elegance, wherever you meet with it, should it be even in the volume of revelation.

Fastosus. I well remember these things, and the learned oration which, at that time, I made in the Sanhedrim; and now we are associated in such a friendly manner, I have a good mind to repeat it to you. You have it in the following manner: "Hearken to me, ye righteous teachers of the law, the virtuous governors of the Lord's inheritance, and I will unfold to you a just state of the matter. You all know that the expected Messiah shall descend from a virgin princess, of the lineage of David; but is this the son of a princess? Is his mother a virgin, being the wife of a carpenter?" Here you will observe how I led them off from the truth, by attending to appearances rather than reality; for Mary, the mother of Jesus, was actually a princess of the line of David, though obscure, and actually a virgin when he was conceived, though after that the wife of a carpenter. Every circumstance attending his birth, corresponded exactly with ancient predictions recorded in the Bible; though, by the way, it was by no means suited to the expectation of the Jews. But, to my great mortification, I must confess, that although the great men of the earth rejected him, the angels of heaven descended to hymn their new-born Lord. The constellations of the firmament showed forth the birth of Messiah. Eastern sages heard the proclamation of the stars, and came to the city of Bethlehem, to offer oblations to the incarnate source of life.

So very clear indeed are the Old Testament prophecies, concerning this affair, that the generality of the Jews were, at that time, in full expectation of the coming of Messiah; therefore it required great address sufficiently to blind their eyes, that they should not see and know him when he came to which purpose my speech was wonderfully adapted "You know, and all the holy rabbins know, continued I that Messiah shall come in power and great glory; shall break the iron yoke of Roman servitude from off your necks and exalt the throne of David, his illustrious ancestor, high above the thrones of the kings of the earth, giving to his happy subjects dominion and great glory, subjecting to your government all those who wish your destruction. Worthy assembly, said I, you have chosen the great Fastosus as your president and director. Hearken, therefore, to me, and I will show you my opinion, concerning your expected Messiah, and his appearance among you. It is most probable, that when he comes, he will be born of illustrious parents, in the family of David, and when grown mature in years, you may expect to see meet in him, a combination of all great and good qualities. By his wisdom and prowess, he will rekindle the martial spirit of the Jewish warriors, leading the armies of Israel to glory and conquest, and his throne shall be exalted above all the kingdoms of the earth. You may therefore expect that when Messiah shall come to your deliverance, you shall see an illustrious prince, attended by a warlike retinue, breathing vengeance against your enemies. But can this be him? could the Messiah, think you, find nobody but poor shepherds to be the publishers of his birth? More likely, if Jesus had indeed been the Messiah, he would have made choice of your reverences for his heralds. Can it ever be supposed, my venerable rabbins, that an obscure person, attended by a few despicable fishermen, can have any legal pretensions to the vacant throne of illustrious David? Or can it ever be thought, that the son of a Galilean carpenter, attended by a few of the riff-raff of the people, is likely to restore the kingdom to Israel?

Besides, continued I, let him be what he may, it would bring dishonor on the princes of Israel, should they submit to be governed by the son of a mechanic

Who knows but the coming of Messiah may be yet more glorious, and ye shall see the heavens open over your heads. he shall appear in the firmament, guarded on right and left by innumerable battalions of armed seraphs, with whom he may descend and stand upon the mount of Olives, before he shall make his triumphant entry into the holy metropolis of Jewry. Then shall he dispatch his flaming soldiers, with full commission to kill, destroy, and cause to perish all such stubborn Gentiles, who refuse to submit to the Jewish empire, now become universal. Your enemies all destroyed, great shall be your felicity and glory, for he shall reign among you in righteousness, peace, and glorious prosperity, unto all generations.

To whom, my worthy rabbins, will he come, but to such generation of righteous men as yourselves? Ye yourselves are witnesses of your own righteousness and devotion. None say longer prayers; none give alms more publicly than you do. So great is your zeal for religion, that ye rob widows' houses for the good of the church. So pious your example, that my life for it, it will be imitated by the clergy in after ages. Your wicked ancestors fell very far short of your piety; for they killed the prophets, and stoned them who were sent unto them; but your reverences so far abominate their murderous deeds, that you build and beautify their sepulchres. You may safely conclude, that you are the righteous generation to whom the Messiah will come." Thus I swelled their expectations so very great, that, when the real Messiah was actually among them, they reviled him as the worst of impostors.

INFIDELIS. The great Fastosus and me, having showed our opinion, the devil Malevolus was humbly requested to speak his mind. And he, by this time, was in a transport of rage; boisterously cried out, "Away with him for an imposing villain! If he were the Messiah, would you ever find him coming out of Galilee? Search, and you will see that out of Galilee ariseth no prophet; neither can any good thing come from thence. Were I in your places, I would rather be subject to the Romans for ever, than suffer this fellow to reign over me. I hate his person; I hate his attendants; I hate his laws and doctrines; and, above all, I hate his pretensions to the crown of Israel. It were low times with you indeed, if an obscure carpenter should be exalted to the throne, to reign over the Lord's inheritance."

FASTOSUS. It is time for us to attend our industrious subjects. Shall we meet here to-morrow, at noon, as usual?

All. Agreed, sir. We will meet.

DIALOGUE X.

ALL THE DIALOGEANS PRESENT.

As soon as the infernal gentry decamped, I went home, and found our parish priest at my house. I thought this a good opportunity of acquainting him with my adventure: but he concluded, with the rest of my neighbors, that my brain was disturbed, and that those imaginary gentry were only the fruits of distraction. However, as I thought myself capable of judging between imagination and reality, I left the parson to his mistake; went to my closet to correct what I had taken down in the former part of the day; and got all ready by the next day at noon, to listen to the sable gentry. Exactly at noon they came; for I found them exceedingly punctual one with another. As soon as they were seated on their ebon thrones, they resumed their discourse; and Infidelis thus began.

INFIDELIS. It happened that the venerable rabbins held another council, to assist at which, the devils, Falax and Perfidiosus were invited. In this august assembly, the main thing to be considered was, by what possible means, right or wrong, they might persecute and destroy Jesus of Nazareth from the face of the earth. The great rabbins and doctors, by this time, began to fear that if some decisive step was not speedily taken, all the country would become Nazarenes. This induced them to apply to those worthy spirits, (who are known to be excellent contrivers) and fervently solicit their assistance. And, as they are by no means bashful, they very soon gave the high sanhedrim satisfaction.

"Venerable rabbins, said they, we are apprehensive that it will be very difficult to accomplish any thing against this Jesus of Nazareth, unless we can stir up enemies against him, among those of his own household, and cause some, who eat bread at his table, to lift up their heel against him; for you all know his conduct is perfectly unblamable. Now we have, at no great distance, a notable limb of the devil, trained up in all the mazes of deep deceit and treachery, fitted for such perdition. Him will we persuade to ingratiate himself into the favor of Jesus, and to become one of his train. When this is done, he shall act the traitor, and betray him into your hands, nothing doubting but you will then take care to destroy his life, how innocent soever he may be."

"Certainly we will, rejoined the high priest; for it is expedient that one should die for the people." Accordingly the devil was dispatched to this son of treachery, whose name was Judas Iscariot, who, being a plodding covetous man, in hope of getting a bag of money, took his instructions from Perfidiosus, went and joined himself to the train of Jesus, and obtained a part in the apostolic ministry. In the mean time, we, and the auxiliary Jews, did all in our power to prevent the advancement of his evangelic kingdom, by bringing the person and ministry of Jesus into as much contempt as possible. We represented him as a glutton, a drunkard, a Samaritan, a wizard; and, in short, every thing that was bad. His doctrine we represented as subversive of the law; notwithstanding we knew him to be holy, harmless, and undefiled, separate from sinners; that he came to magnify the law, and make it honorable. Because his works were such as carried their own evidence with them, and which could by no means be contested, we persuaded many of the Jews, that they were performed by the power of Beelzebub. Others, who were better informed, being stirred up by the devil Malevolus, out of pure malice, fell in with the common cry, and defamed him as one who had intercourse with Satan; and thus they sealed themselves ours; as we need never fear losing a man after he is capable of such transactions.

IMPIATOR. And who were they chiefly, father, who thus acted the devil's part so perfectly as to sin unpardonably?

INFIDELIS. Not the vulgar, who knew not the law, I assure you; but men of priestly reverence, gentlemen in holy orders, gentlemen venerable for their erudition and literature; the doctors in divinity, the scribes of the law, the religious pharisees were the men, and their descendants have in every age been their humble imitators. It is unknown how much the devil has been obliged to gentlemen of the gown, and to scholiasts in general.

It happened, in process of time, our friend Judas found an opportunity to betray him into the hands of the principal priests, for the goodly reward of thirty pieces of silver; for even Judas would not serve the devil for nothing. At the same time my son Slavish Fear, who is a spirit of gigantic stature, fell upon and routed all his followers, so that none of them remained with him in his last temptations. As soon as Immanuel was seized and fettered, they led him in triumph to prison and judgment, where our steady friends, Hatred and Falshood, were appointed witnesses against him in behalf of the commonwealth. So very hard did they swear against him, that he was brought in guilty of death, as had been agreed on beforehand. As soon as the jury of priests brought in their verdict, the devil Crudelis, and Pilate, who sat judge, arose and gave sentence against him; which, for its singularity, I shall repeat.

1. That the Jewish plowers should make their furrows long and deep in his devoted flesh.

2. That his face should be marred with shame and spitting.

3. That his cheek should be bruised by the slavish hand of the barbarous smiter.

4. That he should be delivered over, for further torment, to those who pluck off the hair.

5. That, in mark of the greatest contempt, his temples should be torn with a mock crown of piercing thorns.

6. That he should be crushed to the earth beneath the weight of the cross, to which he was to be nailed for execution.

7. That, in his extreme torture, he should have no drink, but the sourest vinegar mixed with gall.

8. That, in the most barbarous manner which devils, priests, and soldiers could devise, his mangled body should be stretched upon and nailed to the accursed wood. And,

9. As unworthy of either, that he should be lifted up betwixt heaven and earth, a spectacle to devils and men, and there hang till he was dead.

As soon as the sentence was denounced, the devil Malevolus cried out, "Away with him! soldiers, away with him! Come, let us crucify him. His sentence is by far too mild. Away with the varlet to Calvary." So they led him away to crucifixion.

At the same time our infernal nobility were struck with amazement, at the seeming power which man had gained over Immanuel; and great Beelzebub, in the midst of his astonishment, thus addressed his senators: 'Once was the memorable time that we made such an attempt to subvert the government of God, by resisting the power of Immanuel; but great was our defeat, and dismal our overthrow. Our designs were not only frustrated, but we ourselves, in the height of our confusion, fiercely hurled from the resplendent summit of primeval glory, into the yawning gulf of unfathomable perdition, where we are still reserved in these horrible chains, to the judgment of the great and terribl day:—a day, the very thoughts of which make this noble frame of mine to tremble as the quaking asp. But how it comes to pass I know not, these earth-born sons of ours seem exceedingly to surpass us in power: for I saw Immanuel stand fettered at their bar; dumb as a sheep before her shearers, he opened not his mouth. I am much afraid there is some hidden mystery in it.———What is this?———My undaunted mind is not wont to misgive me thus!——— What can this unusual tremor, which now invades my heart, portend?—I hate timidity, and yet I cannot help fearing, that this commotion of my intellects is ominous of some event, fatal to our interest.

"I cannot deem it possible that the God of heaven and earth would patiently submit to such indignities, had he not some ends to answer by it, to which we at present are strangers. Often have I prophesied true; but O may my prophetic mind be mistaken in its present timorous forebodings! Meanwhile, let us, my infernal brethren, harden ourselves in despair; for it is now long since hope took wing and fled from these dreary mansions. Strong in fury, and fired with revenge, let us quit ourselves like devils and avowed enemies of righteousness. As for me, I hold it good that we instantly fly to the assistance of our devoted friends the Jews. Having this unexpected opportunity, let us not fail to improve it to the best advantage; let it not be owing to our negligence, if the state of Immanuel be not overturned. Let us not have the hell to reflect, that we omitted any thing which might tend to promote the interest of darkness."

Great Beelzebub finishing here, and his motion being universally approved of, all the legions of reprobate angels, a few excepted, who were left to look after the affairs of the damned, took wing for earth, to assist at so very amazing an execution. Arrived at Calvary, they formed themselves into an invisible ring around the elevated cross, where, to their unspeakable astonishment and wonder, hung Immanuel, the maker of the world; and you may be assured they did not fail, as far as it was in the power of fallen spirits, to torment his oppressed soul. Ay, ay, so successful were we devils, priests, and soldiers that day, that no less was hoped for than a decisive victory over the Son of God.

But, how shall I speak it? to the everlasting mortification of the infernal peers, just as Immanuel was, to all appearance, ready to expire, on a sudden he exerted his mighty power, seized old Beelzebub and dashed him against the cross, then casting him to the earth, he so bruised the head of the serpent with his heel, that there is great reason to believe he will never recover as long as he lives. It would have grieved the heart of the very Crudelis himself, to see the abuse which our great and venerable parent received on that occasion.

IMPIATOR. Well, sire, I cannot but think how truly the prophetic mind of Beelzebub foreboded his misfortune. But what were the rest of the chiefs a-doing? Why did not all the veterans flee to his assistance?

INFIDELIS. A pertinent question, indeed, considering by whom it is made, my son. But I assure you, we were never so greatly mistaken in our days as at that time. For when we thought ourselves sure of the victory, to our sad experience we learned, that Immanuel was the strongest in death. For even when he was dying, he laid us all under the most perfect arrest; none of us could take one step, either backward or forward, but as he gave permission; so that, being spoiled of all our power, we could not help ourselves, much less the afflicted prince. This done, he cried out with a voice which shook the very foundations of both earth and hell, "It is finished," and was then conveyed by death into an invisible state.

This done, once more we thought the day our own. But here, I cannot omit that fearful stagnation of nature which happened then, and the set of new preachers which were introduced. For, when all under our influence had forsaken Immanuel, who was betrayed by one, denied by another, and forsaken by all his preachers, the indignant sun could not endure that sight; as if angry and ashamed at the proceedings of the sons of men, he covered his face with a sable cloud, and denied one smiling ray to delinquent earth whilst his Lord was ignominiously crucified. As if it had been seized with uncommon tremor, the earth itself fell into a fit of violent convulsions, the mountains reeled, the rocks rent, the graves opened, the dead arose, and all to preach the sufferings of the God of nature. An invisible hand rent the veil of the temple, that cloth of extraordinary texture, in twain, from the top to the bottom; and a voice was heard to say, "The glory is departed from Israel, and now the most holy place is laid open."

Death having conveyed Immanuel to its lonely mansions, the resolute, though maimed Beelzebub, our great prince, recovered himself as much as was possible, his head being incurably broken; mustered his maimed forces and went to the assistance of Death, if possible, to keep Immanuel fast prisoner in the silent tomb. Nothing doubting, but if this could be, we should render all that he had heretofore done and suffered, null and void. The better to succeed in this important enterprise, we sealed the door of the sepulchre and set a watch of faithful soldiers, instructed by the chief of the Jewish priests; and still to make the security stronger, every fiend did his utmost to impose weights on the buried body of Immanuel, to prevent his resurrection from the solitary grave.

But, to our eternal confusion, on the third day of his invisible state, he arose, shook himself from the dust, came to the door of the sepulchre, burst it open, and laid hold on Death, who stood as sentinel next to the door of the tomb, trampled him under his feet, and, by main force, wrenched from him his poisonous sting, that sad repository of all his strength. This done he said, "Henceforth, monster, hast thou no power over the people for whom I have died." Then he broke impetuously through all the lines of martial infernals, who stood in firm phalanx around the tomb, and seized the lately wounded chief, who was very ill with a fever in his mind, arising from his disaster upon Mount Calvary. He took the fiend, the great Beelzebub, chained him to the axle of his chariot, mounted his seat, and rode triumphantly through the gathering crowds of joyful saints, who on golden pinions descended from heaven, in solemn strains, to hymn their all-conquering and triumphant Redeemer.

O my friends, my dear infernals, it must have pierced your hearts with the most poignant sorrow, to see him dragged in triumph through all the hosts of saints and angels, who fearless stood in blazing ranks to see the longed for solemnity; and, at the same time, to see our beloved friend Death lie gasping for life at the door of the sepulchre. Great was the confusion of the infernal brigades, when they saw their principalities spoiled, and Death and Satan so terribly handled: yea, so tremendous was their amazement, that to escape the avenging hand of risen Immanuel, they retreated even to the nethermost depths of hell, and his scattered disciples again resorted to his erected standard. But the greatest disappointment and consternation was, when we understood that after all our diligence and hazardous exploits, we, with our auxiliary priests, &c. had done nothing, but what the hand and counsel of God had predetermined should be done; that by our seeming victory over Immanuel, he had for ever subdued us under his feet; and that all our hatred, envy and cruelty, was fully recompensed into our own bosoms; now deeper damned than ever.

Avaro. Ha! father, these were troubles indeed, such as do not happen every day: but it is not for us to desist from tempting when our designs miscarry; then should we not act the part of desperadoes, such as we are.

Infidelis. Ah, gentlemen, great was the cause of my dismay; for Immanuel gave such demonstration of his Messiahship, that all which was written in the prophets concerning him, was exactly fulfilled in his life and death. Yea, so very striking was the evidence, that many cried, "Truly this is a just man;" and others, "Truly this is the Son of God." Therefore I greatly feared that all the world would become believers in him, and consequently shake off my yoke. But I was much obliged to my good friends, the Jewish clergymen; for their reverences greatly befriended me, and warmly espoused my interest; exerted their utmost power to establish the throne of great Infidelis, and to destroy the early seeds of Christianity, sown by Immanuel, and now beginning to grow.

Immanuel having, in opposition to all the powers of darkness, finished the work for which he came down to the earth, he triumphantly ascended to his native heaven, to the pri meval embraces of his Eternal Father, and assumed all the ensigns of empyrean glory.

Soon after this, the high festival of pentecost drew on, and I, as formerly, attended at Jerusalem, in the midst of many thousands, who, according to the law, came up to worship upon that occasion, not only from Judea, but from nations very remote. I dreaded no harm at the hands of a few illiterate fishermen, having not been informed that any of the rulers, or of the scribes and pharisees, had believed in Jesus; and therefore was at no pains to prevent the multitude coming up to the solemnity as usual. But here was another shock my kingdom sustained; for Peter, the fisherman, who, so very lately, like a dastard, impiously denied his Lord with profane oaths, now filled with the Holy Ghost, stood up in the midst, and clearly proved that Jesus was the very Messiah; and upon this occasion played off the heavy artillery of Sinai on the consciences of my people, which was attended with success so fatal to me, that no less than three thousand were pierced through the heart at once, and fell on the field of action. Now it was that my evil apprehensions were again alarmed, plainly perceiving, that the artillery of the word was levelled against my person, and that the first end of the gospel was the subversion of my diabolical government. However, I drew up all the forces which I possibly could, in the hurry of that surprise, my soldiers crying out as they gave the volley, "These men are drunken with new wine." It was but a poor opposition to doctrine so powerful, I allow; but it was the best that could at that time be made; for we were obliged to retreat in much confusion, and leave the Christian fishermen masters of the field.

As soon as we were a little recovered from the disorder into which that unexpected misfortune had plunged us, I summoned a council of war, in which the self-righteous Jews were the principal, next to our infernal train. I myself gave special orders, that some method should be concerted effectually to destroy the name of Jesus; for, said I, "If we let them alone, all the people will believe in their doctrine." In this council it was resolved, to raise an army of those who were the greatest adversaries to the name of Jesus, to whom orders should be given to kill, destroy, and cause to perish, all who believed in this way, until the Christian religion should be banished from the face of the earth. This army was raised, and the command given to Saul of Tarsus; at that time a mighty zealot for us, and who, for a season, made dreadful havoc of all that believed contrary to the faith of the priests. For it ought to be observed, that the opinion of the priests has been esteemed true orthodoxy, and the only faith, in all ages and countries

But here another sad disappointment and loss befell me; for as this same captain Saul was on his march to Damascus, to fight a pitched battle with the Christians, it so fel out that Immanuel himself was taking a tour in the valley to see how the pomegranates budded, and falling in with trusty Saul on his journey, unveiled his own personal excellencies to him, and laid him under an immediate arrest. As soon as he saw the beauties of Immanuel, he felt the most sincere esteem for his person, and conceived the most exalted sentiments of his friendship and love. Yea, he was even so much grieved that ever he had drawn his sword against him, that he renounced the service of Infidelis on the spot, took the oath of allegiance to Jesus, and thenceforward hated my person and government with the most perfect hatred, and did what he could to overturn our state and subvert our government.

Immanuel having the most tender regard for Saul, gave him a new name written upon a white stone, appointed him one of his prime ministers, and sent him on an embassy to my subjects to negotiate a revolt from me.

You cannot conceive the astonishment the Jewish clergy were in, when swift-winged fame arrived and blowed abroad in every street, that Saul, who was formerly so zealous for our interest, was now become a ringleader of the sect of Nazarenes, and was likely to do us more mischief than all who had gone before him.

By this time several of the Jewish rabbins rebelled against me, and joined themselves to the Nazarenes, who now made it their whole business to go from place to place exhorting my subjects to revolt, exposing my deformity an devilishness, to all they met with. O! those were trying times; for notwithstanding we had forces out against them in every quarter of the world, to impede their progress, the word of God by their means prevailed in such a manner, that it was beyond our power to suppress it: for, if we ourned one Nazarene, two more presently sprang up out of his ashes. Even Rome itself, then the metropolis of the world and seat of pagan virtue; and Athens, where Minerva was said to have been trained up, were soon infested with this new doctrine, and very considerable numbers in them, durst oppose our government and dispute our title to empire; even alleging that the wisdom of this world is foolishness with God, and that all pagan virtue is but dross and dung in comparison of the gospel of Christ Jesus.

However, to cut my story as short as may be, after many hundred thousands of the Nazarenes were slain, my subjects became weary of the war. By this time they saw clearly that persecuting them to death only served to increase their number and strength: so that if those restless devils, Malevolus and Crudelis, would have been quiet, they would gladly have dropped their weapon, and agreed to a cessation of hostilities with the Christians.

IMPIATOR. Little judgment as I am allowed to have of historical affairs, I myself have seen what effect opposition usually hath upon that class of people; for if in any place where my standard is more eminently elevated, there happened to be any of that sect, you shall find them more fervent in their study of virtue, and zealous in their opposition to me, than in those provinces where Morality or Civility preside. Ah! gentlemen, we have had trying times pass over us.

INFIDELIS. Trying times indeed. For notwithstanding the fervent zeal of Malevolus and Crudelis, the many sore campaigns they had served so enervated their arms, that, although their principles remained implacable, they were even obliged to sit down in despair of ever being able to extirpate the religion of Jesus from the world.

But my fertile brain soon produced fresh devices. Seeing many of my temples forsaken, and my idols without mercy thrown to the pavement, I began to think of other expedients to impede the progress of Christianity. I labored to introduce Ease, and her handmaid Prosperity, among the Christians, not without hope, that when they were full they would forget their God. The better to favor this deep contrivance, I persuaded the valiant Crudelis to scabbard his sword for a season, and leave the people of our heart to the possession of their tranquillity.

It was not long that this scheme had been put in prac

tice, ere I began to reap the fruit of my wisdom; for Ease and Prosperity wrought more to my advantage, than all the excursions of the devil Crudelis. When they were at ease from the lash of persecution, they were foolish enough to quarrel among themselves, grievously bit and devoured one another, the cause of their strife for the most part being, who should be the greatest.

FASTOSUS. A very important question, much canvassed, but never as yet resolved. Had I been a clergyman instead of a devil, I had certainly been a great casuist in this part of school theology Never was a point of doctrine more belabored certainly than this, and never were people more divided in sentiments than about this resolution, even from the great church of Turkey down to the smallest dissenting congregation. The divines of the established church in Turkey stand stiffly to it, that Mahomet and themselves ought to preside over all the believing world. The doctors of France, Spain and Italy, are as firmly persuaded that pre-eminence is due to none but his holiness and themselves, and that all who are not of the same opinion, are certainly in a state of damnation.

As for their reverences in England, though they will deny no honor to his popeship, which really is his due, they will submit to none as the leading priest but his Grace of Canterbury, and consider that church which they are the pillars of, as the purest establishment that the lower world can boast of. Others indeed there are who greatly question his Grace's right to preside, and therefore refuse to bow to his mitre, and therefore resolving to be enslaved in their own way. Hence, although the reverend members of the associate synod cannot in conscience submit to the corrupt governors of the kirk of Scotland, all of whom they have long since recommended to the care of the devil, much less can they bow to a metropolitan, whom they call the image of the pope, they can very cordially submit to the government of the reverend Mr. Adam Gibb; because they themselves had the pleasure of choosing him. That goes a great way. And hence it is, every society has its Pope. The venerable —— of —— at —— submit for the same reason to the great ——; and the —— of —— to the rev. ——: so that. it is not submission itself that is objected to, so much as the mode of it: for gentlemen will be submissive enough, may they but choose a pope for themselves. But remember this, whoever is chosen the pope of a party, is by his partisans always deemed the greatest. For instance, at the foundary, none is so great as the Rev. Mr. John Wesley, sometime fellow of Lincoln, Oxon. And at the —— none ever preached or wrote like the great ——, D. D. author of ——, and of ——, and of ——, &c &c. &c. But amongst them all, a very few are found, who consider Jesus Christ as the greatest, and who properly call him Master.

AVARO. I thought Immanuel had settled that point long ago. Did he not establish this rule for the observance of his disciples, "Whosoever will be great among you, let him be your minister; and whosoever will be chief among you, let him be your servant." Did not the divines abide by his determination?

FASTOSUS. No, Avaro. Quite the reverse: for the schoolmen will have it, that he who is chief shall be lord over his brethren. By these means they have annexed a certain degree of nobility to their religion, which Jesus never intended to be joined with his. But we hinder the reverend Infidelis proceeding with his story.

INFIDELIS. Those female fiends, the ladies Prosperity and Ease, as plenipotentiaries for Beelzebub, made great proposals to them; and indeed they soon established kingdoms, principalities, and powers, of the Christian name.

Then were the Christians able to maintain themselves against their pagan neighbors, my professed subjects. This I patiently bore, believing that the martial spirit of the Christians a little indulged for the present, would greatly make for our interest and the final establishment of my kingdom.

Those reverend ladies, Prosperity and Ease, had not been long amongst them, ere many who bore the Christian name were desirous of coming to terms of agreement with me; but upon this express condition. "That in the treaty of amity betwixt them and me, it should be stipulated that they still be called by the name of Christ, for it was now become scandalous to bear the name of another." This request I thought reasonable enough, and that to grant it would be no very great concession on my part; therefore I readily agreed, and the treaty was confirmed. It is an invariable rule with me, that it is not very material whether a man is called a Christian or not, provided I have but safe possession of his heart; for names do not change the nature of things.

This amiable fiend, lady Prosperity, rested not in her pleasing operations, until she had quite reduced the oriental nations to such a degree of reason, that they petitioned my personal return among them; and, as my loving subjects, returned to their allegiance. Having now secured the oriental, the splendid lady and me undertook the conquest of the occidental church; and, the better to succeed in our enterprise, we fixed our abode at Rome, famous both for ancient and modern paganism. As for me, I knew it was necessary I should remain incognito, until a fair opportunity should offer for my emerging out of darkness; but my lady Prosperity decked herself in her richest attire and openly resided among the Christians, who were so ravished with her excellent beauties, that he was deemed the most happy man who could prevail with her excellency to take up her lodging in his house. Her ladyship, you know, is not to be won by every one who addresses her. Here she acted according to previous instructions, and made free with the bishop's house as best suited to our purpose.

Wonderful were the works which she performed there; for, at her first arrival, the bishop was no more than a plain, honest man, having but one congregation in his diocese; but first she created him Reverend; then his lordship; then his grace; and after that, his holiness, &c. Indeed, the vast dominion and immense revenues which she conferred on him, so swelled the haughty prelate, that, not contented with the honors then possessed, he claimed dominion over all as the father of the whole world. Even this was short of giving content, unless he should also reign over heaven and hell; therefore he hath seized the gates of both, and lets in and out just whom he pleases. Nothing short of arrogating to himself the prerogatives of the Almighty could satisfy his ambition, such as his holiness, infallibility, supremacy, &c. The devil himself never aimed at higher things. In the meanwhile, her ladyship, at her leisure hours, waited on those who were of any account among the Christians, who, for the most part, had nothing of Christianity but the name. Some, indeed, were firmly attached to Immanuel, who could not be bribed even by her largest offers; but their number was comparatively small. Seeing the progress which Prosperity made, they went about the streets complaining in some such words as these: "This harlot, Prosperity, will be the ruin of Christianity."

In process of time, I was sent for to the bishop's court, he being entirely reconciled to me. The worthy prelate received me with all the reverence due to my person, and laid before me a beloved scheme, which he had designed, and of which he desired my opinion.

Having maturely digested his plan, I replied, "Worthy and self-adoring sir, has your holiness power sufficient to defend your deityship, providing your divinity should be called in question?" To which his holiness said: "Yes, yes, yes, I have, I have. There are several potent princes, who will conspire to make me omnipotent. They will spend their substance, depopulate their dominions, destroy their bodies, damn their own souls, and the souls of their subjects, in defence of my godhead. There are many wise priests also, who will contribute all their wisdom, for their own emolument, to make me omniscient or infallible." Having such an agreeable account of his holiness's affairs, I resolved all his scruples at once, for thus I addressed him: "Most subtle of all the priests, if thus you are supported, I think all things go very favorably. Therefore lose no time in publishing to the world your excellent scheme of divinity; let it be proclaimed that henceforth you are no longer man."

Impiator. His holiness was in the right of it to disclaim humanity. What mortal man was ever endowed with such qualities as are his? What mere man was ever infallible? Not Peter, he fell low enough. Infallibility is an essential attribute of Godhead, and his holiness being possessed of that, must needs be God. What man ever did, or ever will reign with despotic power over all the priests and princes of the earth, putting down one and exalting another at his pleasure, like his holiness. It is by him that kings reign, and princes decree judgment; and not by the Almighty, as formerly. Therefore his holiness can be no mortal man And yet a mortal god is a strange sort of character.

Infidelis. The great priest thanked me for my good advice, secretly renounced the name of Jesus, and swore allegiance to me; called for Falax, whom he chose for his scrivener, and Perfidiosus, whom he appointed secretary. Then, with all convenient speed, issued forth an edict, in which it was declared—

1. That the word of God is no longer of any force, to decide religious controversies; but that the bare word of his holiness at Rome should determine in every case.

2. That no man, henceforward, should dare to search the scriptures, contrary to the resolution of the apostolic chair; the Bible being condemned as a book full of heresy and Protestant tenets; containing many things pernicious to the souls of men, and very derogatory from the honor of holy mother church.

3. That the pope's Bible, or canons, decrees, and legends, are to be held as the only rule of faith and practice, exclusive of all others, under pain of eternal damnation.

4. That God, who made heaven and earth, hath no longer power to save or damn any man, without the pope's permission; and that the infallible bishop of Rome would save and damn whom he should think proper.

5. Notice was given to all whom it might concern, that the free pardons were already all expended. So that a former proclamation, made from another quarter, which held forth nothing but free pardons, is to be held null and void; and that, in future, no man may expect pardon, unless the full price is paid into the hand of a faithful priest, as delegate of his holiness.

6. That the Holy Ghost is to be deemed incapable of the work of sanctification; all the souls he hath undertaken to cleanse having been found with many spots upon them, before they passed through his holiness's furnace, hereafter to be named.

7. Advertisement: That his holiness the pope has, at great expense, obtained a very large quantity of the most purifying fire in hell, together with a battalion of the most skilful furies of the pit to work the flames, both of which he hath placed in limbo, alias purgatory, where, for a proportionable sum promptly paid unto one of his holiness's vassals, or priests, any Catholic spectre shall be burned as white as a bishop's hand.

8. The better to encourage this branch of priestcraft, it was declared, that no case is quite desperate, but that of

those who abide by the Bible as the only rule of faith and practice.

9. It was declared, that the Almighty has no longer any power to support princes in their sovereignty, that power having devolved upon his popeship; who, for the future, would exalt or debase princes, as they proved steady or unsteady to his interest.

10. It was enacted, that no man should in the least call in question the pope's divinity, his supremacy, and infallibility; and every person thus offending, should be deemed an atheist, an heretic and traitor, and as such should be destroyed.

Now, my brother, having thus far carried on my history, let me beg you to recite some part of yours.

Fastosus. With all my heart, brother; but it must be to-morrow mornir ;. Our time is now spent. Business must be attended, or it will wither and decay.

DIALOGUE XI.

ALL THE DIALOGEANS PRESENT.

Fastosus. Pray, Crudelis, what is this mighty affair, that so highly tickles your fancy? Let your kindred share in your mirth, I beseech you.

Crudelis. Yesterday afternoon I was conjured up by 'Squire Broadfield, to assist in the whipping of a poor man, who, being ready to perish with hunger, unluckily begged a morsel of bread at his door. But, before I give you an account of the whipping, I shall first give you a specimen of the gentleman's character.

'Squire Broadfield is a gentleman, and justice of peace. He is worth five thousand pounds a year; and that is enough to make him a gentleman, even if his father had been a beggar; to make him wise, though born a fool; learned, although a very dunce. Indeed it must be owned, the principal part of his worship's education was had under Dr. Ringwood and Dr. Jowler, the celebrated tutors of his kennel. Their maxims he perfectly understands, and their virtues he has adopt ed. But, five thousand a year, you know, makes the study of the kennel truly classical.

Talk you of Orpheus to him, his worship proposes the virtue of Ringwood to your consideration. Do you admire the ardor which flames in the Iliads, his worship says, no music like the voice of Jowler. Tell him of the majesty of Virgil, he will bid you mind well the gait of his horse, what a majestic creature he is. An emperor, says he, might be proud to ride such another. Do you recommend the pleasures of solid learning to him, he is in raptures about the diversions of the chase. As yet he hath avoided the yoke of matrimony; not that he was ever an admirer of continence, few gentlemen being more conversant with the fair sex than his worship. He keeps in his house a wanton train of over-fed servants, the superfluities of whose table would comfort the bowels of many indigent; besides a pack of hounds, which devour more than serves to maintain all the poor in the parish workhouse. But this miserable wretch, who cannot work, because he is lame, and having no parish to flee to for relief, chooseth to beg rather than steal, for which his worship ordered him to be severely whipt by my good son the beadle, until he shall be made willing, either to steal for a living, or to die of hunger.

IMPIATOR. I am not certain that John Ketch, Esq. of fatal character, had any hand in procuring the law for whipping beggars; but certainly it adds greatly to his revenue. Nor am I certain that it was made on purpose to drive vagrants from begging to stealing, in order more speedily to ease the nation of such a burden; but certain I am, it greatly helps to fill up the Tyburn Chronicle. But what more, cousin?

CRUDELIS. As the poor lame fellow was confronted by the beadle, and was convinced of the reality of his worship's benevolent intention to have him well flogged, he fell on his knees, and implored mercy for God's sake, and for Christ's sake, &c. promising that if he might be forgiven this once, he would never return to these parts any more. He pleaded his indigence, his hungry belly, his lameness, his belonging to no parish, and every thing his fear could devise; but all served only to harden the justice's heart the more. He ordered the beadle to take him away, and to do his duty immediately. The beadle signified to him, as they drew near to the whipping-post, that he felt some relentings of heart towards him; and that if he could only give him a handsome fee, he would favor him as much as his reputation would admit of. But, upon inquiry, finding that the old fellow was so wicked as to have no money, his heart became like brass, and he resolved to ply him thoroughly, to the satisfaction of his worship. Accordingly, when 'Squire Broadfield and me arrived in company to see the sport, there was the poor rascal, whose poverty was his principal crime, tied to the post, and mangled with the cord, which the lusty beadle plied with nervous arm.

Oh! how his worship and me did laugh to see the villain, whose poverty was obstinate, leaping, as his lameness would let him, and writhing his bloody back, as the whip was lustily played about him by the sturdy beadle; who, for his part, would rob, and steal, and do any thing, rather than be whipped by a trusty brother of the trade; yea, would act ten thousand villanies, rather than die of hunger. This fellow must be a most incorrigible rogue, to be sure, if he is not willing, by this time, either to steal and be hanged, or patiently to die of an empty belly.

IMPIATOR. What, Crudelis, have they made a law to whip all beggars that infest your country?

CRUDELIS. No, no, Impiator. I heartily wish there were such a law; for then I would even quit my devilship to become king of the beadles. If all the beggars were to be punished at the whipping-post, (as I know no reason why they should not) perhaps his worship himself, and his reverence the parson of the parish, would not escape a thorough drubbing. And yet, Crudelis as my name is, I think the whip-beggar-law is very partial and unjust, as it lays hold on none but poor petty beggars, who would be content with bread, shins of beef, and table-beer; whilst others may, with impunity, beg and obtain some thousands a year of the nation's money.

What are all the ranks of mankind, but so many beggars? Does not his reverence, the inferior clergyman, beg a living from my lord bishop, or some neighboring nobleman? and do not their lordships beg of the king? Do not the very members of parliament come, hat in hand, and meanly beg of the corporation, having no consciousness of worth in themselves? Do not the pliant courtiers sue to the favorite, for places of trust for sake of the profit?—Beggars all, except the stern patriot, a pelican which does not appear once in a century. But if their lordships, the noble beggars, and their honors, the gentlemen beggars, are to be considered as authors of the whipping law, I should have wondered indeed, if care had not been taken to exempt themselves from its penalty.

The case stands exactly thus. If a gentleman, extravagant beyond his revenue, begs for a thousand or two per annum, he shall not only escape with impunity, but obtain his suit; provided always he would be the humble pliant creature of the minister; but if a poor, helpless, low-born wretch, pinched with hunger, happens to beg a piece of bread in an interdicted place, he shall be exercised at the whipping-post.

Infidelis. I think, brother Fastosus, you agreed to give us some account of your affairs. We should hold ourselves much honored by the favor. But for this, I would beg the history of my son Crudelis, who makes himself so merry at the expense of foolish vicious mortals.

Fastosus. His history might be entertaining enough, I suppose; but doubtless mine must be much more elegant and instructive, as my concerns have been mostly with venerable gentlemen, and with none more than those of the sacerdotal function.

Notwithstanding I prevailed with the Jews, almost unanimously, to contemn the person and testimony of Jesus of Nazareth, the Christian religion gained ground in the world. Yea, the word of God grew mightily, and prevailed over the traditions of both Pagan and Jewish sages; therefore, from thenceforward I found it necessary to deal deep in the things of religion.

I began my trade with ecclesiastical titles, which were altogether unknown in the days of Christ and his apostles: a set of goods very venerable with the populace, and wholly of my manufacture;—an assortment of trifles, which greatly pleased the lords of religion, and forwarded the deep designs of priest-craft.

Impiator. With your leave, sir, I have heard that all the lord bishops are descended in a right line from the apostles; must it not then follow, that the convocation at Jerusalem consisted of the most reverend fathers in God, their graces, my lord Peter, my lord Paul, &c. &c. metropolitans; and the right reverend fathers in God, my lord Stephen, my lord Philip, my lord Timothy, my lord Barnabas, &c. diocesans?

INFIDELIS. Son, you ought not to interrupt your honorable uncle. You may remember that these titles are all of later date.

FASTOSUS. My nephew shall hear, if he will but have a little patience. The famous lady Prosperity and you, brother, had not been a very great while at Rome, before I found sufficient encouragement to erect my office for vending sacerdotal titles there, and I must own that for many years I had a brisk run of trade, until in fact the church had room for no more, from the great infallible priest at Rome down to a Cumberland curate. The first production of this kind was a very brilliant medal, inscribed with these five capital letters, P. A. T. E. R. which having finished, I presented at a general convocation of bishops, who as yet were not become reverend. They were highly pleased with the device, having never seen such a thing before. The worthies examined it, one after another, and all found that the venerable letters, well put together, and properly interpreted, signified Father. And certainly the event has proved, that great is the magical power of this medal.

Every one said to his fellow, "What can be more agreeable to our function than this venerable title? Are not we the fathers of the people?" They forgot that One is the father of the people, even God. I was therefore desired, with all speed, to procure a like medal for every member of this august assembly. Soon after this, I provided medals more highly finished, and inscribed,

P, A, T, R, I, A, R, C, H, A,

one of which I bestowed on the holy bishop of Rome; a second I gave to the bishop of Alexandria; a third to that of Constantinople, a fourth to that of Jerusalem; and a fifth to him who presided in the church of Antioch. In all which places my medals were more highly valued than the finest ruby; and he who could by any means obtain one of them, was supposed to be elevated far above the common rank of mortals.

Long and very successfully had I followed that medallion

trade, when a famous and worthy prelate of Rome, who was a great admirer of my productions, came into my office. After doing obeisance to me, and turning over my pretty devices, he asked me, "If I thought, with all my ingenuity, I could produce a genuine medal with this inscription,

P, A, P, A, S,: S, U, P, R, E, M, U, S.
OR,
EPISCOPUS UNIVERSALIS."

I told him, that if all the artists in hell were to unite their wisdom in one mechanical head, it would be utterly impossible; for, said I, the whole creation doth not furnish sufficient materials. But if it please your holiness, I can make you a sham medal of that sort, which may perhaps answer all the ends you have in view, as well as if it were real. Oh! said he, I care not, for my part, whether it is real or counterfeit, if I can only, by your assistance, my worthy Fastosus, impose upon the credulity of mankind, and make the world believe that I am supreme pope and universal bishop; then I should reign with despotic power over the estates and consciences of all Christians. My good friend, please you to make me the medal, and I will cause the world to believe that I had it from the Almighty, with letters patent under the broad seal of heaven, for the sole use of it to me and my successors for ever. "I well know, returned I, that your holiness means no more, than in a pious manner to impose the cheat upon the world, the better to fill your coffers, and aggrandize your name; in which laudable undertaking your adored Fastosus shall be ever ready to direct and assist."

To work I went, having called in the assistance of several of our friends, and made a counterfeit medal, in the likeness of a treble crown, with certain inscriptions of the cabalistic kind upon it. They were short but pithy sentences, as you shall hear.

On the one side of the first crown was inscribed, He that is honored as the wearer of this medal, is possessed of infallible knowledge. Opposite to that was carved, in fine Italian, He is supreme over all laws, divine and human. On the right side of the second crown, were these words, in large capitals, This is the head of the Church. On the left were these, This is the vicar of Christ, and successor of

Peter. On the third and uppermost crown were the following, The keys of heaven, hell, and purgatory, are in his possession, and used only at his pleasure. Round the edge was this writing, He reigneth supreme over all the kings of the earth, putteth down one, and exalteth another at his pleasure.

When finished, I presented it to the arch-prelate, who received it with all imaginable thankfulness, viewed it with the most exquisite delight, and oftener than once, protested by his infallibility that he had never seen any thing contrived with equal art, nor so suitably adapted to his aspiring principles. Transported with joy, he cried out, "O thou ingenious spirit! bless thee for thy assistance! This precious medal will exalt my name above all that is called God; all the European princes will now become my vassals, and the adorers of my priestly majesty. But, to complete the work, I pray thee, good Fastosus, think of some suitable device for me, by which I may bind all the various ranks of the clergy to my interest; for I shall never dare to show my miraculous medal, nor divulge the delightful inscriptions on it, unless I have something of the like nature to present to their reverences; for this alone will excite them to favor the cheat. As for laymen, the scum of nature, I regard not them. They are asses, upon whom we shall ride with pleasure and profit; and if at any time they ride restif, we will tame them with the rod of discipline, and so belabor them with the cudgel of excommunication, that with gladness they shall submit implicitly to our decisions. Could not the great Fastosus strike me a variety of medals, of different worth and designs, and lodge them safely in my possession, that I may have the sole distribution of them among my depending clergy; for unless they cleave as close to me, as the scales to the back of Leviathan, I shall never be able to support my pretensions to infallibility and supremacy.

To which I replied, "Great priest, in order to bind the clergy inviolably to your interest, let me advise you to take care that your decisions be always in their favor: place your own grandeur in front of all your proceedings, and let theirs immediately follow it." Which advice the good man cordially embraced, and ever since has invariably followed it with the utmost precision.

From henceforth, continued I, I give you full power and

authority to preside over all those medals which I have already issued forth; and for the future, the disposal of them shall be at your holiness' pleasure. I will moreover add to the number, and you shall have more than sufficient to gain all the clergy to your party. But observe, you must receive this power at the hand of great Fastosus; for it is by me alone that you can lord it over the estates and consciences of men. The great prelate heard with attention, and then rejoined, "Mighty Fastosus, if you will oblige me in this, you may depend upon me and all my successors as faithful subjects; implicitly obedient servants to your highness, and your father Beelzebub. Nor do I doubt but the rest of the priests, for the sake of power, will be equally loyal to you, and implacable enemies to Immanuel; therefore your kindnesses shall be gratefully returned on our parts."

"Very well, said I, but be sure that all your villany be carried on under the show of sanctity, otherwise you will do us but little service."

Avaro. Then, sir, by what you say, it may be concluded, the hoary prelate at Rome is very sensible that he is Beelzebub's agent, and that all his pretensions, beyond those of the lowest pastor, are an imposition.

Fastosus. Yes, Avaro, he knows it very well, and that makes him the more like unto us. Indeed the cheat is so palpable, that any one who has read his Bible with attention must needs see through it. But by these proceedings, I soon found I had cut out a great deal of work for myself, so that I was obliged to be doubly diligent. However, my sole delight being to promote the works of darkness, I soon struck off seventy new medals, inscribed Cardinalis. These I presented to his holiness, who examined them with great attention, and was highly pleased with the ingenious device.

"Most noble spirit, said he to me, these medals, I perceive, will raise the gentlemen who receive them next in dignity to myself, and they will be the first and most able to support the see of Rome." You must needs know, my friends, that this prediction has been fully accomplished. For in all ages, since the cardinals have received their medals, they have been truly indefatigable in establishing the power and supremacy of the Pope. His holiness and they being so intimately connected, that they must stand or fall together.

In the next place, I struck off a considerable number, somewhat inferior to the former, distinguished by a Mitre on one side, and on the other by the inscription ARCHI-EPISCOPUS; which, in like manner, I presented to the father of the world, much to his satisfaction. These, said he, shall fix the class next to the former, and I doubt not but every one of them will be sufficiently obsequious, in expectation of a cardinal's hat. The archbishops being thus disposed of, I took all the diocesan medals, which I had formerly produced, and put them under the care and disposal of the prelate; and he was pleased to assign them to those, who were next in place to the archbishops, each one in humble expectation of higher preferment.

AVARO. Hah, uncle! was it you that made those titles, ascribed to the various orders of the clergy?

FASTOSUS. Was it I, do you ask? Yes, it was I indeed! Who ever read in the New Testament, any thing at all about a supreme bishop, or about cardinals, and lord bishops? I made them all, I assure you, nephew; though I will not affirm that every person who has borne these names, has been absolutely under the dominion of pride.

To my great honor I speak it, Avaro, I ceased not when I had made their lordships the diocesans, but went on with my trade, until I had procured curious medals for a very great number of abbots, swarms of monks and friars, jesuits, franciscan and dominican friars, with a long train of et ceteras, who soon appeared in shoals, as numerous as locusts when they ascend out of the bottomless pit. Then followed the bare-headed capuchins, mendicants, penitents, pilgrims, &c. without number. Those religious gentry owe all their dignity to me, unless it may be that Avaro has some little hand in the matter.

AVARO. You do me great honor, sir, in mentioning me as a worker together with you.

FASTOSUS. After all this, the subtle priest thought that the antichristian hierarchy of Rome could not stand upon a foundation solid enough, unless all, or at least some of the princes of Europe were invested with ecclesiastical titles, and so adopted into the new-modelled church. Therefore, I told his holiness, that I had three highly finished medals by me, ready prepared, fitting for royal personages. Here, said I, is one inscribed Rex Catholicus; let it be presented to your servant his majesty of Spain. This second medal, inscribed Rex Christianissimus, will be an acceptable present to your vassal the French king; and this third, inscribed Rex Fidelissimus, I advise you to bestow upon the little monarch of Portugal. His hoary holiness, with raptures, replied, "Very good, most noble Fastosus; this device will doubtless secure all these three princes, as so many pillars, to support my infallibility. But what of the king of England, sir? I dread those islanders. Is there no medallion charm, by which that invincible prince can be secured to our interest? I pray you, good Fastosus, lend me an hand in this.

I shall endeavor to serve your holiness, replied I, and then he withdrew. Soon after I presented him with a medal suited to his wish. It bore the inscription, Defensor Fide, and was given to the monarch of England; but, alas! it has not answered our expectations; for this same monarch, instead of defending the orthodox faith of Rome, was the first crowned head that protested against the supremacy of the Italian bishop.

Avaro. It is somewhat droll, that the king of England, having shaken off the yoke of Rome, should still keep possession of the medal, which his predecessors received as a present from the pope. One would think that when the pope himself was renounced, in strict justice, all his gifts should have been restored, and the title, Defender of the Faith, have been by a Protestant prince rejected amongst the rest of Romish trumpery; but wonders never cease. Did you finish here, sir?

Fastosus. No, Avaro, I assure you, many titles besides these were first issued from my office, such as his grace, a title claimed by many a graceless duke, as well as anti-christian priest. His lordship, a title by which many a profane nobleman and irreligious bishop are distinguished. His honor, claimed by many who never felt one desire after true honor. When a gentleman's honor depends merely upon his estate, table and equipage, such a title as his honor, very ill becomes him, yet many such there are who claim the appellation.

Avaro. If high birth, and an ample fortune, do not entitle a man to his honor, I pray you what will?

Fastosus. An honorable conduct, Avaro, without which

he is only a clown in disguise. And many such fools you may find wrapped in scarlet and lace, with swords dangling by their sides.

IMPIATOR. I beg leave to observe, that according to modern maxims in my country, he is esteemed a man of honor, who can imitate the popish priests in scorning wedlock, and frequenting the company of lewd women. He who is a stranger to every delicate and chaste sentiment; who scorns religion, disregards morality, and thinks it beneath his dignity to keep any of the commands of God; or even for a moment to reflect that there is an hereafter. It would be difficult to persuade some people, that the British senate is too much composed of such men of honor as these. I should be glad, sir, to hear your opinion of a man of honor more at large, for I know that you are wise.

FASTOSUS. A gentleman of true honor, fails not to improve his estate, be it great or small, to the best advantage; for he is neither indolent nor extravagant. His increasing revenues are not heaped up for adoration, nor laid by as useless lumber, but applied to clothe the naked back, and refresh the empty belly. His principal care is not how he may aggrandize his family, but how he may best serve his king and country; for he lives not to himself, but to the public good. He adheres to strict truth, is an utter stranger to impertinent raillery, and perfectly detests the voice of slander. In his civil affairs, he does the same things to superiors, inferiors, and equals, which he would wish others in like circumstances to do for himself. If at any time he is so unhappy as to give his neighbor just cause of offence, he is free and open in confessing his error, and ready to retrieve it to the utmost of his power. The title of his honor is well becoming such a man as this, whether his estate is great or small, his birth illustrious or obscure. But mercenary statesmen, plunderers of the public, ill deserve the titles with which they are distinguished. Happy might it be for Britain, if she could always procure officers for every department, in government, who would prefer the welfare of the nation to their own personal and domestic emolument! And this every man of true honor will be sure perpetually to do.

AVARO. Then, uncle, I am inclined to think, that men of honor are not quite so plenty as some people have imagined.

Fastosus. I am sorry to say it, Avaro; but, bad as the world is, there are still many to be found, who with propriety may be called men of honor: but it is well for us, they are mostly of obscure character. They cannot act the cringing knave, and vilely flatter their superiors, in order to gain preferment. Their countenances, adorned with comely modesty, cannot contend with the impudence of fools and rogues, therefore continue obscure when the most worthless are exalted. But if a truly honorable man should, by some miracle, ascend to an eminent station, and be intrusted with public concerns, his country is sure to find a nursing father, and not an accursed step-dame in him, as is often the case with other governors.

There is, likewise, his reverence the parson, a title ascribed to many men, who lead very irreverend lives.

Avaro. True, sir; but it is the vulgar opinion, that the reverence of the parson does not depend upon his moral conduct, but upon his investiture, received from the hand of the bishop.

Fastosus. I know it Avaro; but it is a prevailing mistake. Imposition of the hands, even of an apostle, could never make any man reverend, whose doctrine is heterodox, or whose conversation is immoral: otherwise our friend Simon of Samaria might have been numbered among their reverences. Indeed, Avaro, were any man hardy enough to attempt it, I know of no subject more proper for satire than the pretended reverence of the parsons. But he must be daring indeed, who would set himself to oppose the orthodox priests of the day, for that would be thought by many the very same as to oppose God Almighty himself, and every body would cry Atheist at him.

Avaro. Pray, sir, what is your opinion of reverence, and to whom may the epithet of reverend consistently be given?

Fastosus. To very few of the leaders of any denomination, Avaro; and yet perhaps to some few of every denomination among Protestants. I hate them, cousin, and could not bear to talk of them were it not to oblige you; for they are avowed enemies to our administration, as you will see by the description of them. For he is a reverend minister whether he was educated at Oxford or Aberdeen, who makes not gold, but the glory of Immanuel, and the welfare of immortal souls, the first end of his labors; who is assiduous in his study, fervent in his ministry, and has a paternal affec tion for his people; who studies not how to please the great, or to gain the esteem of the staring multitude, but to approve himself to God and the consciences of men, not shunning to declare the whole counsel of God, without any mixture of the inventions or traditions of men.

You may follow this man from the church to the market, from the pulpit into his family, and find him all of a piece. His whole conduct is one chain of uniformity. But it is not every gownsman, either papal or protestant, nor even every dissenting minister, whom this description suits. Some there are, and who can deny it, who are haughty and overbearing in their spirits; indolent in study; cool and lifeless in their ministry; thoughtless and unconcerned about the real welfare of their people. Yea, some are so wretchedly lazy, or so much taken up with idle and vain amusements, that it is with difficulty they can bring forth, once a week, an oration, fifteen or twenty minutes long; and that scanty production, perhaps, when it is exhibited, proves no more than a lecture on moral philosophy; or it may be a libel against some different party or denomination of Christians. You may follow some of them from the church to their families, and be fully convinced they are divines only in name. They neglect in their families the very duties which they recommend to others. And what is still more, connive at the same vices in their families, which they expose and condemn in the pulpit. But after all, they have the cure of souls, and are the venerable and reverend clergy, in the same manner as the pope is the head of the church: I mean by craft and usurpation.

Avaro. I have got a noble company of these same parsons in my corporation of Avarice, whose business it is to vend wind in order to obtain wealth. A company confined to no one denomination, but made up of all. Every one of this company has got his own system of priestcraft, but all are intent upon the main point, viz. to get as much wealth by his craft as possible. Indeed, the mother church of Rome very far outstrips the rest, for she may lawfully boast that her clergy, to a man, are the stedfast worshippers of the god Avaro, their great benefactor.

However, the Protestants, both Calvinists and Lutherans, all who are freemen, in the company of Avarice, keep as near as possible to the orthodox priests of Rome, in making a lucrative trade of what they call the gospel. And however they differ about what is, and what is not, gospel, they see eye to eye in regard to making profit of it, and turning the altar of the Lord to their own emolument.

INFIDELIS. How should it be otherwise, my son, seeing there are in some places manufactories, on purpose for making parsons?

FASTOSUS. So I have heard, brother, with this addition, that the making of parsons is reckoned both a lucrative and honorable employment, not unworthy of my own patronage. But, between you and me, the parson-makers are grievously disappointed frequently, however little they are sensible of it: for when they put their materials into the refining furnace, they hope to see at the end of the process, a bright and shining minister of Jesus Christ come forth: but lo! a learned calf is produced, and a fervent adorer of the god Avaro.

INFIDELIS. It cannot be otherwise; for, to our grief I speak it, the unalterable Immanuel hath reserved to himself the wisdom, power, and prerogative, to make ministers of the gospel; and if men, like Jannes and Jambers, will take upon them to imitate the immutable works of the Almighty, they may be permitted to make things which may, for a time, be mistaken for gospel ministers, even as those magicians performed miracles by divine permission.

IMPIATOR. So then, gentlemen, I perceive your opinion is, that learning the languages and sciences unfits a man for being a gospel minister.

FASTOSUS. No, Impiator, no such thing, or the gift of tongues had not been given at the feast of Pentecost: but it may be averred, that if a man has no more learning than the most learned university can give him, he cannot possibly be a minister of Jesus Christ. It is resting in these things as the only qualifications, we think proper to laugh at, Impiator.

AVARO. Among those mercenary orators, there are whom we call the Jumblers. They are such who study not their sermons from the scripture, but compile them from the writings of other men. Being destitute of judgment to direct them in their compilations, they are obliged to rely implicitly on the sentiments of their authors. So it comes to pass, that they contradict on one Sabbath what they asserted and half proved the day before, merely because they happened to stumble on authors of different sentiments. But, alas! poor men, what shall they do? It is their trade; they know not how to get a living without it; they cannot dig, and to beg they are ashamed; therefore are under a necessity of jumbling forward, in the best manner they can. Of late years, indeed, this jumbling tribe have hit on a more happy method of management, by which they both save their reputation and laborious study. Amongst learned men, there have always been some few of genius and industry, who have found means to turn the dullness and indolence of their brethren to their own emolument. They compose sermons, print and sell them to the others, who pay first a good price for them, then preach them, that is to say, read them to their several congregations. Enfield's, and Webb's, and Trusler's sermons have been of great use to many a dull and lazy clergyman.

Fastosus. How is this, Avaro? You speak of the parsons as if they were at best but learned fools. How is it possible they should be so highly revered by the people if they were such?

Avaro. I speak but of some of them, uncle; and to make good what I say, I can tell you that it is not the man, whom the ignorant populace revere, so much as the gown, cassock, and band; and these they would revere if they were seen upon an ass, provided always, his ears were hid with a bush of well-powdered hair. I assure you, gentlemen, amongst the intelligent laity, it is deemed a maxim, that any blockhead will do very well for a parson, if he has but friends to recommend him to a living: as a proof of this I shall tell you a short story. There is one Mr. Provident, a merchant in London, who had four sons at a grammar-school, under the direction of a learned gentleman of excellent sense. It was lately Mr. Provident made a visit to his sons and their tutor, when he took occasion to ask Mr. Teachum's advice, in regard to his disposal of them.

To which the schoolmaster replied: "Sir, I have often, with pleasure, observed a penetrating judgment, solid understanding, and an inviolable attachment to truth, ennobled with the generous principles of true benevolence, in your eldest son. These qualities, sir, are excellently adapted to the mercantile life. I would therefore advise you to train him up in your own business. Your second son, Master Thomas, has genius sufficient for any business; but I hope, sir, you will excuse me, if I tell you that I have discerned one thing in him, which, in my judgment, unfits him for the capacity of a merchant. As I know, sir, you would have me to speak freely, you will not be offended with me, if I tell you that it is a selfishness and contractedness of spirit, together with a violent propensity for lying and equivocation. If he were my son, sir, I would bring him up to the law, in which he will very likely make a conspicuous figure. Your youngest son, Master James, has, if I mistake not, along with a very considerable degree of dullness, an heart that is a stranger to sympathetic feelings; but possesseth genius sufficient for a physician. I would point out the royal college for his residence."

Here Mr. Provident, the merchant, interrupted him, and said, "Sir, you have given your opinion of the two eldest, and the youngest; but you say nothing of Harry, my third son. I pray, what do you say of him?" To which the teacher, with a blush, replied, "If it is agreeable, sir, I would advise you to make him a clergyman." To this the father, with a mixture of grief and anger, replied, "What, sir, do you think he hath genius sufficient for nothing else?" "I am afraid not, said the master; but you can easily make friends with my lord bishop, and procure him a considerable benefice. Take this step, sir, and his lack of genius will scarcely be known, as he may preach and administer the offices of the church by proxy, which you know is very gentleman-like."

INFIDELIS. And do you really think, Avaro, that it is want of abilities to preach, that causeth so many vicars to keep journeymen to do their work for them?

AVARO. With some, sir, want of abilities is the principal cause, and with the rest, an utter aversion to the work; though, by the way, they once professed to be drawn to it by no less an influence than that of the Holy Ghost; but that was when a benefice was the object of their pursuit, and therefore not to be regarded after their end is obtained

FASTOSUS. Cousin Avaro, here I believe we must stop, as we have certainly overstaid our time. I hold it good, therefore that we depart, and meet here at the usual time to-morrow. Business, you know, must not be neglected. Adieu, my kinsmen.

DIALOGUE XII.

ALL THE DIALOGEANS PRESENT.

FASTOSUS. Well, gentlemen, I hope no idleness has attended any of our fraternity, since last meeting. I went directly from you to assist a London jeweller in forming a set of ear-rings and pendants upon a new construction. I made him sensible of the most elegant plan, enjoined him to pursue it, give the praise to his patron Fastosus, and so I left him.

IMPIATOR. I pray you, sir, what is the real use of ear-rings? For my part, I have never been able to apprehend it, unless it is to save a small matter of gold against a day of penury.

FASTOSUS. They are of no use at all to the wearer, Impiator, though they help the goldsmith and lapidary not a little; but they are of excellent use to our government. You know the boring of the ear always was and now is an emblem of servitude. Yea, it is an incontrovertible point that the act of boring, and suffering the ear to be bored, is a token of subjection to the infernal monarch.

IMPIATOR. Ah, sir, how violently the spleen would rage among the ladies, were they to know what you say of them.

FASTOSUS. And let it rage, cousin. What is that to me? —The ladies are too much in love with courtly Fastosus, to banish me from among them, even in their spleenish fits.—But to explain the doctrine of ear-rings, be it observed, that the crafty Beelzebub hath an invisible chain fixed to the ear-ring, by which he leads the wearers a wild-goose chase through all the vanities of the times. No sooner does the sable governor tug a lady by the ear, than she feels an impulse upon her heart, which directs her to the Play-house,

Opera, Vauxhall, Sadlers-Wells, or elsewhere; but very seldom to the church. If, at any time, for the sake of company she takes her pleasure at church, the great deceiver keeps such a gingling of the chain in her ear, that she cannot attend to one word of the service; by these means the Park, the Mall, the Play-house, and the church, are, in effect, the same thing to many ladies of fashion.

AVARO. And are all who wear rings in their ears to be looked upon as slaves to the great Beelzebub, uncle?

FASTOSUS. No, Avaro, not all; for the invincible Immanue hath broken the chains and loosened the bands of servitude from many. Nevertheless, they still wear the rings in their ears, to testify what they have been. And what news from your friends, Avaro?

AVARO. Very little, sir; only that diligence, frugality, and good husbandry, go on as usual. All heads plodding, and all hands active to get and to save; for getting and saving is all the cry with them. I had a little matter to attend to last night at the Swan tavern, where there was a very respectable meeting of manufacturers, by whom some few things, tending to promote emolument, were considered. The first consultation was, "How they might conveniently lessen the quality of their goods, that their profit might be somewhat advanced." In order to this, a plan was proposed by Mr. Dolus, a very great tradesman, which was unanimously agreed to by the rest. The second thing was to settle the prices, and come into mutual engagements, that no one should undersell his brethren; which, after some slight altercation, was as unanimously settled. You must know, mankind are not satisfied with being oppressed by infernal tyranny; but to add to the devil's work, are got into the happy way of joining in combinations to oppress and devour one another. Nor is this practice peculiar to any one set of men, but is common with dealers of every kind and denomination, from the opulent farmers to the dealers in coal and candles.

When this was done, a question was put, How they should finish a certain quantity of goods against a certain day then proposed? For it seems they have large orders at present. To which one of them said, he thought it necessary to advance the journeymen's wages in order to encourage their diligence. But this gentleman's motion was unanimously rejected, as an unprofitable way of proceeding, very ill-suited to the growing demands of their several families. It was then proposed, that a small premium should be given to every workman who should finish a certain quantity of goods in a limited time, then and there to be stipulated. But this also was objected to, it being alleged, that some method might be found that would produce the desired end and yet save all those unnecessary premiums, which, if given, would introduce a very bad custom.

At last, an old gentleman, whose hoary locks shone as silver from under his weather-beaten wig, arose, and most judiciously addressed his brethren in the following manner: "Gentlemen, you all know that such is the indolent disposition of journeymen, that, in general, let their wages be ever so good, they have no notion of obtaining more than will procure them a bare maintenance through the week, and a few quarts of strong beer on Saturday night and Sunday. Therefore, to advance their wages is the certain way to have them work less than they do at present. But let us lessen their wages in proportion to our extraordinary call for goods; for by how much the more we drop the prices of workmanship, by so much the more work shall we have done. A bare living they must have, let the prices be ever so low; and but a bare living they will have, if they are ever so high. If we advance the price, they work less, and if we drop it, they will, they *must* work more. I say then let us drop the prices."

The old gentleman's advice was cordially embraced by them all, and every one blessed the sagacity of the old fox, now grown gray in wisdom. And this day, or to-morrow, the journeymen's wages are to be lessened accordingly.

Fastosus. In the close of our last interview I was going to observe, that my prevalency is great amongst the nobility and gentry. By my indefatigable industry, the greater part of them are rendered altogether insensible of their origin, so that they look down upon their inferiors as a set of despicable creatures, of a species very different from themselves: not considering that my lord Superbo and poor Lazar Askalms are by nature brethren, formed of the same materials, and conceived in the womb of the same earth.

Avaro Yet, sir, if my observations are just, I think they have some kind of an imperfect notion that they were originally formed of the earth; but as one part of the substance of the earth is esteemed much more precious and valuable than another, perhaps the people of fashion have the happiness of being formed of the more rich and esteemed particles, and the rest of mankind the infelicity of deriving their beings from vulgar clay. This is the more likely, as there is a manifest difference between their constitutions and those of people in the lower spheres of life; the first being brittle and feeble, the latter more robust and healthy

FASTOSUS. That is false philosophy, Avaro. The brittleness you speak of does not proceed from any defect in the natural constitution of their frame, nor from any rottenness in the materials of which they are made, but hath its cause from themselves. Many of them, in their infancy, are nearly starved from an infamous notion that enough of wholesome food is injurious to them:* and you will commonly find, that the food which yields the most healthful aliment, is withheld from them, at the instance of Dr. Scrawl, the family physician. This same gentleman has not so little sense under his great wig as not to know that his own personal emolument is intimately connected with the weak constitutions of people of quality, especially the ladies. By his many years' study of physic, he has proved to a demonstration, that if the young gentry were suffered to eat enough of wholesome food, like the farmers' children, his business would not be worth following.

AVARO. I know it well: for there is one of my disciples, a certain physician eminent in practice, who hath acquired a genteel fortune by prescription, and who, if he is indisposed himself, will not suffer an apothecary's drug to pass his gullet; a plain indication that he knows it to be hurtful. I have often thought, a good constitution put into the hand of a doctor, is like a good cause put into the hands of the lawyers; it gets worse with deceitful handling. When a man is, by the force of medicine, fairly got down, the skilful physician knows very well how to hold him betwixt life and

---

* Some learned physicians, those celebrated defrauders of the grave, have found out that bread itself, which has been esteemed the staff of life in all ages, is at last become dangerous to the constitution, and therefore to be used with caution by all sorts of people, especially such as are best able to fee the doctor in case of personal indisposition. As for the poor, it is less matter what they eat, as the faculty can reap but little advantage from their sickness.

death as long as possible; until at last he dies by inches of that prevailing distemper which kills so many people of fashion.

Fastosus. True, Avaro. But farther to prove the gentry the causers of their own infirmity, I would observe, that what, in infancy, penury and want leave of the constitution unconsumed, luxury and idleness well-nigh finish in youth; so that when the lady comes to embrace an husband, the one-half of her remaining days are spent under the hand of the doctor, and the other half in pleasure and dissipation. As for the young gentlemen, before the boyish down on their faces is able to resist the razor, they have commonly contracted such lothesome disorders as render them more fit for an infirmary than for the marriage-bed, and have more need of a surgeon than a wife. Thus, Avaro, you may see by what means the constitutions of the gentry are so frequently enfeebled.

That they are formed of the same materials with their inferiors will appear, when you consider that there were none either noble or ignoble in the original state of mankind; all were on a common level; but when we had made a conquest of them, it became necessary for the Almighty to dissolve the original equality, that the world might be rendered in some measure tolerable to all, amidst the confusion and disorder which our dominion over them had introduced. For if people cry out that the world is bad now, it is certain it would be infinitely worse were superiority and inferiority utterly abolished. Moreover, the Almighty, to manifest the equity of his procedure, has so ordered it, that the system of superiority and inferiority is perpetually upon the change. You may find some persons now asking alms from place to place, who are descended from princes and nobles; and others in the most exalted stations, who had their descent from very beggars.

Infidelis. Ay, brother, that very consideration, to urge no more, if duly attended to, would prevent the contempt which people of elevated rank are apt to let fall on their inferiors. But let them go on until the grand leveller Death approach. He spares neither rich nor poor, noble nor ignoble. Samael knows no distinction, cannot be bribed like temporal judges, admits of no excuses, and is an utter stranger to pity. At prince, at peasant, at the noble earl and his servile groom, at the dame of honor, and the scorched cook-maid, he aims alike his unerring shaft, and brings all again to the dust, from whence they were taken, to rot in their original equality.

FASTOSUS. There is another race, which we distinguish by the name of mongrels, with whom I am deeply concerned. This generation of half-bred gentry includes tradesmen, the gentlemen of the law and of the faculty, together with the farmers. These gentry consider themselves pretty near, if not altogether, on a level with the country 'squire, and therefore affect the manners of their superiors as much as possible. They are gentlemen, their wives are ladies and madams, their children masters and misses. Hundreds of such gentlemen and ladies have I known, who could not boast that any of their ancestors, back to the tenth generation, were proprietors of so much as a cottage with a cabbage. Yet they imperiously assume a title of address, equal to that of the queen's majesty; and no laborer or mechanic must dare to approach them, without a sir or madam in his mouth.

INFIDELIS. I have sometimes thought those ladies you speak of, are either ashamed of their given names, or hold them too sacred for the profane mouths of servants and vulgar creatures; and indeed he would be deemed the most unmannerly wretch that ever trod upon English ground, who should say that Sarah Allgood is his mistress; for Sarah must give place to madam, and she is now madam Allgood, the shopkeeper's lady; and it would be more than her place is worth, for a servant to name her mistress in terms less respectful.

AVARO. Excuse me, gentlemen, you know I love to be concerting schemes of profit, and here is one ready projected, which, if faithfully executed, would either fill the exchequer, or make a distinction betwixt persons of real quality and their apes in middle life.

FASTOSUS. What is your scheme, cousin? let us hear it if feasible.

AVARO. I would advise the nobility, gentry, &c. never to go to an horse-course, cock-pit, or play-house; not to go to Bath nor a bawdy-house, that is to say, never to rest until they have procured a bill, in which it shall be enacted, that every man shall pay the sum of ten pounds sterling per an num who suffers his wife to assume the name of madam. I would likewise have a tax of half the value laid upon every young master and miss, the farmers, apothecaries, attorneys and tradesmen's children, unless the husband or father can make it appear that his annual rent, clear of all encumbrance, is not less than four hundred pounds; if so much, or upwards, he should stand exempt from any such penalty, and enjoy the free use of such names of quality in his family.

Infidelis. Although it is quite foreign to my purpose to dictate any thing to mankind which may be of service to them, I am free among ourselves to say, that my son's scheme is well concerted, and might answer valuable purposes were it carried into execution. The numerous bankruptcies, which make trade so precarious in England, have their spring in this fatal imitation of people of quality, so prevalent among tradesmen. Could this so very pernicious practice, by any means be suppressed, the industrious merchant and manufacturer would meet with fewer losses by their retailing customers.

To your scheme, however, I would add another tax equally necessary, and that is upon every play-house, assembly-room, and place of pleasurable resort. One fifth, at least, of every ticket to Almack's, Ranelagh, every play-house, Cornely's, Sadler's-wells, the Pantheon, and every rout whatever, ought to be sacred to government. Until this, or some such thing is done, it will be difficult for the sensible English to believe that their governors aim at any thing beyond their own emolument. As for the tax upon (madam) it appears indispensably necessary, and can admit of no delay. However, we interrupt you, Fastosus.

Fastosus. I have a great deal of pleasure in stirring up people to quarrel with their Maker, and to say unto him, Why hast thou made me thus? I love not the station thou hast placed me in; I have got parts to qualify me for a better than this in which thou hast placed me; therefore I am not dealt with according to my merit." The poor laborer, who, by the way, is the most happy and contented of his species, is not altogether pleased, because he was not born a gentleman, and heir to a good estate. The 'squire and his lady are almost mad with anger, because they were not descended of noble ancestors. The nobleman himself takes it very unkind that he was not born to govern a kingdom. He that is born heir to a crown hath two things at which he is much offended: First, because the Almighty is so long in taking the father to himself, to facilitate his own accession to the throne: Secondly, he is not well pleased, because it is a regal and not an imperial crown, to which he is born heir. As for the man who is born to imperial dignity, he is angry, because he is not appointed lord of the whole world. And one you know, who, having obtained the sway of the whole world, was angry with God, because he had not made two worlds for him to govern; even so angry, that he is said to have cried again. Thus, in all ranks and degrees of life, I make people quarrel with their Maker.

INFIDELIS. I have often heard it remarked, by our infernal sages, that if the ambitious mind were to obtain what it is now in pursuit of, true contentment would be as far distant as ever; and an Alexander, who covets a second world to ravage, could he get that, would want a third, after that a fourth, and so on, until he had plundered the many millions of worlds which God hath made. Even then, were such a thing possible, his ambition would be as insatiable as ever, and his last effort would be the same as that of father Beelzebub's; I mean, he would attempt to plunder the eternal throne itself. Thus, they allege, that the lowest degree of ambition and discontent in man, if the Almighty were continually to gratify it, would ascend to the most daring attempt of which the infernal monarch himself is capable. After all, I have observed that the greater part of people are so far from deeming ambition to be criminal, they think a spice of it is indispensably necessary to a man of honor.

FASTOSUS. I know it, brother; but that is a striking proof of the blindness to which we have reduced them. Ambition, discontent, &c. reigning in any person, are infallible symptoms of a heart totally depraved, and altogether under my influence. But let them go on to cherish an ambitious spirit, they will find their mistake at last. That judicious pagan, Epictetus, seems very capable of instructing many who are called Christians, and who have the advantage of the Bible. Yes, Infidelis, you and I both know, that ambition is the very vice which ruined our black fraternity: but for it, they would have been in heaven to this day.

As some quarrel with their Maker, on account of their situation in life, I am equally successful in stirring up others, to take offence at the manner in which the Almighty hath formed their bodies: as to their souls, they do not regard them; indeed they seldom consider that they have an immortal spirit belonging to them. If, by chance, such a thought, as that they have an immortal soul, should pass through their minds, it gives them no concern in what position it is found, because they take it for granted that no body sees it. So very inconsiderate and stupid are many, that one who understands the language of hearts, provided he could delight in the voice of discontent and murmuring, might meet with high entertainment amongst our people. For,

One young lady says, O! if the Almighty had made me an inch and a half higher, then my person would have been abundantly more proper. Her neighbor is as ill at ease, because she thinks the Creator has bestowed superfluous labor upon her, in giving her a couple of inches of redundant height, which she looks upon as a very considerable deformity. Another says, Why did he make me with round shoulders? Might he not as easily have made them square? I am ashamed to go into company, because I have not a handsome carriage of the head and neck. What the backboard and girdle can do, has been tried to press in the prominent *os humeri;* but sad experience teaches, that she may as soon wash the Ethiopian white, as make that even which the Almighty hath made crooked. Nor less afflicted is her kinswoman, on account of yellowness in her skin.

Avaro. I have heard several people of allowed knowledge, modestly wish, that all court ladies labored under the same misfortune the last unhappy gentlewoman does; being persuaded that if it were so, naked breasts would never more be brought into fashion, to the annoyance of the gentlemen and the scandal of the ladies: for you know, fashions are all born at court.

Fastosus. Not at the court of London, Avaro, but Versailles; therefore it would indicate better sense in your knowing people, to wish the French ladies the above misfortune. It is held an act of high treason against the French, for the English court to receive any fashion, which hath not had a certificate from Versailles. This policy seems indeed very mysterious, when we consider that the British heroes can so effectually drub the monsieurs, as tc make them cry *peccavi*, and at the same time the French ladies should have the English in such absolute subjection.

It is impossible for any person to conceive the trouble I have, in preparing those ladies for the ball, or assembly, or pantheon, and what art I am obliged to employ, in hiding their supposed defects and redundancies. The lady who fancies her stature to be somewhat too low, obliges me to add to it the whole length of a super-tall pair of wooden heels, and is extremely careful to set off her little body to all advantage possible, so that every beholder must be struck with the most perfect gentility of her appearance. On the other hand, her neighbor, who is over-tall, is as careful, on her part, to have the flattest heels that can be worn, and is equally industrious in decking, to the best advantage, the whole of her extravagant height.

Nor hath their neighbor, who is affected with a dun, or yellow skin, less trouble and anxiety of mind, besides her great toil of body. The waste she makes of wash-balls, and the best recommended cosmetics, together with her own, and her servants' labor, in endeavoring to rub off the native tinct, is not to be conceived. But, alas! it is labor in vain. All the comfort which remains for her, is derived from a black necklace, assisted by two or three well-disposed patches, which she hopes may, in some measure, overcloud the hated yellowness of the adjacent parts.

So absolutely foolish are they, that I have some subjects who say, "Ah me, why were my ankles made so strong and fleshy? O that they had been slender and genteel, then I should not have been thus dependent on the mantuamaker for a covering for them." However, gentlemen, were it not a rule established among the fair sex, that ankles somewhat gross are altogether ungenteel, it would puzzle a philosopher to determine how it is that small feet and slender ankles, come to have more virtue and real worth in them, than those that are otherwise. But certainly it is deemed to be so, and those imperious dames, who have been favored to their liking, do what they can to mortify those who are less happy in their pedestals. Against this disease there is no effectual remedy. Small-sized shoes formerly gave them great hopes of relief; but, alas! they generally made cripples of their wearers.

INFIDELIS. I have always observed, that when people have applied to the artist, to have that mended which they think the Almighty hath marred, the punishment is connected with the crime, as a token of the just resentment of a jealous God, who hath left none of his works imperfect; and who would have them all, as indeed they ought to be, well esteemed. Hence come corns upon the feet, and far greater unevenness in the symmetry of the body, than was before their application to the mechanic.

FASTOSUS. Another of my disciples has got hair of a madder red, and such is her folly, that it grieves her beyond measure. But with all my wisdom, I could never find out the reason why red hair should be any more scandalous than yellow or flaxen locks: or how it is, that scarlet is held to be such a courtly color upon broadcloth, and yet so scandalous for a lady to have her head of scarlet color. But the lady herself is so apprehensive of the scandal, that she is obliged to exchange her native locks, with a neighboring barber, for a set of flaxen false curls; these, she flatters herself, will very well become the native fairness of her skin.

Perhaps, indeed, to spare the natural crop, she may blind the eyes of beholders with powder, which may help to conceal the awful secret. The like expedient is used by women of a coquettish disposition, when to their great grief and inconsolable sorrow, they first perceive old age dying a whiteness upon their temples. In order to prevent the world having any suspicion that she is advanced in years, the coquette procures a defence against the hoary hairs; and thus she keeps herself, as much as possible, from the belief that she is growing old, until the detested wrinkles on her forehead betray the fatal secret, and then she declines faster than other women, because her grief gives swiftness to her decay. Another lady is exceedingly grieved, every time she looks in her glass, because, as she thinks, her face is too much upon the fire to be deemed lovely; but she comforts herself with the reflection that she has good features, and the great artist, when he finished her, has left a dimple in her chin. On the other hand, her cousin beholds a system of agreeable features in her own countenance: but oh! the dejection of her heart, on recollecting the paleness of her lips. To supply the defects of nature in this, before she goes abroad, she has recourse to her pencil and vermilion shell. Thus she has some means of comfort within her power; but her poor sister, who is seamed with the small-pox, is quite inconsolable. If at any time she expresses satisfaction, it is in speaking of the former agreeableness of her features, and fairness of her skin. But alas! her joy is presently clouded with the melancholy consideration, they are for ever gone. Some ladies are highly offended, because their hands are so big, others that their fingers are too short; and now and then you may meet with one who is dreadfully tormented underneath a king Richard back; which is sure to prove an intolerable burthen all the life of the unhappy woman.

INFIDELIS. Nothing more fully demonstrates our dominion in the hearts of mankind, than their being ashamed of their shapes and physiognomy; the supposed deformity of which they could by no means have prevented. Every degree of this kind of shame, is a tacit reproach of the Creator, and therefore daringly impious. Many you may find, ashamed of the innocent defects of their outward frame, who are not in the least ashamed of their vain lives and immoral conversation; to rectify which ought to be their principal concern. And were there but as much pains taken to rectify the disorders of civil life, as there are to hide the supposed defects and redundancies of the body, and to alter the tincture of the skin, the world would be very different from what it is. But you take care to prevent that, Impiator.

DISCORDANS. One who has made mankind no part of his study, would deem it impossible for rational beings to be ashamed of, and concerned for innocent deformities of the body, with which no person of common sense will ever upbraid them, and which never can by any means lessen the esteem of the judicious; (for who can make that straight which the Almighty hath made crooked, or white which he hath made brown?) and at the same time neglect the infinitely more valuable mind.

INFIDELIS. By your account, sir, your vassals have got a wrong notion of beauty, as by our long observation it appears, we may sometimes see a great deal of beauty in a person whose bodily parts no way tend to recommend him. Real beauty lies in the constitution of the mind, and the proper use of its intellectual faculties: every thing else compared with this is like tinsel when compared with the purest gold.

That person appears truly amiable, without external comeliness, who can bear the lack of it with a becoming grace; and who, to make up for all outward defects, is studious to embellish the immortal mind. That is a part of man always capable of improvement; but for the body, they may fret, murmur, and repine at its defects, as much as they will, they plainly see it does not mend the matter, for who by taking thought can add one cubit to his stature, or make one hair whiter or blacker?

Fastosus. Such is my dominion now; nor was it less in the more early ages. I made rude work in the tents of Jacob, between his two wives and among his sons; and by those means I greatly disturbed them whom I could not destroy.

Invidio. I have, until now, been silent; but beg leave to observe, that I think our labor is far from being lost. Seeing, though we are permitted to destroy none who are good and virtuous, we have the pleasure of distressing and distracting them. And certainly no music can be so agreeable to our ears, as the sighs and groans of our enemies. There is something so agreeable in the destruction of infidels, and distracting the rest of mankind, that I have often heard our father Beelzebub say, he would rather aggravate his own torment a thousand degrees than be robbed of that pleasure. His and our happiness lies chiefly in distressing mankind, especially the virtuous and good, notwithstanding he overheard Immanuel, when he said, "I give unto them eternal life, and none shall pluck them out of my hands."

Avaro. One would wonder it did not wholly discourage him from making further attempts against such people, especially if what I have heard is true; I mean that every affliction which they endure by his means, will be an aggravation to his own misery. But his hatred against them is implacable.

Fastosus. It is not altogether his hatred and malice against them, which excite him to persecute them with such unwearied diligence but it happened on a time, that Beelzebub was by, when one of the heavenly heralds declared, "That in all the afflictions of his people, Immanuel himself is afflicted." And at another time he heard another say, "That Immanuel is touched with a sense of human infirmities." Nay, then, said he to himself, they shall not want for afflictions, if I should endure a thousand hells. It will be a heaven of delight to me, to see my fiery darts bound off from the persons to whom they are shot, and strike him whom I have in the most perfect abhorrence. So that it i Immanuel himself, rather than those who believe in him, at whom Satan is so much enraged.

To return to my story. By my means the knot of sisterhood between Rachel and Leah was disunited, and friendship and love fled to a distance far remote from their tents. But this was not the finishing stroke of my artifice; for when one generation passed away, you might always be sure to find me with those, who made their appearance next upon the stage of action. Hence I was found with the sons of Jacob, and made them perpetrate deeds very unworthy of the patriarchal character, and that even in the life-time of their father. The destruction of the Hivites, by the sword of Simeon and Levi, in revenge of Shechem's rape on their sister Dinah, was wholly by my instigation. They grieved, and that justly; but pride alone called up the demons of Revenge and Cruelty, who drenched themselves in Canaanitish blood.

When Joseph dreamed of his future advancement, I prevailed with his brethren to hate him, and give admission to every baleful demon; under whose influence, even at the hazard of their father's life, they sold him into Egypt. There I stirred up Sabrina, the wife of Potiphar, to revenge her slighted charms upon him; Joseph himself to swear by the life of Pharaoh, and to carry it very strangely to his brethren in the time of their affliction, notwithstanding he himself had seen such wonders of Divine Providence, as mentioned by the writer of his life. Just it was that his brethren should have been afflicted for their former perfidy and baseness; but Joseph could never have been persuaded to be instrumental therein, but by my instigation.

Impiator. I am surprised, sir, you should select the history of those reputed the best of men, for exemplifying your dominion; whereas you make no mention of Ham, Ishmae'

Esau, &c. I thought your dominion over them was more full than over the other.

Fastosus. I mentioned the best, on purpose to save myself trouble, cousin. For when you hear my power over them, you will easily conceive that my dominion over the rest of mankind must be absolute. I might indeed do myself honor by telling you of the part I had in the lewdness of Ham, the despite of Ishmael, Esau's revenge, &c. &c. but I understand it as all implied in the present plan of my narrative. Indeed it would be endless to tell you of even a thousandth part of my achievements; and I am persuaded it is more agreeable to you, to hear of my occasional prevalence over the virtuous, than to have a full display of my uninterrupted dominion, over the infidel part of mankind, without it.

Yet it may not be amiss, by way of specimen, to give you one instance of my influence over infidels in general. Amongst the millions I might adduce, I shall refer you to Basuris Pharaoh, king of Egypt, in the days of Moses and Aaron. Notwithstanding the mighty signs and wonders which God wrought by the hands of his Hebrew servants, he was absolutely under my dominion, that he hardened himself against the Almighty, disregarded the voice of his prophets, and would not suffer the people to go into the wilderness to worship. Moses and Aaron wrought works unprecedented in the presence of the king and his nobles; but I persuaded him that the whole was effected by the power of magic, and that Jannes and Jambres, his own enchanters, could do the same, were they called to it.

I had such possession of his heart, before any miracles were wrought, that he thought himself inferior to no being whatever, and scorned subjection even to the Almighty. Pharaoh's magicians, in divers instances, by a divine permission, imitating the wonders wrought by Moses and Aaron, he persuaded himself that he was at least equal to that God who sent them, and in the most haughty disdain he said, "Who is the Lord, that I should obey him?"

You have all heard that no man hath hardened himself against God at any time, and hath prospered: nor did he prosper. I hardened his heart against every divine injunction, until the God of the Hebrews utterly confounded the Memphian magicians, and made the haughty monarch, not only willing to let the people go, but eager to thrust them out of the land. However, they had not travelled very far before Pharaoh, being a little recovered from his consternation, was induced by me to pursue and oblige them to return to their drudgery, alleging the great loss which both his majesty and the Egyptian monarch would sustain, by the departure of such a number of vigorous slaves. Pursuant to this purpose, he mustered his chariots and horsemen, all the Egyptian chivalry, pursued the fugitives by dint of sword to compel them to their spades and wheelbarrows. Every one must praise my noble intentions; for I designed that both hosts should have perished, the one by the sword of the Egyptians, and the other by the thunderbolts of heaven. I conjectured, upon good ground, that if Pharaoh destroyed the Hebrews, the Almighty would avenge their blood upon him and his kingdom.

The host of Pharaoh overtook the Hebrews near Pi-ha-hiroth, where the raging ocean met them in the front, and a vast ridge of impassable mountains inclosed them on either hand: "Glory be on me! cried the exulting monarch. See how my happy stars have hemmed in the fugitives! Now shall they either return to their servitude, or perish on the points of Egyptian swords; and Pharaoh shall no more be upbraided with a God greater than himself." But Pharaoh's boastings were premature; his hopes were blasted before they were full blown: for it came to pass, that the Almighty took the cause of his people into his own hands, wrought salvation for them, and with an high hand destroyed him and all the Egyptian chivalry.

Business calls me hence, gentlemen. I hold it good that we adjourn until to-morrow

DIALOGUE XIII.

ALL THE DIALOGEANS PRESENT.

Avaro. Indeed, gentlemen, what I tell you is true, you cannot conceive how much I am caressed by the grovelling slaves.

Fastosus. Do not boast, cousin, nor let it once enter your mind, that your reception amongst mankind is more cordial and hearty than mine; for where there is one person who prostitutes himself to the devil Avaro, there are at least twenty who fall down at the shrine of the adored Fastosus; though I will still own your craftiness has subdued not a few to your grovelling sway.

Avaro. Not a few, indeed! Every nation furnisheth its quota, to make up the number of my abject slaves, who adore me under feigned names, suitably adapted to the genius of each country. For instance, in Holland, I am called Mynheer Industry; in France, Monsieur Prudence; in Spain, I bear the name of Don Diligence; in Austria and Russia, as also at the Hague, I am known by the name of Good Policy; and in Great Britain and her colonies, I am called Mister Care, alias Mr. Frugality; but my true name being rightly translated will read Covetousness.

Great advantages arise to us from the concealment of our proper names. The word covetousness, you know, is of such a true brimstone color, that unless I had some method of disguising it, I could get but few adorers in comparison of what I have. There are thousands who delight to keep me under their roofs, by the feigned names of Industry and Frugality, who would be afraid to be seen in my company, under the name of Covetousness. They rise up early, sit up late, they eat the bread of carefulness, can never get enough of work done by their servants and laborers; they buy as cheap and sell as dear as they can, and are for ever concerting schemes of money-getting; and yet they are not covetous; all the world could not persuade them that they are the worshippers of the devil Avaro. Even those whose morning and evening desires run in the following strain: "What shall I do to get money? How shall I manage to keep what I have got out of the reach of pilfering rogues?" Such are their desires, and yet they are not covetous. Notwithstanding their increase, they cannot, with pleasure, assist the needy, unless by so doing they can serve themselves; and yet they are not covetous. Such people are very apt to consider gain as a proof of their godliness, and it is difficult for them to believe a poor man is honest. If his honesty is so clear that they cannot deny it, they will tacitly charge him with either indolence or want of economy, as they take it for granted, any man may prosper in the world if he will; and yet they are not covetous.

INFIDELIS. Your disciples, Avaro, it seems, have but little acquaintance with that divine providence which we are constrained to confess; that providence which emptieth the store-house of one and fills that of another, according to the dictates of unerring wisdom. But by long observation, we have learned, that the race is not to the swift, nor the battle to the strong, but to whomsoever the Arbiter of the universe is pleased to give the blessing. What most surpriseth me, is, to see so many of your people among the professors of religion. Do you think they have never heard that those who love the world, have not the love of the Father in them; and that friendship with the world is enmity against God? Or do they suppose themselves capable of serving both God and mammon?

AVARO. With your leave, sir, such texts of scripture are of no weight with our people. Some consider them as interpolations, others mistranslated, others still deem them erroneous, therefore not to be regarded; and all agree that the force of such passages ought to be reasoned away. Yes, brother fiends, you may meet with many, who, if their mental sentiments may be known by their outward conduct, believe themselves capable enough of serving both God and mammon, and that it is very consistent to love both God and the world at the same time. All the week round, they are so earnestly engaged in pursuing worldly advantages, that one would suppose they had got an assurance that for one thousand years, at least, to enter upon, their souls shall not be required of them; or indeed one would think they believe not a syllable of the Bible, or that there is either God or devil, heaven or hell. Yea, so ardent is their chase after gold, they cannot spare so much time as to ask their servants whether they intend for heaven or hell at their death? Whether they serve God or the devil? Whether they read the Bible, or idle plays and novels? Whether they go to church or ale-house on a Sunday; or, indeed, whether they are Pagans or Christians, Papists or Protestants? And yet they are good Christians themselves, members of churches, and worshippers of the God of heaven.

Notwithstanding their fervent zeal for, and unwearied diligence in, the cause of mammon, they will not absent themselves from church on a Sabbath-day on any consideration; but, with all sincerity imaginable, with the devotion of one holiday wipe off the stains of the former six, and on Monday come forth as fresh for the avaricious chase as ever. Thus, you see, my subjects, by their conduct, plainly tell you, they believe it very possible to serve both God and mammon; and thus they give the lie to divine testimony.

It is now as it always was; many people follow religion with the same views with those of the loaf and the fish followers; they take up religion to procure a character among men, that it may serve as a cloak for their mercenary purposes. The person deemed religious, being capable of executing avaricious schemes with greater facility and advantage, than the man who is known to be an enemy to all religion.

Fastosus. It seems, Avaro, your money-hunters can adapt religion or any thing to the great end of getting. I know thousands who would not attend the worship of God at all, if they found not their account in it. I have laughed, many times, at seeing the atheist and the deist come to church and receive the sacrament, to qualify them for places of public concern. It may safely be supposed, that men who believe not the sacrament to be of divine institution, have some ends, no way religious, to answer, by their receiving it. It is not a little droll too, to see many, who, for conscience sake, dissent from the church of England, when they have the prospect of preferment, come cordially to the altar and receive the consecrated elements from the parish priest. Mortal man could not do more to secure all the emoluments of both church and state to their own party for ever, than the authors of the test act did, and yet many dissenters play the devil in cheating them. It must be a close hedge indeed, in which some people will not find a hole to creep through.

IMPIATOR. Ay, uncle, and it is every whit as droll to see many of my subjects, who never attend at church, except upon those occasions; men who spend their whole time in drinking, gaming, and whoring, admitted to the table of the Lord, to serve a turn in politics, contrary to every rule, divine and human; and yet those men commence the pillars and governors of the church, without coming near its assemblies on other occasions. These things make amazingly for our interest.

INFIDELIS. Not many days since, your son Discordans gave us a most agreeable account of some of his operations, by the instrumentality of Prejudice and False-Reasoning. I should be glad, my nephew, if you will be pleased, to go on with your story.

DISCORDANS. I have no objection, sir, if my honored parent will be pleased to permit. But Discordans cannot so much as breathe, without the instigation of great Fastosus.

FASTOSUS. You do me great honor, my son, and have my permission to proceed: but as I have urgent business in hand, and am already acquainted with your story, I shall leave you for the present, and meet you here to-morrow. Darkness and confusion attend you all.

DISCORDANS. This same glass, False-Reasoning, is the mirror in which the Jewish clergy, doctors of law, scribes, and pharisees, tried the doctrines and actions of Immanuel and all his followers. By these means they were fatally deceived, and led to reject the counsel of God against themselves; yea, hardened to that degree, as to say, the light which enlighteneth every man that cometh into the world, is absolutely darkness, and to charge the Maker of all things with being a magician; even to put forth their sanguinary hands, and murder the Lord of life.

You may think I was closely employed in those days, as there was not a pharisee in the whole world, whom I had not furnished with an inverting mirror and telescope. By these means they became quite enamored with their own supposed virtue, and held all besides themselves to be accursed; that is to say, heretics, because they knew not the law; that is, they did not measure length and breadth, exactly according to the standard of orthodoxy, which in all ages has been the traditions of the elders, and not the scriptures of truth, as some have erroneously asserted.

IMPIATOR. Hold, cousin, there I think you must be wrong; for I myself was wont to hear Immanuel, (who you know could not lie) refer his hearers to the scripture for the resolution of all doubts.

DISCORDANS. That is nothing at all to the purpose, cousin. I readily grant, and none can honestly deny it, that the scripture is the standard of truth; but truth and orthodoxy are two things, very different, and sometimes diametrically opposite to one another. Bible doctrine is the same in all ages and nations; but orthodoxy in one nation differs at least as much from orthodoxy in another nation, as the several climates do from one another. To go no farther than Britain, you see what is south of the Tweed accounted the purest religion in the world, is, upon travelling farther towards the pole, deemed corrupt, superstitious, and antichristian. So it is *vice versa*. Moreover, what has been orthodox and apostolic in one age, has had the misfortune to become quite heterodox and damnable in the next; so that there is no certain standard of orthodoxy in any nation: but truth is always the same, and knows no standard but one.

Indeed the synod of Dort, and the reformers of the English church, have done what mortal men could do to fix an everlasting standard of orthodoxy by tying all future professors to subscribe their traditions. But even that is insufficient. For, by the help of mental reservation, many subscribe contrary to their real belief; and others, who have not that address, even go without a benefice, let them believe the Bible ever so piously. Yea, I have known many deemed heretics, and burned at a stake, merely for believing the Bible. Orthodox papists, orthodox episcopalians, orthodox presbyterians, and orthodox congregationalists, have all had the honor of putting people to death for their want of orthodoxy; that is, because they were daring enough to think for themselves, contrary to the known maxims of the orthodox priests, in every age. You know, it is observable, that the orthodox are condescending enough to suffer other people to have thought for them.

IMPIATOR. What, cousin, has any sect of Christians, besides our friends the papists, been found to persecute those who differed from them?

Discordans. Yes, cousin, every sect which has at any time been happy enough to grasp the reins of government for the time being. The worthy papists bore the bell of orthodoxy for the space of twelve hundred and sixty years, during which time much blood was shed by open massacres, secret assassinations, pretended judicatures, acts of bloody faith; and, at last, to finish the bloody reign of antichrist, England, France, the Netherlands, and the valleys of Piedmont swam with the gore of such who would believe the Bible sooner than the voice of the priests. Queen Mary's reign furnished the orthodox in her day with a fine opportunity of discovering their zeal for the church, by murdering those who believed and obeyed the Bible; but her reign being short, and Elizabeth ascending the throne upon her demise, the other scale rose uppermost, and the protestants in their turn became orthodox; that is, got the government into their hands.

O the violence of reputed orthodoxy! Those same gentlemen were no sooner emerged from prison than they also let the world know that they were not to be differed from with impunity; that the formula of their faith and worship must be regarded with as implicit obedience as that in the former reign imposed by the papists. Now the presbyterians, independents, and other congregationalists, felt the weight of their rage, or, if you please, zeal for orthodoxy, and the good of the church. Now the prison-keepers, and their friend Master Ketch, had pretty near as good a run of trade as in the reign of Mary. And now the wilds of America began to be well peopled with English protestants and oppressed dissenters; and the good episcopalians at home, kept the fleece to themselves, and had all the good of the church before them. But those said presbyterians and independents had no sooner crossed the ocean for conscience sake, and found themselves secure from episcopalian rage, than they themselves commenced orthodox and set up their own formula as the standard of religion, to which they required as implicit submission from others as the good bishops of England had erewhile done from themselves; and now the poor antipedobaptists and quakers were taught, that a mittimus is a mittimus, whether it is signed by a papist, an episcopalian, or a presbyterian; and that sentence of death is to be dreaded as much from the mouth of the latter as of the former. Those same dissenters, who had so lately found Old England too hot for themselves, by the glowings of priestly zeal for orthodoxy, soon made New England too hot for the poor quakers and antipedobaptists; who, to escape the rage for presbytery, fled, the one to Pennsylvania and the other to Rhode-Island, that they might not be compelled to worship God according to other people's consciences, and contrary to their own.

INFIDELIS. So then the old spirit of calling down fire from heaven upon heretics, or those who walk in a different way, it seems has prevailed in modern times as well as of yore. O what a mask is that! human rage in the character of godly zeal! It is wonderful to see people glorifying the prince of liberty, but shutting their brethren up in a dungeon for conscience sake; worshipping the savior of men's lives by putting people to death, because they will worship him in a different form; and it is as wonderful that the ambassadors of peace, as they call themselves, should be the principal agents of this violence.

DISCORDANS. But for the ambassadors, persecution had never been known in the world, sir. The laity have so little zeal for God, that they would, if not instigated by the clergy, suffer men to worship him according to the best understanding they have of his mind revealed in the Bible. But the ambassadors are quite of another opinion; for, by them it is determined, that God shall be worshipped in the very mode by them directed, or he shall not be worshipped at all, if they can help it. The honor of persecution, alias punishing of heretics, must all be ascribed to the reverend ambassadors.

IMPIATOR. By ambassadors, I suppose, cousin, you mean popish priests in contradistinction from protestant ministers.

DISCORDANS. I mean both papists and protestants, cousin; and with me it is not very easy to determine which best deserve the honorable appellation.

But to return to my story. I taught the respectable pharisees in general the use of my instruments, which, as you saw in the late experiment, perfectly inverteth every object; and so, by my prudent management, those very people, held to be the most religious of the Jews, were wrought up to such a degree of self-conceit, as to fit them for executing the will of the devil; still supposing that they were doing good service to the God of Israel. Contemplated under the reflection of my ingenious instruments, those pharisees, who were darkness itself, considered themselves as angels of light, and each became so enamored of his own personal excellencies, that all who were not of their sect or persuasion, were held in the most consummate abhorrence; as accursed, and ignorant of their traditions, yea, even enemies to the Almighty.

They viewed Immanuel, the brightness of the Father's glory, and express image of his person, by the help of my glasses, in which, to them, he appeared as one come from Beelzebub, and performing miracles in the spirit and power of the great apostate. His immediate disciples were, indeed, men of whom the world was not worthy; yet, viewed by the help of these notable instruments, they appeared as creatures the most despicable. Although men of peaceful principles, willing to spend and be spent for the good of mankind, they were held to be enemies to the public good, men who turned the world upside down; unworthy of a dwelling in the tents of humanity, and therefore thrust out of the world with violence. Such wonderful works were accomplished of old, by the help of these amazing instruments, and still they are perfect as ever, and fit for operation.

Even at this day, when the whole system of revealed truth is examined by my inverting mirror, it is misapprehended as cunningly devised fables; a well-concerted system of falsehood; or a priestly imposition on the consciences and understanding of the laity. Yes, my fellow destroyers, by my wise government, many who value themselves as the greatest masters of reason, are so absolutely stupid as to suppose that the eternal God has left men at large, without any given law or revelation of his mind, to which their submission is required. Being thus stupidly absurd, you will not wonder, that the same masters of reason have been ingenious enough to find out, that this world, unwieldy as it is, was dexterous enough to create itself, and possesseth wisdom enough to be its own governor.

INFIDELIS. By your leave, cousin, this last part of your account belongs to my administration. You preside only over dissension and division. I want to hear some of your operations of this kind.

DISCORDANS. True, sir. But if I preside over dissensions,

divisions, animosities, &c. you know I must be allowed to use proper means, by which my works are to be propagated; for I am not like those human fools, who expect the end without using the means. Besides, sir, that one devil should assist another, is by no means against the laws of our fraternity. If I, to promote my beloved discord, call in the assistance of your bewildering influences; I also, in a kind return, by the divisions which I foment, greatly strengthen the slavish bands of great infidelity. Our interest being mutual, I hope the worthy Infidelis will never grumble to lend me all possible assistance, in striving to make this earth, as much as may be, to resemble the regions of the damned. Moreover, our great prince and parent is no way careful, about which of his illustrious family is the instrument in damning a soul, so that the work of damnation is effected.

INFIDELIS. I have no objection, cousin, to assist you, or any of our kindred. All I desire is, to have due notice taken of my influence. Our leading view ought undoubtedly to be the destruction of men, in compliance with the will of our great ancestor. But I detain you.

DISCORDANS. The ancient pharisees were not the only dupes I have had in the world. The great man at Rome, the father of the world, and head of the church of antichrist, has been as much my dupe as people of less eminence, as I shall show you in the sequel.

INFIDELIS. What, cousin, have you become acquainted with my old friend? I should like to know how that came to pass, and what acquaintance you have with him.

DISCORDANS. I accomplished it in the following manner. First I presented his supreme holiness with a pair of my instruments, of the right Luciferian construction, on purpose that he might, by their assistance, try all the bulls he should publish, and all the causes which should come before him. For it ought to be observed, the time was when the whole world wondered at his infallible judgment. Infallible, so given out, and so for many ages received. Yea, so powerful, so efficacious has been the word of his holiness, that ere now his very breath has blown the crown off from the head of one prince, upon that of another. So very extensive his sovereign sway, that to give a kingdom to a devoted friend, was no more to him, than to give a snuff of sneezing would be to a trusty highlander.

From the use of my instruments there arises a necessity that his holiness's bulls, &c. should be the most perfect antichristianism; so that in the inverting mirror they may assume the likeness of unerring truth. It is the same with the persons and things which the hoary father is concerned with: the sentence is, in general, contrary to the real intrinsic merit of the party or cause. Hence we find a turbulent Becket canonized for a saint, and placed among the Roman deities; and a pious Cranmer condemned to the stake. Regicide is rewarded as meritorious, whilst walking according to the dictates of conscience is held altogether damnable, both in this and the future world.

From the proper application of this mirror, popish bulls, decrees of councils, canons of churches, human composed formulas of worship, are supposed to be stamped with divine authority; whilst the Bible, that only revelation of the divine mind, is considered not only as insufficient to show to men the way of salvation, but even dangerous to be read by the laity; and it is absolutely forbidden their use, lest, by knowing too much of the will of God, they should perish from the popish faith. So the good old vicar obliges the laity to go to hell blindfold without complaining.

Nothing can be more certain, than that either his holiness the pope, or the writers of the scriptures, must be mistaken. The former says the Bible is dark, mysterious, difficult to be understood, and even dangerous to the souls of men; whereas the latter say, the scripture way of salvation is so plain and easy, that the wayfaring man, though a stranger, though even a fool, shall not err therein. The pope has, for weighty reasons, been pleased to forbid the use of the scriptures, under the heavy penalty of death and damnation; Jesus, the author of the Bible, commands all men to search the scriptures; and his spirit in Paul, applauds this conduct in the noble Bereans. Surely this points out the very person of antichrist. His holiness at Rome, and all other great leaders of the church, are of opinion that the scripture is not of itself sufficient to be the guide of conscience, the rule of faith and practice, therefore canons, creeds, liturgies, &c. are introduced to make the formula of worship more complete. But Paul the apostle tells mankind, that the scripture is able through God, to make them wise to salvation. So that the one or the other must needs be mistaken.

IMPIATOR. His holiness of Rome was in the right, to forbid reading of the Bible, and they find their account in so doing. The old Bible, I am told, tolerates even a gospel minister to lead about a wife, but confines him to one only. Therefore this Bible did not suit my good friends of the priesthood. But the pope's Bible, which forbids to marry, and enjoins an unreserved auricular confession, gives the gentlemen of the cloth an opportunity, under the pretence of being righteous more than others, of being lascivious to the uttermost, and to defile all the nuns in the convent. What full-fed friar would not choose a free admission into such a seraglio, rather than be confined by sacred marriage to one only wife? With them it is a rule, that much pleasure arises from variety.

DISCORDANS. So, cousin, I find you are acquainted with our old friends, the priests of Rome.

IMPIATOR. I have been long acquainted with them. Why, cousin, the greater part of them dwell in my canton of literal fornicators, and they are all freemen in the district of mystical whoredom.

DISCORDANS. I have taken care to furnish every true member of the Italian church with a partial telescope, by the help of which he takes a false view of the members of all other communities whatever; and in the very spirit of the ancient pharisees, holds all to be accursed who are not of his communion. By these means also, the holiness of real saints is called heresy, and the heresy of the papists obtains the name of holiness. The will-worship, superstition, and idolatry, of those sons of the mystic whore, they call piety, whilst the pure spiritual worship of God, in Christ, is by them termed schism and heresy.

In my instruments the papists, in general, view the righteousness of Immanuel, as the ground of man's acceptance with God, and therefore, say they, "It is all a chimera, a mere shadow, a doctrine of licentious tendency, unfit to be published amongst mankind." But when they consider their own personal merit, by the help of my telescope, they are ravished with their own supposed excellency. "A righteousness of their own," say they, "is a work of substance, and will bear our dependence. Here is righteousness of my own working out, enough to obtain the favor of God, and to spare. Blessed be my own hands for working out my salvation, and more than my salvation. Adored be my own heart for possessing more than holiness sufficient to bring me to heaven." Of the same opinion is the Rev. Mr. John Wesley, with whom it is plain, that the grace of God is insufficient to salvation, without the co-operation of the creature; who yet is confessedly incapable of doing any thing aright. There is a very near relation between the old gentleman at Rome, and his kinsman at the Foundry. Both are popes, though the latter is much more diminutive than the former.

There was a time, when the whole assemblage of priests took it into their heads to promote their own religion, and to suppress that which had any tendency to lessen the importance of the sacerdotal order. For their more success they inquired of my mirror, as an oracle, for detection, as to means most proper for the purpose. Answer was given, "By the power of the sword." Therefore, in the popish Bible, it is written, "Those who, in contempt of holy church, shall take upon them to live according to the dictates of conscience and scripture, shall die the death, and their estates shall be confiscated to the prince of the realm, provided always that one full moiety of every such estate shall, without deduction, be returned to his holiness at Rome, the prince over the kings of the earth. Moreover, whoever shall hesitate about yielding his conscience to the guidance of the priest, and shall not with apparent willingness bind his soul to the horns of the pontifical altar, shall be deemed and damned for an heretic; that is, shall be burned out of this world at a stake, and shall burn for ever in the world to come, according to the good pleasure of his merciful holiness."

Infidelis. Ah, cousin, the devil was sadly outwitted in that affair; for although the burning of heretics was a pleasing diversion to our good friends the priests for the time being, it has brought them into contempt which will prove everlasting. Having set the world upon reflection, it is now found, to our grief, that the religion of Jesus has no connexion with a spirit of intolerance, which, wherever it obtains, is known to be the spirit of antichrist. One would really suppose, that the successor of St. Peter had quite forgotten the injunction given his predecessor, to cease from the use of the sword and let it abide in its sheath, seeing he accounts its edge to be the most convincing of all arguments. But I interrupt your story, cousin.

DISCORDANS. Often have I seen the whimsical hermit and fantastical devotee, take an ample view of his own religious proceedings, with this partial telescope and inverting mirror, and thus sounds the voice of self-applause from the hermitical cell at the bottom of Sinai, or on the top of Ararat. "Lo, what a high degree of holiness my own self-denial and assiduity have procured me. Behold! what great good my crucifixion of the flesh, and separation from the world, have wrought out for me; for which I may thank my own resolution. By my pious diligence I have obtained holiness sufficient to qualify me for, and good works more than enough to entitle me to heaven. Happy I, who have made such a good improvement of my time! Unlike to those indolent people who, when they die, are obliged either to purchase their pardons at an advanced price, or to lie for ages in the flames of purgatory, burning away their rebellions; I shall get safe to heaven without so much as touching at that flaming prison on my journey."

IMPIATOR. Dear cousin, how I have laughed; laughed myself out of breath, strong and healthy as my lungs are, to see the papal penitent, after he has in holy zeal whipt himself with the cat-o'-nine-tails, for the length of several streets, till the impious offending gore has laid on the stones. Enamored with his own fortitude in so belaboring the sinful flesh, I have seen him, after his penitential work was finished, examine every stripe by the help of my valuable instruments, and as he viewed, he cried with the voice of exultation, "Ah, how infatuated are those who hope to get to heaven in a whole skin; without mortifying and punishing the wicked flesh! To expose themselves to such severe exercise in the discipline of purgatory, for want of devotion enough to submit to the discipline of the church, how impious! But I shall have a speedy entrance into happiness on my dissolution; for I mortify the members of this body, and these wounds religiously inflicted voluntarily by my own hand, will be so many mouths to intercede for me with the Almighty."

AVARO. So then, cousin, the intercession of Immanuel is

quite out of the question, with your penitents, I perceive. And indeed those people who can whip themselves to heaven cannot have much need of his advocacy and intercession. If the whip, well applied, can save a man from destruction, one would be apt to conclude, that Immanuel might have saved himself the expense of such bloody sufferings and agonizing sorrows as he underwent.

Discordans. That is true, cousin; but their first concern is not with Immanuel, but his holiness the pope. Not about the favor of God, but that of his reverence the priest, who is thought to have all the orators of heaven under his influence. Therefore, those that hope for favor with the inhabitants of heaven, must be very careful not to lose the good graces of the parson; for it is thought, no man can meet with a cordial reception in the other world, but what brings proper credentials with him from the ghostly guide of his conscience in this. But Death is a wonderful instructor, and teaches the poor beguiled criminals, lessons which they never thought of in life; and amongst others, this important one, that the favor of the pope and priest can be of no more service to a dying man, than the favor of Mahomet.

When the true-born sons of the scarlet whore, are pleased to view the Protestants with my telescope, indignation rises in the heart; and thus they give vent to their zeal and vengeance; "Ah, what a goodly heaven would it be to see those heretics broiling in the flames of hell! When shall vengeance fall to the uttermost upon those who dare despise the authority of the church and its holy priest?"

Infidelis. It is allowed on all hands in the church of Rome, that to protest against the pope's supremacy, and disbelieve his infallibility, is the sin unpardonable; for which no dispensation whatever can be obtained from the clergy, however much their so doing may be approved in heaven. And it is an article in the papal faith, that fire and fagot, rack and gibbet, are the most convincing, or rather invincible of all arguments, and therefore never to be omitted in the decision of religious disputes.

Impiator. When we consider, sir, that his holiness of Rome is not such an able logician as Jesus of Nazareth, and hath a religion very different from his to defend, we must allow that he is in the right of it to reason with the edge of the coercive weapon. Fraudulent religion is liable to many disadvantages to which truth is not subject; and although the one will eternally stand of itself, against all the machinations of darkness, the other will require the assistance of violence and intolerance to uphold it. Who then can blame their papal reverences for pulling the sword from its scabbard, in order to convince gainsayers? I have seen many, by dint of sound reasoning, most grievously confound the holy fathers, who became like dumb dogs that could not bark before them, in a moment's time silenced by the end of a cord, or some such irrefutable argument. These are wonderful ways to enlighten the consciences of heretics, gentlemen. But I pray you, cousin, have you no concern among the Protestants?

DISCORDANS. Not a little, cousin, which, to-morrow, I may give you some account of; but at present must forbear, the usual time of interview being elapsed. Adieu, my kinsmen, adieu.

DIALOGUE XIV.

DISCORDANS.

YES, gentlemen, strange as it may seem, I assure you my advantages by these instruments are great, and my influence even over Protestants not to be despised. Though, it is true, I am at no pains to prejudice the Protestants against the Papists, or to make use of my instruments in order to render the latter more disagreeable than they really are. For, whilst in the body, it is impossible to make a thorough-bred papist more diabolical than he is already. I leave it therefore with the Protestants to examine the worshippers of the pope, in the mirror of revealed truth, by which the anti-christianism of that religion is sufficiently detected; and all the fallacy of priestcraft is brought to open light. But, great is the business which I do between one Protestant and another; who, although they unanimously agree to shake off the papal yoke, are most grievously divided among themselves. They abominate the high and arrogant pretensions of Rome; yet they themselves are severally the most orthodox, and drink deeper into the spirit of popery than they are perhaps aware of, even of the precious spirit of intolerance and bigotry.

When a zealous churchman, such as Sacheverel, or his lordship of L——ff, or a Durell, Nowel, or Blackett, examines his own party with my telescope and mirror; how enamored is the good man on the discovery of his own excellency! How much of the self-opinionated strain flows from his boasting lips! "There is no doubt, says he, but our church is truly apostolical; the purest church in the whole world. We hold fast the form of sound words, and are not forgetful of the tradition of the elders."

INFIDELIS. No, cousin, they are not forgetful of tradition; for with all the pompous parade of lordly prelates, there is not a small part of the Episcopalian formula that derives its existence from the traditions of even the Romish fathers. Cringing and curtsying when the name of Jesus is pronounced; worshipping with the face towards the east; keeping lent, and other holidays besides the Christian Sabbath; fasting on Fridays; crossing in baptism; with a great many more, are all sprung from the Italian fountain. In like manner the names of their priests evidently show that the pope stood godfather at their christening. And he that but looks on their canonical robes, must be instantly convinced that they are cut in the true Italian taste. However, they are not the only Protestants who hanker after papal customs; for even the Geneva cloak itself discovers the tailor's acquaintance with the shops of Italy. And yet to hear the Calvinists boast of their reformation from popery, one would think we could not find so much as a shred of the strumpet's garments within the pale of their presbytery.

DISCORDANS. It is a rule with mankind in general, to look out narrowly for the mote in the eye of another, whilst they tenderly pass by the beam which is in their own eye; and, as we have brought the world into such a state of disorder, it is no difficult matter for the eye of jealousy to find faults enough. Sometimes I clap my telescope to the eye of a true son of the church, and direct him to survey the whole body of dissenters; he obeys, and then exclaims, "These same roundheads are schismatics, prone to strife and sedition; self-sufficient, turbulent, and uneasy bigots; haters of apostolic discipline, and lovers of licentiousness, who therefore spit in the face of their mother, and wickedly leave the purest church in the world."

IMPIATOR. I pray you, cousin, are there none apostolical besides the Episcopalians?

DISCORDANS. O yes, cousin Impiator; all are apostolical, if their own testimony is to be credited. All the Romish clergy are apostolical, and give it out that Peter the fisherman was their great-grandfather. The church of Scotland is also apostolical, and the power of the twelve apostles is thought to have been transferred to the Scotch presbytery. The Independents are apostolical also on account of the soundness of their doctrine, and regularity of some part of their discipline. But both they and the north country clergymen labor under some disadvantages; for the latter have lost the deed of transfer, which conveyed the authority of the apostles unto the presbytery; and the former are unhappy enough to be unable to produce either precept or precedent from the apostles for infant sprinkling, which is notwithstanding a foundation doctrine, and by them accounted Christian baptism. The Baptists, or, as the Independents and Methodists respectfully call them, Anabaptists, you may be sure, are not less apostolical than their neighbors, having, besides all the advantages claimed by the Independents, the enjoyment of baptism according to the primitive institution. So that no defect whatever, in point of a gospel spirit, can hinder them from being apostolical.

Even Mr. Wesley and his preachers give themselves out to be apostolical, notwithstanding Mr. Wesley asserts that salvation is by works, which the apostle Paul denied. No contradiction whatever will hinder the teachers of the people from considering themselves as apostolical. When I am used to attend the Sandemanian church, after service-time, and divert myself with their playing at blindman's buff, I confess I could not easily gather from what part of the apostles' conduct they derived their warrant for this game; any more than for cards, skittles, attending plays and masquerades, going to Vauxhall, Ranelagh, &c. &c. and yet this is the only apostolic church in the world in its own esteem, taken in its proper connexions. However, it is said, some of the oldest pillars of the church having had their shins repeatedly broken, and the elders' noses having been smitten even to bloodshed, they have laid aside that dangerous play of blindman's buff, so very apostolical a few years ago, and have found out ways and means of becoming little children, less dangerous and more becoming their infant capacities, by which they may spend the evening of every Sabbath.

IMPIATOR. By your leave, cousin, I have often been puzzled to find out how it is the prelates of the church of England came to be apostolical; and I protest I cannot, after all, unriddle the mystery. I have heard my father say, that the apostles were never consecrated to any see whatever in England, and there was not half the number of apostles there are of prelates even in this island. Moreover, I have heard him say, the archbishops and bishops of the English church are the successors of the archflamins and flamins, the dignitaries of the old British pagan church, prior to the days of Lucius. Now if they hold the honors and revenues of the pagan clergymen, how is it that they are apostolical? Is it because the name is changed from flamin to bishop, or how?

Certain it is, the English bishops must be of a more noble order than the apostles. There are lord bishops; they possess great revenues; they are clothed in soft raiment, and dwell in kings' courts; they are too high, too polite, too dignified, to preach in a common assembly, or indeed in any other, more than twice or thrice a year. But the apostles were men of mean extraction, not lords, not right reverends; plain Paul, Peter, James, &c. They were contented if their revenues would purchase food and raiment for them; they seldom appeared amongst great men, in kings' courts, otherwise than in quality of prisoners; they were willing to spend and be spent, in preaching the gospel to all people, and on all occasions; they had no carriages, no equipages, nothing to glory of but their afflictions, which fell upon them in every place wherever they came.

INFIDELIS. There is some weight in your reasoning, my son, and they will understand it hereafter. But, in the meanwhile, it is not clever in the churchmen, however zealous, to charge the nonconformists with having separated from the church. The church of England, in her rubric, defines a church to be "a congregation of faithful men, where the word is preached, and the ordinances are administered;" from whence it is plain, a church may meet in a house which has never a steeple; and a man may leave the house of parish worship, or what is called the parish church, and yet cleave to a congregation of faithful men and women, where the ordinances are administered and the word preached, which the rubric, as before observed, acknowledges to be the true church. Churches are built of living stones, which never a parish church nor cathedral in England is; therefore a departure from them can never, with propriety, be said to be a schism in the church. My good friend, the high churchman, is somewhat unkind to the nonconformists in this affair.

Discordans. I allow it, sir. But I assure you the nonconformist perfectly understands the law of retaliation, and is an adept in the use of my instruments. In some zealous hour of self-approbation you may hear his thoughts about the Episcopalians. "These Episcopalians, says he, these mongrels, are monsters in religion; like Ephraim, they are neither baked nor unbaked, but like a cake not turned; neither good protestants nor right papists. Partly they worship God, and partly they obey the pope. What consistency can there be in such a jumbled religion? Can there be any good, where there is so much papal dross and refuse? Any true religion where there is so much false traditional superstition? Can there be any thing of the substance, where there is so much of the shadow?" So you see there is never a sect of Protestants, but will occasionally do the devil a kindness, in their treatment of one another.

Infidelis. This language of the nonconformists is not general, cousin; for there are many who believe that a person may really be saved, although even not of their community; and that all who differ from them, are not to be treated as absolutely enemies to God and all religion. The like may be said of the good people of the church of England. For amongst them you will find some who do not really think that every dissenter is absolutely in a state of damnation, and hope at least that a man may escape hell, even though he never sets his foot in the parish church. However, I have often been highly diverted at hearing the church parson on the one hand, railing against the neighboring dissenters as worse than the papists, instead of preaching the gospel; and, on the other hand, the dissenter, with the greatest dexterity, bandying back the curse upon his reverence, as the dog that barks at the sheep of Christ. Prejudice, cousin, deals all in extremes; it never touches on the middle path of judgment, the path reserved for the gentle steps of candor.

DISCORDANS. It is not enough that I persuade the most bigoted part of both conformists and nonconformists, reciprocally to consider each other as the avowed and incorrigible enemies of Christianity, and themselves to be its warmest votaries. But I find means to procure the noncons a sight of each other in my celebrated telescope, and each to treat the different denominations with as much rigor and injustice, as if they were not followers or did not profess to be followers of one and the same Savior. The hottest episcopalian rage ever felt by their forefathers, discovered not more bigotry than what some of them discover against one another.

I was greatly edified the other day in paying a visit to an eminent Quaker, who, when with curious eye he was examining my instruments, was moved by the spirit of self-conceit, to examine, try, cast and condemn all the sects of professors around him, as destitute of the inward power of religion; and thus, having my telescope at his eye, he began: "Friend Episcopalius, I perceive thou art so carried away with the form, that thou carest not for the power of religion. Vain man, shadows are thy delight, and thou little regardest the substance. Dost thou think, friend Episcopalius, that the spirit is in the service-book? Why dost not thee read friend Barclay's Apology? Dost thou suppose that Christian ministers are ever to be seen shrouded in Romish weeds and surplices? How can thy steeple-house be a receptacle of the meek and peaceful saints, when there is such a clinking of bells from the top of it? Is it not more likely a synagogue of Satan, whose servants are turbulent and noisy? Thy ministers preach for hire, friend, they take tithes and offerings from the people, and how can they then be ministers of Jesus Christ? I advise thee, friend Episcopalius, to consider thy ways, and turn to the light within thee; then thy priests will let one shirt at a time serve their turn, and will no longer preach for tithes and offerings. Then shalt thou thyself be led to renounce the fantasies of this vain life, and solicit neither for church nor state preferment, but wilt content thyself with getting money in a way of trade, like our self-denying brethren. I say again, vain man, consider how worldly are thy practices.

"As for you, my friends of the Presbyterian and independent denominations, I allow that ye do not conform to the corrected mass-book, for which some praise is due to you. But, alas! ye conform to the world, notwithstanding. Look ye, friends, your women wear ribbons of unholy colors; rings of gold, polluted by the profane hands of the silversmith; yea, ruffles, furbeloes, and heads frizzled up to an enormous height, of downright French profaneness; your women are ladies, madams, and misses, all of which indicate that ye are destitute of the inward power, and neglect to look to the light within you. Yea, examine but your own clothes, ye who call yourselves gentlemen, and see what irreligion discovers itself in every part of their fabrication. Do you see, friends, your parsons wear clothes of an idolatrous black, and bands starched with superstition, after the manner of popish and episcopalian hirelings. Ye make ministers, sprinkle your infants, use ordinances, and, like all other worldlings, are as much attached to shadows, as if the substance were not to come; yea, your clothes are made of unholy colors, such as are worn by the servants of the flesh; ye wear buttons, made of metal digged out of the bowels of the sinful earth; even pocket-holes impiously gaping in the fore-skirts of your upper garment; and to add to the height of your carnality, your hats are wickedly cocked, after the manner of the sons of antichrist. I charge you all, ye Presbyterians and independents, to turn to the light within you, and that will lead you to the substance. Then will ye forsake all these lying and worldly vanities.

"As for thee, my friend Baptismus, (continued the serious Quaker) thou art worse than all the rest; they have given up some of the ordinances which were in use during the apostles' days, but thou retainest every punctilio; in this therefore thou art formal and superstitious. By leading of people to submit to those primitive ordinances, thou dishonorest the light within thee, which teaches those who obey it to despise ordinances, as thou seest in the case of our brethren. Besides, thy clothes are of a dark color, like those of other hirelings and men-made preachers. Why dost thou not imitate our elders in wearing cloth of a religious color, even of an holy drab? Observe me, friend, thy hat is cocked after a popish manner, and thou wearest a button and loop upon it, after the fashion of an antichrist. Why hast thou not hooks and eyes to raise it only to a half bend, after the manner of the spiritual!

"It appears but too plainly, friend Baptismus, that thou art still in the world. Thy preachers also wear popish cambric on their bosoms, preach for hire, and assume the epithet of reverend. Thee and thy friends make a mighty bustle about what thou callest the scripture. I pray thee, friend, turn thee from that dead letter, to the author of it within, so shalt thou be taught to contemn ordinances, as we do, and to give honor to none of thy fellow-creatures, how much soever it may be due.

"But thou, my friend Wesley, comest more near to the standard than any of thy neighbors. Thy priests are not hirelings, having only food and raiment, and thou wisely takest care of the rest. Neither are they of human manufacture, but are all like unto our elders, sent forth by special commission from heaven, from whence thou sayest that thou derivest thy own commission.

"Thou preachest the free agency of man also, and shuttest none out from heaven, besides those who will not fulfil thy conditions, or, as our elders say, refuse to obey the dictates of the true light within them. Nevertheless, thou fallest short of perfection; for though thou despisest the bishops as dumb dogs, thou art mightily taken with the steeple-house; and, although thou thyself wilt be subject to no ordinance but what thou thinkest meet, thou superstitiously bindest both thy preachers and people to the observance of every rite of what thou callest the church. I pray thee, friend John, why dost thou pinch thy belly on Fridays? What seest thou in the fifth hour more than in the ninth, that thou shouldest set it apart for what thou callest devotion? Why shouldest thou exhort thy preachers to read the scriptures with thy notes, to read thy other tracts in preference to all others, to pray at certain hours, as if the spirit were at their command, and to preach twice every day of their lives? Thou art too formal, friend, and regardest not duly the light that is within thee."

INFIDELIS. And so your friend, the Quaker, is pleased to tell all the world, that he is possest of the spirit of bigotry and self-conceit. However, he is not the only bigot in the world. Bigotry is an epidemical distemper among mankind, and I know no greater bigots than the people who profess to be the warmest votaries for unlimited charity. Who was ever more bigoted than friend Barclay and his quaking brethren? Or who in the world is more bigoted and dogmatical at this day, than the reverend principal of the Foundry, that great votary for universal redemption, and the spontaneous agency of men. So very highly is this gentleman esteemed, by many of his people, that I have heard his labors extolled above those of Paul the apostle; and indeed himself accounted to be one of the two witnesses, spoken of in the apocalypse. But in this they must be mistaken, unless by sackcloth, in which the witnesses prophesied, we are to understand prunella; for in black prunella, instead of sackcloth, have all the prophecies of Mr. John been published.

Discordans. My friend, the Quaker, having triumphantly surveyed the supposed imperfections of his neighbors, turned the telescope towards himself; then gathering his muscles into a smile of self-complacency, he said, Yea, it is evident that I am a true follower of the light within, for I give honor to no man, how much soever it is his due; prince and peasant, noble and ignoble, are all the same to me, my fellow-creatures and equals. In farther obedience to the inward light, I do not pray, not once in seven years, unless moved by an impulse from the spirit. My inward bible I often read; but the dead letter of external scripture I leave to those who are fond of shadows. My raiment too is all made of an approved color, even of sanctified drab; and my linen is plain, though fine and neatly dressed. Yea, and Martha, my good wife, too, is separated from the world, and is a suitable help-meet to a spiritual man; she wears no furbeloes, no profane cardinals, capuchins, dominos, &c. but all her apparel is rich, good and plain, becoming a separation from the world.

Infidelis. With the Quaker's good leave, I think the faults he finds in his neighbors, are but little gnats when compared to the huge camels, which to my certain knowledge he himself can swallow without straining. Besides, the virtues of which he makes his boast, even supposing them to be virtues, are all external, and are no more than tithes paid of anise, mint and cummin, whilst the weightier matters of the law are neglected, perhaps even by this precisian.

AVARO. I have often wondered what it is that makes a drab color more religious and becoming than another; yet certainly it must be so, for the Quakers are wise, very wise, and could not be imposed on, as every tradesman who deals with them is ready to testify. Amongst my disciples I have heard amazing accounts of the wisdom of the Quakers, and the use they are of, in teaching even novices wisdom, by their provident example. However, I have as much wondered what the papists, episcopalians, and every other sect of professors, discern so amiable and lovely in black, as to induce them to make it a canonical color; and almost, if not altogether, essential to the ministration of the word. No doubt they have heard that Beelzebub is said to be drest in raiment of the deepest black; and one would wonder they should desire their ministers to be clothed in the same uniform, seeing they professedly have declared war against him and all his principalities. Yet so it is; for any other than dark-colored clothes upon a minister, would frighten an auditory out of their pews, and the best of sermons would not be worth hearing, if the preacher were not invested in the sacerdotal livery.

FASTOSUS. It is I, my friends, even I, who am at the bottom of that religious whim. But for me, white would be thought to become the pulpit as well as black, and green would be as holy as gray. I call it whim, because the greatest of the Nazarenes, in ancient times, knew no color which was more holy than the rest; and the same clothes in which the apostle Paul made his tents, served him as canonical robes, in which he also preached the gospel. By this you may see that my influence is very extensive, even in religious things.

IMPIATOR. What, uncle, had not Paul a gown and cassock, in which he preached, and a surplice in which he offered up his prayers?

FASTOSUS. No, Impiator. Where should he have them? You may know that the gown, surplice, &c. were contrived by the man of sin, I mean the son of perdition, whose principal seat is at Rome; but in the days of the apostles he was not revealed, notwithstanding the mystery of popish doctrine had indeed begun to work. But all this while we forget our good friend the Quaker.

INFIDELIS. Indeed, brother, we do not use the Quaker handsomely in so long neglecting of him; but to make him some amends, I must tell you, that I have often laughed heartily to hear those precise gentry exclaim against the form of religion by others adhered to, as if they themselves were nothing but spirit, when at the same time they are as formal a people as any upon earth. And in truth very few of them know any thing at all of religion, besides that very imperfect form which they have adopted. But we are wise enough to keep our thumb upon that; for if the cheat were discovered, I am afraid they would be glad to embrace that part of the form of religion which they reject, in order to obtain the power of it, of which the far greater part of them now are destitute.

DISCORDANS. I can tell you, the Quakers are liberally paid back in their own coin. And amongst every sect of Protestants hitherto mentioned, you will find some who seldom or never look at the people called Quakers but through my telescope. Were you by, when the Quaker is examined by the rest of the Protestants, you would almost split your sides with laughing at their partiality and unfair representation. Say they, "The Quakers' religion lies all in their dress, speech, and money-getting. Their religion lies not in the head, but in broad-brimmed half-cocked hats. Not in their hearts, but in their coats. Not in their actions, but in their tongues. All their public meetings are calculated to promote the great end of getting money, and increasing commerce; are not religious, but merely political."

By this you may see, that the Quakers are abused and belied in their turn, as well as they abuse and belie others. The above reflections are just enough when applied only to some or to a great many of them, but will by no means hold as a general rule; seeing you all know, there is now and then a Quaker who breaks away from his subjection to the god of this world; and despising all that we and our sable clan can do to prevent it, gets safe within the palace of Immanuel. Moreover, there are, at those public meetings, some, though comparatively few, who have a truly religious design in giving their attendance. From these things you may see, my friends, that prejudice deals all in extremes, and knows not how to speak favorably.

INFIDELIS. There is a gross mistake, into which we have with great vigilance ensnared the posterity of Adam. When a small number only, of any particular body of people, are found guilty of a certain evil, the crime is usually charged upon the whole; and the precipitate, injudicious conclusion is, "They are alike." For instance, the Munster Baptists were once guilty of certain outrages, with which the whole sect of antipedobaptists are to this day very charitably calumniated. And because very many of the Quakers are amazingly wise to get money, and to keep it when it is procured, it is often said they are all such, and that Avaro is their lawgiver.

Heyday, whither is the rule of moral equity gone, that the professors of religion cannot set their eyes upon it? Where is that candor and benevolence, which the Christian religion everywhere recommends, that you, cousin, have gained such an ascendency over them?

DISCORDANS. By the instrumentality of these glasses, I got the preachers of salvation by grace, traduced as Antinomians, and the doctrines of the word of God bespattered as so many sources of licentiousness. For instance, the preacher, as his duty is, declares, "That salvation is not of works, but grace;" and may thus reason with the people: "You can do nothing that will recommend you to the favor of God; the Ethiopian may change his hue, and the leopard his spots, as soon as you, who are accustomed to do evil, can change your own nature, and learn to do well: for it is not of works of righteousness which ye have done, or can do, that your salvation cometh; but merely by the calling of free mercy." I intantly clap my telescope to the eye of the legalist, and he exclaims, "What an enemy to good works is this same wretched Antinomian! According to him, we may as well do nothing as strive to procure the favor of God; may as well lead lives the most vile and profligate, as study to live righteously and holily; for, according to this same preacher, our wickedness is as acceptable to God, as our most holy and virtuous living. Yea, more acceptable; for he declares, that harlots and publicans shall enter into the kingdom of heaven, sooner than those who do what they can to procure eternal life by their holiness and good works."

Such is the language, not only of the vulgar and ignorant, but of many who profess to know much of religion. Whenever the self-sufficient Arminius is in the humor to try the doctrines of the gospel in my inverting mirror, and the preachers of them in my partial telescope, he very candidly and with great liberality, bestows upon them such as the following reflections: "These wretched Calvinists represent the Almighty God as a partial and unmerciful being, who hides his gospel and withholds his grace from men of virtue, wisdom, and prudence, whilst he reveals himself to the most notorious transgressors. They say, that a man of a regular inoffensive life may perish for ever, when a murderer, like Manasseh; a polluted prostitute, as Magdalen; and a wicked oppressor, like Zaccheus, shall be saved. If this is true, then we had better live notoriously wicked, than sober, righteous and godly lives. What wretched, what dangerous doctrine is this! they make God to be the author of sin too; for they say that nothing comes to pass but by divine appointment or permission. They talk also of some horrible decree, in which God is said to have ordained the things which are coming and shall come. No need of holiness, if salvation is not of him that willeth; no need of diligence, if it is not of him that runneth, but to whom the Almighty showeth mercy. If God hath mercy only upon whom he will have mercy, and hardeneth whom he will, we may live as we please; for if we are to be saved, we shall not be damned. What diabolical doctrine is this!"* Thus the Arminian raves against the doctrine of the scripture, and all its faithful preachers.

Impiator. I pray you, cousin, who are these same Arminians? You know I am but little conversant with religious people of any name.

Discordans. The papists in general, cousin; and all the unconverted, who have any notion at all about redemption through the blood of Christ. Mr. Wesley and his followers, the Baxterians and Neonomians; for none exceed them in enmity against the purity of doctrine. Thus you may see,

* These devils, I perceive, are not very exact in literally copying the expressions, but content themselves with expressing the spirit of preachers and writers. If any reader should think that Discordans does injustice to the Arminians here, he may be satisfied of the contrary, by consulting Sellon against Coles. Fletcher's defence of Wesley's minutes.

that the Arminian party is by far the most numerous, and most honorable among men, and therefore gains proselytes from all quarters. Though, by the way, it is a pretty strong proof that it is the doctrine of antichrist, seeing Immanuel and his doctrines are everywhere spoken against, by men of philosophy and natural religion.

INFIDELIS. You know, cousin Discordans, that we have found out many ways of opposing the pure gospel, and this is one among the rest; under our influence, the grace abusing libertine censures the true Christian as legal, because he strenuously pleads for purity of heart and regularity of conversation. On the other hand, the real legalist, whether he be Socinian or Arminian, alleges, that the evangelical Christian is an Antinomian, because he utterly disclaims the merit of good works in the business of salvation. Indeed, on all hands, those who choose either of the extremes, never fail to censure such as adhere to the middle path of judgment; which you know is the only path of safety.

FASTOSUS. Your observation, brother, fulfils what is written in Immanuel's own word, concerning these same Nazarenes, "As for this sect, it is everywhere spoken against." However the enemies of true religion differ among themselves, they agree in stigmatizing the real Christian. Belarmine, Pucksius, Huberus, Hemengius, &c. holy fathers of the Romish church, heartily belabored them in their days; Dr. Whitby, John Goodwin, Whiston, &c. of the English church, have carried on the dispute with equal warmth, and improved the same chain of arguments against them in latter days; in the present time Dr. Harwood of Bristol, Mr. Wesley of London, Mr. Sellon of Derbyshire, and Dr. Nowel of Oxford, have managed the popish cause with amazing address, and all the while pass for true Protestants. So that everywhere, that gospel which is suited only to the perishing sinner, is spoken against, as pernicious and subversive of holiness.

DISCORDANS. Our friends, the men of this world, always view the sect of the Nazarenes in my glasses, and as they look on them, they say, "What a despicable tribe is this! A set of mean beggarly people, the offscourings of the earth, and the very dregs of humanity. Not a person of any considerable rank among them. Led by the nose by a set of illiterate dogmatical fishermen. What person, possessed of any sense of honor, would frequent their assemblies, or have any connexion with their societies?"

INFIDELIS. Your remarks are very just, my worthy cousin: for mankind in general have forgotten that the scripture says, "Not many wise men after the flesh, not many noble are called; but God hath chosen the foolish things of this world to confound the wise, and the weak things of the world to confound the mighty." So that the very objections raised against them, prove the Nazarenes to be the people whom Immanuel hath redeemed out of the world.

DISCORDANS. True, sir, but they see not the mistake. But to proceed; my instruments farther represent them, as a set of hollow-hearted hypocrites, whom our people thus deride. "What painted deceivers are these, who make such a stir about religion, and affect such an air of sanctity! Hear how they sigh and whine, whilst that rogue of a fanatic tells them his cant story about I know not what. The scripture says, 'Be not righteous overmuch; seek not to be overwise.' And I dare say that we have as much religion as they, though we do not make such a stir about it. I will warrant me these hypocrites are more wicked in private than we are in public; for, although they will not get drunk, curse and swear, as we do, they will cheat and lie like the devil himself."

FASTOSUS. A demonstrative proof of the perfection of our conquest over them; for mankind in general do not only hate godliness itself, but even its appearance. And for this reason true sanctity, devotion and self-denial are commonly censured as hypocrisy.

DISCORDANS. As our good friends of the world are not as yet perfectly agreed in their manner of aspersing good people, it happens that different people pursue different methods, equally absurd and diabolical. Some, for instance, are pleased to say, "These people are melancholy. See how they hang down their heads like bu.rushes as they pass along the streets. One shall never see them look pleasant, nor hear them sing a merry song, as others occasionally do with innocence. I hate that religion which makes people melancholy."

INFIDELIS. People greatly betray their own ignorance, when they assign the cause of melancholy to the religion of Jesus· the end of which is to revive and comfort the melancholy sinner, whose heart is oppressed with a sense of guilt and defilement. To revive the spirit of the contrite, to bind up the broken-hearted, and to make the lame leap for joy, because they obtain the prey. Nor do those revilers of religion consider that they themselves, by their contempt of Christianity, do all they can to excite the grief of the sincere Christian, who cannot see his fellow-sinners walking jocosely in the paths of perdition, without dropping over them a tear of commiseration.

Discordans. No, they never think of the real cause, but with a disdainful sneer continue to say, "See how they melt in sorrow; hark how they sigh and groan, whilst their artful parson tells them an horrible story about death and judgment, heaven and hell, salvation and damnation, with I know not what. They are driven out of their senses with such terrible doctrine. Who would thus subject his conscience to the pedantry of those enthusiastic bigots, their uncharitable parsons?"

Fastosus. The fashionable part of the world hate to think of death or judgment, because the very thought would deprive their beloved pleasures of all their imaginary sweetness.

Discordans. That is just the case, sir; for another of my friends says of the above people, "These ways, which their parsons teach them, are enough to drive a man out of his senses. What man of spirit could endure restraint from all manner of pleasure? According to them, one must not so much as play at cards, spend a cheerful evening at the tavern, nor so much as take a Sunday's airing. Play-houses, balls, and assemblies, must all be laid aside. And pray how is our time to be spent? Read the Bible, truly, the most tiresome of books; pray the one half of their time, and, for aught I know, hear sermons the other half of it. What person of any taste could bear to be bound to the observance of such measures? Let them read the Bible who will; give me a good play or novel. I will have none of their religion, not I."

Infidelis. It is true, plays and novels are light reading, and well suited to the taste of people abandoned to dissipation. Nevertheless, even people of fashion may, if they please, reflect, that reading the scriptures, praying, and hearing sermons, are subjects unfit for their ridicule; though, by the way, I do all I can to promote this irreligion.

FASTOSUS. And as for me, I hold it good we visit our respective divisions, to see that the works of darkness be not neglected; and that we meet here at the usual time.

DIALOGUE XV.

ALL THE DIALOGEANS PRESENT.

PRIVY to their appointment, I watched in my solitary retreat, impatient for the return of the black fraternity, whom I always found extremely punctual among themselves, and observant of every appointment, unless some very urgent business demanded their presence elsewhere. At the hour appointed they arrived at the place of rendezvous, and having seated themselves on their respective thrones, the conversation was opened by

FASTOSUS. I have been thinking of the stupidity and ignorance of mankind, exhibited in our last interview, and cannot but wonder, however dark and blind, they do not see that the very people whom they censure as enemies to holiness, because they oppose salvation by works, are the same identical persons who are said to be melancholy with being righteous overmuch. Reason, even unassisted, might easily discover the palpable absurdity, and for the future avoid a contradiction so glaring. I would have my slaves consistent with themselves, seeing I have given them the name of rationalists. But error will always be inconsistent. However, Discordans, we will leave the blind sons of infidelity to hug themselves in their fancied rationality, and attend to the remainder of your story.

DISCORDANS. My sire, I am all obedience to him who alone could give me being; and to resume the thread of my story, would observe, That, strange as it may seem, I do, by the help of these amazing glasses, make one evangelical minister quarrel with another, and that merely because they do not understand each other's manner of expression. One man, for instance, will have it that Immanuel obtained his personality by eternal generation; another will have it to be by divine filiation; and another still is content to believe him to be the only begotten of the Father, without attempting to explain how, or in what sense he is begotten or filiated. All of those three are firm in the belief of Immanuel's sonship, his Deity, and mediatorial capacity, as well as every doctrine of faith. And yet, strange as it may seem, those very men shall be so prejudiced against one another, that they cannot comfortably have fellowship together; but may even prove injurious to each other's usefulness. And it may perhaps be very difficult to determine which of the three discovers most of a gospel spirit. Every one is in the right, and infallibly assured that the other two ought to come into his opinion.

It is the very same with respect to diversity of gifts. One is led, in a peculiar manner, into the doctrines of faith, well able to state, define and defend them against opposition. Another is widely led about in the wilderness of temptation and affliction, by which he obtains peculiar talents in comforting the distressed, and pouring oil into the bleeding wounds of broken hearts. And a third is kept on the mount of enjoyment: his heart is kept warm by a sense of interest; by which enjoyment he is active and lively in the work, a zealous promoter of practical godliness. All of which gifts seem to be essentially necessary to a gospel minister, and are all by the same spirit. And yet, would you think it, these very men shall treat one another as unsound in the faith, in one sense or other? The first is deemed a dead, dull, and useless preacher, whilst, at the same time, he is effectually stopping the mouths of gainsayers. The second, it is feared, loves to be peculiar, and verges a little towards Antinomianism, notwithstanding many a feeble knee is strengthened by his ministry. And the third is a rambling inconsistent preacher, notwithstanding, by his instrumentality, many are brought to a sense of their sin and danger.

These quarrels are of great use to our government, as they fail not to reproach Christianity, stumble the weak believer, and grieve all good men. But this is not all. You know that two men may have the self-same sentiments in religion, and yet one shall choose to express himself in this manner, and another in that, which difference of expression only may be attended with very serious consequences, if candor is not present on the occasion. This was the case with Trebonius and Theodorus. Theodorus heard Trebonius preach, on a particular occasion, found himself offended with some of his expressions, and thought it his duty to make the preacher acquainted with it as soon as possible. But as Trebonius has too good an opinion of his own attainments, easily to retract a saying, he vindicated not only the doctrine, but the mode of expression. Theodorus was now more than ever persuaded, that Trebonius was unsound in the faith, and was not satisfied with verbally defending the truths of the gospel, that is, his own sentiments, but commenced a paper war with Trebonius. His apology for this step was indeed artful, for he lugged in both Christ and religion into partnership with him, and under their authority, or pretended authority, he did what he could to impeach the orthodoxy, and mar the usefulness, of Trebonius.

When Trebonius read the performance, he found himself aggrieved, and something within him being deeply wounded, he resolved on retaliation. To work he goes: First establishes his personal orthodoxy, which he also called the gospel of Christ; then vindicated his own proceedings, which, by an happy turn of thought, he also linked with the honor of religion. Though the truth is, neither the gospel of Christ nor the honor of religion had any concern t all in the squabble. However, having first set himself and his doctrine in a respectable point of view, he proceeded diligently to search out and expose every blemish in the performance, and in the end did as much for his brother as he before had done for him. Thus those two champions for the gospel, that is for their own honor, went on exposing to the public, all they were acquainted with of each other's weaknesses and folly; never once suspecting that by so doing each was exposing his own want of wisdom, and a true Christian spirit. Meanwhile, the friends of both were exceedingly concerned, and in vain studied a reconciliation between them. But O what pleasure did it afford our society! And how did Ambitiosus and me, and other jocular devils, laugh at their folly and childishness! From sources of no greater importance than this, I assure you, most of the quarrels amongst professors arise. But when the contention is once begun, it is hard to say where it will end.

By these means we get the affections of Christians divided one from another, and instead of being mutual helpers ot each other, as the Almighty designed them, we make them mutual hindrances and burthens; so that, though we cannot indeed destroy them as we would, we disturb and distract to an amazing degree.

FASTOSUS. My son, you would have had, comparatively little advantage over these same people but for my invention of school divinity. That is the great engine of th devil Discordans. But for school-divinity, you might even have retired to hell, or contented yourself with doing business among the laity, or in the unconverted world; for if the professors of religion were content with what is written in the scripture, and chose, as much as possible, to express themselves in Bible language; there would be such a likeness in expression, as well as sentiment, that very probably you would find little to do amongst them.

INFIDELIS. I doubt it not, sir. Notwithstanding, I must assure you, my kingdom has suffered greatly by controversy. For nothing has a more direct tendency to inform the mind than well-managed controversy. But when it springs from blind prejudice, and is carried on in a party spirit, it has a wonderful tendency to strengthen my interest; especially if the contending parties mutually agree to expose each other as much as possible, as in the late squabble between Parson Horne and Alderman Wilkes; and which is, for the most part, the practice of polemic divines. Those two important gentlemen, the parson and patriot, gave as much pleasure to the court party, by flinging rogue and atheist at each other, with so much patriotic zeal, as some divines, in their polemic writings, have given the devil, by throwing heretic, Arminian, Calvinist, Antinomian, &c. in each other's faces. Few divines can dispute without calling names.

DISCORDANS. I have before now stirred up a spirit of jealousy between a minister and his people, and between one minister and another, in a manner inexpressibly masterly. For example, about a century ago, the accurate Camillus preached an excellent sermon at Potheina, which was heard by several of the people to whom Junius was pastor; and they, being greatly affected with the seasonableness of the subject. and the practical manner in which it was handled, invited Camillus to visit them, and preach in Junius's pulpit, not doubting but it would be altogether agreeable to their beloved pastor. Full of the sermon, when they came home, they could not help making Junius partaker of their pleasure. They expatiated largely upon the excellency of his method, the fertility of his illustration, and the propriety of his application; all of which they did not doubt but Junius would admire as much as themselves. But this was not precisely the case. Junius could not help being sensibly affected with what he had heard; but prudence forbid him to deny Camillus his pulpit.

When retired, and reflecting on what had passed, he strongly suspected that his own honor was injured, by his people's high encomiums on Camillus's sermon. "My people, said he, allege they never heard such an excellent sermon as that which Camillus preached. It is something strange, that this one sermon should affect them more than all my seven years' preaching among them. I never heard them say half so much about any sermon of mine. It shows a great want of affection and respect to me, as their own minister, I conceive; and they shall hear of it at a time convenient."

Fastosus. With Junius's leave, I think he discovers a love of praise, which is by no means the offspring of an humble spirit. He would rather be flattered, than his people should be silent in his commendation. But the judicious seldom think it prudent to say much in praise of any person to his face, how well soever they may be affected towards him; and that for two very good reason.—1. Such commendation has not a little the appearance of flattery, however sincere it may be in the party who bestows it. 2. There are but few who are able to bear much commendation, without sustaining damage by it. A man must be led deeply into an acquaintance with his own nothingness and insufficiency, before he can bear to be praised and caressed.*

* It is a very common thing, in gospel churches, that if they have a member of more usefulness than others, they exalt and extol him above his measure; so that he becomes elated with self-conceit, and in the issue, when he cannot carry every point his own way, he turns against his former caressers, and becomes a scourge of the community. In this the righteous judgment of God is manifest, who will have all men to appear in their native nothingness and emptiness, unworthy of the trust and dependence of one another.

INFIDELIS. That is true, brother; and yet people may err even on that head, and be cautious overmuch; for fear of puffing him up by unseasonable commendation, may depress the spirits of their minister, by withholding from him that countenance and encouragement, which his spirit and circumstances require.

People are, in all things, given to extremes; and either a minister is caressed and almost adored as an unparalleled person, or he has little or no notice taken of him. I remember a remarkable instance of this in the last century. There was an independent church, who, having a minister of a lively address and sound doctrine, one who bid fair for great usefulness among them; yet a lineal descendant of the great Diotrephes, who loved to have the pre-eminence; and one who chose to direct them in all the concerns of life, in their families, in their business, as well as in the church. To his government they yielded themselves implicitly, and almost adored the ground upon which he trode. With caresses and favors they loaded him, until they had raised him to the very height of self-sufficiency and importance; from which they themselves at last assisted to cast him down; and the contempt they poured upon him, pretty nearly equalled their former caresses. After him they had another, of an almost contrary disposition. He had but a very mean opinion of his own abilities, either for preaching or governing. He had such constant acquaintance with the power of his own corruptions, that he was commonly low and depressed in spirit. He never assumed any superiority over even the meanest member, firmly believing himself to be the vilest and most unworthy sinner of the whole community: he stood in need of all encouragement possible, in order to hearten him for his work. Yet the same people, who had destroyed the former with unseasonable kindness, suffered the latter to drag on heavily all his days, so that from them he seldom or never heard of his word having been made useful. And I suppose he must have sunk under his discouragements, if strangers, who afterwards came into the church, had not been more free with him in discovering some degree of affectionate regard. Different spirits will require different usage, in order to preserve their usefulness: what was death to the former of those ministers, would have been life and vigor to the latter; and what so exceedingly weakened the hands of the latter, would in all probability have been the preservation of the former. But we forget Parson Junius, cousin.

DISCORDANS. Sir, Junius would have his own humor; and, accordingly, when the time came that Camillus made his visit, any person attentive to Junius's behavior, might easily find that his friend's room would, to him, have been more agreeable than his company, notwithstanding, for decency's sake, he forced himself to carry it to him with some degree of seeming civility: I say seeming, for even Christian people have not as yet learned to be exactly, on all occasions, what they seem. But Camillus is a sagacious man, and soon perceived Junius's coldness, through all his formal civility and seeming deference. He began to question with himself from whence this coldness might have proceeded? In what he might have given offence? But never dreams that jealousy is at the bottom. Is he not offended with my doctrine? said he to himself. What can be the meaning of this distant carriage of his? What have I done or said that might give him umbrage? So Camillus reasoned, but hit not upon the real cause. And as Camillus is somewhat fond of his own sentiments, though a man inferior to few who are accounted good and religious, he could not help being in doubt about the orthodoxy of his friend. By these means, happily invented by me, this well-designed visit, instead of answering the valuable ends of promoting religious friendship, rather tended, by my intervention, to alienate their affections from each other.

Junius would still have his own humor, and from that day forward discovered a shyness to those who seemed most delighted with Camillus; and when occasion offered, he did not spare bestowing on them, what is called a dry rub.

This was not all; for Junius could not leave his prejudice behind him when he went to the pulpit, where he adapted his discourses accordingly. On the other hand, his people could easily see he was not in his usual spirit; and they concluded that they had given him no just cause of offence.

Meanwhile, both parties mutually watched each other's words and deportment. If Junius happened to speak any thing harsh, either from the pulpit or in common conversation, it was said to proceed from a bad spirit. On the other hand, if any of them happened to object to any thing spoken by him, he immediately concluded, either that his people were prejudiced against him, or did not love sound doctrine, for he had not a doubt of the soundness and truth of his own doctrine. And so they went on, until, in the issue, there was a final separation. Behold, gentlemen, how great a fire a little spark of my nature kindleth. Every well-wisher to the Beelzebubian government must acknowledge, that the devil Discordans merits much applause.

FASTOSUS. I speak for the rest, my son, and own that your usefulness is of great extent. I persuade myself your royal grandfather will well reward you, by giving you eternal duration among the people of the nether regions; for certainly your achievements merit the greatest esteem. Why, my son, you make the Nazarenes weak as other men.

DISCORDANS. After all, I assure you, at certain times, I have hard work of it. I mean when Mr. Submission, my avowed enemy, and me, happen to meet. This Submission is one of Immanuel's own children, a very great peace-maker. therefore his business is directly opposite to mine; and although I hate him, I must say, he is one of the meekest persons upon earth. Never is he known to quarrel with any person, except myself. And I confess, that in every scuffle with him hitherto, I have had the worst of it; but I thank my stars, it is very seldom I meet with him. When we do meet, meek as he is, I am quite nonplussed, and am obliged either to flee, which I abhor, or to fall before him, which is yet a greater mortification to a spirit so noble as I am.

INFIDELIS. So then, cousin, I perceive you are as ill put to it when you meet with Submission, as I am when I encounter his elder brother Fides. Fides is a warrior with whom I have maintained a very long, though not doubtful war; not doubtful, because I am worsted as sure as ever I enter the lists with him. With great facility I can overturn the power of every other heavenly chieftain; but this fellow, this same Fides, is Immanuel's champion, and has performed the most unparalleled achievements; such achievements as never were performed by any hero besides himself. He hath subdued kingdoms, wrought righteousness, obtained promises, stopped the mouths of lions, quenched the violence of fire, escaped the edge of the sword, out of weakness hath made people strong, causing even the fainting to wax valiant in fight, turning to flight the armies of the aliens. He hath given to women their dead children again, sustained others under the most cruel tortures, in such a manner, that they would not accept of deliverance; gave a good report of the promised land, to those ancient worthies, who walked about in sheep skins and goat skins, destitute, afflicted, and tormented, of whom, notwithstanding they lodged in dens and caves of the earth, the world itself was undeserving.

These are a specimen of his achievements. But great and heroic as he is, he finds that I also am of noble deeds; a spirit not easily rendered inactive, and more difficult still entirely to subdue. Although he has the promise of the most complete victory in the end, I put him to exert his utmost; for when, to appearance, I am dead as a pebble, and Fides has the sole pre-eminence in the soul of man, I play Reynard with him, and feign myself dead, in order to escape the vengeance of his arm.

In time he finds out my deceit; for I watch the opportunity when he is in the very height of a paroxysm, and can scarcely breathe. He is exceedingly troubled with fits, which will sometimes hold him for a long time together, and in which you would take him to be wholly dead. Then I take the advantage, and rise upon him with all my powers, and beat and bruise him, until life begins to return, which is not always of a sudden. But when he feels the weight of my arm, and the smart of the wounds which I inflict on him, his spirit returns with renewed vigor; he unlocks the magazines of grace, and brings forth such implements of war as I am not able to stand against; so that before he is well out of his fit he is as strong as ever. At other times he is a long while before he is freed from the effects of his fits; weakness, indisposition and languor, hang upon him for many months; at which time he receives no mercy at the hand of Infidelis.

This fellow is of the most amazing constitution; for whereas, on one hand, idleness never fails to throw him into a lethargy, so on the other, hard labor, severe conflicts, and cruel buffetings, never fail to make him strong and vigorous; and what is very remarkable in itself, but very unlucky for me, is that the more he is beaten and bruised, the stronger he grows; and these fits, in which you would take him to be just a-dying, it is said, only tend to make him the more robust and lively; which is the reason that, although I fre quently put him to great pain, I am always discomfited in the issue.

However, gentle friends, you must allow, when circumstances are considered, my valor will at least equal, if not prove superior to, that of Fides. He fights under a certain assurance of victory, and knows, of a truth, that in the end he shall be more than conqueror; I as well know that I shall be discomfited, which would dishearten any besides myself. Yet, notwithstanding the discouragement, I give him many a vigorous turn for it ere I desist, and foully trip up his heels oftener than thrice. Even when I have him down, sprawling and gasping for life, I am conscious he will afterward renew his strength, and give me a most severe drubbing; and, that his victorious hand shall, in the end, put a period to the days of great Infidelis. Yet this noble principle of royal malice prompts me on, and I will not yield an hair's breadth whilst life endures. O the fearful combats I could relate, which I have had with this heavenly champion, this same Fides!

Fastosus. We shall be glad to hear of them, my brother, at another time; but at present, if agreeable, I should like you to resume the story, part of which we have already had, respecting the progress of your kingdom.

Infidelis. You have already heard how agreeable to his holiness my instructions were, as also of the laws by which the whole system of religion was inverted, and how the pious priest had invested himself with the perfections of Deity. I knew that the introduction of this new Christianity might be attended with some difficulty, therefore advised his holiness, the father of the world, to deify some others as well as himself; but, at the same time, lest his supremacy should be in any wise infringed, to take care that none should be deified until after their death, and that only with an inferior rank of godship. He took my advice, canonized a vast number under the title of saints, and ordained masses to be said to them out of his own newly composed Bible: for the old Bible, in use among primitive Christians, having its laws so contrary to those of the pope, was, by his authority, made null and void; and Rome, once the mistress of the world, became the mother of harlots; once more the seat of paganism. But, for distinction's sake, we call the latter

Christian-pagans; because they exercise all their villany under the specious show of Christianity.

In order to support the Christian pantheon worship, slaughter-houses were built, and called holy inquisitions; where every one who was known to deny the supremacy and infallibility of his holiness the pope, or so much as harbor a suspicion concerning the papal faith, was treated with as little mercy as if he had been in hell. By these means, people were kept in the most dreadful awe; so that, if any man happened to be intelligent enough to see through the cheat, he was obliged to keep his mind to himself; well knowing, that one word spoken against the lucrative faith of the priests would have insured his certain death, by means the most barbarous and cruel. By this amazing subtility of priestcraft, with the utmost security they carried on their villany, under the mask of sanctity, for many centuries, and all Europe trembled at the indignation of the priesthood. For by means of my brother's medals, and titles of ecclesiastical dignity, together with my blinding influence, the various orders of reverend fathers clave as fast to his holiness, as scales to one another on the impenetrable back of leviathan.

Yet, terrible as the priesthood were, they could not totally prevent the light of the gospel shining, less or more, in some parts of Christendom, especially in Britain; where Wickliffe and his disciples gave their reverences no small uneasiness; for which they poured vengeance upon his bones forty years after his demise. This same scripture light, kindled in England by Wickliffe's ministry, spread itself to the continent, where first John Huss and Jerome of Prague galled the sides of popish prelates: for which the very pious council of Constance, first recommended them to the care of the devil by excommunication, and then, in the name of the God of mercy, condemned them to be burned to death for believing the Bible. It is amazing to think, with what dexterity they have lugged in the name of the Almighty, to sanctify their murders on all occasions.

About a century after this, a very strict inquiry after truth began, by the instrumentality of John Calvin and Martin Luther, two avowed enemies to popish wickedness. This revival of religion was very alarming to the priests of Rome, and very injurious to my government. His infallible holiness, instigated by the devil Crudelis, voted their immediate destruction, by fire and fagot, by poison, assassination, or any way; for there is nothing dreaded by this same vicar of Christ, so much as the spreading of gospel knowledge.

These measures, however, I withstood; having from past experience found, that coercive measures are by no means the most likely to reduce professors of religion to the obedience of infidelity; and I thought it better to send the devil Discordans to visit them, with instructions to make them quarrel about the forms of religion; this I took to be the most likely method to invalidate the testimony of both, and to baffle and confound their followers. This was done, and they jarred exceedingly about circumstantials; but do what we would, they spake of the doctrines which are absolutely necessary to salvation, with perfect uniformity, which greatly frustrated our dark designs; and this fire of reformation so lately fanned, by degrees spread itself on the continent, and in Great Britain, where it arose in the days of Wickliffe.

The pope and me, being loth to give up the government we had always been accustomed to have in these nations, did what we could to stifle the reformation: but, alas! it went on with rapidity in the days of Edward, and might have made greater advances than it has ever yet done, if, luckily for his holiness and me, that prince had not been taken away in early life. Mary, being a princess just fitted to our turn, no sooner ascended the throne, than I flew to England, accompanied by the devil Crudelis, resolving, at all events, to crush with oppression all who rebelled against me and his holiness. To this salutary purpose, were transported from the pope's arsenal abundance of hempen cord, and fagots beyond number, that we might oblige the people to renounce Jesus Christ, and worship his Romish infallibility.

There were, in those days, two lusty bishops, right reverend tyrants in the devil, Bonner of London, and Gardiner of Winchester, who, hearing of our arrival, came, equipped in their prelatic robes, to do us greeting, and bid us welcome to the British shore. This brace of right reverend prelates, we appointed prime inquisitors in matters of faith, and principal agents of our intended cruelty. Indeed none that ever sustained the office of priest, ever were more trusty friends to the government of Rome and hell, than were those worthy prelates.

The vigilant devil Crudelis ceased not, day or night, from persecuting the saints, so that many of the ringleaders of the sect of the Nazarenes were apprehended, tried, condemned, and tormented to death, at a stake; such as archbishop Cranmer, bishops Hooper, Latimer, Ridley, &c. But as it happened in former persecutions, so it fell out in this, the ashes of burned saints proved such fertilizing manure to the church, that, in defiance both of hell and the pope, the detested Nazarenes became by far more numerous. Wherefore, if our friend Mary, of zealous and scarlet memory, had not been summoned hence to receive her reward, the poor devil Crudelis must necessarily have desisted, merely from incessant and unsuccessful fatigue, and the Nazarenes would have obtained rest solely from our desperation.

But when Immanuel beheld such havoc made of his church, and so many places bathed with sanctified blood, his wrath took the alarm; in his judgment, he cut down the zealous queen and her two trusty bishops, and raised queen Betsy to the throne of England. Now the sword of persecution was wrested from the hands of the papists, and the good [illegible] of the church of England did for the Puritans what the zealous papists had done for them, during the reign of queen Mary. This same queen Elizabeth was a great zealot for high church, and a vigorous nurse of Episcopacy; but the Brownists, and other dissenters, felt the full weight of her regal vengeance. I happily prevailed, unexpectedly, with the divines of the established church, to retain the more refined part of the popish system; which those men who were for a more thorough reformation, both in doctrine and discipline, could not comply with; and, for their non-compliance, we taught them that the arm of Episcopacy is every whit as heavy as that of popery, when it is exerted for the good of the church. And, for my own part, I prompted their reverences to coercive measures, being very apprehensive that the reformation might have been carried on farther than it really was.

Avaro. And I assure you, I myself was not idle in those days, but played my game into the hands of great Infidelis. I met their lordships the prelates, (I shall never forget it) in full convocation, and reasoned with them on the intended reformation, and unto my arguments they lent a willing and attentive ear. "Well, gentlemen," said I, "do you intend to come to a thorough reformation, then, and reduce Christianity to its primitive simplicity? Have you considered, gentlemen, that in so doing you must lose your princely revenues, and descend to a level with plain Peter, Paul, and Barnabas, which must needs be a very mortifying step to some of you? Recollect, I pray you, how long your present profits and dignities have been enjoyed by your predecessors in your several sees. Long before Christianity was known in Britain, even beyond the ken of history, this nation was divided into the several bishoprics and archbishoprics by you enjoyed. Through all the ages of popery, the same division of the nation into archflaminries and flaminries, continued under their present denominations; and will you discover such a degree of mortification, as to give up the profits annexed to your ecclesiastical dignities? That were to show, indeed, that Protestant bishops have less providence than Pagan flamins. Yet, if you are determined to purge your religion from every relic of popery, your profits, gentlemen, must be parted with, your revenues must be enjoyed no more; and how will this be relished by you?" By such sensible and seasonable remonstrances, I won greatly upon the minds of their lordships; and, in the issue, it was resolved, that rather than part with their dignities and revenues, they should submit to many things, which have no foundation in scripture.

Fastosus. You bring to my mind, cousin Avaro, the reception I met with by the dignitaries of the ancient church, on the distribution of the forementioned medals. I went, attired in my robes of state, to deliver one of my arch-episcopalian medals to a certain priest, whom I instantly created "His grace and most reverend." He mumbled over to himself several times, "most reverend, his grace," viewing the medal with the closest attention. It is, it is, said he, a very soft and agreeable mode of address. Most reverend; his grace. Yes, my lord, said I, it is very musical, and what I myself only am capable of composing. A mode of address very becoming the dignity of an archbishop. Humble preachers, such as Peter, Paul, Timothy, and Titus, might be very well contented, without being their graces and most reverend; for they were not, as you are, courtiers, clothed in soft raiment. But for a spiritual courtier, for the primate of a province, to prostitute his name to vulgar mouths, would be highly unbecoming, would greatly eclipse the honors of your elevated station. "But, worthy sir, returned he, you know this is a very censorious world in which we live, and some people may be wicked enough to suppose, that such a title as, his grace, does not so well become a man whose breath is in his nostrils, and I may be censured as ambitious." I hope, my lord, replied I, you will not meditate too much on the gloomy subject of mortality, or that will make your dignity cumbersome, indeed. Honors fade, sir, on the prospect of the grave. As to your being censured, as proud and ambitious, I hold the contrary; it will be deemed essential to your high estate, and the use of the Bible being prohibited, the laity will not know but your order is of apostolical institution. Besides, there is my lord duke enjoys the same title of address with your grace; so that, instead of being censured as proud and antichristian, all ranks of people will revere you the more for it; especially, as it will make you a fit companion for princes. The nobility will consider you as their superior, inasmuch as a spiritual duke is superior to a temporal; so that, in the church, your seat will be next to the cardinal's, and in the senate house, next to the prince himself. The gentry will fawn upon you, spaniel-like, in order to obtain preferment for younger sons, and the vulgar will adore you as a demigod.

I would farther advise you, to lay aside preaching to the vulgar race, and apply yourself wholly to the affairs of state; unless called to it, may be, once in seven years, to preach to the king and his nobles. "Ay, replied the worthy prelate, but how shall I dispense with the obligations I am under, as a bishop, to meditate on these things, to give myself wholly to the ministry of the word and prayer; yea, to be instant in preaching the word, in season and out of season?" Oh, sir, replied I, you need be under no concern about that. "Surely, sir, that is the duty of a bishop," replied he. Yes, very true, said I; the duty of bishops such as were in the apostles' days; such bishops as are appointed in the New Testament. But what has that to do with the diocesan bishop, or an archbishop, of whom you yourself are the first. There were none of them, you know, in the apostles' days; none appointed in the word of God. And therefore the laws which bind scriptural bishops to obedience, can have no manner of power over you, as diocesans; much less can a metropolitan, such a bishop as the apostles never thought of, be under any such injunctions. Surely your grace must know that a lord bishop, or a gracious metropolitan, must have enough to do without preaching the gospel Yet if these things are not sufficient to remove the scruples of your mind, and you should still have a notion, that preaching is a duty incumbent on you, I can put you in a way to satisfy your conscience, without abating any thing of your greatness.

"Pray, sir, be so kind," said he. May it please your grace, replied I, it is neither more nor less than to preach by proxy, as people plead their causes in a court of judicature. You know it is the same in effect, whether you preach in person or by proxy, so that your numerous flock have preaching enough.

Farther, with your grace's leave, I do not think it becoming your dignity, even to say prayers in your own family. How far beneath the character of such a spiritual dignitary, to be down on his knees amidst his servants, worshipping his maker! Let me advise you, either to lay aside family worship altogether, or have it performed by a chaplain. This will have two very great advantages attending it. 1. It will save your grace a great deal of hard and unpleasant labor. And 2. It will make your grace's piety to be admired by the vulgar. Methinks I hear one say to another, "What a good man is my lord, the archbishop! For although he is too high for saying prayers himself, or has got so much that he has no need to pray, he gives a good salary to Mr. Honeylip, duly to perform the offices of religion in his stead."

All this while, the good archbishop continued absorbed in thought. and, awaking as from a trance, he said, with astonishment glowing on his countenance, "Sir, you amaze me! So pertinent your counsel, so persuasive your address! You have more than half brought me over to your opinion, as my future conduct will testify."

Having succeeded, even beyond expectation, with his grace the archbishop, I waited immediately on all the diocesans, within the pontifical jurisdiction, and took the most likely measures to bring them over to our interest.

1. I persuaded them, as I had done the archbishop before them, that the worldly grandeur with which I and his holiness had invested them, was certainly too heavy a burthen for them, to be able to ascend the pulpit stairs, above once or twice a year; and that even then it ought not to be to preach to an ordinary congregation.

2. That they might discharge their duty, to the souls within their respective dioceses, by providing vicars to watch over them in their stead, in their several parishes or divisions, that they might freely spend their time either at the court of Rome, or at the courts of their several princes, without sustaining loss at home.

DISCORDANS. Why, sir, according to your account, the readiest way to stop the mouth of a noisy preacher, is to make a bishop of him.

INFIDELIS. The only way in the world, cousin. Had the king of England given a bishopric to the noisy Whitfield, as he was advised to do by a certain nobleman, it is unknown what mischief might have been prevented. A bishopric would have done him more real injury, than if all the bishops in England had written against him. You remember well how Dr. D——d once threatened our ruin, and promised fair for doing a mischief to our government; until our happy stars fixed him in a prebend's stall, and a r——l chaplainship; since which time he has been quiet enough, and lets people sleep on and take their rest securely.

FASTOSUS. Having secured both orders of popish bishops, I took care to establish deans, abbots, monks, friars, vicars, chanters, prebendaries, canons, minor canons, &c. &c. From thence I proceeded to persuade the higher orders of clergy, to encourage plurality of livings, well knowing that if a country vicar could but procure a fat and fruitful benefice, he would even imitate his betters, and preach as little as possible. I have often, with great pleasure, observed, that if a benefice exceeded two hundred pounds per annum, the poor vicar who enjoys it, finds himself very unable to preach, and is therefore obliged to hire a journeyman, to whom he leaves the bulk of his business. By these means, we got curates introduced into the church; a set of gentlemen sold to slavery and inured to poverty, not for want of parts and learning, nor always for want of piety, but for want of what is by far more necessary to preferment, a patron. A journeyman weaver, watch-maker, or cabinet-maker, can afford a better table than many a gentleman, who lacks nothing but a patron, to make him equal to the very first of bishops.

Happily, it just answered our desire; and it was not long before a sharp conflict between the vicars and curates ensued. As it is not without a vein of drollery, I shall give you a sketch of it. There was a certain vicar, who having obtained a living of about 800*l.* a year, called his curate to him one day, and thus addressed him: "Mr. Curate, I am now in a station which will admit but of little preaching; I must therefore get you to take that part of the service principally upon yourself. I am under a necessity of visiting the neighboring gentlemen, and assisting them in their polite amusements, as has been the custom of my predecessors from time immemorial; so that little of my time can be devoted to preaching or praying, and less still to study and contemplation." Mr. Curate replied, "Indeed, sir, I am but a poor hireling, whose scanty allowance is no way adequate to labors so extensive. I am resolved, sir, to measure my services by my annual salary." The vicar's benefice being sufficient to raise him above preaching, and the curate's allowance so small that he could not afford to preach much, it so fell out between vicar and curate, that the parishioners could not obtain above twenty minutes' preaching weekly, in return for their tithes, many dues and offerings. This, you know, was greatly to our advantage.

Another instance of altercation, between the vicar and curate I well remember, which also was decided in our favor. "Hark you, Mr. Curate, said a certain vicar one day to his journeyman, I expect you shall take the care of all the souls within my parish, upon yourself; as I have much business of a very different nature on my hands." "I take the care of them, sir, replied his curateship; what have I to do with them? I shall take no care of them, I assure you." "Well, but Mr. Curate, said the vicar, I hired you on purpose that you should take the care of them off from me." "Indeed, sir, rejoined the curate, I will not, I am resolved; do you think that, for the scanty allowance of twelve shillings per week, I will put my own soul in the place of your parishioners? No, sir, let him take the care of them, who is best paid for so doing." "Then, said the vicar, let my lord bishop take care of them, for he is better paid than either vicar or curate." By these means the parishioners may go to heaven or hell, as most suits their inclination, provided always the fees are punctually paid.

IMPIATOR. Well, father, I really think those curates were in the right; for as they receive but journeyman's wages for doing the drudgery of the business, it is unreasonable to desire any more than journeyman's labor from them. If they perform the most servile parts of the office, for their scanty allowance, it seems but meet the vicars, who receive the far greatest part of the profits, should take the burthen of souls upon themselves. If I am not greatly mistaken, the far greater part of mankind, the vicars and high-priests alone excepted, are of the same opinion with me and the curate. However, that was all in the days of popery, and the church of England hath since been blessed with a great reformation.

INFIDELIS. It has so, Impiator, and been deformed again, almost far enough. Some time after the reformation, indeed, the gospel was preached almost everywhere in England, which made me apprehend the most dreadful consequences, and made me exert my utmost influence, in order to reduce the clergy to obedience.

This important point was in a great measure carried, by fixing their attention inordinately upon tradition, and kindling relentings in the bosom of many a gownsman, towards the old scarlet lady, whose government had been rejected. So that, by degrees, I drew them to take counsel, as formerly, from the wise Infidelis; one particular instance of which I shall give you, if you think it will not too long detain you from necessary business.

FASTOSUS. That is well thought of, brother. Idleness belongs not to our fraternity; I hold it good, therefore, that we adjourn to our usual time of meeting.

DIALOGUE XVI.

ALL THE DIALOGEANS PRESENT.

Fastosus. When we parted yesterday, you mentioned some particular instance of the clergy seeking to you for direction, brother; will it please you to relate it to us now?

Infidelis. It is only a little confabulation I had with my good friend, parson Out-and-in. The case was this: I set out one morning for Rome, to remove some scruples which infested the mind of his holiness, the father of the world; but, passing by parson Out-and-in's garden, I beheld the reverend gentleman in his morning gown and velvet cap, walking slow and pensive, to all appearance in a dejected manner. Charity bid me stop and relieve the thoughtful divine. At her command I stopped, and called: So ho, Mr. Out-and-in: how do you do? the good gentleman, awaking as from a trance, erected his body into a perpendicular posture, pushed up the snout of his cap from over his eyes, and finding it was me who called, instantly replied, "O my good friend, Rationalis! (for that is the name by which I am known by the clergy, of all denominations) am I so happy as to meet with you, in this so difficult season? I pray you, most honorable tutor, be pleased to stop and give me your advice."

I went to him, and thus the old Levite began: "Most truly noble and intelligent sir, I, and my brethren, the genuine children of learning and science, have long been much grieved at the rapid progress of fanaticism, which now prevails amazingly over the people. So prevalent is it, sir, that fanatical preachers are more followed, more esteemed, than we, the votaries of almighty reason. In these days, sir, there are some, who, in a frantic manner, decry the noble powers of the human soul, which we esteem to be almost divine; who preach salvation, by what they call the righteousness of Christ, contrary to the instructions, which we received from that illumination, which thou hast given us. We have long been studying how to suppress this fanaticism, and to promote the more consistent doctrine of salvation by our own works, and the liberty and freedom of our own will, to perform perfect righteousness. It is intolerable, sir, to hear men of virtue and piety, placed on a level with vile publicans and sinners, who know not the law, and are therefore accursed. Impious in the highest degree, to suppose that the benevolent Deity will not reward our good endeavors to please him, by working out our own salvation, without trusting in the righteousness of another."

To be sure, said I, to gentlemen of virtue and goodness, it must be mortifying to submit to be levelled with those who work not, but believe in him who justifieth the ungodly. Very trying, indeed, to one's own self to be an hell-deserving sinner, when your own reason bears witness, that you deserve the inestimable blessings of everlasting happiness, for your own personal goodness. What man of virtue and moral goodness, what gentleman of a clear head and good heart, like yourself, can bear to be told, that harlots and publicans shall enter the kingdom of heaven sooner than you? I wonder not, my worthy sir, that the preaching of salvation by the works of another, should be a stone of perpetual stumbling, and a rock of invincible offence to you. And this offence will never be removed, until we can so manage it, that this same book, called scripture, is made to truckle to the more consistent dictates of human reason; by which alone the authenticity of doctrine ought to be attested, independently of any records whatever, either ancient or modern.

I myself have beheld the preaching of the cross of Christ, with a great deal of uneasiness. But for seeing the self-righteous Jews break their bones by stumbling upon it, and the wise philosophic Grecians turning merry-andrews, and laughing at it as foolishness, I should certainly have sunk into despair; because I was unhappy enough to see it prove both the power of God and the wisdom of God, to those who felt themselves actually in a perishing condition. But my good Mr. Out-and-in, permit me to tell you, that whatever pain I endure on account of a preached gospel, I can do nothing that will effectually prevent it, without the concurrence of the clergy. By the way, let me not so much as hint any defection of the clergy. No, sir, I thank my auspicious stars, by far the greatest part of them are upon the right side of the question. There are but few, very few who preach those enthusiastic doctrines, with which the ar ticles, homilies, and rubric are stuffed; very few who concern themselves about what is, or what is not the doctrine of the Bible.

But, to the matter of your troubles, sir, I apprehend they may be reduced to these two heads only; to suppress the growth of fanaticism on the one hand, and secure to yourselves the patrimony of the church on the other. "These are all, returned he. If we can but accomplish these, we desire no more." Then, sir, if no more is aimed at, I shall put you in a way, by which you may accomplish them.

Observe me then, my good friend Mr. Out-and-in, the first thing to be done, is, to draw as thick a veil as possible over the personal excellencies, grace, and righteousness of Immanuel; for these, wherever they are preached, have a tendency to eclipse all human glory, and greatly to diminish the profits of the altar; which, you know, are the principal things that ought to be advanced. The holy trade of priestcraft can never prosper, but in proportion to your departure from the doctrine of the cross. Yet, this must be done with caution, lest the eyes of the people should be opened, and the propagation of your rational religion be prevented. The important question then is, "How you may retain the character and authority of Christ's ambassadors, whilst, at the same time, you are laboring to extirpate the doctrine of salvation by his blood, from the rational world?" as you cannot expect to be so much regarded by the people, if ever you lose your claim to ambassadorship. Of this, therefore, you must be very cautious, and by no means declare yourselves avowed enemies to the gospel, in so many express words.

No, sir, you must find out the most glorious names which possibly can be ascribed to the Son of God; yet such names as do not imply his personal divinity; these would spoil your scheme, and therefore must be rejected. For instance, you must not call him Immanuel, the mighty God, the everlasting Father, God manifest in the flesh, Jesus Christ yesterday, to-day and for ever the same; Alpha and Omega, &c. &c. These, and such like names, must absolutely be laid aside, for they make directly against the rational scheme. On the other hand, you must be equally careful not to speak slightly of his person, name, and authority, by barefacedly calling him, but a man, like yourselves, as Dr. Priestley has precipitately done; and by so doing betrayed the cause of rational religion into the hands of the orthodox, to be mangled and tortured after the manner of that wicked Shaver In short, you must consider, that the people are not all rational alike; and therefore a downright denial of the Godhead of Christ, may be attended with very serious consequences. Some people are firmly attached to the Athanasian creed, merely out of deference to the judgment of their ancestors, and others are as firmly attached to the scriptures from an inward conviction of their divine propriety; so that without the greatest care, you may be baffled in your very first attempts to promulgate your rational religion.

In short, sir, notwithstanding you believe him to be but a man like yourself, or at most but a dignified creature, you must of necessity, for fear of the populace, give him a kind of suffragan Deity or deputed Godhead like that of Mars or Mercury, in the pagan theology. Your friend, Mr. Whiston, a man of deep intelligence, has shown you what may be done in this way; do you, my good Mr. Out-and-in, imitate the same Homer-like minister.* You must never omit when you speak of him, to use great and swelling words of seeming respect, as if you had the most profound veneration for his person; call him the only son of the most high God; the first-born, and most exalted of creatures; a being far above men and angels; under God, the great dispenser of all things, both in earth and heaven. Not a syllable of his measuring the seas in the hollow of his hand; of his meting out heaven with a span; of his comprehending the dust of the earth in a measure; weighing the mountains in scales, and the hills in a balance; or of his taking up the isles as a very little thing. That is a description of Jesus, most adverse to what you would have thought to be rational religion, which considers him as no more than a man, like yourselves. It is good, therefore, that such descriptions should never be quoted. By keeping close to those appellations, which are proper to him, only as man and mediator, you will veil his real personal dignity; and, in time, your audience will quite forget all their old orthodox notions, concerning the proper Deity of the Lord Jesus Christ,

* Homer-like minister. Homer was a wonderful creator of gods and goddesses, and so was Mr. Whiston, from his own account of the Trinity which he makes to consist of one uncreated, and two created Gods.

which at present are so very offensive to you and your brethren.

When you happen to hear of any man, who is a zealous and diligent preacher of Christ crucified, as the only foundation of the sinner's hope, you must look to it that something be speedily done, to prevent his success: for such a man is capable of being very injurious to us, and our rational religion. His followers will consider you as no better than hirelings, mercenary priests, and enemies to the gospel of salvation. Therefore you must, but always with the greatest art, attack his character. Stigmatize him with such names of reproach as you think will be most likely to take with the vulgar. However, you must beware of touching his moral character, for that will be like the body of Achilles, invulnerable even to malice itself. His religious character, because less understood by the common people, will be more easily injured; and is, therefore, the most proper object of your attacks.

You may call him an enthusiast, which is a name understood by very few; therefore the greatest part of the people will consider him as some outlandish monster, and avoid him, as they would shun the path of a crocodile. Or you may call him a methodist; this also is a name well calculated to excite popular abhorrence, as you know many would rather choose to be papists than methodists. Or you may call him an anabaptist, or fanatic. In short, you may dress him in what names you think will most effectually stir up the people to bait him, as they would do a bull or a bear from the forest; and so far as your influence goes, you may totally prevent his usefulness; which, you know, will be a great service done to the devil, and to rational religion.

But, my good Mr. Out-and-in, take care that you be not too barefaced in your slanders, as Doctor Priestley has been in his against the orthodox dissenters. His zeal for rational religion is so furious, that it prompted him to rend the disguise, which ought by all means to have concealed his implacable hatred of the orthodox. This, however, he has thought proper to discover in such a manner, that his word, in a way of slander, will now scarcely be taken by anybody, so that even the rationals themselves are ashamed of his rashness. But you, my friend, may avail yourself of his miscarriage, and avoid the rock upon which he foundered under full sail, by considering that, amongst the laity there are always to be found a discerning few, whose penetration may be too keen for a flimsy disguise. Now, should your malice be detected, your very reproaches would bring him proselytes, as in the case of Dr. Trapp, of crabbed memory, and the late Mr. Whitfield. Therefore, let all your reproaches seem to flow rather from pity than malice. Do not fail to commend something of the good that is in him: this will be an excellent cloak, from under which you may with the greater freedom shoot your arrows of calumny. For example, when his name is mentioned in company, you may say, "He is a good sort of man, I believe; but I am sorry for him. Poor man, he hath imbibed sad enthusiastic principles. The poor, weak, well-meaning man, would do good if he could, I believe, but is sadly led away by methodistical notions." Sir, there are a thousand ways of vending scandal, with seeming pity, which some people are perfect masters of: but your divines are too warm, and therefore their arrows fall to the ground before they inflict any wound at all.

I have known an important minister, ere now, ruin the reputation of his neighbor, with less than ten words speaking and those too seemingly spoken in much pity. O, Sir, there requires great art in scandalizing to purpose. Nothing gives such a point to the arrow of scandal, as seeming concern for the welfare of the party whom you want to ruin I could recommend you to certain gentlemen, in great estimation for religion and virtue, as the most accomplished in this necessary art, did not I know that you disdain to learn from any inferior to myself.

If you would invalidate the doctrine of imputed righteousness, you must begin just here, and proceed in the following manner. That it is a doctrine which must be brought into contempt, as you would wish to preserve the honor of the creature, is clear to a demonstration; seeing whenever a man is brought cordially to embrace it, his looks, however lofty before, are brought down, and he lies at the feet of Jesus, as a perishing and lost sinner; which, you know, is inconsistent with the dignity of a philosopher, or a rational Christian.

You must, my worthy Mr. Out-and-in, you must indeed,

declare that man, having received no damage at all by the fall of Adam, and coming into the world in perfect innonence, is capable of having a righteousness of his own, which will justify him before an infinitely holy God. "Ay, but Mr. Rationalis, said he, how shall I manage in this, seeing there are so many plain passages of scripture, which contradict me?" Do, my good friend! You must not mind that, if you intend to be a rational preacher. You must show yourself a man, and leap over them, as many have done before you. Imitate the zealous Dr. Priestley, and like him tell your hearers, that the scriptures do not mean what they say.* What man of reason would regard a few adverse texts of scripture, when the dignity of human nature is the subject in question?

For your encouragement, permit me to assure you, that however adverse the scriptures may be to your rational doctrine, the populace will be very propitious.

You can never please men so well as by clapping them on the shoulders, telling them that their hearts are good, that they need not doubt of getting safe to heaven, whether they believe in the Son of God or not. And I engage, sir your auditory will caress you, for the sake of your pleasing doctrine.

As to the Holy Ghost, I would not have you absolutely refrain from mentioning him, and his assisting influence, because your people read of him in your church liturgy so very often. But be sure roundly to assert, that it is mere enthusiasm for a man to expect to receive the Holy Ghost, in these days; and let them solve the difficulty, how the thoughts of a man's heart can be cleansed by the inspiration of the Holy Ghost, whom they cannot receive, as they shall find opportunity. It seems I proved as a kind of remembrancer here, for he stopped me short and said: "Let me see——I think I should remember something about the Holy Ghost somewhere——Hum—If I mistake not, it was relating to the office of ordination."

Yes, sir, said I, it was; you only professed to my lord bishop, that you were moved by the Holy Ghost, to take upon you the office of a deacon. That was all, sir. He replied: "I believe it was some such thing. But pray,

* Familiar illustration of certain texts, &c.

sir, was it rational in me so to do, seeing I did not then believe that any man receives the moving influences of the Holy Ghost in these times?" Surely, said I, it was. You know, sir, no man can get a benefice without it in your way: and I pray you, who would not do as much as that for a good living? Why should you have any scruple of conscience, seeing you have got some hundreds a year by it? I know many, very many, who did the same, sir, who can hardly procure thirty pounds per annum. On my word, you sold your conscience well. But for those sons of science, they foolishly threw theirs away, without the prospect of any comfortable return. I assure you, a journeyman weaver can afford a better table than many a clergyman of the rank of curate.

Once more; as the works of the Savior of mankind must not be wholly omitted; should you be asked, What Jesus did for his people? you must answer, as it were, in a rapture: "O! he hath done great things for us. He descended from the heavenly glories, and assumed our nature. He hath abrogated the severity of the old, and introduced a new and milder law; lived agreeably to the precepts of it himself, and when his instructions were finished, he confirmed us in his ways, and sealed the truth of his doctrine with his own precious blood." Thus, my friend, you may by good management, if grace prevent not, deceive the very elect. Tears of thankfulness trickled down the old gentleman's beard; he gave me most hearty thanks, and protested, that no instructions could be more agreeable to the dictates of his own reason.

Fastosus. I can tell you, brother, your advice was not in vain, but has been invariably followed, so that this rational religion is now very little injurious to our interest.

Infidelis. It is very moderate, sir, and may well be tolerated even by our governors themselves. It has not the least affinity with the doctrine of the cross; which is justly the abhorrence of every partisan of ours, as will appear from the creed which I composed, and put into the hands of my friend Mr. Out-and-in; which, if agreeable, I shall recite.

Discordans. I pray you, sir, let us have the creed. It may afford matter of entertainment to have the creed of the enemies of all creeds and confessions.

INFIDELIS. Not enemies to all creeds, cousin; only to those creeds which they deem orthodox; those which debase the sinner, exalt the Savior, and thwart the views of human arrogance. But they are very fond of such creeds as tickle proud nature, eclipse the sovereignty of grace, and debase the Savior as insufficient of himself to save to the uttermost those who come to God by him: as you will see in the following.

"I believe in the great God, the Father and fountain of Deity, as an absolute and supreme being, eternal, immortal, invisible, omnipresent, all-powerful, the Creator, Supporter, and Governor of all worlds. I believe in another God, who is not eternal in his existence; not omnipresent in his essence; not omnipotent, but entirely dependent on the great God for his very existence; not supreme over all, as Paul the fanatic thought; but subject in all things to him that made him; not immortal, but actually died about seventeen hundred years agone, for purposes afterwards to be mentioned. I farther believe, concerning this second God, that he was created, as the famous Whiston says, by the great God, in an ineffable manner, before the foundation of the world, far above all angels, and appointed to be the minister of the wrath and mercy of the Creator. I believe in a third God, called the Holy Ghost, created by the second God, or suffragan of the Supreme Deity, and that, therefore, he may properly be called the grandson of the great God."

"I beg your pardon, said Mr. Out-and-in, interrupting me; it would be more rational still, to ascribe no Deity whatever to the Son of God."

O sir, replied I, we shall fit you in that, in the most agreeable manner; then to the article of faith in the great God, add, "I believe in Jesus Christ, as a mere man like ourselves, yet pious and holy. A man sent of God, as a great teacher, whose business in life was to introduce a new mild law, commonly called the gospel; because God had altered his mind, respecting the salvation of mankind, since his giving of the old law, which upon examination and long experience, was found to be too strict and severe, consequently unjust, and fit for abolition. Wherefore, he raised up this same Jesus Christ, a man like ourselves, and sent him to correct the errors, which infinite wisdom had fallen into, in giving what we call the moral law. I believe, that when he obtained a perfect correct copy, he taught it to mankind, and called it the new law, or the gospel. I believe that this good man did actually make such corrections, alterations, and amendments in the moral law, as he saw meet, notwithstanding he positively declared, that, "although heaven and earth should both pass away, not one jot or tittle of the old law should fail," that is, be superseded by any other law whatever. I believe that Jesus Christ, this good man like ourselves, having rendered the old law a perfect system, and having taught it in its purified state, died to confirm the truth of his doctrine, just as Cranmer and other good men have done since then. I believe farther, that he continued under the power of death for three days, and then was raised from the dead, to show that he was no impostor, but was actually commissioned to amend the old law, which, prior to his correction, was neither holy, just, nor good, as the mistaken apostle thought it to be. Farther still, I believe that, in his exalted state, he is, as good Dr. Priestley observes, only a man like ourselves, notwithstanding the orthodox ignorantly worship him as Immanuel, God, with them; God manifest in the flesh; the true God and eternal life; the Alpha and Omega; the first and the last, and I know not what enthusiastic titles, such as that book, called the Bible, ascribes to Jesus of Nazareth.

"Concerning the original state of man, I believe, that Adam did not beget his children in the likeness which he himself bore, at the time of their being begotten, but in the likeness which he bore before he had sinned; that, although the fountain became polluted, the streams continue pure and limpid; and, although the root was depraved by transgression, the branches and fruit are holy and innocent. So that there is no such thing as original sin in any sense; nor have the posterity of Adam any share in the guilt of his transgressions. And, whereas the death of infants is frequently alleged, by fanatics, and orthodox Christians, as a proof of original sin; I do most rationally believe, concerning those that die in infancy, that either God, in an arbitrary unjust manner murders them without cause; or their death is occasioned by some sin of their own, committed either whilst they were in the womb, or before they had being; for no man can die for the sins of another, says your oracle, and yet it is clear that infants do die.

"Moreover, I believe that every man is possessed of power to justify himself by the deeds of the law, and to procure salvation by his own willing and running, contrary to the opinion of Paul, and the rest of the orthodox; that salvation is obtained by works of righteousness of our own performing, and not by the obedience and death of any other person; that the glory of our salvation shall redound to the absolute mercy of God, and our own good endeavors to obtain it; and not unto Christ, whom the orthodox enthusiastically say, has loved them, and washed them in his blood, by which he has redeemed them to God, out of every nation, kindred, people, tongue, and language."

This creed being cordially received by my votaries, I laughed in my sleeve, and said, A fig for you all, my enemies; Goodwin, Charnock, Owen and Crisp, &c. where are you now? A fig for all your snarlings at my principles! Lift up your heads from the dusty pillows, and listen, whilst your own descendants, ye Puritans, with all the force of eloquence, plead the cause of great Infidelis.

IMPIATOR. Honored father, I admire your subtility, and almost adore your craftiness. Who would have thought, when we heard of the old Puritans raving against unbelief and profaneness, that, in such a short time, their descendants would have forsaken the principles of their progenitors. But I give you joy, my sire, your operations have lacked no advantageous success.

INFIDELIS. You are very obliging, my son! But I perceive you are not aware of all the glory of this conquest. Perhaps my friends would think it strange, if I should tell them, that by this device, I have again introduced into Britain, as gross idolatry as ever was preached by the ancient druids, as ever was known at Rome or Athens; and that British divines have arrived at an higher degree of heathenism than ever was known in the celebrated pantheon.

IMPIATOR. Nay, then, my bewildering parent, out with it, and explain yourself. What, idolatry again in Britain! Happy stars!

INFIDELIS. Hold, son. Restrain yourself, I say. Do not you remember the charge I gave you, Impiator, when I sent forth my several worthies to sound my sleep-giving trumpet.

IMPIATOR. I can remember nothing at present, so great is

my joy! O idolatry! How glad am I that the Britons have again embraced thee!

INFIDELIS. This, son, was my charge, and I desire you will remember it. Take care, said I, Impiator, take care what you do. It is a matter of great importance to our infernal interest, to which a blunder of yours might, on this occasion, be very injurious. These men are gone forth upon my business; with a commission from me, your father, to counteract a preached gospel, and as much as may to sap its foundation doctrines. Now, my son, in order to be useful to me, it is highly necessary they should bear the appearance of the strictest sanctity, and be not any wise defective in tithing, anise, mint, and cummin, or how can they impose the cheat upon mankind with success? Whereas, the appearance of devotion and sanctity, will give energy to their arguments, and greatly recommend their doctrine; there is no beating it out of the heads, even of the most ignorant, that there is such a thing as devotion and sanctity, inseparably connected with religion.

Now, my son, thou art but a purblind devil, and at best precipitate; therefore thou mayest overturn my well-concerted scheme. I charge thee, therefore, Impiator, as thou wishest well to our mal-administration, that thou shalt refrain from tempting these men into any of thine openly notorious ways, and to leave them entirely to my government; for they cannot miscarry whilst I have the pleasure of reigning in their hearts.

FASTOSUS. A very necessary caution, and it ought to be regarded.

IMPIATOR. I remember it very well, and have hitherto acted accordingly; notwithstanding, I would rather allure every person to take up his dwelling in some part of my dominions. But, sir, I never knew that your rational divines were properly idolaters.

INFIDELIS. Do you consider, then. They tell their hearers, that Immanuel is no more than a dignified creature, who has no personal claim to the essential properties of true and absolute divinity, notwithstanding many of them pay divine honors to his name. Now, my son, the worship of a creature, how dignified soever, is by all allowed to be mere idolatry.

FASTOSUS. They deny the charge of idolatry, brother,

by alleging, that they offer to Immanuel, only an inferior worship, suited to the inferiority of his person as a created being.

INFIDELIS. The very thing in which their idolatry consists, and is on a level with the ancient pagans. It was an inferior kind of adoration, which the ancients paid to their heroes and common deities, in comparison of that which they offered to Jupiter their great god, the supposed king and father of all the rest. Mars and Mercury, for instance, were never considered as supreme, but as acting under the direction and delegation of Jupiter; as such, and such only, they were adored and worshipped; so that to distinguish between the worship of the father, as supreme, and that of his son, as inferior and subordinate, instead of exculpating them from the charge of idolatry, doth actually enforce it.

FASTOSUS. But, to clear themselves from the charge of idolatry, they allege farther, sir, the command of God himself, for their worshipping the Son, notwithstanding his inferiority. The great God, say they, hath given command, that all the angels of God should worship him, and that all men should honor him; shall then our obedience draw upon us the reproach of idolatry?

INFIDELIS. So they say. But if they knew the scriptures, only half as well as you and me, who have labored all our days to cloud their evidence, they would see that these commands, instead of exculpating them from, do actually bring home the charge of idolatry upon them. God hath expressly commanded, that, "Mankind shall have no other gods before him," as objects of religious adoration, either by office or otherwise. And he would hardly have himself introduced another, of a different nature, and commanded all men to worship him; seeing, in this case, one command would have clashed with the other. This would have been the spring of wild confusion, and everlasting uncertainty; for the two commands being diametrically opposite, no man could ever have known which of the two might be obeyed with safety.

Would we but suffer them to reflect upon the divine commands, they must unavoidably see that their worshipping of the Son of God, as merely delegated, with an inferior kind of worship, is absolute idolatry. When the first begotten was brought into the world it was said, "Let all the angels of God worship him," which they accordingly did at his birth. When he revealed himself to Israel, the Father gave command, that, "All men should honor the Son, even as they honored the Father." That is, with the self-same honor, as is paid to the Father, on the foundation of his being one (in essence) with the Father. Whereas, had the Father ordained divine honors to be paid to any being of a different essence from himself, he would not only have overturned the first commandment, "Thou shalt have no other gods before me," but have given his glory to another, contrary to his own express declaration. I would not, therefore, have those sons of superior reason think it at all strange, if at last they find themselves ranked with idolaters.

IMPIATOR. But, father, if I mistake not, you said, that, with them, paganism is brought to as great perfection as ever it arrived at in the Roman pantheon. How is that, sir, seeing they are rational Christians?

INFIDELIS. Yes, my son, they call themselves rational Christians, because they believe and teach, "That the world by wisdom may know the Almighty," and adorn their harangues with words, which men's wisdom teacheth; but they are pagans, notwithstanding, as will appear, when you consider, that they worship more Gods than one. Arians and Socinians both agree to worship one, whom they say is truly and essentially God, and the king and father of the other Deities. Besides this object of supreme adoration, they have other two, the Son and the Holy Ghost, whom they honor with inferior adoration, just as the ancients did the common Deities. I suppose, gentlemen, you will allow that the worship of two or three objects of different ranks, is as real paganism, as the worship of so many hundreds: but I choose to distinguish the moderns from others, by the name of Christian pagans, because they allow Jesus Christ to be one of their secondary Deities. I am greatly obliged to you, my brother Fastosus, for your assistance, so kindly given, to enable me to accomplish my purposes; without it, I could not have brought my affairs to their present happy situation.

FASTOSUS. No, brother, you could not; but you are at all times welcome to my assistance, in counteracting the simplicity of gospel truth. I myself should greatly suffer, were the Arians and Socinians to discover what part we have in their rational religion; and I am not without my fears, that the capacity of the preachers for making proselytes, the dwindling away of their congregations, and the contempt in which they are in general held, will in time convince them, "That the world by wisdom knew not God," and so bring them to change their present system of rational religion for that of the cross of Jesus, which is truly rational, and ennobles every reasoning power of the human soul.

IMPIATOR. Ah, my sire! What a subtle spirit you are! With what laudable craftiness must you have acted, to succeed in introducing pagan idolatry amongst modern divines, even amongst Protestant dissenters. I have long known that the papists are pagans in disguise, but had no thought of rational Christians being so far in alliance with us.

DISCORDANS. Pagans in disguise, cousin! What do you mean? There is no mystery at all in your father's doctrines; nor is there much difference between the ancient pagans, and modern papists. The principal difference is this: The popish Juno, whom they call the mother of God, is far greater in power, and more exalted in glory, than the wife of Jupiter, the pagan Deity. The pagan Juno acted in all things subordinate to the will of her husband, the king and father of the gods, who bore absolute sway over the heavenly synod: but the popish Jupiter acts in subordination to the will of his virgin mother. He rules the creation, indeed; but then he is still subject to maternal direction; so that it is not God, the savior of sinners, but the virgin Mary the popish Juno, who possesses absolute sovereignty; and what good they expect at the hand of God, is expected as to be done in obedience to his virgin mother.

In all other things, there is little or no disparity between the ancient and modern pantheon worship. The pagans worshipped angels, whom they called Gods; the papists worship them also, knowing them to be creatures. The first had their heroes and heroines, whom they adored under the name of demi-gods; the latter, also, have their heroes and heroines, whom they worship under the name of saints. The ancients had their ambiguous oracles and lying wonders. and the moderns have both, in far greater abun dance; so that he must be blind indeed, who does not see amongst them undisguised paganism.

IMPIATOR. Then it must follow, that the papists are greater friends to my father Infidelis, than the Arians and Socinians; because these bear something of the appearance of truth; but those have cast off both truth and its appearance.

INFIDELIS. That is your wisdom, again, my son. Impiator would make but a blundering minister of state in my court gentlemen. But, my son, you may know, it is with us a maxim of policy, that, "Whoever comes nearest the truth, and is, notwithstanding, destitute of it, is always capable of doing the most essential service to my interest." Popish paganism is by far too barefaced to succeed in England, where its absurdities have been so long detected. English Protestants will not worship a god of the baker's making, whilst their women retain the art of making good plumb-pudding, which will at any time be preferred to the sacramental wafer. But Arian and Socinian paganism is so subtilly invented, and so well refined, that it passeth with many for rational Christianity.

IMPIATOR. I find, sir, you are under necessity, as well as myself, to act wisely, with craft and cunning, finding that the same device will not, with all people, at all times succeed alike. We may sometimes, to some people, appear in our own infernal likeness; and at others we are fain to put on a deep disguise, in order to accomplish our designs. But no matter how, so that we have them safe at last. However, gentlemen, there being such a prospect of plenty, I begin to fear there will scarcely be room left in hell for us devils.

INFIDELIS. Another stroke of my son's wit. It is well, Impiator, that your business is to tyrannize only over the thoughtless part of the human race, or you would be of little service to our fraternity. But have you never heard, that Tophet is wide and large, without either brim or bottom? There is no fear of wanting room. Besides, wherever the fiends may happen to be, they are always at home, being sure to carry their hell along with them.

FASTOSUS. I have somewhere seen a map of that part of your dominions, brother, where the idolaters dwell; if you have got one about you, I should be glad to have a description of it.

INFIDELIS. I have, sir, and am glad it is in my power to gratify my much-honored brother. You see, sir, it is divided into two grand provinces, each inhabited by different sects of idol worshippers. That province on the left contains the various sects of civil idolaters, and this on the right contains the many denominations of their elder brethren, the religious idolaters. And, I assure you, they are two bodies of people very respectable.

The province which contains the civil idolaters, is divided into several counties, all of which are very populous. In the first county live the worshippers of vain pleasure, and this county is divided into several regalities, in which the several sects or denominations of idolaters dwell, according to the diversity of their inclinations. The first regality is appointed to the worshippers of living creatures. This swarms with jockeys, and gamblers of the turf, both of noble and ignoble extraction. Along with them live the worshippers of foxes, hares, and hounds, a very jolly race, I assure you, well skilled in the literature of the kennel. But it is better to be a slave in a Turkish galley, than held as a divinity in this regality; for adoration never fails to procure torture to the idol, as the panting of the hare, and the well-plowed sides of the horse, sufficiently demonstrate. A little nook of this regality is, by royal mandate, made over to sterile wives and maiden ladies, who, for want of more agreeable objects of adoration, worship monkeys, parrots, and lap-dogs. The second regality is the habitation of those who worship the dramatic poets, and their apes, the players. At the shrines of those idols, the worshippers sacrifice health and virtue, under pretence of learning wisdom. They are a very fashionable and honored people, with whom legislators and guardians of public virtue are not ashamed to associate. Here you may find legislators patriotically sacrificing their own virtue, in order to protect that of their nation; their own estates, in order to assist in public economy; and faithlessly wasting their own time, in order to teach industry to the inferior ranks of subjects.

In the second county, you will find all the worshippers of false honor; a set of gentry extremely divided in their sentiments, relative to the object of their adoration. One holy father falls down prostrate, like Cardinal Wolsey, before the triple crown and pontifical dignity. A second is equally devout at the shrine of a cardinal's hat. And a third, less aspiring, pays his devotions to a bishop's mitre or prelatic robes, and the highest of his present ambition is a bishopric. Other reverend gentlemen offer a more humble worship to a deanery, prebend, or vicarage.

It is very observable, that in this county people never worship that to which they have already attained; but having compassed their purpose, burn incense to the idol next in rank, and thus the worshipper goes on, if death and disappointment do not prevent him, until he has worshipped every shrine in the pantheon.

For instance, whilst a curate, a vicarage is the idol; the vicarage obtained, it gives place to a prebend or deanery; which once enjoyed, they also, in their turn, give place to a bishopric; that to an archbishopric, which is the principal idol of the English. But in other countries, there are idols of a superior rank, so that the moment an archbishopric is obtained, incense smokes to a cardinal's hat; which also obtained, loses it worshipper, who is now converted to the worship of the triple crown, the great god and father of all the other idols.

Nor are the laity less devout than their reverend brethren; for one man worships universal empire, like Louis of France, and some others; but it is said that George of Britain is an apostate from this religion. Another worships a crown and sceptre, like the descendants of a certain bricklayer; and many adore the place of prime-minister, chancellor of the kingdom, first lord of the treasury, with every other place of honor and trust in government. Some you shall see fall prostrate before a star and garter, whilst others are all obedience to a coronet. The husband lies in the dust before "his honor," whilst his wife in raptures adores "her ladyship." "His lordship" is bended to by one, and another pays all his devotion to "his grace."

In this county, you may find some men religious enough to worship a corporal's knot, or a serjeant's halberd. Some worship an ensign's sash, others a lieutenant's commission, whilst the captain is absolutely as much devoted to a regiment, as his colonel is to a marshal's staff.

The third county is the dwelling of those who worship

their own bodies, than which, I presume, there is not a more ravenous idol in the synod. Around the shrine of this god, stand the baker, brewer, pastry-cook, confectioner, distiller, weaver, and male and female tailors. Hard by are a constellation of the softer sex prostrate before an Indian shrub, the leaves of which are in great veneration. At no great distance are a cloud of worshippers of Virginia tobacco; they are divided into no less than four different sects. The first of whom worship the tobacco in the neat leaf, cut small, or well rolled together. The second worship it after it is well ground into flour. The third put it through the fire to the dear sensation. And the fourth are of such a Catholic disposition, that they worship the dearly beloved tobacco in all its forms. [Of this last sect the Listener professes himself.]

The belly is worshipped by many, as the principal god, and so profuse are they in their offerings, that its altar is sometimes almost overturned, and the idol, greedy as it is, is unable to bear the fruits of their devotion. The sect of gluttons, a devout race, ransack both earth and sea to bring plenty of offerings to the idol; and that of drunkards, in no less devotion, pour on the wines in such profusion, that all the surrounding trenches are gorged to the brim. This same idol differs exceedingly from most other objects of idolatrous worship; for when it has swilled to excess in the drink-offering, it invites the brain to share in the feast, to which it presents every vaporish effluvia, whilst it reserves for its own use only the parts excrementitious. Moreover, this same belly is apt to resent the profusion of its worshippers, and sends forth the bluest plagues, most chilling agues, burning, putrid and malignant fevers, with all manner of acute and chronical distempers, amongst the worshippers, and thus provides employment for gentlemen of the faculty; whose business positively would be worse than that of a cobbler, but for the religion of belly-worshipping.

In the fourth county dwell the worshippers of gold and large possessions, some of whom you will find lying prostrate, in the deepest devotion, to a fine well-situated house and garden; others worshipping a fertile estate and well-stored barns, a flock of fleecy sheep, or an herd of fattening bullocks. One man adores the brace of nags, which hurl him from place to place, whilst his friend is prostrate before a splendid retinue. Moidores, as well as English coin, is a splendid idol, and attracts the attention of many, whilst some adore a coal-pit, or a mine of leaden ore.

Had I time, I would give you a more full account of the religious idolaters; but as business is urgent, I shall only touch upon some of their gods. The greatest of which is his holiness the present pope, who dispenseth blessing and cursing, casteth down and exalteth at his pleasure. This god, who is exalted above all that is called God, issueth dispensations and pardons, for money and price, contrary to the manner of the God of heaven. The one pardons and gives salvation freely of grace, but the other sells his pardons as dear as he can. Next to his holiness, on the right hand, stands the popish Juno, or virgin Mary, whose powerful command of the God of nature, is greatly adored by every zealous papist. On the left hand stands a Jesus Christ of wood, whom the papists also highly revere; for they are, almost to distraction, fond of wooden deities. Some indeed have a Jesus Christ made of gold or silver, and others, more lowly, worship a paper Savior; but the most humble devotion is paid to the gods which the baker makes. These are the most ravenous idolaters in the whole world; for, with the greatest eagerness and devout veneration, they eat the object of their adoration. Thousands of these breaden gods are devoured annually, and as soon as devoured, they are replaced by others from the sacred ovens. The people, worship, and service of the true Jesus of Nazareth, they abhor and persecute with as much fury as ever their ancestors the Romish pagans did. But if their own godsmiths, carvers, or statuaries, happen to produce a handsome Jesus Christ, or a mother of God, the country will presently wonder after it, in the most profound adoration.

Discordans. I have sometimes thought, brother, that the popish religion is the religion of Moloch inverted. That voracious idol was used to devour the children of his worshippers; but here the greedy worshippers devour their god, after he is well baked in an oven.

Infidelis. The ancient pagans were even foolish enough, in giving their children to that greedy devil, Moloch; and the papists are not much wiser in worshipping the works of the artificer, or believing that they can eat their Maker Here are, likewise, the greatest variety of venerable relics, such as St. Peter's beard, the ear of St. Francis, the milk of the virgin, with a thousand fooleries besides, all of which are in some sense deified.

Besides these already mentioned, there dwell in this province, all who worship their ancestors, which renders the country very populous. I mean those who hold the canons, confessions, and liturgies composed by their ancestors, to be nearly equal to the scriptures in authenticity. Likewise, those who are of this or that persuasion, merely because it was the faith of their progenitors, without giving themselves the trouble of searching the scripture, to know the truth of the doctrine. It is also here that the worshippers of the sacerdotal livery dwell. I mean those who venerate a man merely for the sake of his gown and cassock, without inquiring whether his doctrine and conversation render him venerable.

But I should tire your patience, was I to give you a minute description of my vastly extended country, as well as lead you to imitate the sloth of the children of men. I shall therefore beg leave here to desist. At the usual time I will meet you. Business calls me hence at present.

DIALOGUE XVII.

ALL THE DIALOGEANS PRESENT.

Privy to their appointment, I made business give way to curiosity, and I was as punctual in my attendance as they were in theirs. At the same time before agreed to, they assembled, resumed their seats, and Fastosus thus began:

Fastosus. It is true, sir, your son Avaro hath greatly exceeded my expectations, and proves himself to be an expert devil. He will, I think, do honor to the name of Infidelis, and may greatly contribute to the flourishing estate of the kingdom of pride. I should be glad if Avaro might now a little enlarge upon the hints he has already given, that we may further see the prosperity of our general interest.

Discordans. That will be very grateful to me, cousin Avaro, as your sordid and griping influences have the most happy effect upon the reign of contention. How have I been delighted, when one of your slaves has dropped into the grave, leaving behind him vast possessions, by the discord I have sown amongst his children and kinsfolks! Your slaves dare not think of dying and entering into another world; therefore it sometimes happens, that after the muck-worm has been, by every means, and every kind of rapine, scraping wealth together for many years, he drops into eternity, without leaving behind him any authentic direction how his plunder is to be disposed of. This gives me a fair opportunity of setting his relations together by the ears, about who shall get most of the miser's effects to himself; and I have the happiness, frequently, of planting irreconcilable enmity in the heart of one brother and sister against another, which, you know, is a comfortable sight to our infernal nobility.

Sometimes, the griping miser, that enemy to himself and all mankind, is over-persuaded to make his will, though secretly hoping he shall not die for a great while yet to come; and then the case is very little altered: for when the wretch goes to the place appointed for the covetous, his will is unsatisfactory to some of the relations; one has too much, and the other has too little left him. Here, disagreeable altercation succeeds the funeral obsequies, and division and everlasting disgust sums up the whole. Unless, indeed, that relation who has too little bequeathed to him, should call in the gentlemen of the law to decide the matter in some court of judicature; and who, having fleeced both the fools, as handsomely as the nature of the thing would admit of, refer them at last to an arbitration.

I assure you, cousin, I scarcely ever see one of your industrious slaves, but I flatter a hope of having some employment in his family on his demise; nor do I know any other real use that the miser's ill-gotten money is of to society, besides sowing discord amongst friends and relations The wretch meanly robs his own back and belly, as well as all he deals with, to answer purposes no more valuable by his having. But I prevent you, cousin.

Avaro. I cannot easily depart from the tent of the scarlet lady, whose name is mystic Babylon, without making farther honorable mention of her prudent children. The wise disposal of purgatorial fire has been already exemplified, and the dispensation and pardon market has been glanced at; but one way of getting money besides these I shall now instance. I have laid my claim to the popish clergy in general; but of them all, there are none who exceed the worthy lords, the inquisitors, in veneration of my golden image. This religion of the golden image was first invented by the clergy of Babylon, and I assure you, to this day, the clergy of Babylon invariably follow it. But the inquisitors, of all others, are the most zealous devotees of the golden god, first set up by the parsons of Babylon.

Never did any eagle look out for a dove, nor an hawk for a sparrow, with greater vigilance than their lordships are wont to look out for a prey. If, within their jurisdiction, there happens to be a stranger, whose circumstances are prosperous, and who is likely to be a good bone for their reverences to pick; it shall go hard but they will provoke him, by some of their emissaries, to say something against the inquisitive tribunal, which, in some countries, is deemed the unpardonable sin. No sooner has the insinuating priest, by indirect means, obtained matter of accusation, but he makes information in the holy office, before the fathers, who, on hearing the blessed report, are as much delighted as the wolf, when he has fanged a prey. The merchant is apprehended, his estate confiscated; he is immured in the prison cells until consumed, either by famine or vermin, otherwise he is tortured privately to death, by the hands of their sanctified ruffians.

One instance, of the many which I might produce, shall serve to exemplify the equity of the inquisitors. When Syracuse was in its glory, there was one Bellarius, a foreign merchant, who, in the course of business, had amassed great riches; and who, at the same time, was so circumspect in all his ways, that even the eye of an emissary of the office could find nothing, of which to accuse him to the tribunal. Thus he lived in reputation and affluence for many years, to the great impatience of the holy inquisitors, who could find no plausible pretence, by which they might fang his substance with their rapacious talons.

Bellarius had an only child, a lady about seventeen. Her person was the perfection of symmetry, and her mind a copy of the purest virtue. By her they found means to accomplish their purposes, and bring complicated ruin on the unhappy parent. The family, retired to peaceful repose, were one night alarmed about one o'clock, first by the approach of a coach, and then by a smart rapping at the gate. Bellarius from within asking 'Who is there?' was answered, 'The holy inquisition.' Down stairs he ran, flew to the gates, in obedience to the dread tribunal, and opened to receive those ministers of darkness. Understanding they were come for his daughter, in farther obedience to those leaders of the church, he went himself up to her chamber, brought her down trembling as she was, and delivered her into the hands of the horrid ravishers, who carried her off to the seraglio, in the office of the inquisition; where for the present we leave her, through fear of death, seduced from her virtue, by those pretended patrons of religion, and return to the unhappy disconsolate father.

IMPIATOR. Well, brother, I find then the priests of Rome are not so much addicted to eunuchry as they pretend. It is lawful, it seems, to ravish virgins, however unlawful it may be to have a married wife. I have often heard of the seraglio of princes, but not so often of the seraglio of priests, and those priests too, who, of all others, are the most zealous wanderers after the seven-headed beast.

AVARO. Distressed and comfortless, Bellarius remained at home; forsook all company, and conversed only with the various cogitations of his own foreboding mind. At one time, he conjectured that his hapless daughter, in some inadvertent moment, might have blasphemed either the wooden virgin Mary, or the great high-priest of Rome, or the holy inquisitors; in which case, he gave her up for lost, and doomed her to fall a sacrifice. Yet he could scarcely forgive the rigor of that religion, which had in such a merciless manner ravished her from his fond embrace.

It was not long after this, an Armenian merchant, said to be newly arrived in Syracuse, called on him, under pretence of buying a large assortment of goods. Generous and unsuspecting, Bellarius bid him welcome to his house, during his stay; which he, after some seemingly modest apologies, thankfully accepted. The pretended Armenian, perceiving Bellarius to eat but little supper, and now and then inadvertently to let slip a sigh, took occasion to rally him, in a friendly manner, as if troubled with the hyp', advising him to cheer up and hope for better times.

Bellarius, having but little relish for a jest, seriously replied, 'No, sir, the hyp' is not my present disease, neither have my affairs in trade taken an adverse turn; and yet there is one thing which gives me great distress.' The friendly Armenian was now more importunate to know his grievance, that he might at least sympathize with him in his affliction. Little suspecting that he was conflicting with priestly subtility, he thought he might safely lodge his circumstances in the generous bosom of a merchant. He replied, Sir, I suppose you are a stranger in Syracuse; as such, let me advise you, as you value your life and liberty, to be careful of your words, and every part of your deportment, during your abode; for this is is a place of danger. I have, sir, one only daughter, the perfect image of her lovely mother, whom I had the misery to bury but a few months ago. I know not by what temptation, but my poor girl has said something dishonorable, either of the lady of Loretto, his holiness the pope, or their lordships the inquisitors, for which she is imprisoned in the holy office, and I suppose must answer it with her life.

Oh, sir, I hope not, said the Armenian; the lady's youth will intercede for her, and after some gentle admonition, your daughter will be returned to the house of her father.

Ah, sir, rejoined disconsolate Bellarius, I cannot but fear that her youth and beauty are her greatest enemies and accusers. These are qualities capable of impressing the heart even of an inquisitor. If this is the case, my poor daughter is already either dead or debauched. Or should it happen, that any thing has been alleged against her religious conduct, there are instruments enough in the inquisition, and their lordships want not skill to use them; instruments sufficient to make an helpless virgin confess that, which even never entered her thoughts: so that, at all events, her death or dishonor is insured. No, sir, it is not possible for me to hope for better, seeing the least hint thrown out against the inquisition, is condemned as unpardonable blasphemy.

It was not long after this discourse, before the Armenian feigned a necessity of going out; went straight to the inquisition, and made information, being a Jesuit disguised as a merchant; and that very night a coach was sent to conduct Bellarius to the cells of their dreadful prison. Next day his effects were seized by order of the holy fathers, who now rejoiced that at last they had grasped the long wished for prey. Confined in an abominable cell, he was greatly annoyed by vermin; and, being divers times examined by torture, he died with grief for his daughter, who, as she could never freely yield to the lothesome embrace of those murderers, in a few months tired their patience. Then one of their sanctified ruffians first murdered her, and then burned her to ashes in the dry pan. It is amazing, gentlemen, to what lengths the lust of money and women will carry men.

FASTOSUS. Indeed, cousin, I think your friends, the inquisitors, bid fair for equalling the most subtil of our fraternity. Oh what means of procuring wealth have you taught their reverences of the Romish hierarchy! Selling of dispensations and pardons, begging of money for masses, &c. &c. are profitable articles, and turn to a good account. But, if I remember right, you told me a few days since, your vassals are divided into several companies, or communities, and that people of all kingdoms, ranks, and professions, are, at this day, worshippers of the god Avaro. I should be glad to hear something farther about them.

AVARO. I did so, sir, and shall be ready farther to oblige you, if to give you a brief view of our corporation, which, like all other towns corporate, consists of divers companies, will do it. The first of which is that of

The lawyers. A very wise set of gentlemen; who exceed the children of light, in the art of money-getting, as far as any of the inhabitants of our territories; of course they are held in great estimation, as gentlemen of the first intelligence. In our city of Avarice, there is no knowledge deemed of any avail, no conduct accounted virtuous, besides that of money-getting. He is always the wisest, best, and most virtuous man, who best succeeds in the lucrative art, whether in law, or in trade, or otherwise. There was a time, you know, when the law was as straight, as clear as a beam of light, and needed no expounding, so that every man was his own counsellor. But ever since the kings of England were kept prisoners under a guard, lest truth should become familiar to the royal ear, the case has been quite altered; now it is so full of pleas and demurrers, doubts and exceptions, &c. that it is a perfect labyrinth; dangerous for an honest man to enter. For, in the lawyers' company, it is a standing rule, that, whether the plaintiff or defendan lose the cause, the lawyers, on both sides, are sure to be considerable gainers. Indeed, it is very seldom, but they manage the matter so, that all parties, except themselves, are losers; and if he who gains the trial, finds himself in the end to be a loser, how do you think it must fare with the wretch, against whom the verdict is given? If an honest man has a mind to purchase an estate ever so fairly, and pay for it ever so honestly, he will find it a difficult matter, so to secure his title, but if any succeeding heir be bred to the law, or heiress be married to a lawyer, he may run a risk of being jostled out of his property, by some knavish quirk in law, without any allowance made either for the estate or its improvements.

Indeed, sir, it may be said of my faithful disciples, the lawyers, attorneys, bailiffs, &c. that they pay as little regard to truth as the greatest of ourselves. Right and wrong, equity and oppression, are no objects of their regard, providing the case will yield good advantage, and bring large grist to their mill; an instance of this, if you please, gentlemen, I shall give you.

Contumelius was a Yorkshire gentleman, of distinguished birth and ample fortune, but somewhat akin to the mad Macedonian. His country-seat stood by the side of a lane, through which neighboring farmers passed with their teams, from time immemorial. But so much passing and repassing, of the whistling clowns, following their wagons, at last proved very offensive to the worshipful 'squire, so that he resolved to remove the intolerable nuisance, by blocking up the way. A gate was accordingly put up, and fastened with a padlock, effectually to stop the clownish passengers from passing as before, and turn them by a way considerably more distant.

As soon as the 'squire's proceeding reached the ear of Mr. Loveright, a neighboring farmer, he ordered his wagon to drive directly to the gate, and finding it locked, took an ax, which he brought with him for that purpose, and, to the great mortification of 'Squire Contumelius, hewed it to pieces. His worship, in a rage, posted to Mr. Deceitful, a very eminent lawyer in a neighboring town, for his advice. The worthy lawyer, finding this a proper occasion of serving his own interest, advised the 'squire to send for a writ, and commence an action against the farmer for his intolerable insolence. In a few days, the writ was served on Loveright, who immediately waited on lawyer Deceitful, in order, if possible, to compromise the matter.

He no sooner entered the office, than Mr. Deceitful took him aside, and thus addressed him: I am heartily sorry, my good Mr. Loveright, that I have been in a manner obliged, by his worship Contumelius, to send for a writ against you. But I assure you, sir, in my opinion your side of the question is by much the safest; and might I advise, it would be to stand a trial, and by no means submit to a compromise. Knowing the farmer to be a man of substance and resolution, he continued, There is no bearing with such insolent treatment. For my own part, Mr. Loveright, I would much rather you had been my client, on the present occasion, than the giddy 'squire; but he first applied to me, and insisted on my doing what I have done. If you please, you may apply to my brother Falsehood, who is skilful as any man, and as honest as any lawyer I know. In the meanwhile, sir, you may depend on me as your real friend, ready to serve you, in every thing consistent with my reputation.

As soon as Loveright was departed, Mr. Deceitful took horse, and rode directly to the 'squire's house; told him the farmer had been with him, heartily repented of his folly and was very desirous of coming to terms of agreement. But were the case mine, said he, I would listen to no terms of accommodation, but punish his insolence to the utmost rigor of law. The low-life fellow, having got forward in the world, has forgotten himself; and, if suffered now to escape with impunity, he will be the pest of the neighborhood. Thus the worthy lawyer irritated both parties, until he had made sure of an assize hearing, that, in the debate, he might likewise insure to himself a sum very considerable. For he knew very well, that if ever a difference falls into the insatiable maw of the court, it will never be disgorged, until all costs of suit are amply paid off; for it is impossible for my mercenary scribblers to give any credit. Let them act justly or unjustly they make sure of their fees; and, as the one party must necessarily lose, both counsellor and attorney take care to father the miscarriage of the cause, on something which the client has done, which he ought not; or omitted, which he ought to have done: and, notwithstanding all their fraud and deceit, both of them come off good honest lawyers.

The second company, and next in reputation to that of the lawyers, is the parson's company, which is also very flourishing and reverend. That you may not mistake my meaning, by parsons, I intend all, in general, of every denomination, who are ministers merely for the sake of a living; more especially,

1. All who profess to my lord bishop, that they are moved by the Holy Ghost, to take upon them the office of a deacon, when, in reality, it is the hope of a benefice, by which they are stimulated; and who, afterwards, in the course of their pulpiteering, tell the people that it is enthusiasm in any person, to expect to receive the Holy Ghost in these days.

2. All who, sustaining the sacerdotal character, lead men into sin, or harden those who are insensible, either by conniving at the sins of their people, or by being guilty of the like themselves. These gentlemen are pretty numerous.

3. All who act rigorously towards their parishioners, in regard to temporal things, who evidently show more concern about tithes and offerings than about the everlasting welfare of their people.

4. All in holy orders, who, through covetousness, idleness, or any other unjustifiable cause, withhold from their people the stated ministration of the word and ordinances. Set a mark upon them, for they are all my disciples.

5. Wherever you meet with a gentleman in holy orders, who is so far above the bulk of his auditory, that he will not condescend to converse even with the meanest about the state of his soul, the work of the Spirit, and way of salvation, such are idle shepherds, unnatural pastors, and altogether devoted to the god Avaro.

IMPIATOR. So then, cousin, I find you have parsons of more denominations than one; they are not all engrossed by the established churches in England and on the continent, it seems. Yet I meet with many who, with great warmth, will vindicate their own denomination by wholesale, and deem it little less than blasphemy, to suppose that they embrace any thing erroneous. Yet none more ready to censure and condemn those who are of a different persuasion in religious things.

AVARO. The truth is, my parsons are scattered abroad, among all sects of professors; for the time is not yet come, that any one sect can justly assert, that none of their ministers have any other object in view but the glory of God, and the good of mankind. Nor will the time commence, before that important question, 'who shall be the greatest?' is finally decided; which it is thought will be a great while first, seeing it hath already puzzled the schoolmen and leaders of the church for sixteen centuries back.

But, to return to the parsons' company; wherever you meet with a clergyman, who answers the description I have given, you need not ask him whether he is a churchman or a dissenter. All you have to do, is to put Beelzebub's mark upon his forehead, and take assurance of him, that, at a certain time, he shall not fail to visit the nether regions, and take his abode in the infernal palace.

In this very populous company, there is great diversity of ranks, even where there is an equality of genius; for some, having scarcely finished their apprenticeship, are inducted into livings, and instantly commence rectors and tithe-gatherers. Others, for want of friends, are obliged, much against their inclination, to continue underlings all the length of a tedious life. I have seen a handsome parson, ere now, riding upon four or five steeples at once, and having more in expectation; whilst his fellow-student could scarcely procure brown bread and Welsh butter. And amongst all the pluralists in my acquaintance, I know not of one that has got livings enough; but, Give, give, is still their fervent prayer to my lord bishop, or some other patron, who has a benefice to bestow. Many, indeed, think they should be quite contented, if they had but one more benefice added to what they now enjoy; but I can tell you, could they come by another, there would still be another wanting. It is much, now so many clergymen find themselves uneasy in the trammels, if they do not at last take it into their heads to persuade the legislature, that a clergyman cannot preach in three or four churches at one and the same time; and that it is not perfectly consistent, either with Christianity or reason, that one clergyman should have three or four livings, whilst another has none. Should it come to this, my company must be terrible suffeiers.

IMPIATOR. One would really think, if the cure of souls .s as weighty a concern as some people make it, the parsons would not be so fond of pluralities; of adding living to living, and parish to parish.

AVARO. The cure of souls, forsooth! My parsons care not who take the souls. The fleece, cousin, the fleece, attracts their attention. Give an avaricious parson the fleece, and you may make fairies of the souls of the parishioners, if you will. Many of them do very little of the priest's office, besides collecting the tithes and offerings; at which they are wonderfully dexterous. But as to preaching they have no notion of it, and less still of visiting the sick, were they even in the jaws of death. I assure you, gentlemen, those idle shepherds are of the greatest use to our government. The interest of hell could not prosper as it does, were we not well befriended by many gentlemen in holy orders.

FASTOSUS. Indeed, cousin, I have often thought that without their assistance, we should be ill put to it to maintain our ground, against the votaries of Immanuel. What posting to and from hell is there amongst our sable brethren, when but one faithful and zealous gospel minister arises in a nation? You may remember when Luther and Calvin broke the chain of the pope and devil, lifted up the voice of the gospel trumpet, which resounded through the bowels of hell, and made the pillars of our infernal kingdom totter, what hurly-burly we all were in! What deep consultations in the divan! What diligence in action with our forces upon earth!

AVARO. True, sir, but times are much altered for the better. Many a well-paid parson, now-a-days, is so obliging as to sing a lullaby to his people, when he finds them snoring in the sleep of security, and will suffer no man to attempt their awakening. He kindly tells them, "that they may sleep on now, and take their rest, for the wolf is gone out of the country, and will not for a great while return. Let no man disturb you with idle notions, for you may all go asleep to heaven, without ever knowing what conversion means."

INFIDELIS. It is admirable what power these same gentlemen have gotten over reason and religion. I have often thought, that if ever they were to read their Bibles with attention, they could not be off from seeing that they themselves are the identical persons intended by the idle shepherds, and unfaithful watchmen, against whom so many curses are denounced in scripture. The idle shepherds, you know, are such who feed and adorn themselves with the spoils of the flock, which is suffered to perish unwarned, and to die for lack of knowledge. The idle shepherd is that lordly priest, that downy doctor, who keeps at an awful distance from men of ordinary rank, and is too much of the gentleman to give himself any concern about the souls of his parishioners.

Many of those idle shepherds I know, who possess some hundreds, ay, some of them thousands per annum, who will not so much as ask one of their cure, whether he intends to go to heaven or hell at death, or whether he serves God or the devil; yet if a parishioner die, they will keep as penetrating a look-out for their fees, as an eagle for his prey, and seize it with equal eagerness. Moreover, for the sake of this same fee, they will own the deceased for a brother, which privilege was always denied him whilst alive, unless he should indeed have happened to be one of the fat of the flock, who was capable of yielding a double fleece.

Avaro. It is the fleece, sir, which my disciples regard, and not the flock. How have I been diverted sometimes, both at church and meeting-house, to hear the parson, with an air the most supercilious and contemptful, railing against the most useful of God's ministers, as enthusiasts, fanatics, and methodists! Ah! said I to myself, what poor honest devils were those of old, who confessed Christ and his disciples, and thus declared to the sons of Sceva, "Jesus we know, and Paul we know, but who are you?"

Sometimes I hear them crying with vehemence, against the divinity of Immanuel: one making him some kind of a super-angelical being, and another asserting that he is only a man, like themselves. Then say I, What a pusillanimous spirit was that same devil Legion, who, without receiving either tithe or offering, confessed Jesus of Nazareth to be the only Son of God, to whom the scriptures ascribe every divine honor! But these parsons are well paid for confessing him, and yet deny him with the utmost insolence.

There is never a day but I hear some of this company charging the lie upon one text or other of the Bible. One tells his people that there is no such thing, as one being chosen to salvation more than another; but that the love of God is equal unto, and upon all men, whether Jew or Gentile, Turk or Pagan, Papist or Protestant; nay, then, say I, master parson, you are become a dissenter from your own seventeenth article. And, to speak within compass, there are at least a thousand pulpits in the church occupied by such dissenters.

Then I hear others, railing against those who preach salvation by grace; and, at the same time, assuring their people, that they must be saved by their own holiness and good works. Very well, say I, then I have my desire, for upon these terms they will never be saved at all. But still I am at a loss, how they dare so barefacedly give the lie to Paul the apostle, who taught the church, that, "By grace they were saved through faith, and that not of themselves, but the gift of God." I hear many clergymen of the established church, in entering upon the service, thus address the Majesty of Heaven, "Lord, cleanse thou the thoughts of our hearts, by the inspiration of the Holy Spirit;" and in less than an hour after, telling their parishioners, that it is mere enthusiasm in any man to expect, in these days, to be at all influenced by the inspiration of the Holy Spirit.

So glaring the contradictions, which sometimes they are guilty of, that I tremble with fear, lest the people should be convinced of the truth; but these are favorable times, gentlemen, very favorable; for the greater part of the people have something else to think of, when they go to church, besides either preaching or prayer.

When I hear the parson, whether churchman or dissenter, telling his people how holy and pure the heart of man is by nature; how aptly formed for sentiments of the most exalted piety, and for entertaining the love of God; I am wonderfully at a loss to know, how he came by more extensive knowledge of mankind than Jesus Christ, who expressly taught, that whatsoever defileth the man proceeds out of the heart. Your influences, Fastosus, are of excellent use, in keeping them where they are; you take care to persuade each of them separately, that of all others his own knowledge is the most refined; and hence it is, that Goodwin,

Owen, Charnock, and all such authors, are considered as weak though well-meaning divines.

It is very diverting to hear my parsons boasting of their superior knowledge, even when by their ministrations it is plain, that they are acquainted with almost any writings, better than those of inspiration; when their auditories dwindle away to nothing, and the few people who abide by them are destitute of all religion. Did they but know half as much as the most illiterate devil of our fraternity, they would at least believe, that there may be a possibility of their mistaking the way, and that, after all their pretensions to a superior knowledge, they may run some risk of a final miscarriage. But, as our good friends, the Roman doctors, are wont to say, "Ignorance is the mother of devotion;" so say I of my parsons, "Ignorance is the spring of all their knowledge;" and whilst my father Infidelis can keep them ignorant, my uncle Fastosus can easily puff them up with a sense of the clearness of their heads, and goodness of their hearts; so that I can do very well with them, and retain them amongst our worshippers.

The next company in our corporation is that of the straining landlords, a very noble and reputable company indeed; notwithstanding, they are far from being opulent. In the days of yore, when luxury was but little in vogue, the freeholders were attended with fewer wants, and, of course, this company was less flourishing; but since these happy days commenced, in which people of quality are trained up in absolute idleness and dissipation: in which virtue is of no account, and luxury, pride, and dissoluteness are arrived at their zenith, the people of quality are amazingly poor, and are attended with an undescribable train of necessities. What is very remarkable, their pride has grown in a perfect proportion to their poverty, so that now it is an established law amongst them, to look upon themselves as of a different blood from the rest of mankind. Indeed you cannot affront a person of quality worse, that by likening him to one of those, who are called vulgar creatures; notwithstanding, by the way, it is those same vulgar creatures which enable persons of rank and fashion to support the dignity of their station; and were there no vulgar creatures, there would also be no ladies of quality.

This distinction, which the quality pay to themselves, is

of the utmost use in my administration, as will appear from the following story.

I went, one day, to the house of Sir Fop Mortalis, a very famous gentleman in the country, with a design to pay my devoirs to madam Mortalis, his lady; a gentlewoman, who abhors to have the least comparison made betwixt her and any person of inferior rank. The chambermaid informed her mistress, that good Mr. Prudence waited below, desiring to speak with her ladyship, if convenient. The lady soon descended, and, compliments passed on either side, she conducted me into her parlor, where she and I had the following dialogue.

LADY. Good Mr. Prudence, you have been a very great stranger. It is many months since I saw you at our house but I am glad to see you now, and I wish in my heart Sir Fop Mortalis had been at home.

PRUDENCE. Urgent business, madam, demands my attendance so much elsewhere, that I cannot so frequently as I could wish, pay my respects to Sir Fop and my lady Mortalis. But now, madam, I am come, if possible, to rectify a growing mistake amongst mankind; and must tell your ladyship, that I am heartily sorry to see the world arrived at such a pitch of ambition as it is now. Indeed, my lady, it is become a very difficult matter, in a concourse of people, to distinguish between the farmers' and tradesmen's wives, and ladies of birth and fortune; nor can we more easily distinguish between their several children. Why, madam, the farmers' and tradesmen's children are all masters and misses, young gentlemen and ladies, now-a-days. I know not, for my part, what the world will come to, if some measures are not speedily taken to prevent the confounding of baseness with dignity.

When I was last at church, I was surprised to see, as I thought, Miss Mortalis, your daughter, there; well knowing that neither Sir Fop himself, nor any of his family, go often to any place of public worship. Because you know, my lady, few of you great folks love the tedious duties of religion.

LADY. Not we, indeed. Give us the cards, or musical entertainments, for our money. We hate their whining, doleful cant. Let them choose religion who have taste for nothing more polite. We will have none of it, I assure you, Mr. Prudence.

PRUDENCE. I know it, my lady, I know it, and am mightily pleased with your determination. But, as I was telling your ladyship, being at church, as soon as service was over, I said to a man, who sat in the pew with me, 'I am surprised to see Miss Mortalis at church to-day. Do you think, sir, that anybody has been daring enough to tell her that she really is a mortal?' To which the plain countryman, in his own clownish way, replied, 'Miss Mortalis at church! quoth-a: no, no, sir, you are quite mistaken; for Sir Fop's family are people of quality, and therefore meddle none with religion. What should they do at church, seeing they fear no hell, regard not God, and believe not in the devil. As for heaven, Sir Fop is willing to leave that to the poor, and desires no greater happiness for himself and his, than is implied in an earldom.'

LADY. That is, indeed, what Sir Fop has long been soliciting, and it is believed is now very near obtaining.

PRUDENCE. But I said to the fellow, Pray who is that young lady, whom I took for Miss Mortalis? Poh, lady! quoth-a, why, 'tis John Tillground's daughter, o' the Five Elms. Tillground's daughter! said I; you surprise me. She is as finely drest as I have seen Miss Mortalis, when going to a ball. And pray, continued I, who is yonder lady, with the French head-dress and furred cardinal? I thought you had no people of quality in this parish besides Sir Fop's family. No, sir, returned he, we have none, who are such by birth; but we have many who are quality by their dress. The lady, sir, that you inquire after, is Mrs. Watson, the landlady at the Three Tuns.

Well, madam, I followed them out of church, and was amazed to see the plaitings of hair, the tires of ruffles, and the labyrinthian furbeloes, with which the women were decorated. Indeed, my lady, if the world holds on but a few years, in its present career, we shall not be able to distinguish betwixt the highest and the lowest ranks of people.

LADY. To be sure, sir, the world is now at a sad pitch of pride and ambition; for people of fashion can do nothing as to dress, gesture, manner of speech, or living, but we are mimicked by those vulgar creatures.

PRUDENCE. It must undoubtedly be considered as an insufferable insult upon people of breeding, when they are thus taken off by the vulgar. But, madam, I have a scheme to propose, which, if adopted, will effectually correct their insolence, and soon oblige John Tillground and Timothy Turf's daughters to lay aside their furbeloes, ruffles, and tea-table, and betake themselves to their spinning-wheels.

LADY. What is it? I pray you, good Mr. Prudence, be so obliging; I beg you would, sir.

PRUDENCE. Indeed, madam, your farmers are all become gentlemen of late. They talk of fortunes for their children, and consider themselves as very little inferior to the 'Squire himself. But let me tell you, madam, the fault is not so much in the farmers as in the landlords themselves, who let their farms upon terms by far too low and easy. There is this same John Tillground, and his neighbor Timothy Turf, as I am informed, have both of them money lying at interest, when my worthy and right honorable lord Noble, a gentleman of the first quality, is obliged to pawn his plate for cash, to pay off the four thousand pounds he lost the other night at cards; and whilst his gentle neighbor, 'Squire Fitzfolly, is obliged to fell his timber, to stop the horrid gap which his malevolent stars opened at Newmarket races, where the gamblers of rank and quality occasionally try their fortune.

It is insufferable, madam, that the farmers' circumstances should be easy, whilst people of fashion know not how to keep off the duns from their doors. What right has anybody to any thing besides slavery, except people of quality? Were not those vulgar creatures originally designed as your slaves, madam? And yet, for any thing I see, they will soon be on a level with you, unless some method, lucky enough to prevent it, is speedily devised.

LADY. Ah, sir, I fear it indeed. If you do know of any suitable means to prevent it, I beg, good Mr. Prudence, you will inform me.

PRUDENCE. There is only one way that I know of, madam, and that is to raise their rents to the uttermost. As every lease expires, it will be an easy matter for Sir Fop, in the renewal of it, to advance the rent as high as he pleases. The slaves dare not go away; and if they should, there will be others foolish enough to agree to any terms, rather than miss a farm. This done, and all your tenants settled upon the racked farms, if any of them happens to rear a handsome colt, let Sir Fop himself, or young master, fall in love with it, demand it of its owner for so much, never exceeding half its value; he may privately grumble, but dare not refuse, for fear of offending his honor. By these means, and others, which occasion will suggest, you may make them all humble enough.

Lady. Most excellently spoken, good Mr. Prudence. Then Tillground's wife will be obliged to sell her chinaware, to procure rags for her brats; the daughter must take to her wheel and wash-tub, and my son, master Thomas, will ride a better horse than he now does. This scheme will certainly conquer the ambition of the farmers; but will it do for the tradesmen, good Mr. Prudence? they will still continue an eyesore.

Prudence. Indeed, madam, the same scheme will produce very humbling effects upon tradesmen of every kind; though I dare not assert, that you will ever be able perfectly to subject to your ambition and avarice, that honorable body of merchants, whom you affectedly call cits. No, madam, I am afraid that nobility itself must give place to the public spirit of the merchant; yet even them you may greatly injure, and prevent their being of such essential service to their country, as otherwise they might be. But as to inland trade, by racking your tenants in the manner prescribed, you may absolutely destroy it. That you may see the utility of my scheme, I shall a little explain it to your ladyship.

If the farmers are racked to the utmost, they will be obliged to sell the produce of their lands at an exorbitant price, otherwise it will be altogether out of their power to pay the stipulated rent. And besides selling their crops, &c. for an advanced price, they will be obliged to abridge the wages of all their laborers, smiths, carpenters, &c.

By these means the farmer will find it difficult to live, and of course will rarely visit the mercer's and draper's shops; and as for his laborers and workmen, they will find but little money to lay out in clothes, especially if their children be numerous, as the demands of the back must always give place to the louder calls of the belly. And as you know, my lady, sterility very rarely dwells in the laborer's cottage, it is unknown what misery you may happily introduce amongst them, by the scheme proposed. The draper's goods will lie upon his hands, unless indeed he is pleased to give credit to the poor; if the former, he will be sparing of his orders; and if the latter, we shall soon have him a bankrupt, so that he will be effectually ruined.

You see, madam, that here we affect the manufacturer, equally with the farmer and shopkeeper: for when the retail trade is ruined by the dearness of the provisions, the manufacturer will find little call for his goods; the issue of which will be, the disbanding of many of his journeymen, and abridging the wages of the rest. The disbanded journeymen, being incapable of finding employment, and not having learned the art of living, like the cameleon, on the air, will be driven to thieving, by which means America will be peopled, and Tyburn Chronicle rendered respectable.

As to the manufacturer himself, his capital being soon converted into manufactured goods, he will be obliged to sell them under their value, that he may keep up his credit with the merchant, and be able to carry on a little trade, vainly hoping that times may alter for the better.

LADY. Indeed, sir, your scheme is very feasible; and yet there is one thing that will put the manufacturer absolutely out of our power. I mean, sir, the exportation of their manufactures. I do not know how it is, but these cits of merchants can send goods anywhere, and they, sir, will support the manufacturer.

PRUDENCE. No, madam, I assure you, my scheme, if cordially adopted, and executed with vigor, will put it absolutely out of the merchant's power. There is nothing can recommend the English manufacture at a foreign market, but the price being inferior to that of other nations. Now, if an Englishman must pay twice as dear for his provision in his own country, as a Frenchman does in his, it is easy to see that either journeymen's wages must, in England, be double to what they are in France, or the journeymen must starve; which few Englishmen are fond of doing. The consequence of this is, the French manufacturer can send his goods to a foreign market upon better terms than an Englishman, and, of course, destroy all the foreign trade of the English nation. Thus, madam, I have pointed out a method by which you people of fashion, in order to support your own grandeur, may suck the blood of all inferior ranks of people, and make the British subjects absolutely slaves, even in a country which boasts its freedom. Nay, more, this is a method by which you may ruin the most flourishing nation in the world.

LADY. Spoke like an angel, good Mr. Prudence. I protest, upon honor, I will not sleep until I have consulted Sir Fop on the matter.

AVARO. I took my leave of her ladyship, who could not rest until she had communicated the matter to her acquaintance, and they to their acquaintances, and so they again to theirs, that it had very soon made the tour of Great Britain and Ireland; an ordinance was instituted, in the company of avaricious landlords, that in every future lease, the farmers should be racked to the last extremity. This ordinance has been universally complied with, by the whole company; so that there is reason to hope, in time, all the blessed consequences proposed, will arise from it, as you see to what an exorbitant price all manner of provisions is already arrived. What may not be expected from such hopeful beginnings?

FASTOSUS. A noble company indeed, and near akin to our destroying clan. And yet many of them set up for patriots, even when they are drawing ruin upon the nation, by their pride, luxury, and avarice.

DIALOGUE XVIII.

ALL THE DIALOGEANS PRESENT.

FASTOSUS. No, Avaro; know assuredly that you are not more in esteem with the Dutch than myself. It were strange, indeed, if I had no concern with Mynheer.

AVARO. Indeed, sir, to see Mynheer equipped in his holiday clothes, he makes pretty near as awkward an appearance as a Laplander; and one would certainly conclude, that he is a perfect stranger to courtly Fastosus. But all the world knows, that Avaro is a very respectable personage in Holland.

FASTOSUS. I told you before, cousin, that you have an

ugly way of encroaching upon your neighbor's right. I do not like it cousin, and will assert my dominion. Do you think that Mynheer is not full as proud of his multiplicity of garments, as an English hero is of his scarlet and lace? Or, that he is not the best fellow who can wear the greatest numbers of pairs of breeches? I assert, there may be as much pride under a Dutchman's cap, as under a Scotch bonnet, or even under a Frenchman's hat; notwithstanding there is a very great difference between the first and the last. The first, you know, is a fixed ponderous substance, and the last is mutable, as the weathercock on the top of St. Peter's. Yes, Avaro, I may assert farther, that there may be as much pride under a red cap, as under the coronet of a peer, or even under the mitre of an archbishop.

INFIDELIS. That Avaro is in high esteem in the Netherlands, will not be denied; but to suppose Fastosus excluded from any people whatever, is highly dishonoring: therefore, my son, you must learn to be more cautious, and, for the present, to make atonement for your error, proceed with your account of your corporation.

AVARO. If to retract an error, and endeavor in future to oblige, will procure forgiveness, it shall be done. In order to which you will please to observe that the

Fourth Company of my corporation, is that of the letter retailers, otherwise called mercenary scribblers, and false publishers. The transcribers and abridgers of other men's works, and especially those whose sole aim is to get money by their writings, are free of this company and on the livery.

To give you a proper idea of which, I shall read you a letter, which I stole the other night, from the chairman of a reading society in the country, designed to be sent to the Reviewers, critical and monthly.

GENTLEMEN,

We are what country people call a reading society, into which we had formed ourselves some years before the first Review made its public appearance. We had not long taken in books, before we found several articles of our purchase to be stolen from other authors; and but very few of our titular authors, had either honor or honesty enough, to inform the public from what sources they compiled their volumes. We would advise all writers to live upon their own proper genius, deeming it pity that pilferers should be suffered in the republic of letters. At the last meeting of our club, this question was put and canvassed, "What can induce one writer to steal from another?"

To this important question, one replied one thing, and another said what he could to confute it, as every member was willing to display his abilities; at last, Dick Keene, a testy kind of youth, but of good sense, gave us the following satisfactory answer.

"Very probably, said master Dick, some authors may steal from others, for the same reason, which that celebrated fool of old had, who burnt himself and the temple together, in order to perpetuate his name. There are authors endued with the same laudable ambition, who, not being happy enough to be born free in the literary republic, are obliged to stoop to dishonest measures, in order to gratify their ambition. Their geniuses (if it be lawful to speak of their geniuses) being destitute of every prolific principle, and their fancies fixed as the Pyrenean or the Alps, they cannot possibly gain repute but on the credit of their predecessors. Therefore, what frugal nature, and Gamaliel have withheld, must be supplied by industrious freedom; and as the end proposed, must, at all events, be obtained, honor, truth, and honesty, smoke at once on the altar of ambition. To work goes the writer, plunders every volume in his own and his patron's library, at last completes his scheme; and lo! we have an entire new work, by the learned Mr. Dunce. And so it comes to pass, that we, the honest purchasers, pay three or four times over for the same matter; and perhaps, in almost the same manner likewise.

"There are others, who, as a just judgment on their former indolence and extravagance, are now condemned to live upon their wit; which being dull and tardy, somewhat akin to the brain of an ass, of itself can afford but a very penurious table, and uncomfortable lodging. Bitten with hunger, the unhappy man is obliged to steal where he can, and then sell his ill-gotten collection to the bookseller, in order to procure a good holiday dinner. The bookseller, I believe, is pretty well convinced of the truth of my remarks, as he has paid for his connexion with literary thieves.

"Of these two kinds of pilferers, in my humble opinion, the latter is by far the most excusable. He cannot work, he is ashamed to beg, therefore must either steal or starve. What can he steal with more safety than the works of the learned? in my opinion, there is no more danger in robbing a gentleman of his literary honor, than for a statesman to rob his mother country: few such thieves are conducted, by the county officers, to Tyburn. O solemn tree, what frauds are committed against thee! Of how many necks, equitably thine, art thou cheated annually!"

It was now Bill Candor, a good-natured youth, interrupted him, thinking his reflections somewhat severe. Hold! Mr. Keene, I think your reasoning is too full of acrimony. If all transcripts, extracts, and abridgements, were to be suppressed, it would be a very great loss to the public. Those men, therefore, who take the trouble of such a service, deserve open acknowledgment, for raising up valuable authors from the vaults of oblivion, instead of being lashed with the rod of merciless satire." To which Dick replied:

"That many ancient writings are truly worthy of being introduced to public view, I am so far from denying, that I should deem it truly laudable, for any gentleman of capacity and leisure, to draw forth the remains of antiquity from the cells of obscurity, and should be one of the first to vote him the most public thanks. But I would have it done in such a manner, as to come within the reach of the middle classes of people, amongst whom the bulk of all sorts of readers are found. Moreover, I would have all writings on religious subjects so contrived, as to come within the reach of the poor, for who else give themselves any trouble about religion, or have any pleasure in serious writings? If a commentary on the Bible must go beyond the extent of their finances, it might as well be locked up in Pool's Synopsis, where it was before the commentary was written. Opulent tradesmen, you know, are such slaves to the laws of getting, that they have no time to read, and therefore may prudently avoid purchasing. And people of fashion are generally perfectly satisfied with having such or such books in their libraries, without so much as looking farther into them than the title-pages. Surely, gentlemen, no man is to be vindicated in making merchandise of his neighbor's genius."

Here he concluded, and we were soon convinced, that there was much weight in his reasoning. We must beg leave to tell you, gentlemen, that when your worships erected your tribunal, and every author was summoned to appear before you, we flattered a hope, that all pilferers would have fled out of the republic of letters. But alas! we have been hitherto disappointed, and in reality, they seem to be on the increase, so that a man can hardly claim personal right to a single idea, how justly soever it may be his property.

We earnestly beg that you, gentlemen, will be obliging enough to publish your aversion to this craft; to command all who are destitute both of fortune and genius to reconcile themselves to their destiny, and show their submission to the higher powers, by learning some handicraft business, by which they may gain an honest living. There are a thousand ways to live in this world, if that of an author were to cease. For instance, there is carrying a musket, or beating a drum by land, and furling the sails by sea, either of which are honorable employments, when compared with that of book-stealing.

As we know not to whom we can apply, with any degree of success, but to yourselves, we must farther beg, that you will not only detect the theft when you meet with it, but do as the worthy inhabitants of St. Giles's do on similar occasions. That is, pursue the delinquent with a Stop thief! Stop thief! Indeed, gentlemen, it will not lessen you in the public esteem, should you commence even literary thief catchers. Should it please you to comply with our request, we doubt not but the streets which lead to places of public resort, will in a few years be well lined with many authors, having assumed the more honorable employment of a beggar.

Thus the imposts would be taken off from the studious; real authors would preserve their honor, no one daring to invade their rights, for fear of exposing themselves to public infamy. Perhaps that most villanous of all practices may be put a stop to; we mean the vending of cloudy commentaries on the Bible. Few people, we should think, would be fond of purchasing such books, after they are informed that most of the materials are stolen. Effectually to put a stop to this iniquitous practice, we would recommend the publication of the above named Synopsis in English, and then every reader may take what human sense of the divine word he pleases. We are, gentlemen, your most humble servants,

A READING SOCIETY.

FASTOSUS Indeed, cousin, I think the request of that society reasonable enough, and ought to be granted: for, as the world now goes, it is a difficult matter for a man to know to whom he is obliged, for any profitable hint he meets with in the course of his reading. And flimsy as modern productions in general are, there is now and then a profitable hint to be met with. But when any thing of a recommendatory quality happens to emerge from the teeming press, the whole race of catch-penny imitators swarm about it, and gobble it up, then spew it out, as if it were their own. However, cousin, it must be owned, that there are some of your mercenary scribblers, who are much more honorable than others; and let the public know, that what they write is not the fruit of their own genius, but is borrowed from this or that respectable author, under pretence of making it more public, on account of its great excellency. They desire not to rob the author of his honor! All they deem necessary, is a loan of his genius to supply the defects of their own, and to help them a little forward in the world.

But of all writers, commend me to polemic divines. O! it would be a pleasure to the devil himself, to see with what dexterity they put off their own anger, under the name of zeal for God; just as the industrious tradesmen of Birmingham do their manufacture for the coin of the nation. It is amazing to think how Protestant ministers can lug the Almighty into both sides of their quarrel: and how they would make the world believe that their cause is the cause of heaven, and that they have got authority to dispense the curses of the Most High. Nothing can be more pleasing, than to see men of wisdom and religion, vigorously contending for their own honor, and at the same time making the public believe they have nothing in view but the Redeemer's glory. And I assure you, it is not every divine, even of great parts, who takes time to distinguish between the glory of God and his own reputation.

Next to this, I am delighted to see men of learning and

religion, bickering with each other about subjects which the greatest of all apostles would not presume to pry into. But we have divines so expert, that they understand what never was revealed; and so zealous that they will oblige others to have the same degree of intelligence with themselves, under pain of their implacable displeasure; and yet they are the true ministers of the meek and loving Savior. But a very few are to be met with, who have humility enough to submit to the simplicity of scripture. However, cousin, although I love to set forth my own powerful influence, I would not willingly prevent your proceeding with your story. Meanwhile, I want you to be more explicit, with regard to your company of letter venders. Do you mean by them printers in general?

Avaro. No, gentlemen, I do not mean, either all the booksellers or printers. Printing has been to mankind one of the greatest of all temporal blessings; and will, I much fear, be the total ruin of the kingdom of darkness; as, wherever the freedom of the press is suffered, it carries reformation along with it. But, amongst those concerned in literary affairs, there are many villanous people, who, when their trade runs low, take up with printing corrupting novels, such as the Memoirs of a Woman of Pleasure; blasphemous plays. such as Sammy Foote's Minor; schismatic harangues, like the greater part of political essays; vain disputes about things of trivial import, &c. All such, and many such there be, we rank with the false publishers, because truth and falsehood are, with them, of equal value, and their choice is fixed by what will serve a present turn. The patriotic alderman is a leading man in this learned company. He has not learned so little by the gift of second-sight, which he has had from his cradle, as not to know, that more than truth is indispensably necessary, to support some particular personal characters. Besides, there are others, who will sell both soul and body to the father of lies, in defence of some particular state: and others, to ruin some public character. The celebrated Mr. Maubert, of Brussels, is a great man in this way.

Free of this company, are another set of men, implacable enemies to honest industry, who live altogether by their wit; appear in all shapes and characters, and stick at nothing to get money. Although these people have nothing but grimace to sell, (through a folly, formerly almost peculiar to the metropolis, but now diffusing itself everywhere) they have, for six months in the year, a very plentiful market; and many, who would suffer the miserable to perish unrelieved at their gates, will liberally contribute to support the luxury and libertinism of the players. In the days of yore, the devil Proteus was, but now David Garrick, Esq. is, their foreman; a fast friend to our government, and a faithful disciple of careful Avaro.

Discordans. I think you must be mistaken now, cousin; for the end of all theatrical entertainments, which I perceive you have in view, is the exposing of vice and reformation of manners: consequently, their design was originally religious.

Avaro. I allow, that in the darkness of paganism, the ancients had a religious design, in exhibitions of the stage; but what of that? They had likewise a religious design, in passing their children through the fire to Moloch. I allow, farther, that in the days of monkish ignorance, these blinking priests made use of the stage to convey their instructions; but then it ought to be observed that the same fathers were equally pious and devout, in persecuting the best of men. So then, cousin, the one is as much authorized by ancient practice as the other. Indeed, when you consider that the stage is peopled by extravagant, spendthrift gentlemen, broken tradesmen and lazy mechanics, who always were avowed enemies to moral integrity, they will appear to be a very unpromising race of reformers.

Should you follow them from the stage to their lodgings, and trace their steps through the lanes of private life, you would soon be convinced, that Sir John Fielding's runners bid much more fair than they, for reforming the manners of the people. And you know, the said runners have never as yet been considered as the most respectable characters. Surely it must be thought requisite in those who set up for reformers of others, that, in some tolerable degree, they should moralize themselves.

Discordans. I know it, cousin; and I thwarted you on purpose, to see how you could justify your claim upon the gentry of the stage; and must confess you have done it to my satisfaction. I am highly pleased with the entertainments of the theatre myself, and am greatly delighted to see gentlemen and ladies crowd to them. Gentry, who would worship God in neither church nor meeting-house, can be devout enough to attend the theatres, in Covent Garden and the Hay Market. It is truly pleasing to see gentlemen and ladies, who cannot possibly find money to pay off their tradesmen's bills, find plenty of cash to purchase playhouse tickets.

INFIDELIS. As we came along, cousin Discordans, you mentioned some sport you lately had with two female companions. Pray, what of them?

DISCORDANS. You must know, Leonora and Matilda have been intimate from their infancy; and, as such, continued their friendship even to mature life: but, when both became wives and mothers, I taught them to behave more inconsistently than they did when they were children. Matilda, being quite fatigued with domestic concerns, for attention to which her mind is not very happily turned, resolved one day to spend an afternoon with her friend Leonora. When she went, she found her exceedingly depressed and hysterical, by no means in a talkative humor; a circumstance which frequently happens to the ladies of middle rank, ever since luxury and idleness became so prevalent amongst them.

Matilda, not being sufficiently skilled in physiognomy, to read the sentiments of the heart by the position of the features of the countenance, was led into a mistake, which proved fatal to their friendship. She discovered, or thought she discovered an unusual and unexpected shyness run through every part of Leonora's conduct; which discovery proved no slight mortification to her own sensibility. Said she to herself, 'Well, Leonora, I perceive, notwithstanding all your formal civility, that my company is not the object of your present desire. I wish I had been aware of it in time! Then, I assure you, my presence should not have drawn a cloud over that settled countenance of yours. But, indeed, madam, let my company be ever so disagreeable to you, yours, I assure you, is now very little more pleasant to me.'

Whilst she was meditating some plausible pretext for withdrawing, the tea was unhappily brought in, which precluded her removal for a little while longer. Thus constrained by decency to stay, her glowing resentment of the supposed slight, forbid her to taste a morsel of the toast, or to drink above two dishes of tea. Having finished, she pretended she must retire on some urgent business, which had just occurred to her mind, (for ladies will lie to serve a turn) and after a dry compliment or two she went off resolved never to return.

As she went along the streets, her wounded heart boiled with a thousand cogitations, how or when she had offended Leonora. 'What have I done, or said, that should have given her umbrage? I know of nothing: and therefore I care not for her anger. If people will be so odd in their temper, they must even come to themselves at their leisure. And so your servant, Leonora.'

INFIDELIS. That was a visit more innocent than many I have known, for I hear nothing of slander, or defamation of absent characters, carried on in it, which very rarely happens to be neglected in female visits.

DISCORDANS. True, sir, but the matter did not end here. Poor Matilda, being unable to bear the conceived slight, made free to call on Letitia, on her way home, that she might give a little vent to her turbulent passions. Letitia, being as destitute of innate ideas, as she is of fidelity, readily listened to the plaintive account, how Matilda had been served; without hesitation approved her departure, kindly fanned the flame of resentment, and at last advised her to let Leonora come to herself when she should find it convenient.

Matilda had not been long gone, before Letitia, who burned with impatience to have a little tittle-tattle, went to Leonora, and set Mischief abroad with her also. She told her all the former had said of her, and happily gave it such a turn as to render it very offensive, notwithstanding she kept strictly to the letter of truth. Some people are remarkably happy in talents of this kind: by their manner of representation, they can turn things quite from their natural appearance, as I may perhaps show you in some future conference. Leonora could not but think herself very ill-used, and resolved, weakly as she was, that she should be a slave to nobody's temper.

When Matilda and Leonora met next time, being prepossessed with mutual disgust, their compliments were dry and starched; and each secretly blamed the indifference of the other. By this time, I furnished each of them with a telescope, by which they might thoroughly examine each other's conduct, and so reciprocally strict is their mutual watch, that nothing can escape them. Thus from the smallest beginning, founded too in misunderstanding, I raised perpetual disgust and enmity. Absurd and ridiculous as this is, I could point you out a thousand differences, sprung from incidents equally frivolous and unimportant. Indeed, if Freedom and Submission keep at a distance, I can blow up a flame of contention the most violent, from the smallest matters imaginable. And I thank my stars, Messrs. Freedom and Submission are in no great esteem with mankind. But, wherever they come, they destroy my seeds, and effectually extinguish my flames, for they are irresistible peace-makers.

Fastosus. It is I, my son, who have brought those gentlemen into disrepute. I persuade people, it is beneath them to submit to their equals, how much soever they have been in the wrong. I have, ere now, persuaded one man to do all he could, to ruin the reputation of his neighbor in order to establish his own, when he found it in a tottering condition; and that too amongst those who take themselves to be more righteous than others.

Discordans. I have great pleasure, sometimes, in making parents become the instruments of their children's ruin. Or, as some people say, to kill them with kindness. I make it my business to prejudice almost every parent, so far in favor of his children, that every one considers his own as the most witty and active; or, to use the words of a good woman, concerning her son of two years old, the most manly of any child in the neighborhood, even as the crow conceives her own to be fairer than all the children of the feathered people.

I shall trouble you but with one instance, out of the millions I might produce. Little master Jacky was one of those extraordinary children, whose almost every action was out of the common way, the wonder and admiration of his astonished parents. Jacky must not be chid, when he pinched, bit, or scratched his nurse, but must have his own pretty little humor; it was even pleasing to see his lovely fist darted into his parents' faces. So, you may be sure, the child must not be suffered to cry upon any account, but must always be indulged in whatever he wanted. Thus this extraordinary child, in whom, however, none besides his parents could see any thing out of the common way, notwithstanding every visitor was plagued with the history of his wonderful feats, upon which his parents dwelt with raptures;—I say, Jacky found himself master of the whole family; he acted accordingly, and took his way in every particular.

By these means his tempers gained strength, so that they became habitual, not to be broken by ordinary means.

When he got a few more years over his head, still growing in his humor, the poor parents began to see and lament the errors of their former conduct. Too late: master Jacky being now in breeches and grown a great boy, will not readily give back that dominion they were pleased to put into his hands, when but in petticoats. He thinks it very hard he should not choose for himself now he is ten, as well as when he was but three years old; rightly judging, that he was not more wise then than he is now; and if they thought him fit to be all their masters then, he is sure that by this time he is much more fit to govern.

Apprehensive now of the ruin of his son, the father exhibits exhortations, injunctions, reproofs, and threatenings, with great severity. In vain, for not being bended whilst tender and malleable, master's tempers are not now to be turned out of their native channel. As, in former times, I plied the parents, in prejudice of their darling, it was now time to ply him also in his turn. I furnished him a pair of glasses, and directed him in the use of them; and now the youth began to reason upon his father's conduct.

"What a change is this come to my father? Once he was something like good-natured, but now he is the most self-willed and rigorous man in the world. Surely no reasonable person would impose such laws upon his children as he does on me; laws, such as nobody of any spirit would submit to. I was formerly his pretty lad, his good boy, and every thing I did was right. Times are strangely changed; for now I can do nothing to please him. I could have had what I would, and gone where I pleased; but now I am perplexed with warm exhortations, which I hear unreasonably frequent; and can go nowhere, without his leave, as if I had no more sense now, than when I was little. His reproofs are too harsh; I hear of nothing but my stubbornness and wickedness; of his and my mother's sorrow; and of breaking their hearts, on my account. I should break none of their hearts, I assure them, if they would let me alone.

"Cannot my father and mother grieve for themselves, and not teaze me about their trouble? I am no worse than my neighbors; though, by their account, I might be the wickedest wretch that ever lived. It is not enough that I must go to church on holidays, but we must have lectures on divinity at home; and for me, I am roundly told, that if I go on as I do, I must certainly perish. Yes, I must even be damned and go to hell. Old people are surely very conceited; I will warrant me they think they are so very good, they are sure to go to heaven. It is a brave thing to have a good opinion of one's self, which surely must be their case, or they would never plague me thus with their repeated lectures. Well, for my own part, I am not so vain, and yet I think I am in no greater danger than they are. When they were young, I dare say, they loved pleasure as well as me; but now they get old and cannot relish it themselves, they would absurdly restrain me from it. Reasonable parents ought not to form their commands upon what they now are, but what they were when of my age. But I am determined to submit to no such government. I will even take my pleasure whilst I can have it, and let them grieve on if they choose."

Thus, gentlemen, I persuade many to lay up future afflictions for themselves, in the early ruin of their children, by over-indulgence. I say, early ruin; for, if little master is not taught to submit to government whilst in petticoats, it is much if he ever learns submission after he is in breeches. He who always had his own way when but an infant, will take it very ill to be restrained when he rises towards manhood.* Yet some, yea many parents, will let their children do as they please, whilst but little, and increase in their strictness as they advance in years, so that they become mutual afflictions to each other. In manhood you know children should be used by their parents as friends and confidants, instead of being kept at an awful distance. Yet those very parents, who have laid the foundation of their son's ruin, by early indulgence in his infancy, very often complete it by unseason-

* Vide Locke on Education

able strictness over him, when he is verging towards man's estate. You know parents should always act, so as that their company shall never be burdensome to their children. But I shall become a moralist if I go on thus.

IMPIATOR. Many such youths as master Jacky fall into my hands. If once they can, by any means, be brought to despise reproof, I reckon myself quite sure of them; and when they come, I commonly employ them in my deepest mines.

INFIDELIS. It is always a hopeful sign, when the heart is hardened against reproof. If a young one can be brought to despise the commands, reproofs, and advice of his parents, he bids fair for being one of the devils' companions for ever; and, indeed, nothing but the grace of God can prevent it. It is very agreeable to us to see how happily successful our influences are over mankind, especially in Britain. There, many parents bring up their children, just as if they designed them purposely for the devil. I have great hopes of the next generation, gentlemen.

DISCORDANS. I make myself very merry with the ladies, in another way, which also turns eventually to everlasting separation. I join a little knot of them together so closely for a time, that they cannot be separated, nor bear to be asunder for a day together. I prejudice them so strongly for a while in each other's favor, that they show a manifest slight to those who are not happy enough to be admitted into their society. Family necessity, and every domestic duty, must give place to their firm attachment to one another. When they get together for a little chit-chat, they are as happy as the birds in May; not only examine every absent character, within the circle of their acquaintance, and report to each other all the evil they know of their own sex: but each dwells severally upon the excellencies or failings of her husband; who is, at one time, the best of men, at another time the worst, just as her ladyship happens to be in a good or bad humor with him. Thus they go on, until every one is fully acquainted with the family affairs of the rest, and thus they bring themselves into the power of one another. This is the zenith of that happiness to which I am to bring them; for even the devil will give present happiness, in order to introduce future pain and sorrow; and I assure you,

I am too much akin to my worthy grandfather, to suffer that felicity to go long uninterrupted.

First, I sow a spirit of jealousy among them: says Chloe, "Delia seems more attached to Phillis than to myself or Lucia; Portia is never happy but when her and Arabella are together." And so, round the whole club, the spirit of jealousy happily operates, and gathers strength by every day's duration.

It is not to be thought that a whole society, who can cordially join in picking holes, according to the old proverb, in their neighbor's clothes, can long refrain from doing as much for one another. Now they begin to meet, two and two, according to their various attachments, and those two who happen to meet together, regale themselves with a very pleasant conversation, about the faults and weaknesses of those who are absent, and thus round the whole society they serve one another. By and by it is whispered what Chloe said at such a place about Phillis; what Lucia said of Arabella, &c. until I blow them all up in a pleasing flame of resentment; and every one says the worst she knows of her neighbor, which commonly is a great deal. Out come personal faults along with family affairs, and a hundred etceteras, and those very ladies sit down, just as the devil would have them, in implacable hatred to each other.

INFIDELIS. I pray, what do you smile at, Avaro?

AVARO. I was thinking on an encounter I had with the devil Lunatio, whom I accidentally met last night, with his hair standing upright, and his eyes flaming with madness.

FASTOSUS. And pray, where had that mad-brained devil been? What account could he give of himself?

AVARO. He was quite snappish with me, and ran on in his discourse, as if he had been very angry. There, said he, is my father Infidelis, there is uncle Fastosus, they reign uncontrolled over the greatest part of mankind; they are caressed, even adored, by the most respectable characters in both church and state. You yourself, grovelling as you are, reign an absolute monarch in the will and affections of many eminent personages; but I am hackneyed by the basest, and when I have done, am denied the honor of my labors, and people are taught to believe that I reign only over the bedlams, and other mad-houses of the world. Whereas I could make it appear to all the infernal divan, that there are people who go about at large, and are deemed in their perfect senses, more mad than any in bedlam.

Well then, said I, brother fiend, stop and give me a sober account of your proceedings, and I assure you I shall give you all due acknowledgment.

Lunatio. I have, replied he abruptly, a great deal of business among statesmen, to drive people to their levees, which they dearly love to have crowded, and which never could be without my assistance, For who would attend the levee of my lord Superbo, or of his grace the duke of Parkland, unless he first turned fool? Would any man feed on the promise of a courtier, if he were not mad? The dinner of the cameleon is as weighty as the promise of the greatest statesman, were it even confirmed by a smile of the countenance and a grasp of the hand; for it all means no more than "I am glad to see you thicken my levee." There is never a levee day but I am obliged to bestir myself to drive the fools together.

If the premier, or the head man of any department, finds himself on the decline, and that he shall, without some good assistance, be obliged to resign; that is, be turned out of his place; I am beseeched to procure some verbose, intrepid scribbler, to cry up his abilities and proceedings, as much superior to those of all his predecessors, for time immemorial. But a man must first be reduced to a state of lunacy, before he will venture on a work so difficult, and which is likely to be but very ill rewarded. In the first place, he is likely to have truth and fact to overturn, before the end can be obtained; and these, you know, are stubborn and obstinate. In the second place, if he is happy enough to succeed, and sets down his patron firmly in his chair again, he is soon made to understand that his service has done him little or no good; he is thanked for his good intention; but is given to know, that things would have been just as they are, if no defence at all had been made. If his patron is turned out, the scribbler is blamed for having omitted something which might have been of service, instead of being rewarded for what he has done. So that, at all events, he must come off loser; and therefore none but a madman will venture on the undertaking.

The lawyers also would, but for my influences, be obliged to drive teams, or follow plows; for who but madmen would ever find them employment? But in consequence of their firm attachment to our government, I persuade some to expose themselves, by slowness of payment of their just debts, to the fangs of the lawyers; others, to quarrel about trifles, and refer the matters to them for decision. Sometimes I advise a father to leave his daughter under the guardianship of an attorney, or an uncle to leave his estate to his minor nephew, under the care and inspection of a counsellor; either of which is likely to be a lucrative job to the gentlemen of the law. You know very well, continued he, that none but madmen will ever refer their differences to the decision of those gentlemen, whilst there are three honest men to be met with in the nation; nor will any man in his right mind, ever leave an attorney executor to his will.

There are abundance of people, who live above their revenues, and others still, who have abundance, but dare not make use of it, dare scarcely allow themselves the common necessaries of life, for fear of future poverty. I have known a lady of sixty, possessed of two or three thousand pounds per annum, actually afraid of dying for want. Those gentry are all under my dominion. Besides, a very great share of my influence rests on many others, who are grievously oppressed with troubles that never happen. Some are so remarkably ingenious, as to apprehend difficulties for themselves and offspring, for a great many years to come, as if the evil of the day were not sufficient of itself.

Stop, Lunatio, said I, there you touch me sensibly. I will not thus give up my careful subjects. True, replied he, but you and I may play into one another's hands. And, although I allow them to be yours, it is easy to see abundance of madness in their disposition and conduct. What wisdom, I pray you, is there in any man's burdening himself to-day, with what may or may not happen a twelvemonth hence? Less still, in pretending to foresee what may happen in future; seeing all future events are locked up in the council of the eternal mind.

There are people of property, who sink their rents, fell their timber, mortgage their estates, in giving grand entertainments to hungry visitants and hangers-on, after the example of Timon of Athens, in order to be thought generous and great. Not once considering, that the nearest way to esteem is still to preserve the golden cord in the hands of the owner. Let all be once spent, the insatiable hangers-on, who crowd the plenteous table, will drop off like leaves in autumn; and if the wretch retains the loving regard of Argus his dog, he must expect no more. Away with the fool to Bedlam! He ought to go no longer without shackles.

Parents there are, so dotingly fond of their children, that they strip themselves of their possessions, in order to make them respectable in the world, long enough before their own lives are at a period; leaving their future support to the good-nature and mercy of the dear boy or girl, who, it is thought, are so well disposed as to be incapable of ingratitude to those who gave them being. But, let the dear boy or girl once get the parents' estate into their power, and they will give them occasion enough to lament their folly, when every shilling received shall come with a very intelligible frown. The language of which, to the parent, is, "I wish you were once in your grave." Such parents ought to be provided for at the public expense, and kept in some place of confinement, like other lunatics.

Other parents, to avoid falling into an error which they foresee may be productive of great personal inconvenience, with an equal degree of madness flee into the opposite extreme. They can find in their hearts to part with nothing whilst they live; they will find some plausible pretext or other, for which they will retain the sole possession of their goods and chattels; rather than give a suitable measure of parental assistance, will suffer the young people to begin the world under all possible disadvantages. Send such parents to Newgate, I say; for they are worse than mad!

You do me injustice again, Avaro, in claiming the sole power to yourself, over parents, who will oppress their servants, overreach their neighbors, grind the faces of the poor, and sell their souls to the devil, in order to procure fortunes for their children. This is so far from answering the end proposed, in gaining the love and esteem of the young people, that it has quite a contrary tendency. The greater the estate, the more impatient will the heir apparent be, to be put into quiet possession for himself. The more there is depending upon the death of a parent, the more eager will children be to have him out of the way. So eager have some been, that they have been obliged to use violence, in order to get the cumbersome old man out of the world. Deliver of their being of the least service. Is there no madness in this case? Is it not madness to trifle with a disease in its beginning, the only time, perhaps, in which medicine can afford relief? Is it not equally madness to torment the sick, and throw money away upon the doctor, when the disease is evidently beyond a remedy? And yet you would exclude me from having any share in the government of mankind.

No, Lunatio, returned I, we do not exclude you. We should even be glad to have a full account of your operations in some of our friendly meetings.

LUNATIO. I could give you such an account as would surprise you all, might the honors due to my operations be properly acknowledged. But I cannot stay now, having urgent business in the west end of a certain metropolis.

Pray, cousin, may a brother fiend be acquainted with it? said I. He replied, You know, that almost the one half of the nation is in a starving condition, and are, as it were, on the tip-toe of rebellion, yet are in a very great strait how to act. They think it is hard to famish amidst plenty; to die of hunger whilst the barns are full of corn, and the pastures are well peopled with cattle; whilst their governors can afford to spend thousands at a horse race, or in an evening's play. On the other hand, they think it hard to be shot at, by those who are murderers by profession; or to be hung at Tyburn for seeking to procure bread for their families.

In this dilemma, the poor wretches are raising their voices to government, beseeching their lawgivers to spare so much time from their own pleasure and amusement as to take their wretched case into serious consideration, that they may not die by artificial famine. What I aim at is, to persuade those in power to treat their complaints with neglect, and themselves, as clamorous, uneasy, and turbulent people. Instead of redressing their grievances, to threaten them with the strict execution of the laws against rioters. If I am happy enough to gain this point, as I think I shall, we shall soon see the spirit of madness raving all over the nation, and even the wise will become fools.

Oppression, you know, will make even a wise man mad. Therefore, when their oppressions can no longer be borne, there will go forth a spirit of insurrection among the people; and that shall be followed by a spirit of murder, until all the riots are sufficiently quelled, and the leading insurgents punished by death or transportation. Then will follow a spirit of emigration, and every one, almost, will wish himself to have been transported at the expense of government. At this very time, there are not less than five hundred thousand families, who are kept in their native country, by nothing but the want of means to get cleverly out of it. Neighboring nations will give all possible encouragement to the poor to settle with them; every opportunity will be taken to cross the Atlantic, until the nation referred to, shall become almost if not quite depopulated.

Now, the madness of the scheme lies here. The true riches of a nation are its inhabitants; and the grandeur of the great depends wholly on the number of those in inferior stations. In proportion, therefore, to the oppressions of the poor, will the nation decrease in its strength. Every emigration from the mother country, will either increase the number of colonists, or strengthen the hands of natural enemies; of course, the neglect of the present complaints, will eventually be the entire ruin of the great men themselves, and the translation of the empire to another, and very distant seat. Yet, after all, perhaps it will be alleged, that Lunatio hath no influence. But I shall raise myself an immortal name, upon my own foundation. I deign no more converse with a grovelling spirit. Adieu.

INFIDELIS. This same Lunatio is a spirit active enough, and we give him due respect; but he is, like all his disciples, fixed in his own views, and there is no giving him proper ideas of things. I should be glad, Fastosus, to hear more fully what you were saying last night concerning the Sadducees. It might be informing to these younger devils.

FASTOSUS. You know, sir, they were a sect of deists, among the Jews, who, like the modern deists, did not believe, that there are any angels, good or bad, or shall be any resurrection from the dead. I did not only persuade the scribes, pharisees, and doctors of the law, to lay aside judgment, mercy, and the love of God, in order to establish their own traditions; but wrought upon the Sadducees to prefer their own reasoning to the plainest declarations of the word of revelation. I assured them, that the well-informed author of the book of Job, was under a delusion, when he said, by the Holy Ghost, "I know that my Redeemer liveth, and that I shall stand with him at the latter day upon the earth; and although after my skin, worms destroy this body, yet in the flesh I shall see God." I persuaded them also, that the prophet Isaiah was under the like mistake, when he foretold, that death shall be swallowed up in victory; as also Daniel, who asserted, "that many, who then slept in the dust, shall awake, some to everlasting life, and some to everlasting dishonor." These, together with the testimonies of all the prophets, I persuaded them to reject, merely because they could not comprehend them, nor account for it how the dead should rise. This, you know, is the very reason why modern deists are pleased, under the same influence, to deny the whole system of revealed truth.

Discordans. I have often feasted my mind on the pleasing prospect of that amazement and surprise, which shall overtake those infidels, when the avenues of immortality shall open before them, and the terrors of an incarnate, a despised God and Savior, shall overwhelm them in the floods of horrid despair. Their pretended virtue, their philosophic fortitude, their boasted reason, will fail them, when they see, to their everlasting confusion, that he who despiseth the Son, despiseth also the Father who sent him.

Fastosus. The deist is my faithful, deluded disciple. Wherever you meet with a man of deistical principles, you will easily discern my image at large on his forehead, and my mark on his right hand. Nothing but pride can induce a man to prefer his own reason to the dictates of sacred revelation.

Fastosus here stopped, seemed in a terrible agitation, and thus addressed his brethren: Let us flee, my friends! Let us flee! For yonder comes Michael, the archangel, and with him a numerous train, with whom we are not able to contend. They instantly took wing, shot through the yielding air, and I saw them no more. Nor am I certain if I shall ever have an opportunity of listening to their friendly conferences again: but if I should, as is not impossible, the public may expect to hear what passes among them, so far as may come to the knowledge of a sincere friend of mankind

THE LISTENER.

FINIS.

www.ingramcontent.com/pod-product-compliance
Lightning Source LLC
LaVergne TN
LVHW010227110826
845151LV00004B/1213

* 9 7 8 1 4 2 5 5 2 6 4 0 5 *